**Also available from Amanda Weaver
and Carina Press**

The Grantham Girls

A Duchess in Name
A Common Scandal
A Reluctant Betrothal

The Romano Sisters

Love and the Laws of Motion
Love Around the Corner

Also available from Amanda Weaver

This Book Will Change Your Life
Always
Sky High
The Notorious Lady Grantham:
A Grantham Girls Companion Novella

THE ONE I LOVE TO HATE

AMANDA WEAVER

carina
press

carina press®

Recycling programs
for this product may
not exist in your area.

ISBN-13: 978-1-335-46918-2

The One I Love to Hate

First published in 2019. This edition published in 2020.

Copyright © 2019 by Amanda Weaver

This edition published by arrangement with Harlequin Books S.A.

For questions and comments about the quality of this book, please contact us at CustomerService@Harlequin.com.

Carina Press
22 Adelaide St. West, 40th Floor
Toronto, Ontario M5H 4E3, Canada
www.CarinaPress.com

Printed in U.S.A.

While The Romano Sisters series
is my love letter to Brooklyn, where I have lived
for the past fourteen years, *The One I Love to Hate*
is my love letter to the free press,
and to journalists everywhere who often risk their lives
to shine light into the dark corners of the world.

THE ONE I LOVE
TO HATE

Chapter One

Jessica Romano eyed the line of coffee-starved New Yorkers snaking toward the door of Ému Coffee and Tea with grim resignation. In Brooklyn, it seemed the only constant was change. Ému's coffee was undeniably a step up from the coffee served by the bodega that used to inhabit this storefront. It was too bad the excellent brew had to come with a pretentious name, ironic decor, and jacked-up prices. The same thing was happening all over Williamsburg. Once this had been a workers' neighborhood. Now it was a haven of hipsters, without a workman to be seen, unless you counted the construction workers slamming together glass-and-steel luxury apartment buildings on every other corner. Sure, change was inevitable, but did it always have to obliterate the past?

At least the *Brooklyn Daily Post* still soldiered on in the neighborhood. They might be small, but they were mighty. Media was evolving—or devolving—more and more every day, but there would always be a need for the kind of serious journalism the *Daily Post* produced, and Jess was grateful as hell to be a part of the team.

Serious journalism required fuel, though, so it was time to face Ému. Taking her place at the end of a long line of expensive shredded denim and creative facial hair, she pulled out her phone to kill some time. There was a text from her sister reminding her that Gemma was cooking Sunday dinner for the family this week. Attendance was mandatory. No problem. It wasn't as if she had other plans.

In her inbox, there was a reminder about her student loan payment, which she couldn't afford. Journalistic integrity paid lousy.

After email, she checked in online—Twitter, Instagram, her much-neglected Facebook, and last, the Journalist Collective's message board. The Collective's website was meant to be a place for people in the media to exchange information and advice, but the message boards had long ago devolved into everybody's favorite catty industry gossip site. Jess didn't go a day without checking in.

This morning, most of the usual agitators were online. Festivus3000, NotYourMothersByline, and DeeperThroat were all gossiping about who might be in line to take over at the *Denver Daily Star*. RitaSkeeter93 was complaining about freelancers' rates *again*. Oh, and Peabody was there.

She didn't know Peabody. She hadn't even chatted with him on the message boards, but she'd been watching his handle for ages. Everything he said was so intelligent and reasoned, and he had such clear, principled positions on things. His wry sense of humor was exactly her speed, and while he might snark on politicians or polemicists, he was never cruel to ordinary people. He seemed so smart, so kind, so… Okay, it was kind of pathetic, but she had the teeniest crush on him.

It was a theoretical crush at best, because the rules

at the Collective were strict: everything was absolutely anonymous, to protect reporters who might be posting there. As a result she knew nothing about him. Not his name, or how old he was, or where he might work. But seeing his handle always made her day just a little bit brighter.

This morning he'd posted a link to a short story in the *New Yorker*, and written, This story stopped me in my tracks. Succinct writing that still manages to be stunningly lyrical.

She'd just read that story last night, and then read it again this morning, because she couldn't stop thinking about it. It was a magical story, set in New York on New Year's Eve during WW2, featuring star-crossed lovers, with a dash of art and a sprinkling of fate, all written with masterful skill. Of course Peabody loved it, too, because he had excellent taste.

No one else had responded to his post, so summoning her courage, she typed out a reply under her own handle.

PaperGirl: Right? It was such a gorgeous piece of writing, and I desperately needed a bit of beauty before tackling this day.

His reply popped up immediately, and she let out an involuntary squeak of surprise.

Peabody: Same for me. What are you facing down this morning?

Gah. He was talking to her! She'd finally gotten up the courage to say something to him and he'd replied right away. Eager to keep the conversation going, she typed a response.

PaperGirl: I'm dealing with the supervisor from hell. What about you?

She'd just hit send when someone pointedly cleared their throat behind her. A gap had formed in the line in front of her while she'd been reading. Hurrying forward, she looked back to apologize, but the "sorry" died on her tongue when she saw who was standing behind her.

"What are *you* doing here?"

Alex Drake gave her a broad smile, all dazzling white teeth and carved-from-marble dimples. His starpower hadn't lessened a bit since she'd last seen him.

"I'm applying for a mortgage, obviously. Isn't that why everybody hangs out in coffee shops?"

So he was still the biggest smart-ass alive. That had been her very first impression of him when she encountered him in their Exploring Journalism class during freshman year, and it was still true. Well, truthfully, her *very* first impression had been that he was unbelievably hot. Then he'd taken a swipe at the perfectly valid point she'd just made, taking up an insupportable position just to be contrary, and the second impression erased the impact of the first. "No, I meant why are you in *this* coffee shop, annoying me?"

"I need coffee. And unfortunately this place is closest to the office." Alex looked around at the reclaimed driftwood counters, the uncomfortable-looking galvanized steel stools, and the elk antlers mounted over the cash register. "Are there really no bodegas around here?"

She refused to admit that she'd been thinking the same thing. Then his words registered. *The office...*

She half turned to face him. "Wait...are you working—"

"At my father's latest acquisition? Yes, I am. Thank you for your congratulations." He didn't have to look quite so delighted at her dismayed expression.

"I didn't give them."

"Aww, come on," he teased. "You know you're jealous."

The word sent a jolt through her system. Oh, she'd been plenty jealous of Alex in the past, but she was all done with that.

"I'm hardly jealous." Like she'd ever work for Alex's father, the Genghis Khan of modern media. Never.

Alex pointed over her shoulder. "Line's moving. Keep up, Jess." The way he was grinning, you'd think he'd actually missed annoying her.

Hearing him call her that nickname again was like an ice-cold finger dragging down her spine. "It's *Jessica*." She scooted forward to put more space between them.

"Your friends call you Jess." His phone pinged with a message so he didn't see her scowl as he looked down to answer. His thumbs flew as he typed something—probably buying an island, or whatever it was rich people did on their phones.

"You're not my friend."

He looked up and grinned again, his perfectly tousled red-brown hair falling across his forehead. Stupid Alex and that stupid, bone-melting smile. "So mean. We've known each other for...what? Six years now?"

"Five and a half. That does *not* make us friends. It

just means I had the misfortune of majoring in journalism at the same time you did. I'd have avoided it if I could."

"Miss! The line?" The woman behind Alex was scowling at her over his shoulder.

"Oh. Sorry."

Alex flashed a smile at the woman. "That's my fault. I'm distracting her."

The woman scowled at him, too. Well, at least there was one other female in New York who was immune to Alex Drake's gold-plated charm. He turned back to Jess, still grinning. *Ugh.* It was unfair for anyone to be so attractive. He was tall and beautifully built, his body half the result of good genetics and half the result of years on the college swim team. His high, angular cheekbones, chiseled chin and jaw, sculpted lips, flawless teeth, and aquiline nose looked like they belonged on a Renaissance statue. And his bright green eyes scrunched up in the most disarming way when he smiled.

That smile could fool you. It made him seem like a wholesome boy-next-door, when really, Alex Drake had been born into a kind of privilege few could imagine. His father, Daniel Drake, owned Drake Media and had his fingers in every form of modern media, including a string of cable networks, several magazines, and a sizable collection of major websites. She'd heard he'd recently acquired the "news" website ClickNews, and it wasn't until now that she made the connection. ClickNews had just moved their headquarters to a brand-new architectural atrocity here in Williamsburg.

Right across the street from the historic landmark housing the *Brooklyn Daily Post*.

She thought she'd finally left him behind at graduation, but here he was, popping up in her life again. How could it be so hard to avoid one arrogant rich boy in a city of eight million people?

In her hand, her phone buzzed with an alert. Peabody had replied to her again!

Peabody: I'll be shouldering the weight of the world's expectations this morning. Good luck slaying that dragon, PaperGirl.

Charmed beyond reason, she bit her lip to hold back a sappy smile. Would it be weird to swoon over an anonymous guy's post in the middle of this coffee shop? Probably.

"Good news?"

Alex was still lurking behind her. It would be just like him to try to read her phone over her shoulder. So entitled.

Clapping her phone to her chest, she shot him a glare. "That's none of your business."

Alex held up his hands in defense. "Okay. So what brings *you* here?"

"Same as you. A mortgage and some overpriced coffee."

"No, I meant Williamsburg. Don't you live in Carroll Gardens?"

Alex remembered where she lived? He even knew that in the first place? She opened her mouth to reply, but the woman behind Alex poked her angry face over his shoulder again.

"Miss! You're up!"

"Right. Sorry. Again."

When she had her coffees—one for her and one for

Lina—she moved down the counter to doctor hers. Now that she was out of line, she assumed Alex would wander off to his own corner to wait, but annoyingly, once he'd retrieved his coffee, he followed her to the end of the counter where she was emptying two packets of organic, fair-trade, raw sugar into her cup.

"So you didn't tell me what you're doing in Williamsburg," he said conversationally.

"I didn't?"

"Nope. I'm a trained journalist. I make note of stuff like that. You definitely didn't tell me what you're doing here."

"Huh. So I didn't."

His face when she left him standing at the counter was priceless, worth enduring all his earlier teasing. But her glee was short-lived, because with a few long strides, he'd caught up to her out on the sidewalk.

"Ugh, you're still here."

"Because you haven't answered my question."

"Don't plan to, either. Guess you'll die never knowing."

"Jess, you're going to walk into one of these buildings soon, which is going to give away your super-secret destination. You might as well just tell me."

"Why do you care?"

"I want to be there to gloat when I find out you're applying for a job at ClickNews."

She stopped abruptly. Alex was several feet past her before he noticed and turned back. "Not a chance. I'm using my journalism degree to report the news, not shill half-baked stories with sleazy headlines on the internet."

"ClickNews has higher web traffic than the AP and CNN combined."

She rolled her eyes. "Yes, because web traffic equates to respectable journalism. You know what? I changed my mind. I *do* want to congratulate you, Alex. That place is perfect for you. All flash and no substance."

Finally, she'd managed to wipe that smug grin off his face. As his eyes flashed with temper, Jess gave him a triumphant smile, even though what she'd said was a big fat lie. Perhaps the most annoying thing about Alex Drake was that he was flash *and* substance, just as smart and talented as he was gorgeous and rich. God had been in a really good mood the day He made Alex.

"And what are you doing these days that's so noble?" he challenged.

"Reporting. And if you don't mind, I need to go or I'll be late."

She stepped off the curb to cut across the street, but Alex's bark of laughter stopped her.

"Of course. I should have known."

"Known what?"

"You're working for that old dinosaur, the *Daily Post*."

A spark of righteous anger lit in her chest. "It's the oldest newspaper in New York. We've been publishing since 1822."

Sure the *Daily Post* was small beans now, but once, it had been the voice of a young America. Its gloried history had been largely forgotten, and for decades it had been known as a sleepy little borough paper, covering neighborhood news. But that was all changing.

Alex made a sound of mingled annoyance and boredom. "I suppose you followed your idol, Mariel Kemper, when she took over this relic."

She was speechless for a moment, caught between fury that he'd pegged her so easily, and mystification that he remembered her history with Mariel Kemper after all this time. As far as she could remember, she'd only mentioned it in front of him once. It was on the day they'd met, during that dustup in their first Exploring Journalism class.

They'd gotten in an argument—*naturally*—about the role of journalists in society. Alex had stated, with the casual disregard of privilege, that a reporter's job was to report facts, leaving the crusading to activists. Jess, burning up with righteous indignation, had slapped back, bringing up every "crusading" investigative journalist she could think of—Nellie Bly, Upton Sinclair, Randy Shilts, and finally Mariel Kemper, the woman who was now her boss—to make her point.

Jess had seen up close and personal the power of a good investigative journalist. When her mother had been diagnosed with cancer, she'd been promptly dropped by her insurance company on a technicality. Mariel Kemper, answering a letter from ten-year-old Jess, had dug into the story and exposed the company's shady practices to the light of day. The insurance company wound up under federal investigation and Mariel won a Pulitzer. They'd stayed in touch after that, and Jess had gone into journalism in large part due to Mariel's guidance.

"Yes," she bit out through clenched teeth. "As soon as I heard that Mariel was taking over as Editor in Chief, I submitted my resume. I'm lucky she decided to give me a chance."

Alex snorted, tipping his head back to rake his gaze across the ornate Gothic Revival facade of the building. "They're the lucky ones to land somebody with your talent." Her mouth was still hanging open at his off-handed compliment when he charged on and ruined it. "And your circulation is, what? Ten thousand?"

Bastard.

Seven. It was seven thousand.

"Our circulation is none of your business. At least it's real news."

"I'm reminded of that adage about trees falling in forests. Is it real news if no one reads it?"

"That's right. You measure your worth in Facebook likes."

People were starting to stare at them as they flowed past, probably because her voice was rapidly approaching a shriek. Jess shook her head, frustrated with him *and* herself. She was a nice person, really, but Alex Drake just brought out the worst in her. They weren't in college anymore, though. She was an adult with a real job, and she would not stoop to shouting at him in the street.

"Good luck with the website. I guess I'll see you around."

Alex dropped his eyes from the building to her, looking her over with barely disguised irritation. "Great. It'll be just like old times."

She left him standing alone on the sidewalk as she stormed away. Alex Drake, working right across the street from her! Brooklyn kept changing, all right, and this particular change was going to take a lot of getting used to.

Chapter Two

All the lingering unpleasantness from her run-in with Alex Drake dissipated as Jess passed under the carved stone archway of the Fiske Building and walked through the heavy old brass-and-glass revolving doors. The *Brooklyn Daily Post* had been headquartered here since 1886, when it moved from its original home. The oak-paneled lobby smelled a little funky, but that was the funk of living, breathing history. Working here for five months hadn't yet erased the thrill of ascending the wide staircase to the *Daily Post* offices, with its carved wood handrails and the troughs worn in the pale marble steps from over a century of reporters. Being a part of this, even in her modest, entry-level way, still left her giddy.

Mariel Kemper had a lauded career at the *New York Times* and the Associated Press, both as a reporter and as an editor. She'd made a name for herself doggedly pursuing difficult stories, not stopping until she dug up the truth, no matter where it led her. She was fair, but also brutally honest, not afraid to speak truth to power, or to call out a lie when she saw one. As successful as her reporting career had been—two Pulitzers and a string of other awards—she'd long had her sights set on something more. When the *Brooklyn Daily Post*'s ancient former editor finally retired, she approached the board and pitched her vision. She wanted to turn the *Daily Post* into a small but serious outlet for hard-hitting news, something that was becoming all too rare in the modern media landscape.

The board gave her a chance, and Mariel immediately instituted sweeping changes, hiring new reporting staff and overhauling the paper's platform from the ground up. Jess, having spent her first year after graduation freelancing for a few online sources, applied immediately, desperate to be a part of something so important.

It had been less than a year since the overhaul, so it was too early to know if it would succeed. But it had certainly drawn attention when an obscure borough paper generally known for its front page coverage of playground renovations suddenly began publishing multi-part stories on international events.

"Good morning, Sally!" Jess called out as she passed the receptionist's desk on the second floor. Sally had been with the *Daily Post* so long she was almost as historic as it was, with her tightly permed gray hair and vast collection of appliqued sweaters.

Sally broke off her conversation with Griffin, the *Daily Post*'s overworked, one-man IT department, to wave to Jess. "Good morning, sweetie. Look how pretty you are this morning!"

Jess glanced down at her gray wool skirt and black sweater. "I am?"

"Sure! Your eyes are sparkling and you're all aglow. I'd bet you're in love. Doesn't she look like she's in love, Griffin?"

Griff ran a hand through his shaggy dark hair and pushed his glasses back up his nose. "Maybe she's just cold."

"Ah, you haven't got a romantic bone in your body!" Sally scolded. "She's been talking to her lover, no doubt about it. Isn't that what you kids call them these days? Lovers? Or is it hookups?"

"Hookups," Griff replied with surprising authority.

"I haven't been talking to a lover or a hookup." *Just doing battle with my mortal enemy*, she amended silently.

"You'll have one soon enough, no doubt, looking like that."

"You're hilarious, Sally. I'll see you later."

"Oh, Lina was looking for you a few minutes ago," Sally called out as she headed for the large arched entry to the newsroom.

"Thanks, Sally. I'll find her."

In over a hundred years, the addition of computers was pretty much the only change made to the *Brooklyn Daily Post*'s newsroom. The long, high-ceilinged room, lined with ancient oak desks, was flooded with natural light from the wall of large arched windows to the right, overlooking the street below. Once, the staff had been able to see the Williamsburg Bridge, the East River, and parts of the Manhattan skyline from those windows. Now all you could see was that ClickNews monstrosity across the street.

The desks near the windows were prime newsroom real estate, and reserved for senior reporting staff, which most decidedly didn't include Jess. Her desk was in the corner, next to the cranky copy machine. She'd just shrugged out of her coat when Lina hurried up to her desk, looking frantic. "Oh, thank God you're here. There's no way I'm going into the morning meeting without you."

"And there's no way you're going in there without this." With a flourish, she handed across Lina's soy matcha latte.

Lina's panicked expression transformed into a delighted smile. "You brought me coffee?"

"*That* doesn't count as coffee, but yes, I brought you that green foamy drink you like, for reasons I will never understand."

"Aww, Jess, you're the best."

Being scholarship kids at expensive Ivy League DeWitt University had given Jess and Lina an instant connection freshman year, but battling their way through four years of DeWitt's highly competitive journalism program had bonded them for life. Lina had applied to the *Daily Post* in the same hiring sweep as Jess, and, in a stroke of good luck, they'd both landed jobs. Granted, they were the lowliest reporters on staff, covering the boring city stories no one else wanted, but having your best friend at work made every indignity more bearable.

"Relax, Lina. You're going to kick ass in this meeting." After months of covering city recycling plans, Lina finally had a serious story to pitch today. They'd spent half the night on the phone practicing what she was going to say.

"Are you sure you don't want to pitch your story, too?"

"Right now I don't have a story. I have a rumor."

Not even a rumor, just her aunt Patti, who worked as a secretary for a public school, bitching at Sunday dinner last week about the crappy company that had just been contracted—for a staggeringly large sum—to rebuild the Department of Education's online portal. It was probably nothing—a bunch of administrative assistants griping about stuff at work. But something about it kept eating at Jess. It was such a large contract, and it had been awarded seemingly out of the blue. All the secretaries seemed to know Computer Development Systems already, and their opinion was grim.

"Aren't you going to check it out?"

"Of course I am. But in this case, checking it out means combing through the bid award that's been posted online, and that's three hundred pages of dense financial info. Plus I have to look into CDS's past city contracts. Once I do that, I'll know if there's anything there."

"You're going to do all that research on your own time?"

"I don't mind. Especially if it leads to something good." She snagged her coffee cup from the corner of her desk, along with her notepad. "You ready?"

"I can't believe you went to Ému for me. You hate that place."

"I figured you could use a little fortification. And while I hate their pretentious decor, I have to admit, the coffee is good. I might have to give it up, though, considering who I ran into today."

"Who?"

Jess paused outside of the conference room to deliver the news. "Alex Drake."

"No!"

"Oh, yes. And you'll never guess why. That plastic-

and-tinfoil building across the street? It's the new ClickNews headquarters."

"And?"

"Aaaand…guess whose dad just bought Click-News?"

"Oh, right, I remember reading that somewhere. Wait…did he send Alex in to work there?"

"Yep."

"Some people have all the luck."

"That's not luck, it's privilege. And anyway, it's just ClickNews. It's not like real journalism."

"Hey, speaking of college, how about Josh's party tonight?"

Riiiight. Josh's housewarming party. She'd ignored that event reminder in her inbox this morning. Dealing with Josh always made her feel vaguely queasy with guilt, even though there was no real reason for it. What went down between them had happened during junior year in college, over almost before it began, and they went right back to being friends. He'd been with his fiancée for ages now.

"What about it?"

"We're going, right?"

"I don't know…"

"Come on, Jess, you are *not* going to stay home with your sisters on a Friday night."

"Livie's got a late class and Gemma works at the bar on Fridays."

"Then you're not sitting home *alone* on a Friday night. Just you and that dog and some city financial records. That's just sad."

"Hey, Spudge is great company."

"Jessica, if you're finished gossiping about last

night's episode of *The Bachelor*, there's a staff meeting starting." Mariel's assistant, Lauren, strode by in a tight black skirt suit, her blond hair ruthlessly flat-ironed, and her heels clacking on the wood floors. She sure *looked* the picture of competent authority, but appearances—at least in Lauren's case—could be very deceiving.

"Sorry," Lina chirped. "My fault, Lauren. We'll be right in."

Lauren made a low sound of disapproval, indicating she was still going to blame Jess, no matter what Lina said. They watched her in silence until she was out of earshot.

"Not that I want to be besties with her," Jess muttered. "But I really wish I knew why Lauren busts my balls all the time."

"It's just projection," Lina said in a low voice. "She's barely treading water right now. We all know it. It's just a matter of time before she screws up something she can't hide. Then *Mariel* will know it and cut her loose. Lauren's desperate to crush anyone she sees as competition for her job."

"If we're talking about who could take over Lauren's job, I'm no more likely than anyone else here."

"Yeah, but Mariel has been your mentor since you were ten. Lauren *hates* that you have that kind of history with her."

"As much as I admire Mariel, I don't even want that job. I'm here to report."

"Right," Lina said with a decisive nod. "Me, too. And today I start doing it for real."

"You're going to be so great," Jess whispered to her

as they made their way to their seats at the long table in the conference room.

"Damned right, I am."

Despite Lauren's swipe about their punctuality, Jess and Lina were among the first to arrive. Bill from the Business desk was already there, hunched in his seat, checking stock quotes on his phone and drinking a cup of the foul, bitter coffee the machine in the break room produced. Jess wouldn't touch that stuff even in a moment of desperation.

Zoe, who worked the city beat with Jess and Lina, arrived next with Natalie, who reported for the Lifestyle section. They actually *were* talking about last night's episode of *The Bachelor*. Since Zoe and Natalie were the other two women on staff in their twenties, they often got together with Jess and Lina for lunch. Well, Lauren was in her twenties, too, but nobody wanted to socialize with that barracuda.

Isaiah from International came in next, looking mildly put-upon as Robin from National talked his ear off about something. Tony from the crime beat came in with Caleb, who covered sports, the two of them analyzing last night's Knicks game in exhaustive detail. Dana, the senior reporter on the city beat, was nearly last to arrive, her cell phone glued to her ear as she negotiated something with her husband about picking their daughter up from day care. She threw an apologetic smile at the table as she sorted out the latest crisis in her domestic life.

Mariel arrived last, with a stack of folders in one arm, her notepad and coffee mug clutched in the other hand, and her reading glasses precariously perched on top of her head, holding back her heavy fall of chestnut hair.

"Good morning, all." Struggling to balance her pile of folders, she made her way to the head of the table, depositing her load just before she lost her grip on it entirely. Jess lunged forward and caught her coffee as it slid toward the edge of the table. "Thank you, Jess. That would have been a crisis of monumental proportions."

"I got your back."

Across the table, Lauren glowered at her. Jess glowered back. As Mariel's assistant, *she* should have been helping Mariel, not getting pissed because Jess did it instead.

Sliding her reading glasses into place, Mariel dove in. "Okay, let's start with the news out of North Korea overnight. Yumiko is still tied up with her piece on Russia sanctions, so Isaiah, why don't you take the lead and see what develops? Start with the wire service, but I'd like your own insights on this one, not just a regurgitation of what the AP is reporting." Isaiah nodded and Mariel moved on to the national beat.

When she got to the city beat, she started with Dana. "Dana, how's your piece on the MTA subcontractors coming along?"

Down the conference table, Dana threw her pen on her notepad in disgust. "It was going great until Click-News reported on it this morning."

A collective groan went up around the room.

"They scooped us?"

Dana nodded grimly. "My source was exclusive, but somebody else at the MTA must have talked to ClickNews first. Sorry, Mariel. I can still work it up.

Maybe focus on it as part of a larger piece on the city's aging infrastructure, the kind of context ClickNews would never provide."

"Yes, let's go in that direction. At least it's something." Mariel raked her fingers through her hair in frustration. Robin had gotten scooped on her EPA story just a week before and Mariel was still touchy. "Jess? What do you have on your plate?"

For a second, she considered pitching her story. It would feel so great to have something exciting to talk about at these meetings. But how embarrassing would it be to have to admit it all turned out to be some gossiping by disgruntled employees? No, better do the legwork first. "I'm finishing up the story about the broken parking meters."

"All right, Lina, how's the piece on the Staten Island waterfront rezoning going?"

Lina glanced nervously at Jess before drawing a deep breath to steel herself. "I'll have it finished this morning. But I'm onto something else I'd like to run past you."

"Shoot."

"When I was out the other night, I met a former staffer for Assemblyman Stevens. We got to talking and when he found out I was a reporter, he said he might have a story for me."

Mariel looked up, on alert. "What sort of story?"

"He says Assemblyman Stevens has been taking bribes from developers for years in exchange for pushing through building permits."

"Anything specific?"

"The proposed stadium in Queens, for starters."

Several reporters around the room let out low whistles. When plans for the stadium had been announced, the neighborhoods around the site immediately protested, but somehow the city had approved the plans, anyway. If Lina could prove Stevens had been bribed by the developers, the whole project might get shut down.

"Damn, Lina," Marc muttered with a twinge of envy. "I'd give my left nut for that story." He'd been slogging through an interminable story on tax code reform for days.

"That would be huge." Mariel sat back, considering. "I'm tempted to put someone more experienced on this."

Down the table, Dana looked to Mariel expectantly, and Lina stiffened, her hands fisting around her notepad. Dana was great, a seasoned, talented reporter who'd been happy to share her expertise with younger reporters like Jess, Lina, and Zoe. But this was exactly what Lina had been afraid of—that someone more senior would take her lead and get the story.

Jess held her breath, praying to every saint she could remember from Catholic school that Mariel would give Lina this chance.

Mariel eyed Lina across the conference table. "But I'm going to let you run with it and see what you turn up."

Lina broke into a grin. "Thanks, Mariel."

"I want regular check-ins so I can see how it's coming together. And, Lina, you're going to need to be watertight on this. If he's taking bribes, we need incontrovertible proof. A money trail. Cross every *T* and dot every *I*, understand?"

"Got it. I'm all over it."

"I can help go over the financial records," Jess offered.

Lina flashed her a grateful smile. "Jess is amazing with that kind of stuff."

Mariel nodded. "Sounds like a plan. Good work, Lina. Breaking this would be huge for the paper. For once, we could be first on something."

"Thank you." Lina shot Jess a look of barely suppressed glee. They'd squeal in the bathroom about this later, but they managed to keep their professional game faces on as Mariel worked her way through the crime beat, then Sports, Lifestyle, and finally, Business.

"If that's all for today," Mariel said, pushing to her feet. "I've got a conference call starting in five."

"Jessica," Lauren called out as everyone began to leave. "Stay behind, please."

Like she was a naughty grade-schooler being held back from recess. Jess sat back down with a sigh. Celebrating with Lina would have to wait. Schooling her expression into polite interest, she faced Lauren. "What do you need, Lauren?"

"I need you to take over the paper's social media accounts."

"Me?" Jess blinked at her in disbelief. "Don't we have a PR company for that?"

Lauren kept her eyes on the stack of papers she was shuffling and reshuffling with no discernable purpose. Was she trying to look busy or something? "Launching the new website ate up the PR budget. We're going to have to handle it in-house for now."

"But why *me*?"

"Well, you're the least senior on staff." Except that she and Lina had started at exactly the same time, and only a couple of months after Lauren herself. Hell, aside from Tony and Bill, both holdovers from pre-restructuring, *nobody* had been there longer than a year. "Stories about broken parking meters aren't exactly eating up your days. You should have plenty of time for this."

Her fury was about to burn a hole in her chest. Okay, so maybe her biggest story to date had been about the high number of broken parking meter stations, but it wasn't as if she'd been sleeping on the job. She was here to report, not take on stupid projects that probably should have been Lauren's to begin with.

"I don't suppose I have much choice, do I?"

"No, you don't. Here." Lauren thrust a Post-It at her. "This is the log-in for the Facebook page and the Twitter account. You should probably start an Instagram, too, and anything else you can think of."

"What am I supposed to post on there?"

Lauren waved a dismissive hand. "Just today's headlines. Check some of the other papers' profiles to see what they post. Keep it neutral and upbeat. We've got almost no followers on Twitter, and even fewer likes on the Facebook page. You should probably do some research about growing our audience. Maybe take an online course or two. I'm sure you'll figure it out."

Oh, yes, on top of her regular job, she was *totally* going to self-train as a social media marketer. "Sure." She sighed and stuck the Post-It to the top of her notepad. "No problem, Lauren. I'll get right on it."

This might require a second trip to Ému.

Chapter Three

The parking meter story was back with final copy-edits, and now she had to tackle her new position as a social media manager, but screw it—she was taking five minutes to vent her frustrations online. On the Collective's message board, Jess scrolled to her earlier conversation with Peabody.

PaperGirl: I'm afraid the dragon took a bite out of me instead.

He was still online, since his reply came immediately.

Peabody: Uh-oh. Is it fatal?

PaperGirl: Not unless humiliation is fatal?

Jess took a deep breath. Okay, having this mini-meltdown on a message board, even an anonymous one, was unprofessional.

PaperGirl: Ignore me. Just having a bad morning.

He didn't reply right away this time. Great. She'd scared away the most interesting person on the board after one exchange with him. Good job, Jessica.

But just when she was about to close out of the message board and get back to work, his reply popped up.

Peabody: This might be weird. Tell me if it is. But do you want to talk? Off the board?

Actually, yes, she *did* want to talk, and not just because it was Peabody asking. Lina was busy chasing down her awesome new bombshell story and Jess really needed to vent to someone, even if he was essentially a stranger. If he turned out to be a massive creep, she could always just block him and move on. Although that would upset her more than she liked to admit.

PaperGirl: That would be nice. Thanks.

Peabody: Are you on BulletChat? It's anonymous, too.

PaperGirl: I can be.

Peabody: I'm Peabody there, too. See you in a few minutes.

Jess quickly downloaded the app and set up her account. A search brought up Peabody's name and she fired off her first message.

PaperGirl: I guess I'm PaperGirl here, too.

Peabody: I'm glad. I've grown fond of that name.

She blinked in surprise. Was it possible he'd been following her comments like she'd followed his?

PaperGirl: I didn't know you knew who I was.

Peabody: I knew. I always like seeing what you have to say. You care so deeply about things, and you back up your convictions with solid facts. You turn up with some of the most interesting information—stuff I'd have never seen otherwise. Following your comments makes me smarter.

Oh, *swoon*! Most definitely not a creep. Her smile grew as she read and reread his text. Something eager and new was fluttering madly in her chest. But knowing he'd actually been paying attention to everything she said brought on a wave of nerves.

PaperGirl: So you've been reading all my crusading rants? That's a little embarrassing. I can get carried away.

Peabody: Those rants inspire me. Too many people in this world are more invested in being ironic or sarcastic. Caring is uncool. But the world needs people who care.

PaperGirl: I'll confess; I knew who you were, too. I love reading your posts. They're always intelligent and heartfelt. I know what you mean about snark and irony. It's so refreshing to see someone being genuine, being passionate about something.

Peabody: I haven't always been so genuine. Nice to know I'm improving.

PaperGirl: Aren't we all improving? Nobody's born perfect.

Jess thought back to that confrontation with Alex Drake earlier, lobbing insults and shouting in the street. Not her finest moment.

PaperGirl: Some days (like today) I feel like a walking disaster.

Peabody: Same here. It seems like some days, despite your best efforts, your worst side comes out.

PaperGirl: Exactly!

Peabody: Well, if it makes you feel any better today, you don't seem like a walking disaster. Honestly, you seem pretty great to me.

Jess pressed her free hand to her blushing cheek. Grinning madly, she seized the moment and typed out a reply.

PaperGirl: Thanks. You seem pretty great, too.

Peabody: I'm glad we've finally met, even if it's just here.

PaperGirl: Me, too.

Peabody: Okay, do you want to talk about your dragon? I'm a good listener.

PaperGirl: You're an excellent listener. But are you sure? It's not really your problem.

Peabody: I'm sure. Shoot.

So Jess told him all about Lauren, leaving out anything identifying as she outlined Lauren's general incompetence coupled with her paranoid insecurity, and how all of it seemed to be focusing in on her.

Peabody: It's unfair, I know, but you'll probably have to wait it out. If she's that incompetent, eventually somebody's going to notice.

PaperGirl: It's just tough. I love this job. It's been my dream for as long as I've had a dream.

Peabody: And she's making it miserable for you.

PaperGirl: Worse, she keeps getting in the way of me doing it well. Like this morning. She shoved a totally inappropriate assignment off on me, so instead of doing what I was hired to do, I'm going to be wasting my time on this.

Peabody: That's really frustrating. I'm sorry.

PaperGirl: It's okay. I'll make it work somehow. How about you? How are you holding up under all that weight?

Peabody: You remember that?

PaperGirl: I remember everything you say.

Peabody: Duly noted. I'll try not to say anything too stupid, so I don't spoil your good opinion of me.

PaperGirl: That could never happen. So about that weight… I'm a good listener, too.

Peabody: Well, the weight is…heavy.

PaperGirl: I'm sorry.

Peabody: That's okay. I'm very fortunate. I really have no room to complain.

PaperGirl: Oh, come on! Everybody complains. It's human nature.

Peabody: Well, I shouldn't complain. It's selfish of me.

PaperGirl: The fact that you're aware of that means you're not being selfish. If you want to complain, I'll listen, and I'll never call you a selfish jerk.

Peabody: I'll try never to be one. Assuming you want to keep talking?

PaperGirl: I definitely want to keep talking.

   "Jessica. How are those social media accounts coming?"

Jess dropped her phone on her desk with a clatter and spun around to find Lauren looming over her.

"Geez, Lauren, you scared me." She retrieved her phone and waved it as proof. "Fine. They're coming along fine."

Lauren gave her a tight nod and stalked away.

PaperGirl: I have to go. The dragon just blasted me with a little fire.

Peabody: Careful you don't get burned.

PaperGirl: I'll do my best.

Peabody: Can we talk again soon? This was fun.

PaperGirl: I would love that. And yes, this was fun. Thanks for listening. I needed that today.

Peabody: So did I. Have a good day, PaperGirl.

For several long minutes, she just stared into space, thinking about their conversation. Peabody was *fantastic*. Smart, kind, considerate. If she'd had a teeny crush before, it was a full-blown infatuation now. And he liked her, too! She hadn't felt butterflies like this over a guy since…well, it had been a really long time.

But real life loomed, so Peabody and this crazy new thing they'd started would have to wait until later. She had some social media to manage. Dutifully, she logged into the *Daily Post* Facebook and Twitter accounts.

Lauren had done a slapdash job of opening the ac-

counts and following a handful of obvious media outlets. The *Brooklyn Daily Post* itself had thus far only
tweeted twice.

@Brooklyn_Daily_Post *Excited to join the social media
revolution!*

@Brooklyn_Daily_Post *We report the news you need
to know!*

Wow, Lauren really sucked at this.

Lucky for Lauren, Jess knew a thing or two about
Twitter. Her Facebook languished, but Jess's Twitter
was on *fire*. She was the smartest, wittiest version of
herself there.

But what did a newspaper tweet? After perusing
the Twitter timelines of a few papers, she learned that
most tweeted headlines, just as Lauren had suggested.
But that was so *boring*. Tweeting nothing but headlines and plugs for subscriptions was a death sentence.
They'd never get new followers with content like that.

Still musing, she scrolled through the timelines of
a few papers, and then clicked on their accounts to see
who they followed. More papers. It was like a snake
eating its tail. Halfway down the list of users followed
by the *Syracuse Post*, she saw the Twitter handle for
@ClickNews. She'd seen it before, of course. Click-
News's entire platform was social media. They had
nearly three million Twitter followers and a thriving
Facebook presence. You couldn't be online without
encountering some of their stories.

Already cursing her own curiosity, she clicked the
profile to check out their timeline.

@ClickNews *Beyoncé threw herself a birthday party and she's truly living her best life.*

@ClickNews *This woman's reaction to her husband's big surprise is taking over the internet!*

It was pretty much exactly what she'd expected, except that interspersed with the celebrity gossip and pop culture randomness, there were tweets about some actual news. Well, the *stories* were solid, even if Click-News's delivery made her want to claw her eyes out.

@ClickNews *Climate scientists unveil shocking new findings at Canadian environmental summit.*

Followed by a volcano emoji. Seriously.

@ClickNews *Suicide bombers send Azerbaijan's capital into chaos.*

bomb emoji *sad-face*

Okay, those last two emojis were just in her imagination, but she wouldn't put it past them. It was insulting, the way they took legitimate news and distilled it down to a movie poster tagline…punctuated with *emojis*.

She scrolled a little farther down. Odd, they weren't all headline tweets. Some were almost conversational, the kind an actual person would tweet.

@ClickNews *Halloween was last week & there's already*

Christmas stuff in the stores. Isn't there a federally man-dated blackout window? There should be.

Then a quote tweet, featuring one of ClickNews's own articles about the Prime Minister of Sweden's recent meltdown in the middle of a press conference.

@ClickNews *If the Prime Minister of Sweden is an-noyed by personal questions, maybe he shouldn't have eloped with his twenty-year-old nanny. Just saying.*

That one made her laugh out loud.

It was pretty brilliant, actually. It gave a sense of personality to what was essentially a corporation's public face. Who wrote tweets like that? Not some lowly staffer like her. ClickNews probably paid a high-level corporate PR firm to carefully craft those tweets so they hit the perfect sweet spot between snark and wit. Grudgingly, she had to admit to being a little im-pressed. Plus, despite the new 280-character Twitter limit, they kept their tweets short, which she respected. It took skill to be clever in 140 characters.

She'd lost track of how long she'd been scrolling through the ClickNews feed when one tweet brought her up short.

@ClickNews *New study finds 71% of millennials cite ClickNews as their primary source of news. You're wel-come.*

Ugh. Really? *Really?*

Fueled by a heady flare of indignation, her thumbs quickly typed out a reply to the tweet and she hit post.

And there it was, her first tweet on the *Brooklyn Daily Post*'s Twitter feed.

@Brooklyn_Daily_Post @ClickNews encapsulating everything wrong with the modern world in 140 characters. Well done.

Ah, hell, that was too much, right? Too biting? Maybe she should delete it.

But as she tapped it to send it to the trash, a notification popped up. The tweet had been liked. As she watched, another like popped up.

Okay, it was too late to delete the tweet. It would just draw more attention if she did. Learn from Watergate—it's not the crime, but the cover-up that sinks you. Besides, it had two likes, which was two more likes than any of Lauren's tweets had gotten. Deep breath. Relax. A little attention was good, right? And it wasn't like anyone important was going to see it.

Chapter Four

Spending Friday night at the housewarming party of your ex-boyfriend and his fiancée could have been worse than a dentist visit, if the ex had been anyone other than Josh, and if he wasn't clearly so head-over-heels in love with Caitlin. For Jess, it was a relief, seeing him so happy.

"Jess! So glad you could make it." He leaned down and kissed her cheek. Since he had started working as a junior editor at a TV news station, Josh had trimmed his shaggy blond surfer curls, but that disarming, sweet smile was just the same.

"Of course! I wouldn't miss it."

Caitlin's voice rang out from somewhere behind Josh. "Jo-osh! I need you in the kitchen, sweetie!"

His face lit up with a smitten smile. "She needs me. Come on in and make yourselves comfortable."

"The two of them are sweet enough to give you a toothache," Lina said fondly, watching him go.

"Tell me about it. Now, let's find beers before we have to convince all our old classmates how great our lives are."

Half an hour later, they were catching up on jobs and boyfriends—or rather the lack of boyfriends—

with Brooke, another veteran from the college paper, when Jess glimpsed the one face she'd hoped not to see again anytime soon. Certainly not twice in one day. Everything she'd experienced during their confrontation that morning—the rapid breathing, the pounding heart, the flushed skin—came rushing right back in.

"Alex is here," she whispered to Lina. "I just can't escape him."

Lina followed Jess's subtle head nod across the room. "Damn, he's looking good."

"Lina!" She wasn't sure which was more annoying—that Lina was complimenting her enemy or that she was right.

"He's hot, Jess. It's just a fact. I never understood why you hated him so much."

"I don't hate him. Exactly."

Lina rolled her eyes and laughed. "Sure. Keep telling yourself that. You've had it out for him since he won the Newhouse award."

That's what Jess had let Lina believe, but there was a whole lot more to her animosity for Alex than some college writing contest.

"It's slightly more complex than that," Jess murmured under her breath, but Lina wasn't listening anymore.

"Oh, *no*…"

Another familiar face had joined Alex by the front door. Chase Bennett. Chase was Alex's best friend in college. In fact, they'd come from the same elite prep school, friends since childhood.

Chase was nearly as good-looking as Alex, slightly shorter, with golden blond hair and seductive, dark eyes, his lips perpetually curled into a sexy smirk.

Plenty of women lusted after him, including—for one unfortunate stretch of college best not discussed—Lina. After a lot of flirting, they'd finally hooked up, but when Chase had blown Lina off the next day, Lina's long-standing crush had morphed into righteous hatred overnight.

"Ooh, the golden boys of the internet are here," Brooke said in delight.

Jess and Lina exchanged an apprehensive look. "What do you mean?"

"You know Alex just started working for his dad at ClickNews? Chase was hired on, too. I'm going to go say hi."

"Ugh, Chase is working at ClickNews? Why does the bastard have any sort of career whatsoever? There's no justice." Lina fumed.

"What were you *just* saying about hating someone?"

"I have a very good reason to hate Chase. You never slept with Alex."

Lina was still glaring at Chase across the room, so she missed it when Jess blushed and nearly dropped her beer. Taking a deep swig, Jess fastened her eyes on the floor. It must be the effect of seeing so many faces from college all in one place again. The party, the cold beer bottle in her hand, that pair of beautiful boys across the room…it was all reminding her of the *real* reason she didn't like Alex Drake.

It was true. She'd never slept with Alex. Not quite.

Chapter Five

Three years earlier, DeWitt University

Max Perlman had just thrown up in one of his mother's Chinese vases. That thing had to be worth a year's tuition, and now it was nothing more than a receptacle for Max's beer yak. Nice.

The DeWitt party scene had never appealed to Jess, but putting her second issue of the school newspaper to bed as editor had left her feeling slightly punch-drunk with exhaustion and in a rare mood to blow off a little steam. It was the only thing to explain how she'd found herself at Max's party in his parents' sprawling Upper East Side penthouse apartment, watching Max defile priceless antiques. She should have stayed home with her dog.

"Oh, my God, look who just showed up," Lina hissed under her breath.

Greaaat. Chase Bennett had just arrived at the party with Alex Drake, and *he* was trailing Peyton Tenaway. Of course. Since they'd gotten back from summer break, everywhere you looked, Peyton was following along close in Alex's wake. Not that Jess made it a habit to look. It was just hard not to notice the two of them, with all their tall, gilded beauty, like a perfectly matched patrician Ken and Barbie.

Jess tore her eyes away from Alex and looked hard at her best friend. "Lina, should I tell you again what a supremely bad idea that would be?"

"I *know*." Lina bit her lip. "Chase got so tan. I bet he spent the whole break on a beach."

"Instead of working?" Jess muttered. "I don't doubt that." Chase was the worst kind of lazy, entitled rich boy.

"He's just so *hot*," Lina sighed.

She'd been crushing on Chase since freshman year, but when they'd all started working on the *DeWitt University Gazette* together last year, her crush had expanded exponentially. Not even summer break seemed to have diminished it. Now they were turned loose together at this debauched party, lubricated with a couple of beers…this was a recipe for disaster.

"Lina, you know what Chase is like. He goes through girls faster than a bag of chips. And he's so shitty to them afterward—"

"I know! I know exactly what he's like."

Jess nudged Lina's elbow. "Be smart."

"Ugh, smart is so boring sometimes. Don't you wish, just once, you could be really, really *dumb*?" Lina gazed hungrily across the room at Chase.

"But you won't."

"Probably not."

"Hi, guys. What's going on?"

Jess plastered a polite smile on her face and turned to Josh, who'd just popped up behind them.

"Hi, Josh. How's it going?"

"Great, now that you're here!"

Lina and Jess exchanged a brief, loaded look. Josh's one-sided crush on Jess was becoming so obvious, it was embarrassing. It was too bad, because he was a genuinely nice guy, smart, and not bad to look at. He was no Abercrombie model like Alex and Chase, but he was cute enough. Yet despite all the check marks in the "Pro Josh" column, her stomach stubbornly refused to produce a single butterfly in his presence. Nothing. No flames of lust. Not even a spark.

"Thanks for helping us with those freshman orientation tours, Josh. I really appreciated it."

"All you have to do is ask," he replied, eyes shining. "You know I'll always do anything I can to help you out."

Oh, please, stop.

"Hi, Lina."

Alex. All the tiny hairs on Jess's body prickled with awareness. When she turned back, his gaze shifted from Lina to her, and her nerves zinged with electricity.

"Jessica, did you get my final draft of the opinion piece?"

Oh, so Lina got a "hello" but not her? Typical.

"Yes." Two people could play this "rude and abrupt" game.

"I didn't hear from you about it, so I wasn't sure."

Was she supposed to drop everything to focus on stroking his writer's ego? Editing the *DeWitt Gazette* was a herculean task, and she was still new to it. The last thing she had time for was holding Alex's hand. Metaphorically.

"I got it."

"Did you read it?" he pressed.

Yes. Yes, she read it. Twice. It was brilliant. Breathtakingly good. The way he articulated complicated ideas with effortless linguistic grace made her seethe with envy and appreciation.

"The copy looked clean," she said, refusing to pump him up the way he so obviously wanted her to. The whole world fell all over themselves to praise Alex Drake. She'd be damned if she played into it. "And the word count is fine."

He was struggling to appear unconcerned, but a little muscle in his cheek had started to twitch, giving him away. It was driving him *crazy* that she wouldn't comment on his piece, which made her all the more determined to hold out.

A brittle silence stretched out as they stared each other down.

Lina cleared her throat, breaking the standoff. "How was your summer, Alex?"

Oh, Alex's summer had been *fantastic*, without a doubt. After winning the Newhouse last spring, and then scooping up one of the coveted internships with the *Chicago Tribune*, how could his summer have been less than dazzling?

The Newhouse Student Journalism award was extremely prestigious, but Jess had had another motivation for entering a piece: the award came with a hefty financial prize. Those *Chicago Tribune* internships were unpaid, and Jess had to win the Newhouse if she wanted a chance at interning at the *Trib*.

Then without warning, Alex had sailed in and entered the Newhouse and *won* it. Without a way to pay for it, Jess didn't even bother applying for the internship, but Alex did, and *he* landed one of those prized spots. Of course he did. Did he get it because of his talent or did he get it because of his last name? For a few months last spring, Jess had burned with resentment. Alex breezed from one achievement to the next with such ease, while she and Lina had to fight for every opportunity. Did he even *want* to be a journalist or was this all just a hobby? With his father's money, he sure as hell didn't have to work for a living. It just didn't seem fair.

But being jealous of his successes had made her feel petty and small. She was better than that, right? It wasn't like she was entitled to either the award or the internship. Alex had won and there was no point dwelling on it. She'd done her best to move on since the disappointments of last spring, focusing on her own work and forgetting all about Alex Drake.

It had paid off. She'd spent her summer investigating how the university was investing its endowment, and her explosive story, published last week, was shaking up the university at the highest levels. Maybe she didn't get the career boost the *Trib* internship would have provided, but the work she'd done had made a real difference, and wasn't that why she wanted to write in the first place?

Alex turned to face Lina and his expression transformed, losing every trace of hostility. "Summer was great. How was yours?" After practically beating his chest in her face, he was all smiles and politeness with Lina.

Lina shrugged. "Good. The *Beacon Lantern* turned out to be a great internship. I made so many contacts."

"That's great." He reached up to run his fingers through his hair. It hadn't been that long last spring, had it? It curled slightly at the nape of his neck now. "And you got to flee the city in July. Lucky you."

He really wasn't going to brag about the *Trib*? Jess thought he'd be falling all over himself to gloat. Before she could think better of it, she was opening her mouth and goading him into it herself.

"How was Chicago?"

Ugh, why did she do that? She didn't need to hear all the awesome details. She'd worked so hard to crush her jealousy. Now here she was, poking at something she knew would stir it up again.

Alex's eyes found hers again, wary at her sudden interest. "It was great. I wasn't sure I liked Chicago at first, but Peyton's got some friends there and—"

Her stomach clenched in some awful combination of rage and...yep, jealousy. Seemed she wasn't as immune as she'd thought. "Peyton got an internship at the *Tribune*, too?"

Peyton? C-average Peyton Tenaway—got a spot at the *Tribune*? The only reason Peyton had even been admitted to DeWitt's prestigious journalism program was because she was one of *the* Tenaways. Nearly a century before, her great-grandfather had founded *City Review* magazine, famous for its witty essays by esteemed writers and journalists. Now it was better known as a luxury lifestyle mag, which perfectly summed up Peyton herself.

"Peyton at the *Tribune*?" Alex's lips twitched with a suppressed smile as he shook his head. "Um, no. She was working for a fashion magazine her family owns. But she was the only person I knew there, so we hung out a little."

Okay, so Peyton hadn't been at the *Trib* with Alex,

which was a relief, but she'd spent all summer "hanging out" with him, whatever that meant. Actually, Jess had a pretty good idea of what it meant, especially since Peyton seemed to have become Alex's shadow lately.

Like a good friend, Lina sensed her growing frustration and deftly stepped in to change the subject. "Your article on the student protests last week was really good, Alex."

Good was an understatement. He was undeniably talented. Which meant he probably earned the Newhouse on his own merits. So it was a good thing she'd decided to quit being jealous of him. A very good thing.

"Thanks, Lina. Hey, your interview with the Dean of Arts and Sciences was excellent. Those things are usually so dry, but you did something fresh with it." Look at him, so interested in everything Lina had to say, so complimentary of her work, and it was all absolutely genuine.

It was really too bad they didn't get along because Alex seemed to be an exceptionally nice guy to everybody else. Looking like Captain America's slightly less ripped younger brother wasn't enough. He also had Cap's flawless good manners and innate sense of decency. At least, for people not named Jess Romano.

As if Josh with his inconvenient crush, and Alex with his internship and Peyton in Chicago weren't making this night awful enough, Chase chose that moment to join them.

"Jess, Lina, you're both looking gorgeous tonight." How someone as smart as Lina could fall for such a patently smarmy line astounded Jess, but there she went, lighting up like a candle for Chase. Hormones were the worst.

She'd hoped she could convince Lina to leave soon, but there'd be no chance of that now that Chase had shown up, flinging compliments and flirtation like Mardi Gras beads.

"Hey, Lina, I'm getting another drink."

"Ooh, get me one, too? I'm all out."

"Um, sure." The looks Chase and Lina were exchanging made her reluctant to leave, but it was too late now.

As she headed for the kitchen, Josh called out behind her. "Jess, wait, I'll help you!"

Of course.

Lina had disappeared, which was not good. Because Chase had also disappeared. Bad choices were definitely being made. Jess took another sip from her tepid beer. It was possible this last one had been a mistake, as she was definitely feeling less than dead sober. She rose up on tiptoe, scanning the room for Lina. She was going to have to climb on a table to see over the heads, and since she was just a little bit buzzed, table-scaling was a bad idea.

If she went looking for them, she had no doubt Lina would just chase her away, insisting she had it under control—which was probably true. But shouldn't she make one last attempt to drag Lina off the tracks before this inevitable train wreck occurred? Where was the line between concerned friend and annoying busybody? Well, she was going to find out tonight, because she was definitely hunting down Lina.

Setting her beer bottle down on a side table, she

turned and slammed right into someone. Tawny, high-lighted hair filled her vision. *Peyton.*

Peyton glanced down at her with an arctic smile. "Oh, look, the outer boroughs made it." Classic Peyton. With her beautiful face and honeyed delivery, you could almost miss the absolutely deplorable shit she sometimes said.

Ordinarily, Jess would never let that insult slide, but she'd made that resolution about being a better person and she wasn't wasting emotional energy on Peyton tonight. "Sorry, Peyton, I didn't see you."

With her imperturbable demeanor and her statuesque golden beauty, Peyton always made Jess feel like a baby goat—tiny, jumpy, and overly energetic. Peyton sighed languidly. "It must be impossible to see anything from all the way down there."

Okay, screw being a better person.

"Wow, no one's ever noticed that I'm short before. Clever you. Guess there's more to you than good highlights and a legacy admission."

As she registered Jess's insult, Peyton's china-blue eyes widened with surprise. Most people were either too infatuated with her or too intimidated by her to ever call her out. And sure, Jess was intimidated, too, but she had her limits.

Peyton's smile turned cloying and patronizing. "Be careful, Jessica. While I'm sure certain men find your gritty realness appealing, a snarky sense of humor isn't nearly as attractive to the opposite sex as you might think."

Gritty realness. She supposed that was Peyton code for "poor." *Okay, girl.*

"I wasn't using it to appeal to the opposite sex. I

was using it to underline how tired and clichéd your insults are. Now—"

Peyton cut her off. "Have you seen Alex?" Alex? What the hell did he have to do with anything? There was a challenge in Peyton's flinty gaze, but for the life of her, Jess had no idea why.

"Not for ages."

"Well, if you see him, please tell him I'm looking for him. This party's so bougie. I want him to take me home." She was still staring Jess down, like she was waiting for some specific response from her. Well, tonight was her night for disappointment.

"I live to pass on your messages, Peyton. Excuse me."

Pushing past her, she went in search of Lina. A hallway off to the right of the main sitting rooms led to what looked like guest rooms. In the first bedroom she tried, there was a couple rolling around on the bed in the dark, but it wasn't Lina or Chase. The next room she tried was dark and empty. The third, far away from the noise and activity of the party, looked empty as well, but as she pulled the door closed behind her, a familiar voice spoke in the darkness.

"Wait. Stay for a second."

Squinting into the dark, she made out a shape— Alex—standing by the large plate glass window, silhouetted against the glow of the city outside. She hesitated on the threshold, gripping the door handle. They'd already had one dustup tonight. She should probably just steer clear of him from here on out. But it was weird, him hiding in here, alone in the dark, when everyone at this party was clamoring for a spot at his side. Despite herself, her curiosity was piqued.

The smart move right now would be to back out of this room, maybe say something biting first, close the door, and go find Lina. But something was compelling her forward, making her want to walk into the bedroom and close the door behind her, which would probably be a spectacularly dumb thing to do. Lina was right—sometimes being dumb was incredibly tempting.

"C'mere." His voice sounded different in here, quiet and intimate.

Her curiosity won out. Stepping inside and closing the door, she made her way through the gloom to stand next to him by the window, overlooking the street many floors below. "What are you doing in here?"

Alex gave a shrug, that familiar, elegant gesture of his that she half hated, half envied. "Wanted to be alone. What are *you* doing here?"

"Looking for Lina."

"Ah." He looked away, a rueful smile tugging at one corner of his mouth. The glow from the streetlights lit up his face from underneath, making him look dreamlike, and—if possible—even more beautiful. "I left her talking to Chase."

Oh, Lina. She deserved so much better than what she was about to get. "I figured. I just need to make sure she's okay."

"Lina's a big girl."

That was true. She was an adult, free to make her own choices, even if they were spectacularly bad.

"Hey, your article about the university financial investments was really good."

Alex's words brought her up short. Huh? Two years of animosity had her bristling for a snarky comeback, but no matter how she examined his statement, she couldn't find the dig in it.

"What, I wasn't too strident? Too idealistic?"

He let out a soft huff of laughter. "Maybe a little idealistic, but in a good way. The university has no business investing the endowment money in a company that launders money for a dictatorship. Nobody would have caught it in DeWitt's holdings if you hadn't followed the paper trail. That must have taken you forever to wade through."

Was he really serious? Somehow the gracious Alex he showed the rest of the world had made a brief appearance for her. And yes, it *had* taken forever. The summer she'd hoped to spend in Chicago at the *Tribune* had instead been spent at her kitchen table, surrounded by spreadsheets and complex financial documents.

"Um, thank you." She drew in a deep breath. "Your opinion piece was good. Really, really good." Fair was fair. His piece was brilliant. Refusing to acknowledge that had been petty and a little bitchy on her part.

With the unusual compliments still hanging in the air, silence stretched out between them. Having a normal, nonhostile conversation with Alex Drake was uncharted territory. Having it alone in a dark bedroom with a bunch of beers clouding her judgment was almost too ludicrous to comprehend.

"Peyton's looking for you." Ugh, why did she say that? Just like asking him about Chicago, the words just came flying out of her mouth, her alcohol-fuzzed brain unable to hold them back.

Alex flinched. "Yeah, I know."

What did that mean? If he was hiding from Peyton, why had he asked her to stay? The room suddenly felt small and close and too quiet. Could he hear her heartbeat? It had taken off like a racehorse. A bubble of panic welled up in her throat, making it hard to breathe. When she could manage words, they spewed forth in a rushed jumble.

"It's really late I should probably go home now."

"You're leaving?" He turned to face her again, the city glow casting the side of his face in extreme light and shadow. There was something new in his voice, a note of uncertainty. If she didn't know any better, she'd have said he was nervous, but what the hell did Alex Drake ever have to be nervous about?

"It's a long subway ride back to my house."

Alex's eyebrows furrowed. "You shouldn't take the subway this late at night by yourself. Take a cab."

A bark of nervous laughter broke free. "Um, a cab to Brooklyn from here will cost me as much as my weekly Metro Card. No way."

His gaze drifted back to the window. "Right. Sorry. I didn't think."

No, he probably never did think about stuff like that, because he didn't have to. A moment later his eyes found hers again, but he said nothing. He just watched her with a steady intensity that set her nerves on edge.

No, not nerves—*butterflies*.

Those stupid butterflies, which refused to show their faces for Josh, were putting on a freaking party in her belly as she stood here staring at Alex.

This was stupid. What was she doing here, staring up at him like some besotted fool, yet another member of the Alex Drake fan club? Tomorrow morning, she was going to be really embarrassed about this weird moment.

She took a step back. "Okay, well—"

"Jessica… Jess."

The low rumble of his voice, caressing that single syllable, stopped her retreat. He'd never called her that before, and she was glad, because it was lethal. That murmured name slithered down her spine like molten gold.

"Yeah?"

In the dark, without a sound, he leaned down and kissed her. And everything—the whole wide world— just stopped turning. Like gravity had released them all, and she was floating up while the stars outside were falling to the ground.

A soft, warm press of his lips on hers, and then, at the end, a ghost of movement. It was just a slight caress, his lips gently urging hers apart, enough to let her breath escape into his mouth, and for his to land on her tongue, before he pulled back to look her in the eyes.

The bewilderment she saw there mirrored her own. How could something so extraordinarily unexpected have felt so very perfect? "What…why did you do that?" And why did he stop? She liked it better back there, suspended in that moment, instead of here, blinking at each other in bafflement.

"I wanted to," he said simply. Such a brief, gentle kiss, and yet his breathing sounded like he'd just run a mile. Or maybe that was hers. Her lungs felt too tight to let any air in.

"Are you drunk?" *Please say no.* The best kiss of her life should not be someone else's drunken mistake.

"A little." He paused, licked his lips. "Are you?"

"Maybe." She was lying. Because "drunk" made this excusable, understandable…forgettable. Take away that excuse and all that was left was—*oh, no.*

"Is that why you did it?" Her breathing stopped entirely as she stared into his eyes and waited for his answer. Nothing had ever felt so important as his next words.

He took a deep breath while she still held hers. "No," he said quietly, like he was telling her his darkest secret. "Is that why you let me?"

Did she let him kiss her because she was drunk? No, because she wasn't. He'd just laid himself on the line. Now it was up to her.

His face was too close to hers to allow her to see the whole thing, to read his expression. There were just his eyes, looking into hers, and his mouth, still just inches away from hers. The heat of it, the electricity, still tingled on her lips.

Heart pounding, she stared back at him, digging through the tangled jumble of her emotions to sort out what she wanted. But of course it was right there, once she allowed herself to acknowledge it. She'd always wanted him, from the minute she'd laid eyes on him. She wanted to kiss him again, then again, then never stop kissing him.

Her voice was barely a whisper when she answered him. "No, that's not why. I wanted you to k—"

The rest was lost under his lips, because they were kissing again—*seriously* kissing—open mouths and stroking tongues and mingling breaths. Wow, Alex could kiss. *Really* kiss. One hand came up to her face, fingertips just barely touching her skin, while the other landed firmly on her waist, turning her until her back was to the window. Cold glass pressed against her back as the solid warmth of Alex's body pressed into her from the front. He leaned in just enough to tease her with his weight, making her imagine lying down, with the hard, gorgeous length of him pressing her into the bed and…*oh*. Her fingers curled into his biceps as lust pooled in her stomach. She sighed into his mouth.

His hand slid around her back, pulling her away from the glass and into his chest—his broad, perfect chest. She stumbled into him and he stepped back to catch her. Then they were moving together across the room, an awkward dance as he bent low over her to kiss her. The bed loomed up behind him, a hulking shape in the dark. She wanted to tumble down onto that bed with him and not stop until they were both naked.

Swaying to a stop beside it, he held her steady as they kissed again, then again. She was the one to tip backward onto the silk duvet, pulling him down with her. The softness of the expensive, plush mattress cradled her as Alex pressed down on her from above. Somehow her legs found their way to either side of his. Lost in his endless kisses, before she knew it, they were grinding on each other, hips against hips.

"We can't do this here," she murmured.

He kissed the side of her neck and exhaled, his hot breath rifling through her hair and making her nipples go hard. "I know."

"Someone could come in—" His kiss silenced her, his tongue making her momentarily forget the reasons they should be stopping.

"Let me get a cab and take you home," he murmured between kisses. His fingers slipped up under the edge of her shirt, skimming across the sensitive skin of her stomach, making her tremble. "Let me take you home, Jess."

She'd heard that nickname every day of her life, but it sounded so different when Alex whispered it in the dark—soft, sexy, intimate.

It was Saturday night, which meant Dad and Gemma would be tied up at the bar until last call at three a.m., and then probably another hour for cleanup and closing. Livie was away at college. The rambling, shabby family town house in Carroll Gardens was empty right now, and would be for hours. If she let Alex take her home, they'd be all alone there. There was little doubt what would happen next.

"I have to find Lina first."

Alex reared back and licked his lips—licked the taste of her off them. Desire curled in her stomach like a fist. If there wasn't a good chance of someone walking in on them at any moment, she'd strip his clothes off him right here and right now and keep going.

But Lina was her best friend. She was somewhere in this party, mixed up with a truly lousy guy. Her conscience demanded that she check in with Lina one more time before abandoning her to her dubious choice.

"I gotta talk to someone, too," he muttered grimly.

Peyton. He was going to ditch Peyton and leave with Jess. Oh, God, she'd just nodded yes. She was leaving this party with Alex Drake, taking him home with her. What was happening right now? No, don't think too much about it. If she stopped to think, it might all end, and whatever else happened, she did *not* want this to end.

"See you in a minute," she whispered, slipping out from underneath him. Alex let out a frustrated groan as he rolled away from her. His fingers dragged across her belly as she sat up. She felt it between her legs, a hot, heavy pressure. She staggered to her feet, keeping her eyes averted. If she looked back at him, she'd never leave.

Outside, the hallway seemed too bright, too loud, after the soft, cocooning darkness of the bedroom. Reality rushed back in like a wave, and she had to touch her lips, still tingling and slightly swollen, to remind herself that it had been real. Alex had just kissed her, touched her, set her on fire. And he was going to do it again before the night was over.

She pushed her way through the overcrowded living room, looking for Lina. No one she asked had seen her in ages. After an endless circuit of the room, and then the kitchen and dining room as well, she still hadn't located her. That left just the bedrooms on the other side of the apartment.

The hallway was unlit and quiet. The first door on the left wasn't quite closed. She'd grasped the handle and was about to step inside when she heard voices.

"I just don't understand what you were doing in there with her."

Jess froze. *Peyton.* And for once, all that languid boredom had vanished from her voice. Had she seen Alex leaving the bedroom after her?

"Come on, Peyton, leave it alone." Alex sounded dismissive, bored, not a hint of the breathless urgency she'd heard a few minutes ago when he'd begged her to let him take her home. It was like he was a different person.

"Alex, I'm trying to look out for you. As a friend. She's an absolute *nightmare.* The worst kind of self-righteous, crusading do-gooder."

Heat flared in Jess's cheeks as she listened to Peyton diss her. But who cared? Let her say what she wanted. She was about to be shocked into silence anyway when Alex told her what had just happened.

"Peyton, it's nothing—"

Nothing? Unease prickled along Jess's skin.

"You can't trust her, you know. She's such a little hypocrite, wearing that outer-borough working-class thing on her sleeve while she chases after the richest guy at DeWitt. It's really so transparent—"

"Peyton, knock it off!" Alex snapped. "I was just messing around. It's a little fun, that's all."

Fun? It hadn't felt fun a minute ago. It had felt urgent, passionate, intense…

Peyton shifted gears, letting out a trill of laughter. "Oh, it's a *joke*. Why didn't you say so?"

There was a rustle of fabric, as if she was brushing up against him. Jess bit her lip, not breathing, waiting for Alex's reply.

"Sure," he said flippantly. "A joke. She's so easy to wind up. I was just having some fun with her."

The roar in Jess's ears was so loud, she almost missed Peyton's low purr. "Alex, you know I love it when you drop the Boy Scout routine and let your wicked side show. Now, are you taking me home or not?"

Her face burned and her eyes pricked with tears. She'd heard more than enough. Time to find Lina and get the hell out of here.

How could she have been so *stupid*? Of course Alex Drake wasn't into her. Well, he'd have slept with her if she gave him the opportunity. And she'd given him plenty of opportunity.

But when she imagined the next day, she felt sick with humiliation. He'd give her that smug, knowing

smirk as he and Peyton laughed at her foolishness—
how hilarious, Jessica Romano thinking she had a shot
at someone like Alex Drake. Thank God she hadn't
done it. She'd never have lived it down.

Lina. She had to find Lina and get the hell out of here
before he came back out to the party. Facing him—
facing both of them—would be unbearable.

"Oof!" She'd been so distracted, pushing her way
through the crowd, that she'd run right into someone
again.

"Hey, there you are! You disappeared!"

"Josh. Sorry, I was…um…"

Josh lightly held her shoulders and crouched down
to look her in the eye. "Is everything okay? You seem
upset."

He was so, so nice. Why couldn't it have been him
that let loose those butterflies? Why hadn't he been
the one to press her against the window and kiss her
until she forgot to breathe? Why couldn't Josh be the
one she wanted to take home?

She *hated* Alex Drake for making her feel this way,
for making her want him when he was clearly never
meant for her. She might not ever give him the satisfaction of acknowledging what had just happened,
but she would hate him for the rest of her life for it.

"Nothing's wrong," she muttered, desperately trying to rein in the emotions Alex had sparked tonight.
There was no place for them. She'd burn them down,
stomp them flat, bury them deep, then forget all about
them. He was dead to her.

"Were you looking for Lina?" Josh asked. His
thumbs gently caressed the curves of her shoulders.
Nothing. No tingling skin, no flush of arousal.

Over Josh's shoulder, she saw Peyton slipping back into the room, an indolent smile on her face as she towed Alex after her. Look at the two of them together. That's where Alex Drake belonged, and she was a fool for thinking otherwise.

Nausea roiled through her as his gaze met hers. Peyton turned back to him, saying something over her shoulder. He answered her without looking, his eyes still on Jess. Was he waiting for a reaction from her? Some hopeful smile from her that he could mock? That was never going to happen. She might not have his money or his privilege, but she'd be damned if she'd let him make a fool of her.

She tore her eyes away from Alex and looked back to Josh. Fine. He wanted to watch her? Let him watch this.

Forcing her mouth into a brittle smile that almost hurt, she reached out and curled her hand around the back of Josh's neck, her fingers sliding into his gold curls.

"I wasn't looking for Lina," she murmured. "I was looking for you."

For a split second, she saw Josh's eyes go wide with surprise as she pulled his face down to hers. Then she closed her eyes, blotting out everything and everyone, as she kissed him. She might as well have been kissing that vase over on the table, for all the resemblance this held to what she'd done with Alex a few minutes ago. But that didn't matter, because what happened with Alex was never, ever happening again.

When she came up for air a minute later, Josh was smiling at her like she was the sun, moon, and stars combined, and Alex was gone.

Chapter Six

"They're coming over here." Lina's voice snapped Jess out of that unpleasant trip down memory lane. By the time Alex and Chase reached them, she'd schooled her face into impassivity. She'd never breathed a word of what happened in that bedroom, not to Lina or anyone else. She wasn't about to change that now. It was still too humiliating to even think about.

"I don't see you for a year and a half and now twice in one day," Alex said. The words were casual, as was his stance, one hand stuffed in the pocket of his pants, but there was an edge to his voice and a spark in his eyes that she didn't trust. He took a sip of his scotch, never taking his gaze from hers. Scotch, still. Alex had always been weirdly anachronistic. He wore a vintage wristwatch with a leather band when everybody else their age just used their phone to check the time. He drank aged scotch when all the other college students had swilled beer from Solo cups. On anybody else, it would have been a pretentious affectation, but on Alex, it just worked, like he'd been born forty and fused to a leather club chair.

"Josh invited us." She tossed the words out like a challenge.

"Right. Your old friend Josh."

It almost—but not quite—felt like a dig. If she called him on it, he'd deny it, pretending nothing had ever occurred between them. For all she knew, he didn't even remember it. It was years ago, he'd been drinking, and by his own admission, it had meant nothing to him. She was an idiot for thinking he might be bothered.

"Lina, nice to see you again." Chase didn't even try to hide the once-over he gave Lina. She gave him a glacial smile in return. "So I'm sure you've heard, I'm working with Alex at ClickNews now."

"Hmm. I think someone did mention that."

Her pointed lack of a congratulations hovered in the middle of the conversation. Any normal person would be aware of the awkwardness of the exchange and change the subject, but Chase had never been sensitive to other people.

"Yeah, it's awesome, being in on an organization like this right as it's going viral. ClickNews is changing the face of journalism. We're going to put the final nail in the coffin of print media, right, buddy?" He slapped Alex on the back, full of bro camaraderie.

Surely that *thunk* made by Jess's and Lina's jaws hitting the floor was audible, right? Had Alex not told Chase where they worked or did Chase simply not care? Or maybe Alex was gloating about destroying print media, too.

"Well!" Jess said brightly. "I guess me and Lina and everybody else at the *Brooklyn Daily Post* should be dusting off our resumes, huh? Maybe Starbucks is hiring."

Chase managed to look mildly chagrined. "Hey, I didn't mean—"

"Sure you didn't. Lina, I'm getting another beer. Do you want one?"

"Yes. I'm going to the restroom."

Jess took off in one direction, and Lina in the other, leaving Chase and Alex alone in the middle of the room.

The kitchen was nearly empty, and since she couldn't face those two smug assholes again anytime soon, she pulled out her phone to kill a few minutes. To her delight, Peabody had messaged her again earlier in the evening.

Peabody: Did you eventually tame your dragon?

PaperGirl: Survived the battle only a little bruised. The war is ongoing. On many fronts.

She didn't expect him to respond. After all, it was Friday night. Normal people were out having fun. So she was surprised when his reply came only a moment later.

Peabody: More dragons looming on the horizon?

PaperGirl: More like a bunch of entitled knights.

Peabody: I thought the knights were supposed to slay the dragons for imperiled maidens.

PaperGirl: Not these knights. Too busy staring at their reflections in their armor and congratulating themselves. Useless in dragon-slaying. Not that I need or want their help. I can handle my own dragons.

Peabody: I'm pretty sure I already guessed that about you.

PaperGirl: Sometimes I wish I had some of that armor myself, though. Must be nice to be so impervious. Sure they don't care about anything, but nothing bothers them, either.

Peabody: It would be criminal to hide your heart in armor. What would the world be like if it was nothing but uncaring, impervious knights? They need to be more like you, not the other way around.

PaperGirl: Ha, that'll be the day. I think these knights are irredeemable.

Peabody: Oh, well, then, nothing for it. You have to slay them.

PaperGirl: Damn, and I left my slaying sword at home tonight.

Peabody: Now I have the funniest mental image of you wielding a giant sword. Which is odd, since I have no mental image of you at all.

Jess drew in a deep breath, bracing for the worst. Here it came. He'd want to know what she looked like, and from there it would be just a short hop to an unsolicited dick pic. But once again, Peabody defied her expectations.

Peabody: So tell me more about these narcissistic knights. Maybe I can help you find the fatal weakness in their armor.

Oh, Peabody was dangerous, all right, just not in any of the ways she'd come to expect. Not only did he refuse to default to the lowest common male denominator, he kept asking her about herself and being funny and charming as he did it. She could very easily find herself over her head with this guy.

PaperGirl: They're just some jerks. No one worth thinking about. What about you? Have you managed to set down the weight long enough to enjoy your Friday night?

Why did she ask that? He was probably out. He might even be on a date, which sent a little tremor of unease down her spine. She hadn't thought of him being taken, but for all she knew, he was married with kids. Oh, that would be awful. Maybe she didn't want to know.

PaperGirl: Sorry. Forget I asked that. I shouldn't intrude into your private life.

Peabody: You're not intruding into anything. To answer your question, yes, I'm out, but I'm not exactly enjoying myself.

If he *was* on a date, then it wasn't going very well. He wouldn't be texting her in the middle of it otherwise. She shouldn't be so happy that he wasn't having a good time.

PaperGirl: Sorry to hear that. Is it the place or the people?

Real subtle, Jess. That didn't sound at all like she was digging for info.

Peabody: The place is fine. So are the people. The problem is me.

PaperGirl: In what way?

Peabody: Everybody seems to be going after what they want in life except me.

PaperGirl: Why can't you do the same?

Peabody: It's complicated. I work for the family business, so that's what I do with my life.

He had no idea how well she understood that. Her older sister Gemma had skipped college and a career to help run the bar with their dad. Gemma didn't seem to mind, but being the oldest by several years, she hadn't had a lot of choice, had she? Somebody had to do it. Since the loss of their mother, that somebody was always Gemma.

PaperGirl: Ah, I see. I understand exactly what that's like. We've got a family business, too.

Peabody: Do you work for them?

PaperGirl: No, but my sister does. That might be worse.

Peabody: In what way?

PaperGirl: Remember when I said I had my dream job? She's the one who makes that possible. She works there so I don't have to.

Peabody: Yeah, you're right. That would be worse.

PaperGirl: But it really sucks that you can't do what you want. It's never fair.

Peabody: Hey, don't get the wrong idea. My situation is hardly grim. My issues are just that. Mine.

PaperGirl: Still, you're entitled to feel how you feel.

Peabody: Thanks. There's no one in my life I can really talk to about this.

PaperGirl: Anytime. I'm sorry you don't feel like you can talk to the people in your life.

Peabody: Well, my family is out. And I don't have a lot of friends I can confide in this way.

PaperGirl: And there's no one else?

Ugh, that was pathetically transparent. And Peabody wasted no time in calling her out on it.

Peabody: Is that your way of asking if I'm involved with anyone?

PaperGirl: Um, maybe? Sorry, I'm a journalist. Nosy by nature.

Peabody: Just journalistic curiosity, huh?

To keep it light and teasing or to tell the truth? Putting herself out there was scary, but they obviously had a connection, right? It was entirely reasonable to be curious about his relationship status.

PaperGirl: Okay, fine. I'm asking. Are you seeing someone?

Peabody: No, I'm not.

…

…

Peabody: Are you?

PaperGirl: No.

Peabody: Okay. Good to know.

"Jess. Why are you hiding in the kitchen?"

She looked up to see Lina standing in the kitchen door, hands on her hips.

"Um…sorry. I was just texting someone."

Lina's eagle eyes darted to her phone and back to her face. "Who?"

Did she want to spill about Peabody already? Well, if she was going to tell anyone about him, it would be Lina.

"A guy, actually." She could feel the silly smile taking over her face. She could hear it in her voice.

"Yes! You finally got back on Tinder!"

"No, I didn't meet him on Tinder."

"So you actually met a guy in real life? In New York? Wow, I didn't know that was possible."

"No. And I haven't actually met him. I don't even know his name. It's Peabody. From the Journalist Collective."

Lina was on the Collective message boards, too. Everybody in the industry was. And she'd mentioned Peabody to Lina once or twice, just commenting on his intelligence or humor. Lina knew she was a bit of a Peabody fangirl. Now Lina's face settled into a stony frown. "Oh, no. You are *not* flirting with some rando from a message board."

"Why is it any different than all those guys you talk to on Tinder?"

"There's a picture, for one. And personal details."

"Which they could be lying about."

"I can tell when they're lying. At least I know *something* about them. What do you know about this guy? Maybe he's some fifty-year-old creepy suburban guy, married with kids, fishing for hot young girls on the internet."

"Listen to yourself. If he was looking for young hotties on the internet, I seriously doubt he'd do it on the message boards of the Journalist Collective. We don't even post pictures there."

"Okay, maybe not," Lina reluctantly acknowledged. "But my point still stands. You don't know anything about him."

"I know plenty already. He has a family business, just like me. He's a journalist, just like me. And he's single."

"Oh, my God, he's sending you dick pics, isn't he?"

"No! Lina, no dick pics. Can you stop being so suspicious just this once? This is…" She looked down at her phone, smiling again in spite of herself. "Actually, he's kind of amazing."

"Just be careful. Protect yourself, okay?"

Jess had tried out all the apps that connected people in the modern dating world, but after just a few months of insipid text exchanges and horrifying propositions from strange men, she'd given up and deleted her profiles. Lina, on the other hand, was a pro at all of them, from Tinder to Bumble. The upside was, at any given moment, she was juggling half a dozen potential new men. The downside was that she'd seen the very worst the dating pool had to offer. She laughed along with everyone else as she related her hilarious stories of dating disasters, but Jess was worried that Lina was growing jaded, that she'd lost her belief that good guys even existed.

Maybe she was right. Maybe they didn't exist. Or maybe Peabody was one of the last good guys out there. Jess knew which possibility she preferred to believe in.

"I'll be careful. But, Lina, he really is great."

Lina still looked dubious, but she relented. "Just keep me filled in on all the juicy details."

"You know I keep nothing from you."

"I'm holding you to that. Now, I didn't drag you to a party so you could hide in the kitchen texting."

Jess grimaced. "Are they still out there?"

"Chase is running his mouth about how super-amazing their website is to his posse of adoring fan-girls, and Alex has disappeared somewhere, so we're safe to mingle. Now get out here."

Laughing, Jess pocketed her phone and followed Lina out of the kitchen. But nothing the party could offer was more appealing than what was waiting for her on her phone. She couldn't wait to get home so she could get back to Peabody.

Chapter Seven

Peabody kept texting her all weekend. While she spent tedious hours poring over a dry, dense city contract for computer services, she kept her phone next to her on the bed as their endless text conversation spun out. They spent forever dissecting their favorite pieces of investigative journalism, and then moved on to a lengthy debate on who made the best Batman. She knew he loved Mexican food but didn't much care for sushi. He knew she hated greeting cards because they were too sentimental, but she wept uncontrollably at the first ten minutes of *Up*. But she still didn't know his name, his age, or even where he lived, outside of "the tristate area." He didn't offer and she didn't ask. And it was funny how little any of that stuff seemed to matter.

Gemma invited half a dozen family members to Sunday dinner, filling their house with the familiar hum of conversation and laughter. But tonight, Jess didn't want to spend the evening surrounded by family. She wanted to escape to her room, her phone, and Peabody.

She half listened, her leg bouncing up and down under the table, as Aunt Elena, her mother's older sister, argued with Uncle Richie, her father's younger brother, about the subway system. Ordinarily, she'd be in the thick of the debate, but tonight, she couldn't make herself focus.

"Don't you think so, Jess?"

Jess blinked. "What?"

Aunt Elena was staring at her expectantly. "You ride the subway every day. What do you think?"

"Um…" She shook her head. "I don't know."

Her whole family stared at her in mystification. If there was one thing Jess had never been short on, it was an opinion.

"Everything okay, Jess?" her father asked, eyeing her closely. John Romano had been forcefully thrust into single parenthood over a decade earlier, and he'd learned to read all three of his daughters like books.

"Everything's fine, Dad," she promised him. The last thing he needed was more worry.

Elena returned to her conversation with Uncle Richie. Her father watched her for another moment before joining in with his brother and sister-in-law.

Gemma leaned in beside her. "What's wrong with you tonight? You're about to jump out of your skin."

"Nothing. I'm just…distracted. Livie's distracted, too, but you're not giving her a hard time."

Currently, Livie was bent over the table, scribbling out a list of arcane symbols and numbers on her napkin. She'd been puzzling out some sort of astrophysics problem before dinner and it looked as if the answer had just hit her.

"Livie was born distracted. You weren't. And usually you like nothing better than bitching about mass transit. So what's up?"

"I told you, nothing." Jess glanced down at her phone in her lap. There was a tiny red bubble on the BulletChat icon. He'd messaged her again.

Gemma followed her gaze and arched one eyebrow. "Oh, I *see*," she murmured with a smirk.

"Hush," Jess hissed. "He's just a friend."

"Oh, *he* is, is he? Well, he's going to have to wait. You know how Aunt Elena is about cell phones at the table."

"It's not even her table," Jess grumbled. "And Livie's doing math."

"You sound nine. And that's different. Do what you want, but I'm not gonna save you from Elena."

Jess sighed and stuffed her phone back in her pocket before taking another bite of Gemma's astoundingly good lasagna. Gemma spent her life pulling taps and sparring with Romano's grizzled old patrons, but she could create magic in the kitchen.

"So is he hot?" Gemma pressed.

"I'm not discussing this with you." Gemma would be even more suspicious of Peabody's motives than Lina had been. Older than Jess and Livie by several years, she was both big sister and mom, and fiercely protective of them.

"Come on, you know I'm just gonna keep bugging you."

"Aunt Elena," Jess said brightly, breaking into the larger conversation. "Didn't you say Kendra has a new boyfriend?"

Elena's eyes lit up with glee as she launched into her favorite topic ever—the marital prospects of her daughter. "She does, and this one is a keeper. He's a cop, and *so* handsome. I think I hear wedding bells.

What about you, Gemma? Anybody new in your life?" Elena's second favorite topic was the marital prospects of the Romano sisters, especially the eldest.

"I am going to *kill* you," Gemma muttered to Jess under her breath before replying to Elena with practiced nonchalance. "Nope. Working too much for all that stuff."

"You're not getting any younger, you know. Those eggs of yours won't last forever." Elena's third favorite topic was motherhood.

Okay, maybe it had been mean, throwing Gemma to the wolves, but Jess wasn't ready to open up this thing with Peabody to outside eyes just yet. Not to Gemma and *certainly* not to Aunt Elena.

After dinner, Uncle Richie, Aunt Elena, Uncle Michael, and Richie's girlfriend, Sheila, headed to the living room to watch football. Their father, oddly, slipped out the back door.

Jess and Livie, in the middle of clearing dishes, paused, watching him pass.

"Where is Dad going?" Livie asked.

Jess peeked through the kitchen window. John Romano was standing in the bare, cold backyard, head tipped back, talking on his cell. He was facing away, so Jess couldn't see his face, but a shiver of unease skittered down her spine. Her father was not secretive by nature. "He's making a phone call. Outside. What the hell is that about?"

Gemma eyed the closed door uneasily as she packed up leftovers. "He's been acting weird lately. I don't know."

"Is he okay?" Jess pressed, feeling guilty that while

she'd been obsessing over Peabody, something might be legitimately wrong with their father.

"He seems fine. Just keeping to himself, sneaking off to make phone calls in private and stuff."

"That's weird," Livie said.

"Very weird. Is it the bar?" Jess pressed. "Are things bad?"

Gemma shrugged. "No worse than they ever are. You do the books, Jess. You know better than anyone."

Yes, she did. The truth was, Romano's barely broke even most months. And in some months, it didn't. Business wasn't good, but as Gem said, no worse than usual.

"So what's he sneaking around about?"

"Who knows? What are *you* sneaking around about?"

"I'm not sneaking."

"So who's the mystery man on your phone?"

"When did this become about me?"

"Since now. Who is he?"

"None of your business."

Gemma chuckled. "Look at you, all worried about Dad when you're just as secretive."

"Look, I promise I'll tell you when there's something to tell. Right now, it's just…new. And maybe nothing."

Livie, up to her elbows in soapy water at the sink, rolled her eyes. "Just let her go talk to her mystery guy. I'll clean up."

Jess turned to stare at her sister. "You weren't even paying attention at dinner. How do you know about him?"

"I notice things, you know. Especially when it's you."

Ah, Livie. With her brilliant, expansive mind and the obsessive way she sank into her work, everyone assumed she was oblivious to what went on around her. Jess knew better, though. The two of them were very different, but less than a year separated them and Jess understood Livie better than anyone. The middle Romano sister might be quiet, but she saw *everything*.

"You sure?"

"I'm sure. Go."

"Just promise you'll tell us all the details when it gets juicy," Gem added. "And take Spudge with you before somebody trips on him and breaks an ankle."

"Thanks, Livie. I owe you one. Come on, Spudge."

Upstairs, she settled down on her bed with her phone. Spudge stared longingly up at her, too old to jump up on the bed as he once had.

"Come on, you pathetic baby." She heaved Spudge up next to her and he collapsed with a delighted doggy groan. With Spudge's head in her lap, she leaned back against the headboard and opened up BulletChat. Peabody had replied to their earlier conversation about the latest literary fiction critical darling they'd both read. The mental shift—from her loud, sparring family downstairs, back to such an esoteric subject—was jarring.

Usually Jess loved living at home. It was a comfort, having her father and sisters waiting here in this familiar place, ready to wrap her up in their loving care after a terrible day. And knowing there was a vast network of aunts, uncles, and cousins to call on had helped them all hold it together when their mother died and through the years since. Plus, there was Spudge. He wuffed in his sleep, nuzzling further into her lap.

On the other hand, still living at home sometimes made her feel like a fraud. When she was little and imagined being a grown-up with a job at a newspaper, she thought the rest of her life would look different. What did Peabody imagine about her? Did he think she was some sophisticated New York reporter, hanging out with the media elite discussing weighty topics of great journalistic merit? Would he be disappointed to learn the truth, that she was just a bottom-rung staffer at a tiny paper still living in her childhood bedroom?

She looked around her room, trying to see it through outside eyes. The faded old wallpaper, cream with tiny clusters of violets, dated from her grandmother's time in the house. None of the furniture matched, some left over from her childhood, some passed down through several generations of Romanos. Jess had done her best to dress the place up, banishing the stuffed animals and childhood awards to the basement, and adding some cheap framed posters and a modern Ikea bedspread, but it was still clearly a little girl's room whose occupant had never left.

PaperGirl: Hey, do you ever feel like everybody else became an adult while you weren't looking, or is that just me?

Peabody: Every day.

He'd answered right away, so she supposed *he* wasn't out having great intellectual conversations in hip watering holes, either.

PaperGirl: I'm so glad it's not just me.

Peabody: What brought on this bout of existential angst?

PaperGirl: I thought being twenty-three with a full-time reporting job would feel different. Adultier.

Peabody: Adultier is not a word.

PaperGirl: I know that, genius. I do have a journalism degree.

Peabody: I was teasing. Adultier is a great word. Everybody should be using it. I predict Merriam-Webster adds it next year.

PaperGirl: I still live at home. Did I tell you that?

Peabody: No, you didn't. I do, too.

Jess let out a sigh of relief. See, they really did have so much in common.

PaperGirl: It can be nice sometimes, though, right?

Peabody: What do you mean?

PaperGirl: My family's always here. No matter what happens out there in the big, bad world, they're always on my side, you know?

There was a pause before he replied, and for the first

time, she wondered what his family was like. Being tied to his family business had reminded her so much of Gemma and the bar, she'd just assumed the sense of suffocation was the same—stealing your breath but replacing it with unconditional love. But maybe he didn't come home to a team of adoring cheerleaders like her.

PaperGirl: Is your family not like that?

Peabody: Not exactly. I'm loved. I know that. But the forms love takes don't always make you feel better about yourself.

Wow. That was cryptic. She was still turning his comment over, trying to parse his meaning, when he texted again.

Peabody: Why are you so glum all of a sudden? Did something happen?

PaperGirl: The holidays always make me a little maudlin.

She wouldn't burden him with the details of her mother's death, between Thanksgiving and Christmas of the year she turned ten. In her experience, people often got weird when she told them. She'd learned to keep it to herself until she knew someone well.

Peabody: Right. Holidays.

PaperGirl: Thanksgiving is coming up. Are you going away?

Peabody: Away?

PaperGirl: To spend it with family?

Peabody: Oh. No. It'll just be us, I guess.

Again, when he'd mentioned family, she'd imagined her own, complex and sprawling. Peabody gave the impression that his gathering, such as it was, would be much smaller. And lonelier.

It was on the tip of her tongue to invite him over. Gemma had been planning the menu for weeks. The bar would be closed, so her father and sisters would all be home. A herd of uncles and cousins would plant themselves in the living room with her father to watch football all day. Aunt Cynthia would pop in and lecture Gemma about her gravy until Gemma threw her out of the kitchen. Every other relative in Brooklyn and a handful from Jersey would stop by to exchange family gossip, reminisce about past Thanksgivings and Romanos who were dead, and everybody would have "one more drink before we go."

She hated the thought of Peabody feeling lonely on the holiday, but inviting him into her inner sanctum felt a little too much, too soon.

PaperGirl: Well, I hope it's nice.

Peabody: I'm sure it will be. Hey, I meant to ask you, did you know Anna Petersen has a new book out? You said you liked her stuff, right?

PaperGirl: I'm a huge fan. But I didn't know it was out yet.

Her phone buzzed with an alert.

A photo.

Peabody had just sent her a photo.

Holding her breath, she tapped on the icon to open it.

It wasn't him. But it was his hand, holding a brand-new hard copy edition of Anna Petersen's book on Robert Kennedy. Well, it was part of his hand. Just four fingers, curled around the edge of the book in the very corner of the picture. He probably hadn't even realized she could see them.

But she could. And now she was obsessively cataloguing every tiny detail. Like there was no wedding ring. Like they were obviously not an old man's hands. That they were long. Beautifully shaped. Short, tidy nails, a couple of tiny freckles on one knuckle. He had very nice fingers. A girl could spend a lot of time fantasizing about fingers like that. And she was pretty sure she was about to.

Taking a deep breath, she tapped out what she hoped was a light-hearted response, nothing to give away how much her heart was racing just because she'd glimpsed his digits.

PaperGirl: I'm so jealous. Guess I'm hitting Amazon tonight.

Peabody: I'd loan it to you, but…

But that would require meeting face-to-face, and neither of them had suggested that yet. She wanted to. More than ever, now that she'd gotten a tantalizing glimpse of those fingers. But maybe it was a little soon.

So, as deftly as she could, she made another joke, putting that discussion off to another day.

PaperGirl: You could just photograph every page for me and text them to me, one by one.

Peabody: Brilliant idea. I'd love to, except it's 700 pages and I have to work tomorrow.

PaperGirl: Shucks. Amazon, it is, then. I have to work tomorrow, too. I'd better go. I still have some work to do.

Peabody: Me, too. Talk to you tomorrow?

PaperGirl: Of course. I want to hear all about Petersen's book. You can text me your favorite bits on your lunch break.

Peabody: Will do. Sweet dreams, PaperGirl.

Reluctantly, she closed out of the app, rubbing Spudge's head. That was…wow. Who knew a glimpse of a couple of fingers could make her so giddy?

But she hadn't been lying about having work to do. She hadn't checked the paper's social media accounts all weekend, which was bad. As crummy as it was getting stuck with such an onerous task, it would be even worse to fail at it.

With an irritated sigh, she opened up the accounts. Post a headline on Facebook, cross post it on Instagram, onto Twitter…

Oh, no. ClickNews had *replied* to her snarky tweet from Friday.

@ClickNews @Brooklyn_Daily_Post *Yeah, the geriatric crowd loves using twenty words when five will suffice. Explains so much.*

Geriatric crowd? Did they mean *her*? They were calling her old, frumpy, out of touch. Well, the paper. Same difference. Fine, you want to play it like that? It's *on*.

@Brooklyn_Daily_Post @ClickNews *If you're implying it's quality over quantity, first that requires some level of quality.*

Was that too mean? She read back over the "geriatric crowd" bit. Nope, not too mean at all. She was scrolling through her timeline when her phone buzzed with a notification. ClickNews had replied to her again. *Now?* Their social media manager had less of a life than she did.

@ClickNews @Brooklyn_Daily_Post *Quality? You're a paper that covers recycling schedules on the front page.*

She was going to throttle this guy. Girl. PR person. Sure, she started this argument, but didn't they have bigger things on their plate than to keep taking swipes at her? And besides, the city recycling schedule hadn't made the front page in *months*, thank you very much.

@Brooklyn_Daily_Post @ClickNews *You noticed? Starbucks just released a new signature Frappuccino, and yet you still found time in your busy schedule to read a newspaper. You get a gold star.*

Take *that*, fancy PR firm.

Chapter Eight

Monday morning, she was still floating along on her Peabody high, which was why she didn't realize she'd forgotten her travel mug of coffee until she came up out of the subway in Williamsburg. Guess it was Ému Coffee and Tea again.

She was peeling off her gloves just inside the door when she spotted a familiar tangle of rust-brown hair near the end of the line. Damn. Suddenly he was *everywhere*. In the moment of hesitation as she debated ducking back out, Alex spoke, without ever glancing up from his phone.

"Don't bother running away. I already saw you come in."

Sighing, she took her place in line behind him and pulled out her phone, intending to ignore him the way he was ignoring her. Maybe Peabody had texted.

Abruptly, Alex turned to face her, seeming so much closer than she'd thought. "Are you stalking me, Jess? First the coffee shop, then Josh's party, and now the coffee shop again."

Did he *have* to look so good this early in the morning?

"I could say the same thing about you. At least I

had a good reason to be at Josh's. You guys weren't even friends in college."

Alex scowled. "Nope. We weren't. Not like you, anyway. I mean, you guys dated forever, right?"

"Two months. Actually, not even two months. Watch the line."

"What?"

"The line." She pointed to the gap in the line that had appeared ahead of him, smugly satisfied to be able to call him out on it this time. "Pay attention, Alex."

"Right. Was it really just two months?"

"Oh, my God, why are you so obsessed with this?"

Alex jerked back in surprise. "I'm not obsessed."

"Then drop it."

"Fine. What should we talk about instead?"

"There's no law that says we have to talk at all. I'm sure you'd rather not."

"Come on." He flashed her that winning smile he had to have been practicing since puberty. "You know how much I love annoying you."

"Oh, I know. That's why you've always been the one I love to hate. So what's on the agenda for today in the exciting world of cut-rate internet journalism? A Kardashian scandal? Or maybe a new cat meme went viral this weekend and you can devote an entire news cycle to it."

His eyes flared with anger. Nothing like hitting him where it hurt.

"Actually, one of our staffers is about to break something big."

"Like…?"

"You'll just have to follow ClickNews to catch the latest."

"It'll be a cold day in hell." Which was a lie, because she already followed ClickNews from the *Daily Post* account.

Alex chuckled—this patronizing little laugh that grated on her nerves—as he stepped up to the counter. "Hope the air isn't too thin to breathe up there on your mountain of moral superiority."

A cold gust of air rushed into the coffee shop as the door opened to admit someone new.

"Alex, there you are."

Jess turned to look, along with everyone else in the coffee shop, because the famous Dan Drake had just walked in.

Alex Drake had long since given up trying to analyze his complicated relationship with his father. Even the unexpected sound of his voice in the coffee shop set off an avalanche of conflicting responses. That was bound to be the case when your father was also your boss, your best friend, and your cross to bear. Complicated.

Dad was looking in top form this morning, in an impeccably tailored charcoal suit, crisp white custom-made shirt, and a blue silk tie from his favorite maker in London. He broke into a wide, white smile when he spotted Alex, and strode toward him, oblivious to the stares. As the owner of a media empire, he shouldn't be a household name, or a face people recognized on the street, but Dan didn't do anything the ordinary way. His private life—and the string of beautiful, sometimes famous, women who passed through it—was discussed in the press as much as his business successes. Alex might have gotten used to it, but he was never fully comfortable with the attention his father drew.

Dan paused beside him, leaning across the counter to address the wide-eyed barista. "Extra-large Red Eye."

There were still half a dozen people behind them, but Dad never let a little thing like waiting his turn hold him up. It was infuriating, but that trait had undeniably worked for him. Dan Drake didn't wait to be asked. Dan Drake stepped up and made it happen.

The barista eyed him warily, and for just a moment, Alex thought she might tell him he had to wait. Then Dan slid a twenty across the counter toward her. Her eyes flicked down to the cash. Then her hand slipped out and snatched it, and she wordlessly began making his coffee. Another Dan Drake trait; if charm and confidence didn't work, just buy what you wanted.

Dan winked at the barista. "Thanks, Ava."

Another trick. Absorb personal details—even just a name on a tag—and use that info to gain trust. The barista fought back a smile, falling prey to his charm seemingly in spite of herself. It never ceased to amaze Alex how well it worked. As always, he was both embarrassed and impressed.

"What are you doing here, Dad?" Although he had a pretty good idea already.

"I decided to sit in on the staff meeting this morning. You don't mind, do you, son?"

Through a tight smile, Alex replied, "Of course not. It's your company."

His father grinned and clapped him on the shoulder. "But I don't want to step on your toes, do I?"

Alex couldn't even feel resentful, because that was the truth. Dan wouldn't do a thing to get in the way of his son's running of the new company. He would look on proudly, and compliment his business acumen and decision-making, and he'd cheerfully tell everyone not to get too used to Alex's presence at ClickNews, because his son was destined for bigger and better things.

Jessica was still behind him, no doubt absorbing every second of his exchange with his father. He could feel her presence, could feel her stare, could feel the weight of her judgment. It made his skin prickle all over. From the first day he'd met her, there had never been an instant when he wasn't aware of those things.

On one hand, he wanted to keep his father as far away from her as possible, for both their sakes. On the other, if he ignored her now that Dad was here, it would just prove her right on so many fronts, and one thing he could never abide was Jess being right about him.

Stepping slightly to the side, he nodded his head in her direction, trying to keep it casual. "Dad, you remember Jessica Romano? We were on the college paper together."

He didn't miss the flash of surprise in her eyes. She'd fully expected him to ignore her. Good. Nothing better than defying her expectations.

"Sure I do. How are you, Jessica?" His father turned his charming, bright white smile at Jessica and extended his hand. Here it comes—the smile, the deliberate, sustained eye contact, the firm handshake—he made everyone he spoke to feel important. He might not remember Jessica at all, but he'd never show it.

Jess stared down at Dan's extended hand, caught off guard. Her teeth bit into her bottom lip briefly, her unconscious tell that she was unsure of herself. Alex cleared his throat and looked away.

"Don't tell me my son's got you working for Click-News, too?" Dan said, as Jessica finally shook his hand. "Did we hire the whole college newspaper staff?"

"Oh! No, no. I don't work for—"

"No! She doesn't work for us. Dad, Jessica works for the *Brooklyn Daily Post*. It's right across the street from our new offices, remember?"

Jess had been abundantly clear that she wouldn't be caught dead working for ClickNews. And the truth was, for all the grief he gave her, she was right. She was far too talented to be wasted at ClickNews. Smug and infuriating, but undeniably, astoundingly, talented.

Dan still hadn't released her hand, as he nodded slowly, still smiling. "Right. Cute little old local paper. I remember."

Alex glanced at their hands and scowled. If his father even *thought* about flirting with Jess, he might have to physically drag him out of the coffee shop. Jess was off-limits and out-of-bounds, for a million reasons too complicated for Alex to sort out. Just… no. Forever and always, *no*.

Before he was forced to come to blows with his own father, Jess disengaged her hand and tilted her chin up in challenge. Oh, he knew that aggressive chin tilt so well. It always preceded a blistering set-down or an impassioned rant. "Well, we don't intend to stay a little old local paper for long, Mr. Drake. Mariel Kemper's got big plans."

"So I've heard. She's quite a spitfire, that Mariel."

Internally, Alex winced. Did he *have* to use that word to describe a woman as accomplished and intelligent as Mariel Kemper? Especially when that woman was Jess's mentor? Predictably, Jess bristled in reaction, every inch of her flaming up defensively. It was a sight to behold, and Alex felt an old, familiar stirring deep inside. He'd always been a sucker for Jess when she was on an outraged tear. Frankly, he'd always been a sucker for Jess, period. Seemed that time, circumstances, and her unrelenting disdain for him had done little to change that.

"Ms. Kemper is one of the most talented people working in journalism today. I feel honored to be working for her."

"I bet you do." His father gave Jess another toothy grin. It bounced off her like rubber, which gave Alex a curious flare of satisfaction. If there was one woman on earth who could withstand Dan's charm offensive and come out unmoved, he was weirdly glad it was Jess. Proud of her, even, although she'd probably deck him for thinking that.

If possible, she grew even more outraged at his father's patronizing smile. *Oh, Dad, never underestimate Jessica Romano.* Forget having to drag his father out in a choke hold. Jess was going to take him out herself in another minute.

But before he could step in and divert Dan, Jess hiked her messenger bag higher on her shoulder and turned toward the door. "I have to go," she muttered darkly, shooting a glare first at his father, then at him.

Ah hell, she was really mad. She wasn't even going to wait for her coffee. His instincts had him nearly reaching out to stop her and apologize on behalf of his father, but if he attempted it, he suspected she'd take a swing at him.

Jess was almost out the door when his father chuckled and nudged his arm. "She's quite a little spitfire, too, huh?"

Even from behind, he could see every inch of Jess stiffen in fury. Of course she heard that. She let the door slam shut behind her, and through the glass, he watched her storm off down the sidewalk, long dark hair snapping in the breeze behind her.

"Dad—" Alex began.

But Dan was already turning toward the door with his coffee. "Better get going, son. Car's waiting outside. Don't want to be late."

Then Dan was gone, too, leaving Alex with his rapidly cooling coffee and a shop full of stunned patrons still waiting for their coffee.

"I'll pick up the tab for them." He passed a fifty to the barista before following his father outside. Drake Media waited for no one.

Chapter Nine

"If I could just get a minute of his time—"

"Who did you say you were again?"

"Jessica Romano, from the *Brooklyn Daily Post*."

"Mr. Gallagher doesn't give interviews to college papers."

"The *Post* is *not* a college paper. It's been in continuous operation since 1822."

"Well, *I've* never heard of it."

"I assure you, we're a legitimate—"

"I think you should speak to the Office for Media Relations."

"I'm not looking for press releases," Jess pressed, losing her patience after going twenty rounds with Frank Gallagher's secretary at the Department of Education in Albany. "I have questions of a serious nature to ask Mr. Gallagher—"

"And I told you already, Mr. Gallagher doesn't give interviews."

"But—"

A resounding *click* met her protest. Jess pulled the receiver away from her ear and stared at it in dismay.

Well. That was that.

Days of parsing through CDS's bid had definitely

raised some questions. And CDS's past record of service only raised more. Something was not right about this contract. The next step was to lay it all out for Frank Gallagher in the Department of Education, and see what he had to say about it. But she couldn't seem to get to the guy. There was no direct way to reach him and his secretary guarded him like Fort Knox.

Jess set her phone down and looked up to see Lina approaching her desk.

"You look miserable. What's up?"

"Just ramming my head into a brick wall all morning. The usual."

"Well, take a break from that and come to lunch with us. Natalie says the new place around the corner has amazing mac and cheese."

"I should go over this contract again, and—"

"Jess, it's cheese and pasta. Your two favorite foods. Let's go."

Lina was right about the cheese and pasta. Frank Gallagher's impossible secretary would still be there if she took a break for half an hour.

Shoving herself to her feet, she reached for her coat. "You're right. Let's go."

"How's your Assemblyman Stevens story coming, Lina?" Zoe asked when they were all settled at a table.

Lina blew out a breath. "Good, I think. There's definitely some shady stuff in his campaign contributions, but I'm still digging through all of that. It's going to take me a while."

Jess nudged her elbow. "Let me know if you need a hand, okay?"

"I will totally take you up on that once I've got it all pulled together. The financial stuff is daunting."

"How much longer until you think you can break it?" Zoe asked.

"Definitely by Christmas. Maybe sooner if I get lucky."

"I'm so excited for you, Lina. What a killer story."

"Thanks, Zoe. I'm just so nervous. It's got to be perfect, you know?"

"You'll kill it," Zoe assured her. "Okay, Jess's turn. What's got you so miserable?"

Jess shook her head. "I'm just having a hard time making progress on this story. There's something there, but I can't get at the guy who might have the answers."

"Well, explain the problem," Zoe said. "Maybe we can help."

Dubious, Jess looked from face to face. "Are you sure?"

Zoe's pale blond corkscrew curls were piled up on top of her head today, but several had escaped and danced around her face as she nodded. "Women have to stick together. Let us help."

"Okay, so I heard that the Department of Education has just awarded a massive no-bid contract for building and maintaining the new online portal for city schools, and I decided to look into it." Jess pulled her printed copy of the contract from her bag, littered with Post-It flags and scattered with highlights and notes scribbled in margins.

"You're carrying it around in your bag?" Natalie interjected before she wolfed down another forkful of mac and cheese. She might look like a willowy runway model, but she ate like a starving trucker.

"I work on it during my commute," Jess said defensively. "So I looked into similar projects in other major school districts, and it seems unusual to have so many different projects lumped into one contract to one vendor."

"What do you mean?" Zoe asked, reaching for the contract.

"These guys are building the software for the new portal, but they're also providing new desktops to school administration offices across the city. It's unrelated hardware. Why isn't that a separate bid? And look at the price per unit they're charging. You could buy it retail from Dell for half that. There are a million line items like that. Stuff that has literally nothing to do with the new portal, a lot of it wildly overpriced."

Zoe scowled as she flipped through the contract. "Jess, did you seriously annotate this whole thing?"

"Jess kicks ass at this kind of stuff," Lina said. "You should have seen this article she did in college, tracking the investments of the school's endowment."

"Thanks, Lina, but the contract is just the start. There's also this company's history with the city."

"If they have a solid reputation as a vendor, maybe that's why they got the contract," Natalie interjected. "I mean, my stylist costs a fortune, but she always gets my highlights perfect. I'm willing to pay more if I know it's going to be done right."

"See, that's just it. This is where it gets shady. I had to really dig, because CDS has been reincorporated a few times, but if you follow the paper trail, the name changes, but all the executive officers stay the same, and they're based in the same office park on Long Island. CDS, in various incarnations, has been fined three times for either failing to complete city contracts on time, failing to provide the services as agreed upon, or doing substandard work."

"And they still got this contract for the new DOE portal?" Zoe asked.

"And with a whole bunch of tasty extras thrown in, all at a price tag of nearly a billion dollars."

"That's a *billion dollar* contract?" Lina's voice was strangled.

"With no public review period, and with the bid posted online, unannounced, just a week before the vote to award it."

"Wow. So who voted on it?" Zoe asked.

"A panel at the city Board of Ed approves things, but as far as I can tell, they usually don't even see the full bids."

"You mean nobody but you would be willing to wade through three hundred pages of this stuff?" Natalie laughed. "Shocker."

Jess laughed, too. "Yeah, I get that. They don't have time. They usually get a summary from the Department of Education, which is a state agency, and they tend to rubber-stamp their recommendations."

"They probably assume someone at the state has already done the legwork on the contract by the time it gets to them," Lina mused.

"Right. And someone should have. But that's state info, and they're pretty opaque about their practices. And there's another thing. It turns out one of the executives at CDS happens to be married to a highly placed staffer at the Department of Ed. Now, I don't know if this guy oversaw this contract. Could be unrelated. But if this guy had anything to do with the review of the contract…"

Zoe finished her sentence. "That's a massive conflict of interest."

"And probably illegal," Lina added.

"So I figured I'd go to the guy in charge of that office at the state DOE—that's Frank Gallagher—and just ask him. Who put this contract together? Were they *ever* open to bids from other companies? Who gave it the greenlight before it was passed on to the city panel for approval?"

"Sounds smart." Natalie snatched a French fry off Lina's plate as she spoke.

"But his secretary refuses to give me even five minutes with him. I guess I'm not important enough for her. She just keeps referring me to the state's press office, which is worthless."

"What you need to do is get in this guy's face when he's not in the office," Lina said, pushing the rest of her fries toward Natalie. "Figure out where Frank Gallagher lives, where he hangs out, and just show up."

"Nice idea, but I don't have weeks to hang out in Albany and follow this guy around."

"I can ask my dad," Zoe said.

All heads swiveled to Zoe. "Your dad?" Lina asked.

Zoe shrugged. "Sure. You know he works for the governor."

Okay, so Zoe got a little career boost over the rest of them, having a father who worked for the state government. But Jess wasn't going to complain if she wanted to flex those muscles on her behalf.

"Oh, my god, that would be amazing. Thank you so much, Zoe."

"No problem."

"We're all in this together," Natalie said.

Zoe nodded in agreement. "It's a tough business for women. We've got to have each other's backs. Let me talk to my dad and see what I can do."

"Zoe, you're the best."

The late fall sunshine felt even brighter as the four of them made their way back to the paper after lunch. Jess was full of bubbling optimism. If Zoe could get her this interview, she was onto a story that would bring the paper a new kind of recognition, and would propel her to the next level of her career. A story like this would mean she could tell Lauren to go stuff her social media accounts in her ear.

But not yet. She hadn't checked the accounts in a couple of days. While Zoe, Natalie, and Lina chattered away about the new Max Irons movie, Jess slipped her phone out of her pocket and quickly did the rounds. Link to an article on Facebook, cross post it on Instagram, then over to Twitter, where— ClickNews had replied *again.*

@ClickNews @Brooklyn_Daily_Post Does it count as "reading" when you're using it to pack your dishes for a move?

This was probably not the kind of attention she should be drawing to the paper's social media accounts, which meant she should, under no circumstances, reply again. But how could she let ClickNews get the last word? That would be letting them win, and she just couldn't stand for that. Then again, didn't Lauren tell her to grow the audience? ClickNews had tons of followers. If the *Post* picked up even a few of them, it would improve their numbers, right? Yes, she was being a little argumentative, but honestly, no one was paying the slightest attention to what she was posting. Nobody except ClickNews's social media manager. Who was a total jerk.

@Brooklyn_Daily_Post @ClickNews Does your website count as "news" when 80% of your visitors are taking a quiz to sort their pets into Hogwarts houses? (My dog is totally a Hufflepuff, btw.)

That was fun, but definitely a stupid move. Eventually somebody at the *Daily Post* was going to notice her exchanges with ClickNews, and that would be bad. Which was why she was absolutely not going to tweet at them again. Well, not unless they tweeted her first. Because no way were they getting the last word in.

Chapter Ten

As Jess exited the subway in Williamsburg several days later, her phone pinged with a message from Peabody.

Peabody: I have the funniest thing to show you. You have to read it now.

There was a link to a blog post, some tourist's nightmarish experience with street food in New York that had her howling with laughter.

PaperGirl: That was disgusting and hilarious. But I take exception with the unfair slandering of hot dogs.

Peabody: But…street meat. That hot dog water is horrifying.

PaperGirl: You're a terrible New Yorker. Street food is a New York tradition.

Peabody: I prefer my food served indoors, by a place that's passed a health inspection.

PaperGirl: Hot dogs and me go way back. It's true love.

Peabody: One day I'll take you to a proper restaurant and show you the light. Maybe I can win your heart away from hot dogs.

Jess stared at her phone, stunned. He'd very nearly asked her out. Not quite, but almost. She was still giddy over it when she walked into the *Daily Post* front office a few minutes later.

"Good morning, Sally. You look nice. Did you get a haircut?"

Sally patted at her tidy silver curls. "Ah, just a trim. Nothing fancy."

"What's with the smile?" Lina asked, coming to perch on the corner of Sally's desk.

"What smile?"

"That smile. She's smiling like a cartoon character, isn't she, Griff?"

Griffin popped up from under Sally's desk looking like he'd spent the night in his clothes, which was typical for him. "Your monitor was unplugged, Sally. Try it now. Who's smiling?"

"Her!" Lina pointed at Jess. "Oh! I know. It's *him*, isn't it? You're still talking to him, aren't you?"

If Lina only knew. It felt like talking to Peabody was all she'd done for days. "I don't know what you're talking about."

"Have you got a new boyfriend, Jessica?" Sally asked eagerly. "I *knew* you were in love! Didn't I tell you, Griffin? Didn't I say I could see it all over her face?"

"No, I do *not* have a boyfriend. He's…just a friend."

"She's never even *met* him," Lina said to Sally.

"Oh, is this one of those internet dating things? My niece met her husband that way. He's not much to look at, but at least they ran a background check on him for her."

"A background check isn't foolproof, you know," Griffin said. "Ted Bundy didn't have a criminal record."

"Oh, be careful," Sally said to Jess. "You don't want to be dating someone like Ted Bundy."

"I'm not dating anyone! I haven't even met him."

"Right. Because he probably looks like Freddy Krueger." Lina waved her fingers like knives. "That would make for some interesting sex."

"If you're going to have sex with someone with blades for fingers," Griffin interjected, "it seems Edward Scissorhands would be a much better choice than Freddy Krueger."

Lina sighed. "You're so right, Griff. Those cheekbones? Those dreamy eyes? Oh, yeah. I'd go there, blades and all."

"Oh, my God, he doesn't look like Freddy Krueger or Edward Scissorhands." Jess thought back to that photo of his hand holding the book, the photo she'd saved in her phone. Definitely nothing like Freddy Krueger. Not a chance.

"How do you know?" Lina smoothed the front of her sweater. "I'll point out again, you don't know anything about this guy."

"I know plenty! I know he's brilliant—"

"You already said that."

"—and he's a reporter, like me." *At least, he wanted to be.*

"Where does he live?"

"Here in New York."

"How do you know?" Lina pressed.

"He calls hot dogs 'street meat.'"

"Okay, he's a New Yorker," she conceded. "And is he in print, like you? Online? Cable news?"

As far as she knew, he wasn't doing any of those things, because he was busy working for his family business. But he must have at least *trained* to be a journalist, if he was on the Collective, even if he wasn't currently working in the field, right?

"We don't share specifics, you know that."

"Where did you meet him?" Sally asked.

"I already told you, I've never met him."

"No, which site? Was it OkCupid, or Match.com, or Tinder, or—"

How on earth did Sally know about Tinder? Lina turned to fill her in, sparing Jess the trouble. "She was stalking his posts on this message board—"

"I'd hardly call it stalking!"

"—and then she finally got up the courage to talk to him. The next thing you know, he's got her texting him, and now look at her. Swooning over some stranger."

"I'm not swooning." Not much, anyway.

"He hasn't asked to meet you?" Sally asked.

"No. Um, not really." Which hadn't struck her as odd until Sally put her on the spot about it. There was that moment when he nearly did this morning, but then nothing. He didn't actually do it. She didn't feel so giddy anymore.

"If you get along so well, it seems like he'd want to

meet you in person," Sally mused, straightening the message pad and pen on her desk.

"Maybe he's married," Griffin said.

"He's not married." There had been no ring. Definitely not married.

"Or he has a girlfriend," Lina added. "You know all men are lying dogs."

"Hey!" Griffin protested.

"Present company excepted, Griff."

"But he could be anybody." Lina was warming to the subject now. "I mean, you met him on the Collective. You might already know him."

"There's no way I already know him, Lina." Surely she'd know, right? She'd be able to tell? She'd seen his *fingers*! Those were not the fingers of anyone she knew.

"How do you know? Maybe it's Marc. Or Caleb. Or maybe it's Isaiah."

Jess rolled her eyes. "For God's sake, Lina, it is not Isaiah. He's over forty."

"But—"

"And gay."

"Okay, it's not Isaiah. All I'm saying is that until you meet him, you don't really know who you're sexy texting with."

"Jess is sexting with random strangers?" Zoe asked from the doorway.

"No, I'm not," Jess insisted.

"Yet," Lina said. "Mark my words, it's just a matter of time before he asks you to send nudes."

"I'd never do that. So can we stop speculating about my sex life with strangers now?"

Sally hiked an eyebrow as she sorted the mail. "According to you, there's no sex happening at all."

"Okay, that's enough!" Jess laughed. "I don't know about the rest of you, but I have newspaper stories to write."

"Not yet, you don't." Zoe waved the paper in her hand. "Memo from Lauren. Expense reports are due by noon."

"What? I thought they were due on Friday." Lina snatched the memo out of her hand and skimmed it quickly. "*Receipts* is *ei* not *ie*. And why does she pass out photocopies? Has she never heard of email?"

"Bookkeeping asked for receipts early for the end-of-the-quarter close-out."

"They gave us *three hours* to get them done?"

"No." Zoe took a step closer and lowered her voice. "They told *Lauren* two weeks ago. Lauren forgot to tell *us* until this morning. Hence the panicked memo."

"Oh, great." Lina rolled her eyes. "Once again, we're all going to have to drop everything to cover her ass."

"Sorry." Zoe shrugged.

"It's not your fault, Zo."

"Well, let's get it over with," Jess said, following Lina toward the newsroom.

"Um, Jess, can I talk to you for a minute?" Zoe's eyes flicked toward Sally and Griffin. "In private?"

"Yeah, sure. Out here." Jess led her back out onto the stairs. A few people were filing past, headed to offices on other floors, but no one from the *Post* was out there.

Only now did Jess notice how anxious Zoe looked.

All her usual perky energy was missing, and she was twisting her hands together. "What's going on?"

"I have something to tell you that you're not going to like."

"Is this about the interview? Gallagher's not going to talk, is he?" Disappointing, but not that surprising. She'd just have to keep at him herself.

"Um…" Zoe's eyes drifted to the side. "That's not it. He was willing to talk." Hesitantly, Zoe looked back to her. "But only to me."

"Oh." Jess blinked, trying to sort out the implications of that.

Zoe began speaking in a rush. "Dad introduced me and he was really friendly, but when I explained what I was there for, and that my colleague at the paper had uncovered some issues, he closed right up. You'd done all that research, Jess, and I was afraid if I walked out of there without telling him about it, he'd call in the lawyers and there would never be any answers. So I told him what you'd uncovered in the bid, and about CDS's history with the city and the personal connection to his staff. He was completely dumbfounded. It turns out his comptroller is the one who's married to the CDS staffer, and he was the one who oversaw the whole process. As of this morning, the comptroller is on administrative leave, and they're launching an investigation into possible criminal wrongdoing."

"Oh. Okay, well that's a pretty big deal. I'd better get going and—"

"There's more," Zoe said quietly. "I called Mariel from Albany as soon as it happened, and she told me to write it up, so we'd break it first. It's in today's edition."

Zoe's words slammed into her like a physical blow.

"She told *you* to write it up? Did you tell her it was my story?"

"Yes! I did! But she said that since I'd landed the interview, it was my story now. I insisted that you get credited for the research, though. It's not a by-line, but—"

"So you wrote my story?" The back of her neck prickled and her throat felt tight.

"I'm so sorry, Jess. I swear, I didn't know it was going to work out like this. I feel terrible."

"No, it's not—" Jess had to stop and swallow down a raw knot of devastation. "It's not your fault. You were trying to do me a favor."

Her face burned with humiliation. She'd screwed this up. She should have run Gallagher down herself, then everything would have been different. She'd have been the one there when he discovered the shady bid process, and it would be her name on that byline right now. But she'd let Zoe run interference for her and lost her first major story because of it.

"Jess?" Zoe tentatively reached out and touched her hand. "I can't tell you how sorry I am. You worked so hard—"

"No, it's fine." Shaking her head, Jess forced the most brittle smile of her life onto her face. She was the one who'd dropped the ball. It wasn't Zoe's fault that she was the one to pick it up. "You landed the critical interview. You got the story. That's how it works."

Zoe gave her a sad smile and squeezed her hand. "Your time is coming, Jess. I just know it. And I owe you. Anytime you need me, just say the word."

"Sure. Congratulations, Zoe."

Zoe dropped her eyes to her feet. "Guess we'd better get in there and finish our expense reports, huh?"

"You go on. I'm going to—" She had no idea what she was going to do, but whatever it was, she was getting out of the newsroom until she could sit at her desk without breaking something in frustration. "I'm going for a cup of coffee."

She headed back downstairs and outside. She needed to talk, and not to Lina, or her sisters, or anyone else in her real life. Regardless of what everyone seemed to think about Peabody's role in her life, right now, she needed him.

Chapter Eleven

Peabody hadn't been online when she'd gotten Zoe's terrible news about her story, and her disappointment had been profound. Somehow, being unable to talk to him about it made the whole thing even worse than it already was.

But later that night, when she settled on her bed and checked her phone, she saw he'd messaged her, just an hour earlier.

Peabody: I thought about you today. I think about you a lot, actually. Sorry, did I just get weird? Too much? Whatever, it's the truth. Anyway, today, something happened. Someone said something to me, and I had this overwhelming urge to turn to you to see your reaction. Isn't that crazy? I could picture you right there next to me, and I just knew what you'd say. Which is funny, because I can't really picture you at all. I don't know what you look like, or what your voice sounds like, but it feels like I do. Without knowing anything specific about you, I could still feel you right next to me. I'm not even making sense to myself.

Oh. It took her several long moments to draw in a full breath, never mind marshaling her thoughts enough to manage a coherent response.

PaperGirl: It's not crazy. Not at all. I must have thought about you at least a dozen times today. I got some terrible news at work today, and even though I could have vented to a dozen people about it, you're the first person I wanted to talk to.

Peabody: I'm sorry about work. I'm here now. Vent away.

PaperGirl: I'm past it now. I'll survive, and next time I'll get it right.

Peabody: You amaze me. It's been a long time since I've met anyone as determined as you.

PaperGirl: You really have a knack for making me feel good about myself.

Peabody: Well, you make it easy. You do the same for me, you know. Having you to talk to is becoming the best part of my days.

Okay, maybe it was time to give him a firm nudge in the right direction.

PaperGirl: It's the same for me. What are we going to do about this?

She hit send before she could talk herself out of it.

A few minutes went by without a reply and she tried to imagine what he was doing, what he was thinking.

Peabody: I think the best part of our days could be even better if we were face-to-face.

Jess let out a long exhale and clutched her phone to her chest. *Yes.* He *did* want to meet her. The idea made her nervous, but she was far more excited than scared. He texted again before she could reply.

Peabody: But not yet. I'm not ready yet.

In an instant, her hopes deflated, and a speck of doubt wiggled its way in. Maybe everybody at work was right. What did she really know about him? He'd said he was single, but maybe his idea of single and hers were two different things. Plenty of guys would do that, but she hated to think Peabody was one of them.

PaperGirl: Is there a reason you can't?

Peabody: It's not what you're thinking, I promise you. I'm not involved with anybody.

PaperGirl: Then what is it?

Peabody: There are things about me you don't know. Things I haven't told you. Once you know, things might change.

PaperGirl: I can't imagine anything you tell me changing what I think of you.

Peabody: I've just had some past experiences that make me wary. This isn't about you. It's about me.

PaperGirl: Okay. I don't want to push you into something you don't want.

Peabody: It's not a matter of wanting. I want it.

His text glowed on her screen with its almost-confession, the almost-words. *I want you.* She desperately wanted to believe that. But her more rational side was being eminently sensible right now, reminding her that while he'd been a perfect gentleman in their every interaction, she didn't really know him. In the beginning, she'd thought this intellectual connection was enough, but it turned out she needed more than words before she could fully trust him.

But she also couldn't blame him for being cautious. It was scary, meeting someone face-to-face that you'd only known online. Maybe she'd be disappointed, or he would. Maybe the chemistry they had when they were messaging would fail to materialize when they were sitting across from each other.

His hesitation was perfectly understandable, and he'd given her every indication of being a good guy. She owed him a little more time to sort things out for himself.

PaperGirl: It's okay. I understand.

Peabody: I'm sorry. I don't want to lose this.

PaperGirl: You won't lose it. I'm still here.

Peabody: You have no idea how much that matters to me. I don't have a lot of people I can call a friend and really know it's true.

Friend. What a ghastly word. But that's all they were for now. Friends, burgeoning with the promise of something more.

She honestly valued his friendship. Even if all she ever had was this online communication, that was okay. Yes, she had a bone-deep sense that there could be much more between them…something really special. But only when he was ready. So they'd stay friends until Peabody was ready to take things to the next level. She just hoped it was soon.

Chapter Twelve

"Jessica! Mariel's office, now!" Lauren bellowed across the newsroom.

Jess groaned in frustration. What now? Did her fingers make too much noise when she typed? As she made her way to Mariel's office, everyone she passed gave her commiserating smiles.

"You wanted to see me, Lauren?" she asked brightly. Mariel, Lauren, Isaiah, and Hassan from Circulation were clustered around Mariel's desk, looking at something on her laptop.

Lauren spun Mariel's laptop around. "Do you mind explaining this?"

She took a step closer to see. Oh, no. The paper's Twitter account was open on the screen, and there was the back-and-forth exchange she'd been engaged in with ClickNews. Okay, in retrospect, that had been very unwise.

"They've been goading me." And now she sounded like a child. How could she have been so stupid? So irresponsible? Why couldn't she have just ignored them?

"The *Urbanist* wrote a goddamned post about it!" Lauren clicked to a new tab and imperiously pointed to the screen.

"What?" Jess was filled with dread as she moved closer to read. The *Urbanist* was possibly the most popular site in the five boroughs for New York–centric pop culture and gossip. The headline said "Old Media Takes on New Media in Everybody's Favorite New Flame War." What followed were screen caps of her tweets with ClickNews, along with screen caps of other users, commenting on the argument. Sometime since she'd last replied to them, their exchange had gone viral. In a major way.

@cece978 *Daaaamnnn, @Brooklyn_Daily_Post, school that asshole hard!*

@victorious_mel *Hey, @ClickNews, you gonna let them talk to you like that? Come on, dude!*

@spronks_in_Queens *This is my favorite thing on Twitter right now.*

@stephanie679 *Is it weird that I'm kinda shipping these Twitter accounts?*

@allison_smith *@stephanie679 Me too!*

"I'm afraid to ask what *shipping* means," Mariel said.

Hassan saved Jess from having to explain. "It's when someone is a fan of a relationship, real or imagined, between two fictional characters. Or in this case, two Twitter handles."

"What do you mean, a fan of the relationship?"

Hassan shrugged. "Like, you wanna see the relationship happen. Get it? Relationship? Ship? It's a verb."

Mariel scowled. "No, I don't get it."

"It's like in *Vampire Diaries*. Some people shipped Stelena and some people shipped Delena."

Mariel's expression was blank. "Are you using real words right now?"

Hassan took a deep breath. "Okay, obviously we need to go older. Did you watch *The X Files*?"

"Everybody did."

"Were you rooting for Mulder and Scully to get together?"

"Sure. Everyone was."

"Then you shipped them," Hassan explained. "Just like Maddie and Dave in *Moonlighting*, or Han and Leia in *Star Wars*."

"But that was part of the plot."

"Sometimes people ship characters who *don't* get together in the plot."

"Like Han and Luke," Isaiah interjected, with a slightly guilty expression on his face. "Or Han and Lando."

Hassan gave Isaiah an approving nod. "Nice."

Mariel blinked. "People *do* that?"

"Oh, yeah," Hassan and Isaiah said in unison.

"And they're doing that about the *Daily Post* and ClickNews?"

"And they're having loads of fun doing it." Hassan looked at Isaiah. "I bet there's already fan fic."

"Mmm-hmm. You know it."

"Dare I ask what fan fic is?"

Hassan shook his head. "It's too soon. The fic would blow your mind. Hey, Mariel, I know it's new territory for you, but this is going viral in a big way. You can't buy this kind of coverage. It's pretty amazing. Good work, Jess."

"What are you talking about?" Lauren fumed. "This is a *disaster.*"

"Lauren, this thing is blowing up our feed. Think about it. The *Urbanist* is writing about us."

"Not for anything good! Just her Twitter bullshit. I knew I never should have let you take over the accounts."

What? No way was she going to rewrite history. "Let me? Lauren, you didn't *let* me—"

Hassan cut her off. "People are following the paper's Twitter in droves. We've got over two thousand followers as of this morning."

Jess gasped. "Two thousand followers? We had forty-seven when I started tweeting."

"And it'll go up all day as people read that *Urbanist* post," Hassan added. "I bet we crack ten K before the end of the day."

Mariel pressed her palms down onto her desktop. "Obviously I'm a little behind on this social media stuff." She glanced at Isaiah. "And a lot of other things. Do these Twitter followers actually translate into a readership? That's all I need to know."

"We've gotten fifty-two online subscriptions since I logged off last night. And I haven't checked the hard copy delivery subscriptions yet."

"Fifty-two new subscriptions?" Jess echoed in disbelief.

"Well." Mariel sat back in her chair. "That answers that, I guess."

"You want her to keep doing this?" Lauren asked in disbelief.

"We do what works. I've been looking for inventive new ways to increase our readership. Looks like we've found one, however distasteful I might find it personally."

"So you want me to keep it up?" Somehow, miraculously, she didn't seem to be in trouble. For the first time since she'd walked into Mariel's office, Jess exhaled.

"Don't go nuclear on ClickNews, but yes. Jess, you seem to have a knack for… Hassan, what did you call it?"

"A Twitter feud."

"Right. You seem to be adept at these Twitter feuds. And, although I have no intention of emulating anything about ClickNews, the fact of the matter is, they court a much younger demographic. A demographic we're going to need if we want a hope of turning this paper around. So yes, go forth and tweet with my blessing."

Lauren huffed. "But, Mariel—"

"Lauren, Jess has done more to improve the paper's circulation in the past twenty-four hours than anyone has since the restructuring. While I wish it was our hard-hitting and insightful reporting responsible for the numbers, I'll take success any way I can get it. Good job, Jess. Just try to talk about our headlines once in a while, too, so we're at least attempting to make this about journalism."

"I will. Thanks, Mariel." This time, she couldn't help but throw a smug smile in Lauren's direction before she left.

Apparently having the discussion in Mariel's office hadn't been the least bit effective in keeping it private. As Jess started back toward her desk, the newsroom broke out in scattered applause and whistles. Everybody had found their way to the *Urbanist* post and were calling out their favorite comments as she passed.

"'Whoever is manning the *Daily Post* Twitter feed is my new hero.' Kick ass, Jess." Caleb gave her a thumbs-up.

"'I've been refreshing my Twitter feed all day, just waiting to see what they say next,'" Dana read off her monitor.

"'New Yorkers haven't had this much fun watching two titans go head-to-head since Macy's took on Gimbels in *Miracle on 34th Street*,'" Marc shouted.

"Hey, look at that!" Natalie laughed. "We're a titan now!"

Jess spun in a little circle and gave a silly curtsy to her clapping, cheering coworkers. Like Mariel, she'd have preferred it if it was her kick-ass reporting and incendiary writing that was bringing the accolades, but she'd take success anywhere she could find it, and right now, this success felt *great*.

Chapter Thirteen

It was too cold to go out for lunch, Alex thought, as he walked headfirst into the brutal wind blowing off the East River. But Chase and Andy had been trying to drag him out to lunch, and he just wasn't in the mood for it today. Frankly, he was never in the mood to listen to Chase brag about his latest sexual conquest, and that was pretty much all he ever talked about. How had he once found the guy fun to hang out with? It was a mystery.

Samaira, one of the ragtag team of writers euphemistically referred to as ClickNews's "reporting pool," had mentioned a new sandwich place around the corner, so Alex seized the opening and escaped. Now here he was, freezing his ass off instead of ordering in, all to avoid Chase. He should really figure out a way to shed the friendship. Then again, he hadn't heard from Chase in ages before they started seeing each other every day at work, and soon enough, he'd be moving on from ClickNews, so the Chase problem would likely take care of itself.

The Jessica problem, however, wasn't going away. In fact, it seemed to dog his every step. Inside the sandwich place, there she stood, blowing on her hands to warm them up, cheeks pink from the cold and hair tousled from the wind. It always amazed him that someone so prickly and hostile could still manage to look so cute. Like an adorable woodland creature who would claw your face off when you reached a hand out to pet it. He'd developed a healthy respect for Jess's face-clawing abilities long ago.

Alex stepped up silently behind her. "First the coffee place and now you're stalking me in my favorite lunch place, Jess?" So maybe he'd never stepped foot in the place before today, but he'd never waste an opportunity to provoke Jess Romano. It was way too much fun.

She jumped and let out a small gasp of surprise. Something thumped in his chest at the sound. It did it again when she turned those large, dark brown eyes on him.

"I was here first," she pointed out tartly. "Which means you're stalking *me*. What are you doing here, anyway?"

"I'm here to see the new *Avengers* movie. Is this the right place?"

She rolled her eyes before turning her attention back to the menu board. Her teeth dug into her bottom lip as she considered. Those teeth. That lip. Annoyed with himself, Alex dragged his eyes away from her mouth and focused on the menu board, too. He could do without getting his face clawed off today.

When Jess learned ClickNews had moved into the neighborhood, she'd never dreamed it would mean crossing paths—and crossing swords—with Alex this often. It seemed everywhere she turned, there he was, impossible to avoid or ignore.

Now they were both examining their phones like it was their job, pointedly not interacting, but that hardly meant she was unaware of him. How could she *not* be aware of him, standing a foot to her left, being all impossibly tall and handsome? Nobody should look so good in a winter coat. No shapeless puffy coat, flattened hat-hair, and dripping red nose, like the rest of the New Yorkers. Nope. With his hair freshly tousled by the wind whipping off the East River, he looked like a model advertising winter instead of an ordinary human enduring it.

When it was her turn to place her order, she hurriedly stepped forward, happy to escape Alex's nerve-jangling presence. After she ordered, she moved down the counter to wait, perusing last night's text exchange with Peabody. They texted every day, sometimes stupid stuff, sometimes long, heartfelt exchanges. They were still no closer to a face-to-face meeting, but he was still the first person she talked to in the morning and the last one she talked to at night.

Next, she popped over to Twitter to check in. Not her *own* Twitter, of course. In the weeks since her *Urbanist* triumph, she'd abandoned that to focus all her energy on the *Daily Post* Twitter. Last night, she'd had another dustup with ClickNews, a rapid-fire series of tweets and replies that left her heart pounding with adrenaline. This morning, her mentions were full of fan replies. Excellent. Jess fired off a pithy response to ClickNews's most recent tweet—just moments ago— to set the tone for today's battle.

"Good news?"

Alex had placed his order, too, and instead of waiting in the opposite corner and ignoring her, like a proper New Yorker, he'd followed her. "What?"

"You're grinning at your phone like a Disney villain. Is your evil plan for world domination finally falling into place?"

Feeling triumphant and magnanimous, she gave him a broad, genuine smile. "You could say that."

Alex blinked at her in consternation. It was a delight throwing him off his game. In her opinion, the world didn't throw Alex enough curveballs. Being confused was good for him.

"Speaking of world domination and evil plans, how are things at ClickNews?"

Was it wrong, striking up an idle conversation with her sworn enemy hoping he'd drop a tidbit about the Twitter feud? It would make her day, her week, her *year*, to hear him bitch about it, all the while hugging to herself the secret knowledge that she was the one behind it all.

He raked a hand through his hair. It fell into a disordered, cinnamon-highlighted, perfect mess. "Great. Page views are skyrocketing. Ad revenues are through the roof."

"Oh." Not exactly what she wanted to hear. "Good for you. Bet your dad is thrilled."

"And the *Daily Post*? You guys changing the world yet?"

"Our subscriptions are up forty percent over this period last year." And all due to her, although she couldn't share that part.

"Wow. Forty percent. So that means another sixteen subscribers? The *New York Times* better watch its back."

"Hey—"

"Sir? Your order's ready."

Somehow, even though she'd ordered before him, he'd managed to get served first. How very Alex Drake.

"Hold that nasty thought," he said with a wink, striding away to pick up his food.

Fine, let him take his lunch and go. When she looked back down, intending to text Peabody, she saw Alex had left his phone on the counter where he'd been standing. She picked it up and stepped forward, intending to call out to him, but then she saw what was still glowing on his unlocked screen.

He had his Twitter app open to his mentions. And there, at the top of the column, was her last *Daily Post* tweet from just a few minutes ago. But...how... That would mean...

The dots connected with swift and stunning certainty. This could *not* be happening.

The only way Alex could be seeing her tweets in his mentions was if *he* was the one logged into the ClickNews Twitter account.

No. *No!*

She snatched up his phone and scrolled down. There were all the same mentions from the fans that she got, and when she swiped back to his timeline, there was ClickNews's tweet from just a few minutes ago, when Alex had been standing next to her in line—on his phone.

"What are you doing with my phone?"

She looked up. "It's *you!*"

"Excuse me?" He held out his hand. "Are you finished invading my privacy? Can I have my phone back?"

She spun it around, shoving it in his face. "Click-News's Twitter account is on *your* phone. It's *you*!"

With an annoyed scowl, he snatched the phone out of her hand. "So what if I'm logged into the site's Twitter? Why do you care?"

"But…it's *you*! I can't believe this!"

Slowly, he looked up at her with dawning horror. "Wait…is it… Tell me you're not…"

She turned her own phone to face him, their exchange from last night glowing on her screen.

"It's *you*." Color tinted the tops of his cheekbones, a dead giveaway that he was rattled.

"What the hell are you doing manning ClickNews's Twitter feed? Aren't you like the Editor in Chief or something?"

"I was unhappy with what the PR firm was doing with our social media so I gave it a go myself."

She would never, ever admit to him how impressed she'd been by those tweets. Or that she was impressed he did the work himself rather than paying someone to do it for him. It was so annoying when Alex turned out to be good at stuff.

"Why are *you* doing it?" he challenged. "I thought you were a reporter."

That was embarrassing to admit, too, but she had no choice. "The paper couldn't afford a social media manager this year."

"That's too bad. Must be driving you crazy not to be tackling the real news." With a falsely sympathetic frown, he air-quoted "real news."

It was all she could do not to smack that arrogant, taunting, beautiful face of his. Ugh, how dare he throw her own words back at her? How dare he be *right* about that?

"Yeah, maybe I won't win a Pulitzer on Twitter, but the paper's subscription rates are through the roof because of me, which helps everybody, including our staff reporting on the *real news*."

He shook his head sadly. "Be careful, Jess. Sounds an awful lot like rationalizing."

"Says the guy using his journalism degree to write tweets for a gossip website."

Now it was his turn to look furious, and she *reveled* in it. That incendiary glint in his eyes made her every last nerve ending stand at attention. Electricity crackled through her bloodstream. What was it about baiting Alex that was so exciting…dangerous…fun?

"Yeah, well, those tweets caught the attention of the *Urbanist*, in case you missed it." He was practically swaggering with pride as he took a step closer, all tall and loose-limbed, towering over her.

"You think *your* tweets did it? I'm the popular one here. I *own* you on Twitter."

Alex scoffed. "In your dreams."

Jess thrust her phone in his face. "I smell a challenge. You ready for me?"

He startled, leaning back. "What, here? Now?"

"What's the matter? Can't come up with a good tweet without twenty-four hours and four drafts?"

"Brace yourself, Romano." He furiously typed something out on his phone.

She glanced down to see what he'd tweeted.

Witty, succinct, and biting. Not that she'd ever tell him so. "Not bad."

A wicked smile spread across his face, and Jess felt it in her toes. "So?"

"So, what?"

"Are you going to show me what you've got?"

Jess wasn't quite sure how it happened. Before she knew it, she and Alex were across from one another in a corner of the cafe, the remains of their lunch scattered between them, as they sat, phones in hand, and slammed each other on Twitter.

She hit send on her last tweet, glancing up to gauge his reaction as she polished off her chips. One sharply angled eyebrow hiked up in a perfect inverted V and he tipped his head to the side. "Decent."

"That was brilliant and you know it."

His brows furrowed as he leaned forward, typing furiously. "Sweetheart, you haven't seen brilliant yet."

He was just poking at her, she told herself. That *sweetheart* was completely sarcastic, an insult, not an endearment. Apparently her heart didn't receive that message, though, because when he looked up at her, green eyes flashing and a grin lighting up his face, it did a totally unexpected somersault in her chest.

It was just…hormones…pheromones…whatever. Some primordial lizard brain response to a hot guy smiling at her. A hot guy whose devastatingly good kiss she could still remember like it was yesterday. A hot guy she'd once had a complicated, reluctant crush on. No matter how ruthlessly she'd squashed that crush all these years, some of the wiring remained in place, and when Alex was this close to her, smiling at her like that, the switch got flipped on those ancient, forgotten feelings.

A prickling heat was spreading up her neck that had nothing to do with the radiator clanking out steam heat in the corner. He was still grinning at her, waiting for her to read his tweet and respond. The air seemed to contract around her and suddenly, it was hard to draw a deep breath. Alex's expression shifted, his smile sliding away, the gleeful glint in his eyes turning into something else altogether.

Just when it felt one of them was going to have to say something to dispel this unbearable tension, someone else did it for them.

"Well, this is interesting."

Jess startled and turned to see Lauren looming over their table. "Lauren…"

"Taking a meeting with ClickNews? I'm sure Mariel will find this fascinating."

She and Alex started speaking in unison.

"It's not—"

"I didn't… This isn't a meeting," Jess stammered helplessly. But it sure would look like one to Lauren, wouldn't it? Her stomach twisted into knots as she reached for some sort of reasonable explanation.

To her surprise, Alex stepped in to save her. "Jess and I went to college together. We ran into each other getting lunch and we were just catching up."

Lauren's frosty blue gaze swiveled back to Jess, pinning her like a butterfly to a board. "You have a friend at ClickNews?"

"We're not friends."

"Not at all," Alex helpfully chimed in. "In fact, I'm pretty sure she hates me."

"I do. And he hates me, so—"

"You hate each other so much you're having lunch together?"

"What can I say?" Alex said, throwing out a practiced, gorgeous grin. "Even my enemies can't resist me."

Lauren's eyes raked scathingly over Alex, then landed back on Jess. "Jess, is that Twitter on your phone?"

Jess fought down the urge to hide it. "Um, yes, I was just—"

Lauren glanced at Alex. "It's him, isn't it? This stupid little Twitter feud you've got going with Click-News. It's with him."

"I—"

"We didn't know at first," Alex interjected. "Isn't that crazy?"

"Crazy. What a coincidence." As she turned toward the counter to order, she tossed over her shoulder, "See you back at the newsroom, Jess."

What a disaster.

Jess scrambled to wrap up her trash. "I gotta go."

"Hey." Alex reached out and dropped his hand over her wrist to still her, and it was like a hot iron had just branded her. Her eyes flew to that point of contact and she couldn't drag them up to look at Alex if she tried. "Are you okay?"

Sliding her hand out from under his, she busied herself with shrugging into her coat. "Lauren doesn't like me, that's all." At least, she hoped that was all.

Alex leaned back in his chair, watching her as she buttoned up. "Okay, well… I guess I'll see you soon."

Her fingers fumbled with the last button. She looked up at him in confusion.

He waved his phone in the air. "Twitter."

"Oh. Right." She now had a standing arrangement with Alex Drake. Seemed she'd had one for a while now, she just hadn't known it.

Regaining a bit of her equilibrium, she slung her bag over her shoulder and grinned at him. "Brace yourself. I'm just getting started with you."

He pinned her with another one of those electric stares that hit her like a fist behind her rib cage. "You have no idea what I can do, Romano."

Her mouth felt dry and her skin felt too tight as she forced a cocky grin. "Looking forward to it, Drake."

Chapter Fourteen

The New York Newsmaker award ceremony and banquet was the industry highlight of the year. Every major player in New York journalism, all in one room, and this year, thanks to Mariel's generosity, Jess got to be a part of it.

Naturally, due to a stalled train at Jay Street, she was late. She just prayed her hair, carefully coaxed into smooth waves, wouldn't be a frizzy mess by the time she made it inside. She ditched her coat at the coat check and hurried to the ballroom, finding Lina waiting for her outside, chatting with Hassan.

"Hey, sorry I'm late. Wow, you look fantastic." Lina had poured her stunning curves into a skintight red knit dress, its demure knee-length hem and long sleeves offset by a plunging back. Jess's feet hurt just looking at her impossibly high heels.

"I know, right?" Hassan said, giving Lina an appreciative once-over.

"Hands to yourself, mister." She gave Hassan a playful shove before looking Jess over. "You look so cute in that dress, Jess."

In Jess's experience, girls who barely cleared five feet were never described as "sexy" or "stunning," just "cute." She'd long since resigned herself to it. But Lina was right. In her black beaded minidress with its deeply scooped neckline, she looked pretty good, if she said so herself. And while she wasn't sporting Lina's skyscraper stilettos, her strappy black heels did great things for her legs. "Thanks, it's *vintage*. Which really means it was my mom's."

Lina laughed. "Well, your mom had good taste. You look great. Let's get in there and get our free drink on, yes?"

"Yes! I've been looking forward to tonight for *weeks*."

All her enthusiasm for the night ahead nearly shriveled up on the spot when they walked into the ballroom and were immediately confronted with Alex Drake and Chase Bennett, standing just inside the door.

"This is getting ridiculous!" Jess hissed in a whisper to Lina. "Everywhere I go, there he is."

"I wish *Eternal Sunshine of the Spotless Mind* was real," Lina sighed wistfully. "And you could just erase annoying people out of your life."

Hassan elbowed in between them. "Who are we talking about?"

Alex and Chase turned to face them, and there was a moment—it came and went so fast, Jess was sure she imagined it—when Alex's eyes slid down the length of her body in undisguised appreciation before they found their way back up to her face. That must have been when he realized who she was, because the admiration leached away, replaced by the stone-faced expression he always reserved for her.

"We really need to stop meeting like this, Alex. It's becoming embarrassing."

"What are you doing here?"

She waved a hand at the room behind him. "It's the New York Newsmaker awards. I'm a New York newsmaker. And I guess you are, too. In theory."

The glare he shot her could have melted the beads off her dress, but Chase spoke before he could zing her with a biting comeback.

"Lina. You're looking gorgeous tonight, as always."

Lina sniffed. "I know."

"Is this your brother?" Chase asked, indicating Hassan.

Wait...*what*? Jess looked from Alex to Chase. Surely that was a joke? A seriously bad, racist joke?

Alex flinched. "Jesus, Chase..."

Lina's eyes flared with rage. "This is Hassan. He's not my brother, because *he's* Pakistani and *I'm* Puerto Rican!"

Chase, not the least bit shamed, held his hands up and grinned. "Sorry. No offense."

Lina rolled her eyes. "Ugh. Come on, guys, I need a drink."

"See you around, Lina!" Chase called after them.

"Not if I can help it!" she shouted back.

Hassan collared a passing waiter and snagged three glasses of champagne. "So who's your asshole friend?"

Lina nearly growled as she slugged back half her glass. "*Not* my friend. I would happily chop off Chase Bennett's dick before I called him a friend."

Jess took a sip of her champagne. "We're not going to let either one of them spoil our night."

"No," Lina declared. "No, we're not."

The *Brooklyn Daily Post* staff had been seated at

the same large, round table. Jess took a seat beside Hassan and Lina.

Mariel smiled across the table at them. "Jessica, Lina, Hassan, nice to see you all here tonight."

"Hi, Mariel," Jess said. "Thanks so much for the invite. I'm really excited for this."

"Don't thank me yet." Mariel reached for her wine. "You might feel very differently after you sit through Peter Volk's keynote speech. He's a sexist old windbag and his jokes are terrible."

Everyone laughed and the chatter around their table continued to be light and fun. Another glass of champagne and Jess was starting to enjoy herself in earnest. The reporting staff were one-upping each other with the most embarrassing stories they'd ever covered, while Hassan showed Lina and Isaiah pictures of his last cosplay at Comic Con, and Lina teased him ruthlessly about the size of his light saber.

Then she saw the one thing that could destroy her evening coming toward their table. Well, the three things—Alex Drake, his father, and Chase trailing in their wake.

Dan Drake, dressed impeccably in a tux, threw his arms wide. "It's the *Brooklyn Daily Post*, New York's favorite underdog story!"

Mariel scrambled to her feet, clearly unwilling to have Dan Drake tower over her as she sat. Dan cast an imposing figure, but so did Mariel, in her way. Her dress was an ivory beaded sheath that hung straight down on her slim body. Her hair was swept up in a French twist, and the only jewelry she wore was a chunky gold circlet around her neck. She looked like an Olympian goddess, casting judgment down on all the lesser mortals huddled at her feet.

"Mr. Drake," she said, her own smile like an ice-cold blade compared to Dan's mega-watt grin. "It was so kind of the organizers to include your website in the invitations."

Everyone at their table sucked in a breath. "Sick burn," Hassan whispered appreciatively.

ClickNews might be one of the biggest names in internet news, but Jess was far from the only traditional journalist questioning their credibility. Drake's new website didn't hold much cachet in a crowd of serious journalists like this and he knew it.

But Dan easily absorbed Mariel's swipe, something flaring in his eyes, a kind of sharpened awareness, like a shark who'd just smelled blood in the water. "Yes, well, it's all due to my secret weapons. Have you met these two brilliant young men?"

Alex had been hovering silently behind his father. Now he stepped forward and politely shook Mariel's hand. "Nice to meet you, Ms. Kemper. I'm Alex Drake."

"You're the one running the news department at ClickNews these days?"

"No, that would be me," Chase interjected, extending his own hand. "Chase Bennett."

"I see." Mariel managed to pour an ocean of judgment and scorn into those two little words.

"We're doing some really exciting things in journalism, right, Mr. Drake?" Chase asked, clapping Dan on the shoulder with far more familiarity than Alex showed.

Mariel's eyebrows lifted. "Exciting? That's one way to describe it, I suppose."

"We'd better get back to our table," Alex murmured to his father.

"Yes, I'm presenting, so I'd better get ready," Mariel replied.

Another dig. She was a respected member of this establishment in a way the Drakes weren't. Dan Drake, no matter how many networks he acquired, would never be asked to present at this venue.

Dan gave her another smile. "I look forward to it. It was…a *delight* to see you again, Mariel. Enjoy your evening."

"Oh, my god," Lina breathed. "He's totally checking her out."

When they were gone, Mariel dropped back into her chair with a growl. "Insufferable, presumptuous, arrogant, egotistical, obstreperous, bombastic, insolent *asshole*!"

"Too many adjectives, sweetheart," Isaiah drawled as he refilled her wine.

The table erupted in laughter, which broke the tension.

Jess pushed back from the table. "I'm getting food before this thing starts. You coming, Lina?"

"Not just yet," Lina turned back to Hassan. "Maybe later."

Okay. Hassan. That was surprising.

The buffet table held an unappealing spread of pasta, limp vegetables, and overcooked meat wallowing in gravy, steaming in silver trays.

"I'd stick to the salad."

She jumped and turned to glare at Alex. "Really? Again? I thought we'd agreed to avoid each other tonight."

"We did? Sorry, I didn't get the memo."

She snatched up a plate and started indiscriminately plopping food onto it. "It was implied."

"Listen, I'm sorry about Chase."

"Keep him away from Lina or he might lose a limb."

"Deservedly. That was pretty bad."

Well, at least he knew that. "Yep, pretty bad."

"And sorry about my dad. He's…hard to corral sometimes."

"Your table is a handful tonight."

Alex blew out a frustrated breath. "You could say that. I'm sorry if Dad pissed you off."

"He didn't piss me off."

"He pissed off Mariel and I know you're protective of her."

"Mariel can take care of herself."

Alex let out a snort of laughter. "That's putting it mildly. I can't remember the last time somebody took the skin off my dad like that, and she barely even said anything."

"She's very smart."

"Yes, well… I just didn't want you thinking that was my idea. I know we have…"

"We have what?" She dropped the spoon back in the gooey tortellini alfredo and turned to look up at him. A tuxedo was a dangerous weapon when deployed by Alex. It was all Jess could do not to take a step back just to give herself room to breathe.

He waved a hand between them. "Past history? Present resentments? Open hostilities? A declaration of war? Take your pick."

"E. All of the above."

Alex chuckled again, sparking a curious little curl

of satisfaction in her stomach. Making him laugh was almost as good as making him mad. "Well, I promise I'll keep him pinned down at our table. Enjoy your night."

And just when she was gearing up for a good scrap with him, he smiled politely, turned, and left. Jess clutched her plate, feeling oddly deflated as she watched him make his way across the room.

Fine. He could stay on his side of the room and she'd stay on hers so she could enjoy her evening.

"Was that Alex Drake?" She startled at the sound of Mariel's voice behind her. She was arranging a tidy little pile of salad greens on her plate. "I didn't realize you knew him."

A frisson of alarm raced down Jess's spine. Damn Alex Drake, forever landing her in these awkward situations. But at least now she knew Lauren hadn't ratted her out to Mariel after she caught them together. That was surprising, honestly, but she wasn't going to question her good fortune. "Um…we went to college together."

Mariel's eyebrows lifted expressively. "Really? You went to college with Alex Drake?"

"And Chase Bennett. So did Lina."

"That's some graduating class."

"We weren't exactly friends." Ugh, now she sounded defensive, which wasn't helping.

"He seemed friendly enough just now."

It's just an act, she wanted to scream. *Don't fall for it!* But that would be rude and immature. "We don't run in the same circles at all. I've barely seen him since graduation. He was just saying hello." *Oh, my God, shut up, Jess*. She sounded wildly guilty to her own ears.

"Of course. This pasta looks a little suspect, doesn't it?"

Jess let out a shaky exhale. Disaster averted. "Sure does. I'd avoid it if I were you."

Jess fully intended to do the same. She'd avoid the pasta, the buffet table, and every single man in this room with the last name Drake.

Lina pounced as soon as Jess made it back to their table. "What was Alex saying to you?"

"Did Lauren see us?" She glanced quickly at Lauren, who was halfway across the room. The last thing she needed was for Lauren to see her talking to Alex again. That might provoke her into telling Mariel all about that disastrous lunch after all.

"Nah, she's been too busy kissing asses all over the room. You're deflecting."

"He didn't say anything. Well, he apologized for Chase and his dad."

"Chase is the one who should be apologizing."

"Yeah, I don't see that happening. Do you?"

Lina chuckled. "Chase? Self-aware? Perish the thought. Still, it was nice of Alex."

"Strangely nice. He must be coming down with something."

"Jess, I know you hate him—"

Jess let out an ungraceful snort.

"—but he's not so terrible."

"Lina, he's an arrogant, entitled—"

"You sound like Mariel talking about Dan."

"They're exactly the same."

Lina shrugged and sipped her champagne. "Maybe when we started college, but Alex grew up a lot in those years. More than *Chase* did, obviously."

She set down her fork and twisted in her seat to face Lina. "What are you suggesting, Lina?"

Lina fiddled with her champagne flute, turning it in circles. "Just maybe give him a chance?"

Prickles of uncomfortable awareness broke out across her skin, making her feel weirdly cold and burning up with heat at the same time. "A chance for what?"

"He was checking you out when we came in."

Thank God her skin didn't flush easily, because she felt the heat start in her belly and race up her chest and neck. "That doesn't mean anything. It was just a male libido stretching its legs. Chase was blatantly leering at you, and you know how sincere that was."

Lina rolled her eyes. "Chase and Alex might be friends, but they're not the same person at all."

"I can't believe you're suggesting I should—"

"I'm just saying—"

"Lina, I have Peabody."

"He's not *real*!"

"Yes, he is! Just because I haven't met him yet, that doesn't mean I imagined him. I've shown you his messages, Lina. You know how amazing he is."

"Jess, he might be amazing, but right now, all he is is a screen name. Are you willing to pass up a flesh-and-blood real-life opportunity for a bunch of texts?"

"Alex is *not* an opportunity."

"He could be." Lina pushed her chair back and laid a hand on Jess's shoulder as she passed behind her chair. "Think about it. I'm going to get something to eat."

"Stick to the salad."

Lina's words ate away at her. Not the Alex part. That was patently ridiculous. The Peabody part.

Was she being foolish, considering herself already half-committed to him when he was avoiding meeting her face-to-face? Was she passing up "real life" opportunities for a guy who might, in the end, never be more to her than a username on her phone?

Did Peabody not count as "real," no matter how much she enjoyed what was happening between them? Maybe. And maybe she wasn't really satisfied with texting, despite convincing herself she was. She wanted more. And if he didn't, then she had a real problem.

Chapter Fifteen

Monday dawned cold and damp, the sky a leaden gray blanket hanging low over the city. A frustrating morning trying to corner a city commissioner for an interview that never happened did little to improve Jess's mood.

When she got back to the paper, Lina was sitting at Sally's desk. Sally was standing behind her, a comforting hand on her shoulder as she pressed a cup of coffee into Lina's hands. They were both staring at Sally's computer monitor.

Cautiously, she approached Sally's desk. "Hey, guys. What's going on?"

Lina looked up from the monitor. Her dark eyes were glassy with unshed tears.

"Lina, what is it? What happened?"

"I got scooped," she murmured helplessly.

"What? Your Assemblyman Stevens story?"

"My source talked to somebody else."

Jess hurried around Sally's desk so she could see for herself. A cold tendril of dread unfurled in her stomach when she saw the screen. ClickNews. The assemblyman's ex-staffer—the source Lina had been so painstakingly developing—had spilled everything to a ClickNews reporter.

"Lina, I'm so sorry."

Lina inhaled shakily. "It's fine. I'm fine."

Jess rubbed her shoulders. "No, sweetie, you're not."

She shook her head fiercely, swiping away a tear. "This was going to be my first big story. Something that wasn't filler about building code violations and Christmas tree mulching. It was a byline I could brag about. And now—" Another tear slid down her cheek.

"Okay, we're taking an early lunch." Jess tugged Lina to her feet and marched her into the newsroom toward her desk. "Grab your stuff and let's go."

"But—"

"No buts. You need to get out of here for a little bit. As your best friend, it's my job to cheer you up. I'll even buy you a drink. You deserve one today. Coat. Purse. Let's go."

With a chuckle, Lina relented, sliding her arms into her coat and retrieving her purse from her desk drawer. "Okay, okay, I'm going."

"Good. Hassan, are you coming? And you, too, Zoe. This is an emergency. Lina needs a distraction."

Zoe scrambled out of her chair and grabbed her coat. "I am *excellent* at distractions. Ohh, let's go back to the fancy mac and cheese place. You can't be sad when you're eating mac and cheese. Natalie? Grab your stuff! Early lunch!"

Across the room, Natalie squealed in delight.

"Wait, I'm the only dude," Hassan protested. "Caleb, you have to come. And somebody find Griff."

Caleb stopped typing midsentence and swiveled

around in his chair. "You don't need to ask me twice to take an early lunch."

Lina spread her arms out for a hug. "You're the best, Jess. Thanks."

"No problem," Jess replied, folding her best friend in the world into a firm embrace. "What are best friends for?"

The long, rowdy group lunch did wonders to revive Lina's spirits. She was actually laughing as they made their way through the newsroom.

"Thanks for this, guys." She dropped her purse on her desk and began unbuttoning her coat.

"Anytime," Zoe said. "We've gotta take care of each other, right?"

"Here here! Solidarity!" Caleb said, raising his fist in the air. Caleb had had a couple of beers with lunch, so he was a bit more celebratory than the rest of them.

Hassan grabbed his arm and tugged it down. "Easy, there, Norma Rae. Have a cup of coffee and a mint before you go back to work. You smell like a brewery."

Jess looked around at her fellow reporters, hard-working and supportive, every single one. Maybe her career wasn't yet setting the world on fire, but she was so grateful to be working here.

She touched Lina's arm. "Are you going to be okay this afternoon?"

Lina smiled. "Yeah, I'm good. Thanks again, Jess."

Isaiah appeared in the doorway of the newsroom, looking funereal. "Good, you guys are back. Mariel's called an emergency staff meeting."

"I guess that's not surprising," Lina sighed.

Jess followed her to the conference room, where the

rest of the *Daily Post*'s reporters were rapidly assembling. Mariel, looking grim, sat at the head of the table.

"Good afternoon, everyone," Mariel said. There was a bit of rustling as people shifted in their seats, and one or two cleared throats, but no one said a thing. "So, Robin's EPA story was just business. Multiple reporters are often chasing the same story. Dana's MTA story might be reasonably chalked up to bad luck. But now, with Lina's story on Assemblyman Stevens breaking on ClickNews's site instead of ours, we officially have a problem. This was more than a source talking to more than one reporter. I've compared the story to Lina's notes and much of it appears word-for-word."

Beside Jess, Lina sucked in a breath. Not bad luck. Not an unfortunate coincidence. *Theft.* This was so much worse than she'd thought. A pin dropping would have sounded like cannon fire in the brittle silence following Mariel's words.

"Now, it's clear we've got a flow of information leaving the *Daily Post* newsroom and landing in ClickNews's lap. Let's start with tech. Griffin, is there any way they're accessing our internal server?"

Griffin leaned forward in his chair. "It wouldn't be impossible to get past my security firewall, but it would be extremely difficult and eventually I'd find it. The payoff doesn't seem worth the risk. I'll run a full diagnostic, but I doubt I'm going to find anything."

Mariel shook her head wearily. "I don't think so, either, but thank you for your diligence. I had to ask. All right. Moving on. If they didn't break in and steal the information, that means someone's giving it to them. And that someone has to be in this room."

Again, deafening silence met her pronouncement.

But she was right. The internal server only allowed access with a password, and only the reporters in this room had passwords. It meant one of the *Daily Post*'s own reporters was giving their stories to the competition.

Maybe she was guilty of being too idealistic sometimes, but Jess assumed everyone in this room had a minimum of ethical integrity. But someone—someone close to her—had betrayed them all.

Which one of her colleagues had done this? Jess looked at everyone in the room with new eyes. Griffin? He was the one person in a position to cover up any weirdness on the server. Or Isaiah? He was so talented. Maybe he thought he deserved more compensation than the *Daily Post* could ever afford to pay him. Robin had more experience than anyone in the room, outside Mariel. Maybe she was tired of playing second to Isaiah? Marc? He was young and ambitious, and he'd been openly envious of Lina's lead on this story. Dana? She had the baby at home and Jess had heard her complain about her tight finances more than once. Maybe someone was paying her for their stories and she leaked her own story to throw off suspicion—

Ugh. *Stop!* She would not give in to this impulse to distrust everyone, not without proof. If anyone deserved her suspicion, it was ClickNews. They were the thieves.

She had her own complicated opinions of Alex Drake, but never once would she have seriously considered him capable of something like this. It was possible he didn't know. Maybe there was a staffer there who wanted to make themselves look good and didn't have any scruples about how they accomplished it. But what if he knew?

She thought about all the times she ran into him at Ému, bickering and sniping at each other while they got coffee together. Saturday night at the banquet, when, for just a second at the buffet table, he'd seemed genuine. Or the Twitter feud. Did he do that to distract her, to divert attention away from the *Daily Post* articles that kept showing up on his site? She scolded herself for her paranoia. Of course not. How could he have known she was on the other side of that Twitter account? Besides, she was the one who started it. He didn't know about this. Suddenly, she very much needed to believe that.

But he worked there, and not just as some flunkie. His father owned ClickNews. With a sick, sinking feeling of horror, she remembered sitting with him in the cafe and looking up to find Lauren standing over them. And Mariel seeing them together at the banquet. Shit. Suddenly a lot of innocuous encounters looked a lot more suspicious in the light of these latest revelations.

Her association with Alex was entirely blameless, but that didn't stop her from feeling this creeping prickle of guilt across her skin. Well, there was nothing she could do about the past, but she had full control of the future. From here on out, if she so much as caught a glimpse of Alex, she'd turn around and run in the opposite direction. Maybe he was entirely innocent, but that was a chance she couldn't take.

Chapter Sixteen

If there was one thing worse than being guilted into doing a favor for a family friend, it was having that favor turn into an ambush, and right now, Alex Drake was definitely feeling ambushed.

When his father asked him to meet Georgia Gates, the daughter of Michael Gates, owner of a network they were hoping to acquire, it had seemed innocent enough. The girl had just finished college and moved to the city to start an internship. She didn't know anybody. Would he please meet her, give her a few tips on navigating the city, and make her feel welcomed? Remembering how isolated he'd felt in Chicago doing his own internship, Alex had agreed.

But this was all starting to feel suspiciously like a date, and he was the only person who hadn't known that.

Georgia leaned forward on her elbows, her smile gleaming in the light from the votive candle. Her teeth were alarmingly white, and all exactly the same small size, like a row of Tic Tacs. "So, Alex, what made you suggest this place? Is it, like, the restaurant everybody's talking about right now? Is it super hard to get into?"

Her eyes darted eagerly around the narrow Brooklyn eatery, as if hoping to spot a celebrity any second.

"It's close to your apartment, it fit your dietary requirements, and Yelp said the food was good," he replied flatly, before looking down at his plate of organic farro with pan-wilted locally sourced winter greens and a beet root reduction. That second part was definitely up for debate.

"Oh." Georgia deflated slightly, which made him feel bad. She wasn't *awful*. With her long, shiny blond hair and big blue eyes, she was attractive enough, in that highly groomed way, like a glossy doll. But her pointed questions about his father, his role in the company, and his life in New York set him on edge. He'd been subjected to this kind of interest from women way too many times in his life. She wasn't here to get to know *him*—Alex. She was after the Son of Daniel Drake, and all that entailed.

Georgia rallied fast shaking her hair back over her shoulders, making sure as she did so that her cleavage was visible. The skimpy little halter top she was wearing left her arms and back entirely exposed. It was December. She had to be freezing.

"So, are you doing anything fun for Christmas?"

"Just the—" But Georgia didn't let him finish before charging on.

"I'm going to Tulum in Mexico with my sorority sisters. It's totally been discovered, so it's a little *over*, if you know what I mean, but Stacia's parents have a condo there, so—"

Alex tuned out everything that came afterward. This was the other problem with Georgia. Even if she *had* been interested in learning about him, she was too busy trying to convince him of her own awesomeness to find anything out.

He snagged the drinks menu, because there was no way he was getting through this night without alcohol. It was printed on artfully stained parchment, in old-fashioned typeset, the paper then pinned to a small plank of wood with fig leaf push pins. This place was Ému Coffee and Tea all over again, but with a liquor license. His eyes skated down the list of cocktails, all with fanciful names and even more fanciful ingredients. Muddled thyme, rosemary sprigs, fennel greens, lemon zest…he wanted a glass of scotch, not a damned garden salad.

Georgia prattled on about which Mexican spas were the best ones, and how hard it was to find a decent place to get her highlights done in the city, as Alex morosely worked his way through a thoroughly unsatisfying plate of flavorless grains and blanched greens and willed the night to be over.

He was filled with annoyance, but not really at Georgia. None of this was her fault. Right now, his irritation lay squarely with his father. Dan had known exactly what he was doing when he asked Alex for this "favor," and it wasn't the first time. Being Dan Drake's son meant being part of his sales pitch, sent in to smile, charm, and glad-hand where Dan's own powers of persuasion wouldn't work. If Dan couldn't sweet-talk the father, then Alex could sweet-talk the daughter. Except Alex wasn't interested in sweet-talking anything other than a glass of good scotch and some red meat. Seemed he wasn't going to get anything he wanted tonight.

When Georgia paused to take a breath, Alex pointed at her plate. "Are you going to finish that?"

She glanced at her barely touched salad. "I'm not really hungry." Because, of course, she had to demonstrate to him that she subsisted on nothing more than air and CrossFit. Why had she insisted on eating at a vegan restaurant if she had no intention of eating? He'd kill for a cheeseburger right now.

"Great. I mean, fine. I'll get the check."

Georgia's eyes widened in alarm. Guess she'd planned on this "date" lasting longer than the time it took him to down his entree. But really, this was all pointless. She seemed to know her way around the city just fine, and she'd casually mentioned going out with her fellow interns after work several times, so she wasn't home pining away with loneliness. He'd been dragged into this by his father for one reason, and one reason only, and tonight, he refused to play ball.

As he paid the check, Georgia fiddled with the zipper on her coat. "I'd invite you back to my apartment to hang out, but I have roommates, which is *so* stupid—"

"It's okay." Gently, he herded her through the restaurant and out onto the sidewalk.

"But we could go to your place." She paused outside to look meaningfully at him. "If you wanted."

Damn. He'd really, really been hoping he could get out of here without having to flat-out reject her. He forced a polite smile as he buttoned his coat against the cold. "My place is really far away."

"I don't mind!"

"And I have an early morning tomorrow."

Georgia fixed him with her most seductive stare. "I'll make sure you get enough sleep."

Okay, he was done here. "I don't think so. Listen, it was nice to meet you, Georgia—"

"But—"

"Good luck with your internship." He extended his hand to shake hers, and after a pause, she reluctantly took it.

"Thanks for meeting me tonight. It was really nice of you."

She looked so deflated that he found himself regretting getting short with her. She wasn't a bad person, she was just trying way too hard. "No problem."

Then he leaned in and kissed her good-night on the cheek, which was a mistake, because she immediately brightened, as if he'd just thrown her a bone. "So I'll text you sometime!"

"Um…" *Get out of here, Drake. Just get out.* "Sure. I'll see you around."

"See you!" she chirped.

He turned around and walked away before she could rope him in again. What a waste of an evening. He didn't even get a decent dinner out of it, because he was still *starving*. He wasn't familiar with this pocket of Brooklyn, but there had to be a place that served real food. At the very least, a proper drink.

The block he'd been on had been peppered with trendy bars and restaurants, interspersed with newly built modern apartment buildings, but as he continued, the flavor of the neighborhood changed around him. There were a smattering of old-school Italian businesses, all closed for the night, looking like they'd been in business since the middle of the previous century. There was a baker, a cheese shop, a butcher—a real honest-to-God butcher shop, with ham hocks and salamis hanging from the ceiling and everything.

Up ahead, across the street, a little bar inhabited the

corner. The plate glass window in front cast a square of inviting golden light onto the sidewalk. A neon Michelob sign was the only decor. Not a chance of fennel greens in your drink in a place like that. He crossed the street and headed for the door.

Chapter Seventeen

He stepped inside and stopped in his tracks as his insides lurched.

Jessica Romano was sitting at the bar.

She had her laptop open in front of her as one hand idly turned a glass of beer in circles on the bar next to her. What the hell was Jess doing—

As he stood frozen in utter confusion, she glanced back over her shoulder to see who'd come in. Her eyes went wide and her mouth dropped open as she registered his presence.

"Alex?"

"I was just… I came in to get… I didn't realize…" He pointed helplessly at the mirror behind the bar, where *Romano's* was painted in flaking gold paint. This was her family's bar. He'd known they owned a bar in Carroll Gardens, but he hadn't made the connection—or realized that's where he was—until this very moment.

Jess shifted uneasily on her stool. Right. This was her bar, her home turf, her safe space. It was the last place she'd want him invading.

"I should go—" he began, just as she said, "You might as well come in."

They both stopped speaking and stared at each other.

"You sure it's okay?"

She shrugged dismissively. "You want a drink. We serve drinks."

After another moment of hesitation, he cautiously crossed the room, unbuttoning his coat. He hung it on the old-fashioned coatrack tucked into the corner, debating where to sit. Jess was sitting at the corner of the bar, her back to the front window. There were two open stools next to her. Or he could sit on the long side, facing the mirror on the wall, where he'd be too far away for conversation. It might be weird to sit next to her, but it would be even weirder to sit in her bar pretending she wasn't there. He sat next to her.

Eyeing him warily, Jess closed her laptop and pushed it to the side.

"What brings you to my neck of the woods?"

"I was having dinner with…" He did *not* want to discuss that awful dinner with Georgia. "With a friend at this place down the street. Trestle?"

"Right," she muttered. "One of the new places."

"Friend of yours, Jess?"

The bartender had materialized in front of them, and now stood with her hands braced on the bar. She was tall and angular, with her long, dark brown hair caught up in a messy ponytail.

Jess waved a hand between him and the bartender. "Alex, Gemma. Gemma, Alex. Alex is my stalker."

Alex shot her a scowl before instinctively swinging into charming mode, and extending a hand across the bar. "Hi, Gemma. Nice to meet you."

Cautiously, she took his hand and shook it in a firm

grip, her dark brown eyes roving over him. She wasn't at all swayed by the charm offensive or the smile. Jess never had been, either. A light bulb went off in his head. The familiarity of her exchange with Jessica, the similarity in their coloring, the same prickly defensiveness...this must be one of her sisters, which she confirmed in the next instant.

"Same. I'm Jess's sister. So you're a friend of Jess's?"

"We're not friends."

They'd said it in unison.

Gemma's eyes shifted between him and her sister. "Okay, not-my-sister's-friend, what are you drinking?"

"Scotch?"

Gemma nodded and turned away to pour it without asking which kind. Guess Romano's only served one.

Alex rubbed his palms down his thighs, trying to dispel the adrenaline flare that Jess always seemed to spark in him. He didn't want to argue with her, not tonight. "So, do you work here?"

There. That was neutral. She couldn't possibly take offense at that.

"I cover shifts now and then. It's mostly Dad and Gemma. I'm just here to get a start on our end-of-the-year paperwork."

"Oh, sorry. Do you need me to go?"

"No, it's fine."

Gemma returned, sliding a highball glass with a healthy pour of amber liquid in front of him. "Have you eaten?"

He glanced around Romano's. Nothing about the place gave any indication it served food.

"This is a restaurant, too?"

Gemma shook her head. "No, but I keep stuff cooking in the back, just for family and friends."

"He just came from dinner, Gem," Jess protested.

"But I'm starving," he interjected quickly.

Gemma gave a brisk nod. "I'll make you a plate."

"I don't want to inconvenience her," Alex said as Gemma departed.

"You're not. She feeds everybody. She can't help it."

Silence descended on them. Okay, so a neutral conversation with Jess. This couldn't be so hard. Alex had chatted up and charmed titans of industry, powerful politicians, and everyone in between. Surely he could manage a reasonable conversation with Jessica Romano.

"So this is the family business, huh?"

"Yep. This is our bar."

He took a sip of his scotch—most definitely not top shelf—and looked around. It all dated from much earlier in the century, and from the looks of it, nothing had been updated, with the exception of a large flat-screen TV mounted in the corner, broadcasting an old football game. With its white-and-black tiled floor and aged mahogany bar with a brass rail, the place was unfussy and functional. It was a locals' place, with no pretensions to more.

Fancy decor would have been wasted on these patrons, anyway. The place was nearly empty, just a few guys at tables and two more down the bar, looking like they'd grown roots there. Guys like this came to drink, watch the game, and shoot the shit with their friends. They weren't into mood lighting and fancy cocktails.

"I like it."

She snorted dismissively.

Okay, so much for neutral conversation. "What's that supposed to mean?"

Jessica shot him an appraising sideways glance. "It's not exactly your kind of place."

"Maybe you don't know what my kind of place is."

And here it came. They were already butting heads. Wasn't this at the root of all their earliest conflicts? Jessica had made assumptions about him from the start. And he could acknowledge now that maybe she'd been right. He could look back on his younger self and see the privilege-tinged arrogance she'd despised.

But in the intervening years, he'd changed. Jessica hadn't been interested enough in him to find that out, which had pissed him off. And now here they were, barely able to speak without fighting, which was a shame, because, well, things could have been very different, otherwise.

Jessica sighed and took another sip of her beer, pulling his focus back to the present. "Maybe I don't really understand anybody the way I thought I did."

"Sounds cryptic."

She carried on as if he wasn't there. "I mean, you *think* you know people, but clearly not. And meanwhile there's *you*."

"Me?"

"Lina's going on and on about how you're not the same as you were once and I should just give you a chance and—"

"You were talking about me to Lina?" An unexpected flare of heat bloomed in his chest.

She chuckled, tipping her glass back and draining her beer. "Don't get too excited, tiger."

Right. Probably the only thing Jess had to say about

him to Lina was an insult. But, still, knowing she'd *discussed* him, thought about him…that was…

Jess wasn't looking at him, so he stole a glance at her, looking at her—*really* looking—in a way he hadn't let himself look in a long time. Her lashes, thick and dark, cast long shadows on her cheekbones as she fiddled with her empty beer glass. Color tinted the slight hollows of her cheeks. If she'd had lipstick on earlier, it was all gone now, but she didn't need it, not with those lips. Jess would probably expire on the spot if she knew how many of his college classes had been spent surreptitiously studying her mouth. He knew the lush and delicate shape of it better than his own.

Gemma reappeared and set a large shallow bowl full of steaming pasta and sauce on the bar, startling him. "Eat up." She retrieved a fork from under the bar, then left to refill someone's beer.

Stop staring at Jess and change the subject. Alex cleared his throat, trying to get a handle on the last few moments. "Does she cook like this all the time?"

"All the time."

It looked amazing, and smelled even better. When he took a bite, he closed his eyes and let out an involuntary moan of pleasure as the taste exploded across his tongue.

"I know, right?"

When he opened his eyes again, she was watching him. "Is it always this good?"

She cleared her throat and looked away, toward the flat-screen, where some Giants game from the '80s played out on ESPN Classic. "No, it's usually better. It's a Monday night. She's taking it easy."

"This is the best thing I've eaten in years."

"Says the guy who probably orders Nobu for lunch."

"I hate sushi."

She glanced back to him in surprise. "Really? You're the second person who's told me that recently. Didn't you just come from dinner? How can you eat like that?"

"Wilted lawn clippings and gravel. But artisanal and locally sourced, of course."

Jess let out a bark of laughter. He'd just made Jess Romano laugh. That had to be a first. "So why'd you go there, anyway?"

Alex didn't look up from the freaking amazing food he was devouring. "It was near her place," he muttered dismissively. The less said about that disaster with Georgia, the better.

"Right," Jess murmured.

He took another mouthful, unabashedly stuffing his face. "I'm serious. Your sister's an amazing cook."

Now he did look over at her. She shrugged, a small smile playing around her lips. Some of that eternally defensive tension seemed to have dissipated in her. Nothing he said to her could get her to lower her guard, but a compliment to her sister seemed to do the trick. He wasn't sure when he'd actively begun to try getting her to lower her defenses, but he had to admit this was nice, talking without fighting. A vast improvement over the state of war they'd inhabited for far too long.

She wasn't drunk. Two beers wasn't enough to accomplish that. So intoxication didn't explain it.

As she watched him carefully wiping up a drop of sauce off the bar, she pondered the possibility of a rip in the space-time continuum. Because that would be the only thing that could explain what was happening right now. Alex Drake, here in Carroll Gardens, here in her bar, meeting her sister, eating Gemma's food, and actually being a decent human being.

You always wanted to see him here, her subconscious whispered seductively to her. *Yes, but that was years ago*, she snapped back, *before I knew better, before I knew that someone like him didn't belong in a place like this. Didn't belong next to a person like me.*

Except here he was, in this place, next to her, making himself at home. And he seemed to fit in just fine.

"Do you like having a bar?" he asked, chasing the last of his food around the bottom of the bowl with his fork.

"I guess. It's all I've ever known."

"Your dad started it, right?"

"No, my great-grandfather, in 1935."

"Seriously?" He looked up long enough to cast his eyes around the bar. She braced for the sarcastic comment she felt sure was coming—some dig about it being long overdue for a renovation, or it being more of a quaint artifact than a business. "That's amazing. What a legacy," he said, before returning to his food.

Oh.

"She'll bring you more if you want." She indicated his bowl when he glanced up in confusion. "She always makes enough to feed an army."

"Oh." Pushing his empty bowl away, he shook his head. "I'm good. Any chance of getting another drink, though?"

One glance down the bar told her Gemma wasn't coming back soon. Frank was talking about his ex-wife again, and once he started down that well-traveled road, it was almost impossible to get him to shut up. "I'll get it."

Jess slid off her stool and ducked under the pass-through at the end of the bar. After she'd poured herself another beer at the tap and fetched Alex's Dewar's from the shelf, she came back around and hopped back onto her stool.

"That food was…wow." Alex splashed more scotch into his glass. "Sorry, I should—"

She stopped him as he fumbled for his wallet. "Forget it. On the house. It's a perk."

"Thanks. Have you guys ever considered expanding? Serving food?"

"Um… Gemma looked into it. It would cost a fortune to renovate. Building the kitchen, installing everything for health and safety, bringing the building up to code, applying for all the permits… We couldn't swing it."

Jess had never been ashamed of her family's financial standing. So what if they were always a hair's breadth away from being broke? They worked hard and they'd managed a lot with very little. Working-class Italians helped build this city, and she was proud of that. But somehow she'd always hated admitting the truth to Alex. It felt like confessing a weakness, letting him see that she was vulnerable in a place where he was so impervious.

"That's too bad. She's really talented."

Ah, hell. It was hard to keep hating him when he was being so nice about Gemma. It was hard to keep hating him for much of anything these days. All those reasons which had seemed so black-and-white for years had started turning a hazy gray lately.

"So, back to you and Lina."

She startled out of her mental floundering. "What? What about Lina?"

Leaning forward, forearms crossed on the bar, he angled his upper body toward hers. The bar was nearly empty tonight, but his nearness made the air feel close, almost too warm. "Before you were interrupted, you said Lina had told you I'd changed."

Panicked, she averted her face as mortification ripped through her. Oh, *why* did she have this tendency to say whatever she was thinking when she'd had a couple of beers? "I'm not—"

"So when was this?"

"When was what?"

"You and Lina talking about me? Was it at the banquet?"

"God, can you just drop it?"

He chuckled, a low, warm sound that made something in her stomach tighten. She ran a hand under her hair, across the back of her neck, prickling with humiliation, and then took another long sip of her beer, just to have something to do. Not like she needed *more* at this point. There was no telling what she might confess to before the night was out.

"She's right, you know," Alex said quietly, the humor erased from his voice.

"About what?"

"I'm not the same person I was when we first met."

"No?"

She chanced a glance at him, catching his offhanded shrug. His hair was elegantly mussed, like he'd had his hands in it for half the day. A very faint late-day stubble shadowed his jaw. Usually Alex was ruthlessly clean-shaven, which highlighted his sculptural features. There was something a little thrilling about seeing his perfection so subtly marred. He looked approachable like this. Still heart-stoppingly beautiful, but the kind of imperfect, rumpled beauty you could imagine waking up next to in bed. She took a hefty swig of beer to deal with her sudden dry tongue and nearly choked on it.

"College changes everybody, right?"

What? What had they been talking about? Once again, she'd lost the thread of the conversation, caught up in imagining the feel of that stubbled jaw under her fingers. "Um, sure. Right. College."

"Before I started at DeWitt, I'd spent my whole life at Reynolds Academy. Do you know Reynolds?"

"I went to Sacred Heart, the Catholic school down the street."

"Reynolds is in Westchester. It's K through twelve and it costs six figures a year."

Ugh, just when he was becoming almost bearable. "How nice for you."

"I'm not telling you that to brag. I'm explaining. The only other people at Reynolds were kids just like me."

"Rich ones."

"*Very* rich ones. It can…" He trailed off, running a hand through that wrecked hair again. "I went to school with some good people, but there wasn't much opportunity to experience the world outside of our very rarefied circle."

"I can see how that would happen," she conceded.

"I didn't really break out of that until I went to college."

"Where you hung out with Chase, who's *nothing* like you." She hadn't meant to be sarcastic, but it had turned into something like a default when she was talking to Alex. It was safer, somehow, to keep him at the end of her barbed judgment.

"I wasn't talking about Chase. I was talking about you."

"Me?" Mystified by the turn in the conversation, she blinked at him in confusion. Where was he going with all this?

Alex chuckled and drained his scotch. "You were so…" Shaking his head, he stared into space, apparently remembering her at eighteen, which was uncomfortable.

She finished that unpleasant thought for him. "I'm sure I was completely insufferable. I only saw absolutes. Compromise of any kind meant moral bankruptcy."

"You were idealistic. The world was full of injustice and you wanted to take it all on with your writing. And you really believed you could. You were terrifying with all that passion, all that confidence. I had no idea how to deal with someone like you."

Okay, yes, she might have been a little *intense* back then. "No wonder you hated me."

"I didn't hate you. I had a massive crush on you back then."

Her heart lurched to a stop. "What?"

"Come on," he said, elbowing her gently. "You knew that."

Was he serious right now? After everything that had happened, how the hell was she supposed to *know* that? "Um, no, I didn't know that."

"Jess," he said patiently. "I entered the Newhouse just to get your attention."

She couldn't believe what she was hearing. "You entered the Newhouse just to impress a *girl*?"

"I entered the Newhouse to impress *you*. Didn't work, though. You just hated me more after that."

"I needed that prize money to pay for an internship at the Chicago *Trib*."

Alex swiveled to stare at her. "You wanted to intern at the *Trib*, too?"

She nodded, fingers curling around her glass hard enough to crack it.

"Well." Alex turned his attention to his scotch. "That would have changed a lot, huh?"

Her mind spun. Would it have? Would everything have happened differently if it had been her in Chicago with him instead of Peyton? It was too much to contemplate.

"I guess it doesn't matter in the end. You were into Josh." He was curled over the bar, staring into his highball glass as one long-fingered hand deftly turned it in circles.

"I wasn't, though."

His head turned just enough to shoot her a wry smile. "Come on, Jess. That party?"

A full-body flush flooded her system, mortification swirling in her brain, making her tongue too thick to form words. All these years, that night had lain buried back there in their past. She'd been half-convinced he'd forgotten all about it, just a drunken fumble with a girl he enjoyed teasing. Everything was starting to shift in her memories, each thing she thought she knew like a colored chip in a kaleidoscope, constantly moving and forming new pictures, until she didn't know which picture to trust. What was real?

"You were all over Josh that night. Believe me," he said, letting out a self-deprecating chuckle. "I remember."

"That was *your* fault!" she blurted out, before she could fully think things through. "You and Peyton!"

His features screwed up so tightly that she would have laughed at his comical confusion if they were discussing anything else. "Peyton Tenaway? What does she have to do with anything?"

"I heard you with her!"

Alex waved a hand, encouraging her to keep going. "What did you hear?"

"You told her it was just a joke. You and me." Oh, God, here she was, bringing up *that* moment herself. How had she gotten here? "You said you were just playing around, winding me up, to get a rise out of me."

Alex blinked slowly at her, his jade green eyes narrowed in concentration. When the memory hit him, his eyes fell closed. "Ah." Wearily, he passed a hand over his face, and then left it there, as if he couldn't bear to open his eyes again. "You heard that."

"Yes, I heard that."

His hand dropped into his lap and he turned to face her fully. "It was a lie."

"What was?"

"I was lying to her. Peyton… I know she seemed nice, but believe me, there was a nasty side to her. She was fine when we were hanging out in Chicago that summer, but then she wanted more and when I didn't, this whole other side of her came out. Peyton's not used to hearing no, and when she does, she can get ugly. If she'd gotten wind of how I felt about you, she'd have been really vicious to you."

"She already was. I can't believe you'd think I *didn't* know about Peyton's nasty side. That's the only one I ever saw."

"I was just trying to throw her off the scent, get her to leave me the hell alone and keep her away from you."

"Oh." Those kaleidoscope pieces collapsed into a pile, shifted, then shifted again. No clear picture yet. "I kissed Josh to get back at you."

"What?"

"I was angry…humiliated. I thought you were just jerking me around. And then Josh was right there in front of me, and I thought 'You know what? Fuck him,' and I kissed Josh."

"That was for *my* benefit?"

"Yep."

"But you dated him for two months."

"I *had* to! He had a huge crush on me. If I told him I'd used him, he would have been devastated."

"So you *pity-dated* him for two months. Nice. He must have been just as devastated to get dumped by you eventually."

She had to hand it to Alex, he never let her off the hook about anything. "He dumped me."

"Excuse me?"

"He met Caitlin and it was…you know…love at first sight, or whatever, and he broke up with me."

"I'm sorry…" A sputter of disbelieving laughter burst from his lips. "Josh. Dumped you? For *Caitlin*?"

"Yes, he did, because she was absolutely perfect for him and I wasn't. So you see? I got my payback."

"That's just…" He dropped his head, his shoulders shaking with barely constrained laughter.

"Oh, shut up. It's your fault I ended up dating him, anyway." She tried to fight it, but his laughter was contagious. Because it really was hilarious, if you could step away from the bruised feelings and anger, and time had done a lot to dull those edges. Before she knew it, she was laughing, too, so hard that tears streaked down her face.

"It's not funny," she wheezed.

"Yes it is." He threw his head back as he laughed, long and loud. Had she ever seen him laugh like that? She didn't think so. "You dated a guy you didn't like for two months all because a girl I didn't like couldn't take a goddamned hint. Sorry, but that's hilarious."

Her laughter subsided into a few hiccuping chuckles. "God, I hated her."

"Peyton? She really gave you a hard time?"

Jess swiped a finger under her damp lashes and took another sip of her beer. "Oh, yes. I thought it was just because she's a snob, but now I suspect it was because she'd sniffed out my crush."

At her side, Alex stilled. Oh, shit. There she went again, her mouth spilling out things she hadn't even consciously thought yet. "What?"

Tossing back some more beer, she tried to play it off with a casual shrug, but suspected she failed. "I had a crush on you, too. Back then."

Alex took a long sip of his scotch. "Well. I thought that Ivy League degree was supposed to mean we're smart, but we seem to be a walking disaster."

"You could look at it that way."

Nothing about that night had been a lie. *Nothing had been a lie.*

What were you supposed to do when the event that entirely defined a person in your mind turned out not to be true? Well, other things had helped form her opinion of Alex years ago, but he was steadily taking ax swings at all of those suppositions, too.

"I always wondered how you and Josh stayed so friendly," Alex said, many minutes later. "After he started dating Caitlin, I mean."

His hands busily turned that highball glass in circles on the bar. Jess kept tracing lines in the condensation on her glass. Even the air around them felt electrically charged after everything that had just been said.

"It was such a *relief* when he dumped me." She took another nervous sip of her beer. "And Peyton?"

"What about her?"

"Did you guys eventually—"

"I told you, that was all her. I kept putting her off and eventually she slept with Chase and lost all interest in me. Thank God."

"That Chase. His libido sure comes in handy."

"Look, I know his personal life is pretty questionable—" Jess let out an ungraceful snort of laughter, and Alex nodded in weary agreement. "Okay, very questionable. But he was a good friend to me growing up."

"He must have been or you'd have never gotten him hired at ClickNews."

The shift in Alex's expression was subtle, easy to miss, unless—like Jess—one was busy obsessively cataloging every inch of his face. His eyebrows furrowed slightly and his lips flattened out. Not quite a frown, but almost.

"What?"

He threw a questioning glance at her, the almost-frown vanished. "What, what?"

"What I said, about getting Chase hired at Click-News. Your face went all…" She scrunched up her fingers to demonstrate his expression.

The corner of his mouth twitched with a suppressed smile. "That's what my face looks like? No, I was just…" He trailed off and looked away, taking another thoughtful sip of his drink.

Elbowing him lightly, she pressed on. "Come on. Tell me."

"I wanted that job," he said at last.

"Chase's job?"

"Yeah. Head of journalism."

One less beer would have made coming up with a tactful reply somewhat easier. Instead, she blurted, "You're hardly missing out. It's not much of a journalism division."

"That's the point. I had this idea…this…dream…" Pausing, he shook his head. "Never mind."

"Tell me."

His eyes roved quickly across her face and whatever he saw there made up his mind. "ClickNews has an amazing platform. Even before we bought it, the page hits and web traffic were off the charts, and it's only gotten better."

"Yeah, I'm well aware of how many people read your site every day." Not that she was jealous. Or bitter. Well, maybe just a little.

"So just imagine, instead of just pulling stuff off

the wire services and padding it out with our weak local stuff, we had a real journalism team providing original content. Hell, with our structural organization and resources, we could put together investigative journalism teams to rival the biggest names out there. We've got the money to finance in-depth investigations. We've got the platform to publish multi-part stories that would leave the *Times* and the *Spotlight* guys in the dust. ClickNews has already built a loyal following. People check in every day, and they read everything we post. Imagine if we gave them something *real* to read, made them aware of issues no one else is talking about. We could change everything, the entire direction journalism has gone in this country. We could restart the national dialog, and make a whole generation of people fucking *informed* again. Can you imagine that?"

Oh, hell…he had *integrity.* Alex's gorgeous face was potent enough. But with that brain? That passion? Jess suddenly felt herself on very dangerous ground. Her heart beat hard in her chest in a visceral response to him.

"Alex—your idea sounds amazing. You've got to do it."

Just like that, the fire in his eyes went out, like it had never been there. With a dismissive wave of his hand, he turned back to his drink, sipping morosely from it. "It's not what we acquired the site for. They've got a good business model in place. It would be insanity to mess with it when it works."

"Yes, it's good now, but it could be so much better. With you in charge, it could be brilliant."

He shook his head. "Not me. My stint there is temporary. Chase's the one staying on."

"It'll never happen under Chase. Chase wouldn't know solid reporting if it bit him in the ass."

"Hey, he's not as good as you—"

"Or you."

"But he's not bad. He's been doing good work there since we hired him."

In a rush, the day's events came back to her. No one knew who was behind the ClickNews thefts, and both Chase and Alex were too close to the situation for comfort.

Her gut told her it wasn't Alex. Yes, he had a dream for ClickNews, but let's be real—he was talented enough on his own to achieve it. He didn't need to steal from anyone. Chase, on the other hand... She wouldn't put it past him. Maybe Alex wasn't involved, but he was close to someone who might be. Which meant sitting here talking and laughing with him was supremely stupid.

"I have to go." She slid off her stool, but the floor was farther away than she'd guessed and she stumbled. In a flash, Alex was off his stool, his arms around her, holding her up. And holding her tightly against his chest.

Oh. A flush crept up her neck to her cheeks. Alex looked down at her and licked his lips.

"Um..." She pushed herself away from him unsteadily. He reached a hand out to her, but thought better of it, raking his fingers through his hair instead. The silence was so loaded, it hurt.

Without warning, Gemma sailed into the strange, electric atmosphere they'd just created.

"You doing okay?" Gemma asked. "You almost fell off your stool."

She rubbed a hand across her forehead, feeling a little punch-drunk with beer and laughter. "I'm fine. But I should go home. I have to work tomorrow."

"I can kick these guys out and close early," Gemma offered. "They're just warming chairs, anyway."

Jess shook her head. "No, it's okay."

"I'll walk you home," Alex volunteered. Jess and Gemma both swiveled to stare at him. He shrugged. "It's not far, right?"

"A couple of blocks," Jess murmured.

"You okay with that?" Gemma asked her.

She nodded. "Yeah, he's fine. Not an ax-murderer."

"You said he was a stalker."

"I was kidding. Mostly."

Gemma pointed a finger at Alex. "We have four cousins on the police force. That's just *cousins*. Half the regulars in this bar are former cops, and Jess is the baby of the family. You got it?"

"Gemma—"

Alex held up his hands in defense. "She'll be safe. I promise."

Gemma nodded slowly. "Okay."

"Thanks for dinner. It was amazing."

Of course, Alex knew exactly what to say to any woman to charm her, even Gemma in full-on Mama Bear mode. "Thanks. See you around."

She shrugged into her coat, watching Alex do the same. When they were both buttoned up, he smiled tightly, wordlessly holding his arm out, indicating that she should take the lead. She did, feeling like she was sliding sideways off the edge of reality as she knew it.

Chapter Eighteen

Outside, the night had grown colder, the air sharp and bracing on her flushed cheeks. Shivering, she tugged her scarf tighter around her neck and stuffed her hands in her pockets. Alex let the door swing shut behind him and came to stand next to her. He glanced up at the sky, glowing orange as the sodium streetlights reflected in the low-hanging clouds.

"Feels like snow," he said, hunching his shoulders against the cold.

"It doesn't snow before Christmas."

"Sometimes it does."

"Yeah, sometimes it does."

"Remember that year it snowed the day before Halloween?"

"That was wild."

"Yeah."

Wow, they'd chattered away for two hours without stop inside, and now they were having this painful conversation about *snow*?

"Where do you live?"

"Oh. Um, this way."

She started walking up Court Street toward home. The shops they passed were a mix of old Italian businesses she'd known all her life and trendy restaurants and boutiques that had moved in as the neighborhood gentrified. The familiar storefronts—DiPaola's Bakery, Vinelli's Meats, Russo's Pizzeria—were comforting. She'd grown up running in and out of those shops. The DiPaolas, the Vinellis and the Russos were like her extended family. Because she didn't have *enough* family all on her own.

The Christmas decorations were already up, with white lights hanging in swags over the street and giant glittering red-and-green holly leaves adorning every lamppost. Once, Court Street would have been a ghost town at this hour, but now that it had gentrified, it stayed busy late into the night.

"Will your sister be okay on her own at the bar?"

"Gem? Oh, sure. She wasn't kidding about half those guys being former cops. Nobody touches Romano's."

"Right."

"Plus she's armed."

Alex spluttered in disbelief, making her smile.

"Never mess with a Romano girl. Everybody in Carroll Gardens knows that."

"I think I'm beginning to understand that. So you grew up here?"

She nodded. "The same great-grandfather who opened the bar bought our house. Angelo Romano. My family's lived there ever since."

"It's…"

"What?"

"It's nice. Your history. That you have so much history. And family." They walked side by side, hands in their pockets, shoulders brushing now and then.

"You don't?"

He shook his head. "It's just me and Dad."

"Where's your mother?" she asked cautiously. She knew better than anyone what a loaded question that could be.

"Connecticut, occasionally. She and Dad divorced when I was a kid."

"Oh, I didn't know that. Except I guess it's obvious that he's single, what with all the…" She'd been about to say "with all those women he hooks up with" before she managed to stop the word vomit. At least there was one embarrassing thing she managed to *not* say tonight.

"It's okay. You can say it. When it's everywhere in the press, it's hardly a secret. He likes women. He liked them when I was eight, too, which is why they got divorced after my mother caught him with the lady planning my birthday party."

"Oh. Ouch."

She looked up just as he flashed her one of those easy, disarming grins. "It was a long time ago. She's remarried now. Her husband is Swiss, works in banking, so they spend a lot of time overseas."

"And your dad got custody of you?" Dan Drake had never, even slightly, struck her as a hands-on father.

"I split time between both of them when I was growing up. Actually, with nannies, to be honest. You can board at Reynolds starting at twelve, so I mostly lived there after that. It was more fun. Then when I started college, I moved in with Dad, because DeWitt was in Manhattan."

"He lives in the city?" She didn't know why that was surprising. Dan Drake seemed like the kind of person who only existed on a private jet, flying from one metropolis to another. Either that, or he lived tucked away on some estate or private compound, the kind of place tourists took pictures of from tour buses. But she really had no idea. She'd never thought about it. She'd also never really thought about what Alex's childhood was like. His description of it was casual, but it sounded lonely and cold, at least compared to what she knew.

"Well…" He reached up to scratch his ear. "He has a few properties—"

She laughed. "Forget it. I forgot who I was talking about for a minute."

"But yes, he lives primarily at the place in the city."

Biting her lip, she tried to keep her voice casual. "Just out of curiosity, where are the others?"

He hesitated, and she immediately regretted the question. He must get invasive questions like that all the time, for all the wrong reasons.

"Never mind. You don't have to answer that."

"No, it's okay. Um, there's a house in LA, an apartment in London, and one in Paris, and there's a small estate in St. Croix. That's really just for vacations."

Wow. There was knowing Alex was rich and then there was *knowing*. She was almost sorry she'd asked. It was much easier to poke at him and take verbal swipes when she had no concept of his net worth. Now she felt like a butterfly who'd been teasing Godzilla. He could scoop her out of the sky and squash her flat with a flick of his wrist. Except that was all in her head, wasn't it? Alex was just Alex. And, as tonight had made amply evident, she'd gotten a lot of things wrong about him.

"I don't visit them too often," he hurried to add, a touch defensively. "I'm almost always here in the city."

"Funny, me, too," she quipped. "It is nice to get out of the city now and then, though. Sometimes we go out to my uncle Richie's place on City Island, just for the weekend."

"Cut it out," he groaned, elbowing her, and she laughed.

"This way." Unthinkingly, she snagged his elbow and tugged him into the turn onto her street. And now her hand was tucked into the crook of his arm, sandwiched up against the warmth of his body. She'd have to tug to get it free, which might be more awkward than just leaving it there. Or maybe not, because now she was obsessed with her hand on his arm. It felt like every atom in the universe had changed its course around them, drawn into the powerful black hole forming where she was touching him.

"Your neighbors like Christmas, huh?"

Almost all the houses on her block were lavishly decorated for Christmas. Colored lights twinkled from every hedge and window frame. All manner of reindeer pranced across front yards and no less than three yard signs pointed the way toward the North Pole. Two houses even had inflatables in the yard, which was actually possible in Carroll Gardens. It was a quirk of the neighborhood that the town houses were set back off the street, with little front yards, instead of fronting right onto the sidewalk, like in most of Brownstone Brooklyn.

"Yeah, everybody decorates here. It's kind of a big deal."

They'd left the foot traffic behind when they turned

off Court. Here, they were the only two people on the block and the night was quiet around them.

"It's nice. All the lights. What's that?" He was pointing at the Blessed Virgin in Mrs. Maratelli's front yard, currently draped in festive multi-colored twinkle lights.

"Um, that's a Bathtub Madonna. Well, that's what we call it. I don't even know if it has a real name. Bathtub Madonnas are an old-fashioned Catholic thing. Mrs. Maratelli is eighty."

"You know your neighbors by name?"

"Sure. I've lived here all my life. So have a lot of them. You don't know any of your neighbors?"

"Well, with security—"

"Say no more. I get it." Which she didn't, but she could pretend to be sophisticated enough to understand his life.

Her hand was still in the crook of his arm. She'd made no move to take it away, and he'd made no move to shake her off. Despite the bone-chilling cold, she could feel nervous sweat prickling along her hairline. It was that third beer. It was still swimming in her head, giving everything a weird dreamlike quality. At least, she thought that was the beer. Through the flush of heat on her face, she felt the sting of something cold and wet.

"Oh." Tilting her head back, she watched the snow start to fall around them, soft and silent. "It's snowing."

"I told you so."

"Alex, do not ruin this magical moment by saying 'I told you so.'"

"Magical?" She didn't have to look at his face to

know that eyebrow was arched dramatically, or that he'd aimed another one of those deadly, teasing grins in her direction.

"Snow is always magical."

And this snow was particularly magical. The night was twinkling with a thousand lights around them, and her hand was still resting on his arm as the snow drifted down around them, catching on their clothes and hair.

When she looked at him, Alex was watching her, his expression unreadable.

"This is me," she murmured, drawing to a stop at their wrought iron gate and finally letting go of him.

He looked up at the house. "It's dark. Is anybody else home?"

"Dad is at Uncle Richie's on City Island." She smiled back over her shoulder as she moved through the gate and up the walk. "I wasn't making him up."

"Do you have aspirin?" His words came out in a rush as he followed behind her.

"Aspirin?"

"Those beers might give you a headache tomorrow. You should take some aspirin before you go to bed. It might help."

Right. Beer. That had to be why he looked like some sort of mysterious, modern-day dark angel, standing there on the bottom step of her front stoop, the collar of his black wool overcoat turned up against the cold, his eyes fixed on hers. There's no way she'd be having these trippy, fanciful ideas about him if she wasn't a little buzzed, right?

She turned and unlocked the door. "Come on in. I'll get you some aspirin."

"I didn't mean for me. I meant for you." But he followed her inside.

No one had been home to turn on the lights since night fell, so the only light on was a small decorative wall sconce, next to the coatrack bench in the front hall. When she turned to face him, he straightened away from the door and took a step toward her. Her nerves and anxiety exploded at once, waging a battle as they raced through her bloodstream. Frozen, she stood rooted in place, unsure if she wanted him to stop where he was or come much, much closer.

He took a step closer. Her stomach clenched in almost painful anticipation.

"Wuff." Spudge let his weight fall against her ankles like a sack of flour.

Alex backed up and looked down, chuckling. "Who's this?"

As she ducked down to scratch his ears, she let her hair fall forward to cover her face and hide her confusion. That was a *moment*. It had flared up as clear and bright as day. She had no idea what might have happened next, but it hardly mattered, because her geriatric dog had lumbered in and put an abrupt end to it.

"This is Spudge."

"Spudge?" he asked, unbuttoning his coat and hanging it on the rack. "Where did that come from?"

"I have no idea. He came with that name as a puppy and it just stuck. Spudge sort of fits him."

"Yeah, it does." Alex leaned down and ran a hand across Spudge's bony head. "Hey, Spudge. You're the Hufflepuff, I take it?"

"You remember that?"

He straightened back up. "I remember." He was

staring at her again, that focused gaze that made her whole body erupt with nerves. "Let me guess. You're a Ravenclaw."

Right.

"The kitchen's back here," she said, a bit too loudly as she abruptly turned away.

She led the way to the back of the house, not even pausing to draw a breath, not exhaling until she'd passed through the dining room and flipped the light on over the sink. She left the overhead kitchen light off. It would be like shining midday sun into this weird little bubble she'd fallen into, and she wasn't sure if she was ready to do that yet. In this dim half-light, she didn't have to face the reality of what might be happening head-on.

Alex rested one hip against the kitchen counter as she retrieved two glasses from the cabinet and filled them at the sink. After sorting through a million half-empty packs of cough drops and expired antacids in the pantry by the basement stairs, she found the aspirin. Alex was still there, leaning on the counter, when she turned, pills in hand.

Not even back in the beginning, when she'd been fighting her forbidden crush on him, had she ever gotten as far as imagining him in her kitchen. It was like trying to imagine Prince Harry in your corner bodega. He just didn't belong there, no matter how much mental photoshopping you engaged in.

But there was Alex, leaning against the scuffed, silver-flecked white Formica counter her great-grandmother had chosen, his very expensive black shoes standing on the ugly harvest gold linoleum floor her grandfather had laid down. As she approached him, holding out a glass of water and two pills, he set his phone down on the counter and reached out a hand. He was wearing a snug black sweater, something that looked luxuriously soft to the touch and painfully pricey. Even his dark denim jeans looked expensive. Alex, so beautiful, so golden, so out of reach.

But he was the same guy who'd bounced between multiple million-dollar homes with no one there to talk to but his nanny. Who'd happily gone away to boarding school at twelve just to have some company. He was the guy who'd confessed to her, an hour ago, that he'd nursed a secret and hopeless crush on her since they'd met.

His eyes, so vivid green in the daylight, were dark in the shadowy room. They never left hers as she tossed her aspirin back and downed half her glass of water in one go. Okay, he hadn't been wrong about the water. She was wickedly thirsty. Because of the beer. Which was why it was probably a dumb idea to have invited him inside. And why it was an even dumber idea to stand here in the dark, in her empty house, practically willing something to happen.

Carefully, she set her glass on the counter, sensing him watching her over the rim of his own glass.

"Looks like it's starting to stick," she said, glancing at the backyard through the window over the sink. Back to talking about snow. Excellent, Jess.

Out of the corner of her eye, she saw him set his glass down, too. "Maybe we'll get some accumulation."

Her eyes had accustomed to the sight of him in her kitchen but the sound of his voice sent a shiver down her spine. When she brought her eyes back to meet his, all the other warring thoughts and conflicting emotions simply fell away, as insubstantial as smoke. He lifted his eyebrows, a question. She ducked her chin, a nod.

Alex made some small movement in her direction, no more than a straightening of his tall athlete's body, a shifting of his weight toward her, and she was moving in response. All it took was her own step forward, just a matter of will, and they connected.

One of his hands touched hers, fumbled past it on its way to her waist. The other brushed her arm as he lifted it to her face. His fingertips were cold on her cheek, but they slid away quickly, his warm palm replacing it, holding her face firmly, tilting her face up to meet his as he came down to find her mouth with his own.

Snow, cold water, warm scotch…sensations tickled across her lips at the first soft brush, the slight urging to open. For a moment, they just swayed there, barely moving, scarcely breathing, the shock of ending up here drowning out every other thought or sensation. Then his mouth moved over hers and she forgot everything else.

His tongue, warm and tasting of scotch, stroked along hers, the caress setting off a dark lick of fire deep inside. His arm slipped around her back, pressing her body up against the length of his. She gave herself permission to touch anything she wanted, at last. Her palms shaped the hard muscles of his arms and shoulders under that soft black sweater. Her fingers traced the tight tendons of his neck, and then she went higher, plunging deep into that glorious hair, gripping, holding his head to hers, as the kiss deepened.

He made some small sound of surrender, falling into her, pressing her back against the counter. Then his mouth was momentarily ripped away from hers as his hands gripped her waist and he lifted, setting her on the counter. Their height difference vanished, but before she could look him in the eye from this vantage point, his mouth came back to hers, hungry and hard. Greedy, she took as much from him, indulging in something she felt like she'd been craving in desperation for years.

His hands were everywhere, and nowhere she needed them. On her face, in her hair, gripping the back of her neck, sliding down the length of her thigh. But her nipples hardened and she ached between her legs and he wasn't there. Not yet.

Wrapping her calves around his hips brought him flush to her center, driving a soft huff of mingled pleasure and pain from his throat. His hand slid from the back of her knee up the length of her thigh to her ass, squeezing, dragging her closer. This time, the sound he made into her mouth was nothing but low, animal pleasure. As he angled his mouth across hers, his teeth scraped along her bottom lip, the sharp-edged pleasure of it cutting like a knife through the lush soft warmth of the kiss.

Her insides felt combustible, like all it would take was a single touch from him in the right place, and she'd go up like paper in an open flame. She writhed against him, wrapping her arms around his broad shoulders and pressing her breasts to his chest. His large hand splayed across her rib cage, fingertips barely brushing the underside of her breast. A caress of her skin through her sweater, his hand gentling her, before he slid it higher to palm her. She arched in anticipation, her breasts aching for his touch.

"Wuff," said Spudge, from somewhere down near Alex's feet.

Slowly, their lips parted, letting in air, and a tiny bit of sanity. Drawing back, she opened her eyes and looked into his. Lust slowly gave way to confusion. His eyebrows drew together just the way she felt her own doing.

"Um," she whispered.

"I don't—" he murmured.

He took a step back. Her hands dropped away from his shoulders, gripping the edge of the kitchen counter instead. She looked down, needing a moment to clear her head, even though it seemed impossible.

"I…there's someone. A guy." She hadn't thought about Peabody all night, but he still existed, and right now, she was struck with a disorienting sense of guilt. Did she owe him her loyalty when they hadn't even met?

Alex scowled, pinching the bridge of his nose. "Yeah, I'm sort of…"

Did he have a *girlfriend*? Is that what he was trying to say? He'd been at dinner with her tonight, though, hadn't he? He'd told her so. That was so much worse than whatever nebulous understanding she had with Peabody.

At that moment, his phone, lying forgotten on the counter, vibrated. They both looked toward it. It was from someone named Georgia.

I had so much fun tonight! <3

Jess slid off the counter, her feet hitting the floor with a dull thud. "You should probably go."

"Right." Alex snatched up his phone and stuffed it in his pocket.

Alcohol and secrets and a magical snowfall made for one heady drug and she'd just fallen head over heels under its spell.

Alex threw her one tight half smile. "I'll see you around."

The cold caught up to her all at once, chilling her to her bones. "Okay."

"Good night."

"Good night."

She stayed where she was, hands gripping the kitchen counter to hold herself up, feeling cold and alone as she heard the front door slam behind him.

Chapter Nineteen

Lina was perched on the corner of Sally's desk, chatting with Sally and Hassan, when Jess made her way to the front office at the paper.

"Goodness, what happened to you?" Sally cried when she saw her.

Jess's hand flew to her face. She knew she didn't look her best this morning, but she hadn't thought it was that bad. "I, um…"

"You look like you didn't sleep a wink last night," Sally fussed.

"Right. That's it. Terrible night's sleep. Lina, can I talk to you?"

"Sure!" Lina was chipper and smiling this morning, a far cry from yesterday.

When Lina didn't move, Jess jerked her chin in the direction of the break room, on the other side of the newsroom. "Alone?"

"Oh." Lina hopped off Sally's desk. "See you later, Hassan.

"Okay, what's going on?" Lina asked when they'd reached the empty break room. "You look really freaked out."

Nervously, Jess began tidying up the random salt

and pepper packets left over from people's takeout. "I don't even know where to start."

"With the good stuff, of course."

Turning back to Lina, she gripped the edge of the counter behind her with both hands, bracing herself to force the words out. "I made out with Alex last night."

Lina's eyes went wide. *"What?"* Then she squeezed them shut and shook her head. "Forget the good stuff. Start at the beginning, because I need to know everything that happened."

"I'm still not sure myself." But Jess did her best, starting with Alex unexpectedly blowing into the bar, all the way through kissing him in her dark kitchen, to the badly timed text from his maybe-girlfriend, to his abrupt departure.

"Wow."

"Yeah, I know."

"That came out of nowhere, huh?"

The time had come to spill every sordid detail. She swallowed hard, eyes on the floor. "Um…not exactly."

Lina was silent for a moment. "Okay, what are you not telling me?"

"Just…" Jess stopped, flinched, then took a deep breath. "We sort of did it once before. In college."

"Did what?"

"Made out."

"What? When?"

"It was just a dumb thing that happened at some stupid party."

"What happened after?"

"Nothing happened. Because I thought…and then he thought… Anyway, we got our signals crossed. But it didn't matter because by then, we hated each other."

"Wow. I can't believe you never told me about this, Jess. I told you all about Chase. You brought me Ben & Jerry's and sat with me while I cried."

A pang of guilt had her shifting uncomfortably. Keeping that ill-advised college encounter to herself hadn't seemed like a big deal before. Denying it to herself meant denying it to the rest of the world, too. But she'd never thought about how that would make Lina feel.

"I'm sorry I didn't tell you. I just wanted to forget it ever happened."

"I guess I get that. So…you and Alex, huh?"

"Did you miss the part where his girlfriend texted in the middle of it?"

"You don't know that for sure."

"I know he had dinner with her last night. And I know she's texting him emoji hearts."

Lina frowned. "Right. That's pretty bad. I'm sorry, Jess."

Jess huffed and waved her hands, like the memory was smoke, and she could just whisk it away. If only it were that easy. "It didn't mean anything. We obviously have some physical chemistry and it got a little out of hand. I should never be alone with him when we've been drinking."

"What are you going to do?"

"Nothing. I have Peabody, anyway."

Lina rolled her eyes. "Right, that guy you've never even met."

"Yet." Although this morning, the thought of meeting Peabody didn't cheer her the way it usually did. He felt almost like a character in a book she'd read, instead of someone she'd been talking to for weeks.

"Enough about stupid Alex and his stupid girlfriend. How are you today? You seem much better."

"I am. I went home and felt sorry for myself for the night, but now I'm done crying about it. Time to find a new story."

"Good for you."

"Thanks for yesterday. That was just what I needed."

"I'm here for you, Lina. You know that. You're my best friend."

Hiking one mocking eyebrow, Lina drawled in exaggeration, "Such a good friend that you withheld the juiciest piece of gossip of our entire college career?"

"Guilty." Jess laughed and covered her face with her hands. "Next time I make out with my mortal enemy, I promise, you'll be the first to know."

Jess was deep into an online city archive, pulling parking stats from past years, when she sensed someone approaching her desk. One glance from the corner of her eye told her it was Lauren. Great. Just what she needed.

"Hi, Lauren."

Lauren's face was a wall of disapproval, which was nothing unusual. "Jessica, can you come with me?"

"Is it important? I'm in the middle of something."

Lauren's eyes flicked dismissively to her computer monitor. "Leave that. Mariel needs to speak with you."

Suppressing the roil of nerves in her stomach, Jess pushed to her feet. "Sure."

Beads of sweat prickled along the back of her neck as she followed Lauren through the newsroom to Mariel's office. Her fellow reporters didn't spare a glance for them as they passed, caught up in phone calls and transfixed by their computer monitors. Casting her eyes around the room, she strained for a glimpse of Lina, but she was nowhere to be seen.

Lauren paused at the door of Mariel's office and waved Jess ahead of her.

"You're not coming in?"

Lauren's reply was clipped and hard. "No."

Every one of her spidey senses clicked into overdrive. Dread settled over her skin like a cold, wet shroud. Whatever was about to happen in Mariel's office, it wasn't going to be good.

Steeling her spine, Jess lifted her chin and tapped briefly on Mariel's door before opening it.

"Mariel? Lauren said you wanted to see me." Keeping her tone light took every ounce of willpower she had, but there was no way she'd creep in cowering in fear, since she hadn't done anything wrong.

Mariel glanced up from the notes spread out across her desk, her expression grim. "Come in and close the door, Jessica." Gone was the friendly, familiar "Jess" that everyone else in the newsroom used. Suddenly she was "Jessica"?

"Is something wrong?"

"Sit down."

She took the chair on the other side of Mariel's desk, pressing her palms flat against her thighs to still the slight tremors in her fingers.

"I'll get right to it," Mariel said briskly. "It's been brought to my attention that you've got long-standing connections of a troubling nature with high-ranking staff members at ClickNews and that you are, in fact, the source of our leak."

Mariel's words knocked the breath clean out of her lungs. "Mariel…" The name came out as a gasp as Jess struggled to speak. "I swear, I didn't do it. It's not true!"

"You haven't been meeting up with Daniel Drake's son every morning?"

The room felt tiny and close as panic raced through her body. Shit. How could something so innocent look so treacherous? "It wasn't like that. I haven't been meeting him on purpose. We get coffee at the same place and—"

"Lauren saw you taking a lunch meeting with him."

"That wasn't a meeting—"

"And it seems you and he cooked up this whole Twitter feud together."

"What? No! I didn't even know it was him behind that until weeks later."

"Then would you like to explain this?" Mariel slid her laptop across the desk. Twitter was open to the *Daily Post* accounts. All the tweets she'd made in the past week were there. Then the one at the top popped out at her and every inch of her body went cold with horror.

@Brooklyn_Daily_Post *The only people reading this sorry paper are old white people from Canarsie. Making way for modern media, it should put itself out of it's misery.*

"I didn't write that!"

"Jessica, you've been manning the paper's social media accounts for weeks."

"And the log-ins for all of them are on a Post-It

taped to my computer! Anyone in the newsroom had access to them!"

Mariel hiked one eyebrow wearily. "You're trying to tell me you were framed? Really?"

Of course that sounded insane. Looking at it objectively, Jess knew it did. Stuff like that only happened in the movies. But there was no other explanation.

"All I know is that I didn't write that last tweet."

"Taken as a whole, there's no other reasonable explanation. Your relationship with Drake dates back years. You told me you barely crossed paths with him when we spoke about him at the banquet, when in fact, you've been meeting him nearly every morning, just blocks away from here. You set up this entire Twitter scenario to bring attention not just to us, but to Click-News, and, when the time was right, you torpedoed the paper, making sure ClickNews came out clean. The only conclusion I can draw is that you've been feeding Drake our stories in preparation for jumping ship to their organization. I'm quite sure they've offered you more money than you'll ever earn here."

"They haven't offered me anything, because none of that happened. I would never betray this paper that way. I would never betray *you* that way. You have to know that."

Mariel shook her head wearily. "I'm not sure what I believe anymore where you're concerned. Which is why I'm afraid we have to let you go."

Jess jerked back, as if Mariel's words had physically struck her in the chest. An awful cold horror prickled across her skin and her mouth dropped open in disbelief. "What?"

"I'm terminating your employment at this paper, effective immediately."

"But…you've known me for years. You have to know I'd never do this."

"I have known you for years, which makes your actions even more repugnant. It's a betrayal of everything I've done for you."

"But—"

"Jessica, there are no other explanations for your actions."

"I didn't *steal* from you!" Hysteria tinged her voice as she struggled to hold it together and think clearly. Just…*think*.

"The evidence tells me otherwise. I'll give you thirty minutes to collect your things. After that, security will be called to escort you from the building, if you haven't already left."

Tears burned in her eyes. Jess blinked furiously, willing them not to fall. *Don't cry, don't cry.* She wouldn't make this moment any more humiliating by crying. Somehow she managed to command her frozen limbs, stiffly standing up. Her fingernails cut into her palms as she fisted her hands in a desperate attempt to steady herself.

"You don't have to call security. I'll go. But I didn't do this. I swear I didn't."

"I don't wish to discuss it any further," Mariel said.

Jess clenched her teeth together. With one tight nod, she turned and made her way out of Mariel's office, the door clicking closed behind her with an awful finality.

Lauren wasn't waiting outside, but that didn't make it any easier to face the newsroom. Every head swiveled to look at her, and Jess could tell from the expressions of shock and anger confronting her that word of what went down had spread quickly. Lauren's handiwork, no doubt. These people had been her friends—practically her family—half an hour ago, but it was clear that was all over.

Summoning all her strength, she willed herself to put one foot in front of the other. One by one, her coworkers looked away from her, as if tainted by her presence. Zoe and Natalie were huddled by the windows, heads together, watching her. When Jess looked over at them, they both hurriedly turned away. How many cups of coffee and take-out sandwiches had they laughed and gossiped over? Just a few weeks earlier, they'd talked about how they needed to look out for each other in this tough business. And now, in an instant, they'd turned their backs on her. Humiliation burned in a knot in her chest.

At her desk, she fell into her chair, gripping the edge of her desk with both hands so hard her knuckles went white. Her things. She had to gather up her stuff and leave before someone called security on her. This was already an unimaginable nightmare, but that would make it exponentially worse.

Hands shaking, she jerked her desk drawers open, rifling through the contents for anything personal. Functioning on autopilot, she hurled her belongings blindly into her bag. Spare headphones, an extra sweater, lip balm, an assortment of flash drives, a bottle of aspirin, last month's *New Yorker*…a notepad emblazoned with the *Brooklyn Daily Post*'s logo found its way in, but she fished it back out and left it on her desk. There was no way she'd give them cause to accuse her of stealing office supplies, too. A paperback Natalie had loaned her that she hadn't had time to read yet…she left that on her desk as well. Let Natalie come retrieve it when she was gone, so she could avoid her tainted presence.

All that was left was the framed photo of her father and sisters, but when she tried to wedge it into her overstuffed bag, it toppled back out and clattered to the floor. The sound was like a gunshot in the mostly silent newsroom. Jess gritted her teeth against the threatening tears. They were all watching her, and she would not cry.

Suddenly, Lina was there, crouching beside her, picking up the picture.

"Here." Briskly, Lina made room for it in her bag.

"Lina…"

"Let's get you out of here."

She kept her eyes on the floor as Lina guided her out of the newsroom. She couldn't bear to look up and see the way people were looking at her.

Sally wasn't at her desk, which was some small relief. One less person Jess had to see turn on her. The front office was empty and quiet.

"Lina, I don't know what's going on. What am I going to do? I didn't do this. Not any of it."

"Yeah, I know."

But Lina's words sounded oddly flat, and she wasn't looking at Jess. Her arms were crossed tightly over her chest as she stared at the floor.

"You believe me, right?" It hardly seemed necessary to ask, but suddenly Jess had a dreadful fear that maybe Lina didn't.

Lina was silent for a moment, just staring at her

feet. A wall of misery and rage hit Jess like a freight train. "Lina?"

"It's just—" Lina started, then trailed off.

"It's just *what*, Lina? Exactly what have I done that would make my *best friend* believe me capable of something like this?"

"You've just been keeping all these secrets!" Lina blurted out.

"Secrets?"

It was like a dam had broken as the words spilled out of Lina. "If I'm your best friend, why didn't you tell me what happened with Alex in college? And apparently you've been hanging out with him every morning at that place you swear you hate. And why didn't you tell me he was the one you've been fighting with on Twitter? I had to find that out from *Lauren*. It's like maybe I don't know you as well as I thought I did."

Jess stared at her in shock. Lina felt this way about her? *Lina?*

"I didn't realize keeping a few personal things to myself would make you believe I was a thief and a liar." But she'd kept the truth from Mariel, too, hadn't she? Trying to explain her complicated interactions with Alex had been too hard, so she'd pretended they didn't exist. And now she looked every bit as guilty as they alleged she was. Even to Lina, apparently.

"You know that's not what I think."

"I don't know what the hell you're thinking! All I know is I can't believe my best friend would doubt me like this, even for a second. I guess I don't really know you, either."

"Jess—"

"Save it, Lina. Lucky for you, you don't have to deal with me anymore after today."

"But, Jess—"

Jess couldn't stay to see the doubt, the uncertainty, in Lina's eyes for another second. Losing Lina's faith hurt worse than anything that happened in Mariel's office. Before this moment could get any worse, she turned and fled down the stairs, leaving the Fiske Building and the *Brooklyn Daily Post* for the very last time.

Chapter Twenty

It was after noon by the time she got home. Dad and Gemma were both at the bar, so the house was quiet. Spudge was crashed out in his favorite sunny spot by the back door in the kitchen, barely raising his head when she dropped into a kitchen chair. Elbows propped on the table, head in hands, Jess watched her tears plonk down onto the Formica and tried to think.

I've been fired.

Fired.

The words chased each other around her brain ceaselessly, but she couldn't seem to get a good grip on them. It was all too much to comprehend. The accusation itself wasn't all that surprising. Lauren had it out for her from the beginning, looking for any reason to bust her. Of course she would willfully misinterpret what she saw.

But Mariel, the person she most admired in the world, thought she'd betrayed her. Lina thought so, too. At the very least, she doubted her, which had been inconceivable this morning. Right now, she was hard-pressed as to which hurt more.

How could this be happening?

It was unjust, unfair…she knew that. But even still,

the sting of the humiliation was brutal. She'd never been fired before. She'd scarcely ever even gotten into trouble. Remembering the judgment and suspicion in the eyes of her coworkers as she'd left had her writhing in misery. And Lina…

Every time she flashed back on that moment, she felt physically ill. They'd had each others' backs since that first day in college, but when Jess was in crisis and needed her, Lina had looked at her with doubt in her eyes, and Jess wasn't sure she could ever forgive her for that. Not that she'd ever get the opportunity to. She'd been cast out of the *Daily Post*, and everything she'd thought she'd had there was gone. Her career, her colleagues, her best friend…it was all gone.

This time, when no one was here to see her break, she gave in to the sobs welling in her throat. Collapsing onto her folded arms, she buried her face in the darkness and wept until she could barely breathe.

Her weeping even penetrated Spudge's usually impervious sleep cycle and she felt the heft of his body settle in along her leg.

"Wuff," he said softly, laying his head on her knee.

"Sorry, Spudge." She rubbed his ears by way of apology, swiping at her hot, tear-stained face with the other. Stroking his bony head, she stared out the back window at the winter-bare backyard, feeling more alone than she ever had in her life.

The buzz of her phone in her hand startled her out of her reverie. It was a text from Peabody.

Peabody: Hey, did you read that crazy article in the Times this morning?

Peabody. God, that all felt a million miles away. His innocuous question was like a message in a bottle from a past that ceased to exist an hour ago.

Her gaze drifted to the corner of the kitchen counter, where Alex had been standing last night just before he kissed her. And right there…that's where he picked her up and sat her on the counter, the better to reach her mouth…

Ruthlessly, she stuffed those memories in the box with the ones from college. Alex had bolted on her last night, right after *Georgia* texted him her love in emoji form. Alex Drake, once again, was meant for someone else, in some other life.

And here was Peabody, still reaching out to her just when she needed someone to talk to. As always.

PaperGirl: Been a little tied up this morning.

Peabody: Busy day?

PaperGirl: You could say that.

Peabody: Is everything okay?

PaperGirl: No. Not at all. I got fired.

Peabody: What?? I don't understand.

Jess laughed out loud, a wet, rusty sound.

PaperGirl: That makes two of us.

Peabody: Do you want to talk?

Yes, she did, but for the first time, Peabody's words on her phone weren't enough. She needed a friend in real life, someone who understood, who would hold her hand and tell her it would be okay. Lina seemed to be right about that much, at least. Whatever she and Peabody had, it wasn't enough anymore.

PaperGirl: No offense, but an online friend isn't going to cut it right now.

The clock over the sink ticked away the minutes as she stared out the back window. The kitchen tap dripped, the water making a tiny *splonk* every time it hit the coffee cup her father had left in the sink. Outside, a cardinal landed on the bare branch of the lilac bush in the backyard. Wasn't seeing a cardinal supposed to be good luck? She could certainly use some of that right now.

When her phone vibrated with an alert, she was so lost in watching the little red bird hop from branch to branch that she startled. Spudge did, too.

Peabody: I meant in real life. Meet me tonight.

What? He wanted to meet *now*? Tonight? After all this time? She thought about it for a moment, attempting to weigh the pros and cons, but linear mental debate was simply beyond her at the moment. Why not? She needed a friend, and at the very least, she knew he was that.

PaperGirl: Okay. When and where?

Chapter Twenty-One

The name of the bar Peabody had given Jess was on the Upper East Side, where the sidewalks were wide and even, and the avenues lined with shops where her paycheck would barely cover a T-shirt. Her former paycheck. Despite being born and raised in the city, she rarely made it to this neighborhood, and she'd most certainly never been to this bar.

Standing under the brown awning, she took a moment to run a hand over her hair. She'd picked a navy knit mini dress, dark tights, and knee-high suede boots to wear tonight. A little dressier than a day at work, but hopefully she didn't look like she was trying too hard. A quick glance at her reflection in the highly polished brass and glass door told her that the redness and puffiness had mostly faded from her eyes. She looked a little hunted and panicky, but not like she'd sobbed her eyes out a few hours earlier.

It was a few minutes past their agreed-on meeting time. Peabody was probably inside waiting for her right now. Nervously, she licked her lips and tried for the thousandth time to imagine him. Once again, her mind refused to come up with a picture. He could be anything. Short, tall—heavy, thin—hot or…not. She'd known that all along, and she'd always insisted his looks didn't matter. And they didn't. Really.

But now that she was finally here, just moments away from putting a face with his name, she had the recent memory of Alex Drake's stunning face muddying the waters. The memory of Alex's perfect lips on hers, the memory of Alex's gorgeous hair wrapped around her fingers…

Ugh. It wasn't fair. Ordinary human males couldn't compete with Alex, and she wouldn't expect Peabody to. She just wished she could reach into her mind and erase Alex out of it. Then she really would be meeting Peabody with a blank slate. Right now, she was afraid that whatever she encountered inside was bound to disappoint in comparison.

"Miss? Are you going in?"

A well-dressed elderly couple was standing expectantly behind her, the white-haired gentleman gesturing at the door.

"Oh! Sorry. Go ahead."

Stepping aside to let them enter, she noted the woman's fur coat and the sizable diamond bracelet winking on her wrist. This was probably one of those superfancy bars where a glass of wine cost twenty bucks and they'd sneer if you ordered a beer. Was he trying to impress her? She thought he knew her better, that she'd never be impressed by something like— Ugh, *stop*! Without any real-life interactions to go on, she'd taken to reading an ocean's worth of meaning into every word and gesture. It was time to stop looking for clues and confront the reality.

Taking a deep breath, she pulled open the door and stepped inside, stopping to let her eyes adjust to the low golden light. The inside of the bar was almost whimsical, with what looked like children's book illustrations on every wall. Tearing her eyes away from the colorful murals, she scanned the rest of the room, finally ready to see Peabody in person.

There was a grand piano dominating the center of the low-ceilinged room, and someone was playing—playing well, too. Semicircular banquettes lined the room, and tables were scattered throughout. The bar itself took up most of the far wall. The bartender wore a suit and tie. Gemma and Dad would never believe this place.

Her eyes roved over the patrons. This early in the evening, there were less than a dozen, almost all easily ruled out. The elderly couple who'd come in before her were settling in at a table near the piano. Two middle-aged women with teen daughters—tourists—were cheerfully chattering away in one of the booths. Two older couples occupied tables. One man sat alone at the bar with his back to her. There he was. *Peabody.*

But something was wrong…

She knew the shape of those broad shoulders. She knew that long frame, leaning casually over the bar. She knew that tousled auburn hair. She'd had her fingers buried in it last night as he'd—

As the realization sank in, and kept sinking, down to her stomach and lower, all the way down to her feet, a cold, blooming horror spread through her body. She couldn't breathe, couldn't move. How could this…how could he…?

He turned to glance over his shoulder.

Their eyes locked, and Alex Drake surged to his feet. "What the hell are you doing here?"

Except they'd both said it, at the exact same moment, and now the words were just hanging there, any rational answer impossible to produce. There was no way he could have possibly known about her plans with Peabody unless he *was*…

Jess found her voice first, advancing toward him, her fury bubbling up like lava about to spill over. "I don't know what kind of sick joke you're playing here, Alex—"

"Me?"

All of their past encounters came rushing at her, tangling into one massive, unthinkable, ongoing betrayal. "Do you get off on humiliating me? Is that it?"

"You think I *planned* this?"

"What the hell else am I supposed to think?"

He straightened, his eyes blazing to life with anger. "One of us planned this, all right, but it sure as hell wasn't me."

"You think *I* set this up?"

Something passed in Jess's eyes, but it wasn't guilt or panic. If he didn't know any better, Alex would have said she looked hurt. It was the first time since he'd turned to find her standing inside the door of the bar that he felt anything other than a blinding sense of betrayal. Betrayal of *what*, he couldn't even answer.

His head had been a mess since last night in Jess's kitchen. Although he *liked* PaperGirl, and valued their online connection, he'd been even less inclined to meet her in real life. It felt…wrong, somehow, in the wake of his encounter with Jess. But then she'd needed someone and he'd felt compelled to reach out, as a friend, to help. After all the time they'd spent talking, it was the least he could do for her.

But now somehow, inexplicably, Jess had shown up *again* to fuck with his head, and possibly his life. Because the years had taught him that "coincidental" encounters with women rarely ever were.

"It wouldn't be the first time somebody's manipulated their way into my life."

She scoffed. "Of course. Because everybody in the whole world is out here scheming to get a piece of Alex Drake."

He shrugged. "Well, actually, yes, in my experience."

"God, you really are arrogant." She took another step closer, close enough to poke her finger into his chest. "Listen here. You might have women falling all over themselves to lure you into traps, but I'm not one of them, understand?"

Somewhere deep in his chest, buried inside this burning knot of anger and confusion, something eased. Because he *did* know that. He had no idea what the hell was happening here, but weirdly, even when they were furious and yelling at each other, somehow, he knew he could fundamentally trust Jess. He'd always known that.

That still didn't answer any of the hundreds of questions crowding his brain.

"Then how the hell did you get here?"

Her dark eyes burned with fury as she glared up at him. "The same way *you* did."

"Excuse me?" An unfamiliar voice cut into the brittle tension surrounding them.

Alex and Jess both turned to look at the bartender.

His personable smile and polite demeanor had vanished. "I'm going to need you two to take this outside."

Shit. They were shouting at each other in the middle of goddamned Bemelmans Bar. This was not the kind of bar that witnessed fights. Every other patron in the bar was gaping openly at them. Even the piano player had stopped playing to stare.

Color flooded Jess's cheeks and she took a step back, her chest rising and falling as she fumed. "Not a problem. I was just leaving."

Then she spun around and strode out the way she'd come.

"Jess, wait!" He was stuck scrambling for his coat, digging in his pocket for a wad of cash to throw on the bar, before he could sprint out after her. She'd only made it a dozen feet or so down the sidewalk, shoulders hunched against the cold, hair whipping in the sharp breeze, as she marched up Madison Avenue.

"Jess, stop. Just stop."

He'd caught up to her in a few long strides, reaching out for her arm. She spun to face him, slapping his hands away. "Don't touch me!"

Hands up, he took a step back. "Okay, I won't. Just stop, so we can figure this out."

"Oh, I've figured it out all right. Somehow, some way, you…you're…"

"I'm Peabody," he finished for her.

Saying the name out loud had the effect of defusing her anger, like puncturing a balloon. Jess turned her huge eyes on him, glassy with confusion and hurt. Now that the shock had passed, the answer was staring him straight in the face, impossible and obvious. "And you're PaperGirl."

Looking away, she let out a soft huff of humorless laughter, swiping at the tears she was determined not to let fall. That was Jess, never wanting the world to see her vulnerable.

"I think we should talk."

Jess kept her eyes averted, breathing heavily. He could almost see the wheels turning in her mind, coming to grips with the situation.

"I suppose we should," she said at last. She jerked her chin toward the bar, behind him. "But it's cold as hell out here and I think we've been banned from that bar."

Alex sighed. "And it was my favorite."

Well, there was nothing else to be done. He was in uncharted waters from here on out. "This way." He turned and gestured for her to walk with him, which she did. She was silent as they walked side by side around the corner onto 76th and up the block. When he reached the town house, he paused to fish his keys out of his pocket.

"Where are we?" Jess stared up at the white brick facade of the house in confusion.

"My place."

"*Your* place? You live here?"

"Where'd you think I lived?"

"Nowhere. I just…" She shook her head in confusion. "It's fine."

He pointed her toward the stairs leading to his entrance. "This way."

Chapter Twenty-Two

There was a wide set of steps leading up to the carved wooden doors of the main entrance, but Alex led Jess around to the side of those, to a narrow set of five steps leading down to a more modest door. He keyed something into a keypad and pressed his thumb to a sensor.

"Are you kidding?"

"Dad's security is pretty tight," he murmured without looking at her.

"This is your *father's* house?" She looked up again at the wide white stone five-story edifice. She didn't think real people even lived in this area. She'd thought it was all foreign embassies and plastic surgery offices.

Alex shrugged, keeping his eyes on the door. "I have my own apartment on the ground floor."

Inside, Alex flipped on a light. Not that she'd given much thought to where Alex lived, but if she had, it would have looked just like this—luxurious and understated at the same time. A hallway faded into darkness in front of her. An arched entrance to her left opened onto an open-plan living room with a kitchen tucked into the back of the room, all stainless steel and dark wood cabinets. The living room held an overstuffed sofa and a pair of club chairs in rich brown leather. A low coffee table was scattered with newspapers and magazines. A mahogany shelving unit housed a large flat-screen TV and an impressive-looking sound system. On the wall, there was a framed edition of the *Chicago Daily Tribune*'s famous "Dewey Defeats Truman" front page, no doubt the real thing.

His voice startled her back to reality. "Do you want a drink?"

"Absolutely." Right now, alcohol was definitely in order.

"I have…" He peered into his fridge. "I have beer. And scotch."

"Beer."

She shrugged out of her coat and left it on the back of the sofa before following after him to the kitchen.

He handed her one and took one for himself. She twisted off the cap and took a sip. Anything to fill this painful, tense silence. She tried to keep her eyes averted from Alex, but it was impossible to ignore his presence in this small space, leaning against the kitchen counter just a few feet away, fingers picking at the label on his beer bottle.

God, she'd sat next to him last night, watching those same fingers turn his glass in circles on the bar and she'd never once realized that she'd seen them before, that Peabody had sent her a picture of those very fingers.

Alex was Peabody. Her mind had accepted the obvious, but her gut still gave a brutal lurch when she thought about it. All this time, when she'd been pouring out her heart and soul to Peabody, Alex had been on the receiving end. She felt raw, exposed, vulnerable. Would it have been this terrifying if Peabody had turned out to be a complete stranger? Or anyone else she already knew? Did she feel this scared because it was *Alex*?

She tried to remember everything she'd revealed to him, every secret she'd entrusted to him, and to imagine Alex reading it all, but it was impossible. The Peabody of the past several weeks was still at war with the Alex she'd known for years, the Alex of last night.

She should probably just go. What could they possibly say about this unbearably awkward situation, anyway? They'd box up this embarrassing discovery, along with that thing that happened in her kitchen last night, and pretend none of it had ever happened.

But wait a minute. About last night...

"Hey, what the hell?"

Alex blinked in confusion. "What?"

"Um, *Georgia*? You're flirting with a girl online when you have a girlfriend?"

Alex set his beer bottle down with a clunk and straightened away from the counter. "She's not my girlfriend. I just met her last night."

"Seems long enough for Georgia. I saw her text."

"She's a little overeager, but definitely not my girlfriend. She's the daughter of a business associate." He paused, looking steadily at her. "I wouldn't do that, Jess. You and me. Last night. I wouldn't have done that if I was involved with someone else."

She swallowed hard and dropped her eyes. Funny, she already knew that. Whatever *very* complicated stew of emotions she was wading through where Alex was concerned, deep down, she knew he'd never do something like that. Maybe she hadn't always felt so certain of him, but after last night, and everything he'd revealed, she did.

Setting down the beer she'd found impossible to drink, she rubbed her hands together. "So."

Alex inhaled deeply. "So."

"That's your favorite bar."

"What?"

"Explains why Peabody would pick a place that's not at all my speed."

"That's not the only reason I picked Bemelmans."

She looked back at him.

"Do you remember? The first time we talked on-line, about that short story in the *New Yorker*?"

Jess reached back into her memories for that beautiful short story she and Peabody had bonded over. It had taken place in New York, and then—

The last scene, were the GI meets the army nurse on the night before he ships out to war, took place in a bar on the Upper East Side. A romantic little place with piano music and children's book illustrations painted on the walls. Her throat closed up with a sudden rush of emotion. Peabody had loved that story—because it was Alex's favorite bar.

"This is hard," she confessed. "Knowing that you know all that stuff I told him."

He blew out a breath. "No kidding. I've never told anybody some of the stuff I told PaperGirl."

It was so strange, hearing him talk about Paper-Girl—about *her*—like she was someone else. Jess struggled to identify this curious flare of heat she felt in her chest when he mentioned her. It felt suspiciously like jealousy. She wasn't going to examine that one too closely. Not yet, anyway.

Alex shifted his weight as he leaned against the counter, crossing his arms over his chest. "So...the family business that PaperGirl's sister runs...that's Romano's. And Gemma."

She nodded. Then out of nowhere, a frantic little huff of laugher burst from her lips, and she clapped a hand over her mouth to stifle it.

"What's so funny?"

"Nothing." She shook her head. "It's just... I thought you worked in a hardware store."

"What?"

"Your family business. I thought it was a hardware store or something."

This time she couldn't hold back the burst of laughter. Alex's mouth quirked, the first smile he'd allowed himself all night. "Nope. Media empire."

She laughed again, and then she couldn't stop as the tension of the last half hour ebbed out of her body. Then Alex had joined in, laughing so hard he had to bend over and brace his hands on his knees. She laughed and laughed, until tears streamed down her face and she could barely draw breath.

"It's just so *unbelievable*," she gasped.

Alex's laughter ebbed, although he was still grinning widely, his white smile dazzling her for a moment. "What is?"

"You and me...all this time."

His smile softened but didn't disappear. "Not so unbelievable, when you think about it."

"What do you mean? Of course it is."

He shrugged, then straightened away from the counter. Jess's pulse leaped in response. The laughter faded away, leaving her breathless and tingly.

"I mean, you and me." He waved a finger back and forth between them. "We know how this works. And PaperGirl and Peabody. We know how *that* works." He took a step toward her, and her stomach swooped with a sudden rush of nerves. "Maybe we should try them together."

"This is crazy." Her voice had gone all soft and breathless. "All we do is fight."

Alex raised one eyebrow, in that enviable, sexy way of his. "That's not *all* we do."

Memories of last night, of his mouth on hers, of his hands on her body, came rushing back in. She couldn't move, every muscle frozen in place as Alex took another step, closing the small distance between them. Her heart was about to beat its way right out of her chest.

"Jess?" he asked.

"Alex?"

"Are we going to do this? You and me? No more secret identities or misunderstandings?" He was closer now, looming over her, close enough to touch. She could almost feel the heat from his body.

If she thought too hard about it, that was a big question, with a big answer. So she didn't think beyond the next moment, and in the next moment, she really wanted Alex to touch her.

"I think we are."

"So?"

He leaned in and every inch of her skin prickled with anticipation.

"So… I think you should kiss me."

That was all it took. His hands were reaching for her and she was tumbling headlong into his arms. She leaned up to him as he leaned down to her and their lips met in the middle.

Everything about Alex and her had always been so complicated. But when he kissed her, it all became so very simple. Lips parted, tongues touched, heat licked up her body, and for the moment, nothing else existed.

She gripped his shoulders, feeling her way across their solid expanse, to the tendons of his neck, and up to trace the hard line of his jaw, the elegant slant of his cheekbone.

He held her so tightly she was pulled up to her toes, left leaning on him for support. He felt solid and steady. Tonight, Alex wasn't going anywhere.

"You're so tiny," he muttered against her lips as he backed her up against the counter. She opened her mouth to object, but the words cut off abruptly when he hauled her upright and set her on the edge of the counter, just like last night. Sliding his hands up the backs of her thighs, he pulled her legs apart and moved into the space he'd made. "It's so fucking hot," he said, before capturing her mouth again in another brain-melting kiss.

Alex saying "fucking," now *that* was hot. What was also hot was making out with him on his kitchen counter, with his hands kneading her ass and the hard length of him pressed right between her legs. Against her will, a helpless little moan broke from her throat and was lost in his mouth.

His fingers curled around the back of her knee, pulling her leg up, making more room for him. He was the one to groan this time, a ragged, hard-edged sound so very unlike Alex.

"Jesus, Jess…" He broke the kiss, gasping for air, searching her face.

His hair was wrecked from her questing fingers, his eyes half-closed, his lips parted as he panted through his fierce arousal. The sight of his sex-starved expression, and those eyes, so intent and hot, made her nipples tingle, competing for urgency with the ache pulsing between her legs. There was probably still a lot they should talk about, issues they'd have to work out with words. But none of it seemed particularly urgent in the face of this tidal wave of desire.

"Where's your bedroom?"

He blinked. "Are you sure?"

As her hand tightened in his hair, she brought his mouth back to hers, kissing him with a sensual, almost obscene thoroughness. She was no longer sure of a single goddamned thing in her life, but she was absolutely sure she wanted to have sex with Alex. Right now. Tonight. "Yes, I'm sure."

Instead of immediately dragging her off to the bed, he took her face in his hands and kissed her again, altogether more gently than she'd kissed him. The romance of the kiss was at odds with his body, pressing against hers with an unabashed sensuality, stimulating her everywhere without ever touching exactly where she needed him.

"Alex…" she panted, as he left her mouth to drop kisses across her cheek and down her neck. Hooking a heel over his hip, she tugged him in tight against her.

"You're driving me crazy," he muttered into the soft skin in the hollow behind her collarbone. "I want you so much."

His tongue stroked across her skin in the wake of

his words and she arched against him, needing more than she was getting with all of these clothes between them. For five years, she'd denied herself even the dream of Alex. The time had come to have the dream and the reality, too.

"Then take me to bed and have me."

He leaned back to look at her, a lazy, satisfied grin on his face. Then, as easily as if he was picking up a bag of groceries, he swept her off the counter and into his arms. Now *that* was hot.

"Bedroom?" he asked, giving her another chance to change her mind. Which would have been very gallant of him if she hadn't been reduced to a trembling pile of lust by that little display of strength. Frankly, he was being a gentleman just taking her to his bed, when she wouldn't have stopped him from doing it right there on the kitchen counter.

"Bedroom," she forced herself to reply. His chest rose and fell as he looked down at her. Then, with one more brief, hard kiss, he carried her down the hall and into his room.

"Should I leave the lights off?" he murmured as he set her down inside.

She shook her head. Alex was here with her and she didn't want to forget it was him for a moment. He drew her along behind him to the side of the bed, where he flicked on one small lamp. It cast a dim circle of light, which didn't reach to the corners of the room.

Like the rest of his apartment, it was much simpler than she expected. The far wall was completely concealed in floor-to-ceiling curtains. Opposite, a wall of overstuffed bookshelves. His bed, a huge king-sized expanse of navy duvet, had a simple, dark upholstered headboard. Nightstands flanked it, one holding a scattering of personal items, intimate in their ordinariness…a paperback thriller, some change, a watch, its leather band still curled to the shape of his wrist.

He turned to her, the low light casting his beautiful face in dramatic light and shadow. Before he could say anything or touch her, she lifted a hand and ran her fingers over the landscape of dark and light, tracing his features with her fingertips. His eyes fell closed and he sighed.

"I've wanted you forever, Jess." The words were whispered, almost like a secret he was confessing. He opened his eyes, smiling down at her, running a hand over her hair as he spoke. "Since the first time I saw you. Peter Jakes sat back in his chair and I could finally see your face, and for a minute, I couldn't breathe. All I could do was stare at you, your gorgeous dark eyes, this hair…"

Her heart stumbled to a stop as his words sunk in. Peter Jakes was in their freshman-year Exploring Journalism class. He'd transferred out after a couple of weeks. Alex was talking about the first day of Professor Hughes's class, that moment when an innocent classroom discussion had flared into a heated argument between the two of them. It seemed as if arguments had stood in for every other intimate encounter they both wanted and couldn't have.

"Since then?" she whispered.

He nodded, his eyes roving over her as he carded his fingers through her hair. "From the first."

"Then I opened my mouth and spoiled everything."

His mouth tugged into a lopsided grin. "Then you opened your mouth and I knew I was in *real* trouble.

Because I'd fallen head over heels for a brilliant, passionate girl who was never going to give a rich, useless brat like me the time of day."

She thought back to those early days, when he seemed like some golden god a girl like her could never hope to touch, and a host of terrifying, tender, new emotions blossomed into blazing, emphatic life in her chest. Taking his face in her hands, she pushed up to her toes and kissed him, pouring into it all the feelings she couldn't yet express in words. He kissed her back, the heat from earlier morphing into something darker and rich, full of the promise of everything to come.

His hands slid from her waist, slowly over her hips, and down the backs of her thighs, curving her body against his as he bent over her. The hem of her dress rode up in his clutched hands, but he made no move to lift it or take it off her.

When she couldn't take it anymore, she pushed against his chest and took a step back. His hands hung in the air for a moment, his expression questioning. Never looking away from his eyes, she slowly bent over and unzipped one boot, toeing it off. The heavy knit neckline of her dress gaped away from her body, giving him a clear view of her cleavage down the front. She knew it, tossing her hair over her shoulder and out of the way, so nothing would impede his view. As she moved to unzip the other boot, she noted the prominent bulge at the front of his dark jeans, and she pressed her thighs together against the ache of pure desire.

When her boots were gone, she slid her hands up under her skirt without lifting it, working the waistband of her tights down over her ass and hips. She'd just started wiggling them down over her thighs when his voice stopped her cold.

"Lie down." Not a request.

Okay. That was a side of Alex she hadn't expected, and it made her so hot, wet, and ready for him.

She moved to the side of the bed to sit. When she made to scoot herself back, he stopped her again.

"No, right there." Pausing, she looked up at him as he came to stand between her feet. "Lie back."

Ufff... Who knew being bossed around by him would be such a turn-on? She did as he asked, her back flat on the bed, her knees bent, legs hanging over the edge of the bed. Slowly, Alex bent and grasped her feet in his hands and raised her legs, until both of her heels were settled on his shoulder. Her breath was coming in short pants as he slid his hands back down the length of her legs, shaping her ankles, cupping the curves of her calves, fingertips dipping into the sensitive hollows behind her knees, palms scraping deliciously down the length of her thighs.

He'd been watching his own hands as he touched her, but now his gaze came up to meet hers, and it never wavered as his fingers curled around the waistband of her tights and he slowly began to peel them down her legs. Inch by inch, her pale skin was revealed, stark against the charcoal gray knit. Every bit of her that was exposed sent her temperature up another degree, until she felt like she was on the verge of combustion by the time he tugged her tights off her toes and tossed them away.

His hands came back to her ankles, the heat almost searing against her already tingling skin. The urge to press her thighs together against this aching need was almost overwhelming. Lifting her left foot, he shifted it to his other shoulder. Still looking straight into her eyes, he turned his face and pressed a kiss to the inside of her ankle. Moaning, she arched off the bed, as aroused as if he'd touched the very center of her sex. But Alex wasn't done. Slowly, he moved down her leg, his mouth never leaving her, unless it was to kiss the other leg, his lips and tongue tracing heated tracks over her calves, knees, and down her thighs.

"Alex…" Her voice was a thin, reedy pant as her hands fisted into the duvet on either side of her head.

"Almost there," he murmured against the inside of her thigh.

When he was nearly to the top, he gently pushed the hem of her dress up over her hips. But he bypassed the main event, instead, pressing a kiss to the little bow at the top of her panties, on her lower abdomen. She moaned, arching again, and he took advantage of the space under her body to push her dress farther up, chasing it with his mouth, dropping kisses up her stomach as he went.

Her shaking legs wrapped around his rib cage as he moved up her body. Her dress was rucked up under her arms, her bra partially exposed, but not enough to allow his mouth access to all the places she wanted him. With a quick sideways wiggle, she grasped the bunched up fabric and drew it up over her head and off her arms, flinging it away into the darkness.

Alex paused, gazing up at her from where he'd been kissing her rib cage. Her breasts, swelling above the cups of her plain black bra, heaved with every breath.

With slow deliberation, he slid his palms up her sides until they'd settled over her breasts and he squeezed. It forced another ragged moan from her throat, and she threw her head back, eyes closed. Could she come just from his hands on her breasts? Right now, it felt like she might.

The pleasure of his touch over the fabric was enough to drive her out of her mind, but then he added his mouth, tracing the edge of her bra with his lips and tongue as his fingers kneaded and stroked her. When he shifted slightly to the side and closed his mouth over one peak, she nearly shot up off the bed. Writhing, she grasped at his hair.

"Alex, *please*." Begging. He had her begging and he still had all his clothes on.

One hand slid under her body and she arched to give him access. As his mouth teased her nipple through the damp satin, his nimble fingers flicked open the hooks of her bra. Drawing it down her arms, he barely drew a breath before taking her in his mouth again, this time nothing at all between her tender nipple and the hot, wet pleasure of his mouth.

His body pressed down on hers, delicious weight between her legs, but he was too low to be where she really wanted him—needed him. With infinite thoroughness, he moved from one breast to the other, using his fingers when his mouth was busy, rolling and tugging on her nipples until she felt on the edge of combustion.

"Oh… Alex…*stop*."

In an instant, he slid back, lifting his head to look at her in question. Her tongue skated along her bottom lip before she drew it briefly between her teeth. His lust-filled eyes tracked every tiny movement.

"What's wrong?" His voice was low and gritty with need.

"Stand up." It was his turn to get bossed around.

A wicked grin unfurled across his face, his teeth flashing white in the dim light, and he pushed back, rising to tower over her, her legs hanging limply to either side of him.

"Sweater," she murmured. "Take it off."

"Yes, ma'am." Still grinning, he lifted an arm over his head, grasping a handful of fabric at the back of his neck and peeling the sweater off over his head with a casual, purely masculine shrug that made her mouth water.

"So polite."

He shrugged, and the light played over the wonder of his torso, the broad shoulders, defined abs, flat stomach, and tapered waist. God bless the college swim team. "Manners matter."

She laughed, her eyes roaming down the length of his body. There was only a smattering of hair across his pecs, but a narrow trail started below his belly button, disappearing under the waistband of his jeans. Her palms itched to trace every inch of sculpted muscle and bone. Her tongue ached to trace that delicious trail down to its conclusion.

But she made no move to touch him as she lay back on the bed, staring up at him. "Jeans, too."

"As you wish." Automatically, his hands went to the fly, flicking open buttons with an easy confidence.

"Did you just *Princess Bride* me?"

"That depends," he replied as that delicious trail

was gradually exposed, and then the waistband of his boxer briefs. He began to push his jeans down, but stopped just as a very tantalizing V of muscles was coming into view.

"Depends on what?" Jess was breathless with longing and anticipation.

"Did you like being *Princess Bride*-ed?"

"Yes."

"Then I was totally *Princess Bride*-ing you."

She forced her eyes up from what he was almost revealing, to meet his. "All off," she commanded softly.

His eyes were on fire as he stared down at her. In a moment, his jeans and briefs were gone. As he straightened, her eyes zeroed in on his cock, hard and curving up toward his stomach. *Oh.* Who knew he was hiding all of that? She might have wondered more than once, but she'd never dared dream it was so—

"Jess."

Her name, spoken in that low rasp, jerked her eyes back to his face. "Come down here," she murmured, holding out a hand to him.

"One more thing."

Grasping her panties at either hip, he shimmied them down, taking away the last scrap keeping her body away from his eyes. When they were gone, his eyes slowly raked down her, from her heavy dark hair spread out on the duvet around her head, down over her breasts, nipples still hard and damp from his mouth, down over her stomach, to the V between her legs, and down the length of her legs.

"I've wanted this for so long…" he murmured, trailing off as he lost the words.

Then he slowly slid a palm up her thigh. Every muscle in her body went tense, but this time, he didn't skip over the good stuff. One arm braced next to her head, he leaned over her as he dragged the fingers of his other hand over her mound, then down, down, down.

"Oh," she gasped, at the same moment he groaned.

The touch of his fingers to her most sensitive skin was like an electric shock. He leaned down, his mouth hungrily claiming hers as his fingers swiftly and confidently explored her. She was already so worked up that it felt like only moments until she was trembling on the edge of an orgasm, her thighs shaking as it neared. She moaned into his mouth, her hands clutching at his rock-hard biceps, needing something stable to hang on to as he pushed her ever nearer to the edge.

His fingers never stopped or slowed, and he didn't break the kiss until she did, gasping and throwing her head back. Pleasure flooded through her like warm honey, and everything fell away for a few breathless minutes. There was just Alex and the bliss he was bringing to her body.

When she opened her eyes again, flushed with her climax, he was still leaning over her, smiling down into her face.

"That was amazing to watch."

"It was amazing to feel, too."

His sexy smirk started spreading across his face.

"Don't gloat," she warned him.

"I wouldn't dare." Then he hooked his hands under her arms, lifted, and tossed her fully onto the bed like she weighed nothing. She was so shocked—and turned on—she couldn't speak. He was crawling up the length of her body, the hair on his thighs pricking the sensitive skin of hers, his hard chest teasing the points of her breasts. The feel of him, alternately arousing and unfamiliar, overwhelmed her senses. Then he was lying over her, naked body pressed to naked body. How could she want him this much already when he'd just given her an orgasm so good her wits were still scrambled?

"Do you have…?"

"Yeah, hang on." Leaning to the side, he retrieved a condom from the nightstand. She ran a hand up the tightly corded muscles of his arm as he braced himself and rolled it on.

He came back down over her, kissing her briefly before pulling away enough to look down at her.

"Yes?" he murmured.

If she hadn't been a thousand percent ready, his pausing to ask one more time would have convinced her. She wrapped her legs around his hips, pulling him in where she wanted him, urging him forward with her body. "Oh, yes."

There was a nudge, a delicious moment of anticipation as his body gently began to breach hers. She held her breath, desire thrumming through her veins. Alex pulled his lips from hers, kissed her cheek, buried his face in her hair, and with one hard thrust, he drove home.

Her moan split the still, quiet air of the room.

"Ah, God…" he groaned. "Are you okay?"

"I'm *so* good. Don't stop," she whispered. "Whatever you do, just don't stop."

"I won't stop." He began to move in her, long, slow strokes, each one another shock to her heated nerves, until she was lost to it. As his pace picked up, a coil of desire began again, low in her abdomen, drawing in tighter and tighter until she could barely stand it. Everything ached, striving for release. Alex's strong body surged over her, leaving her helpless, tossed on the waves like a leaf on the breeze. He groaned as he drew closer, his hips snapping hard against hers.

"There. Right there," she whispered, as he hit some new, perfect spot. Her eyes were squeezed shut, but when his palm came up to cradle her cheek, she opened them again to look at him.

"Jess," he whispered. Nothing else. Just her name, spoken softly in the heat of passion, his eyes looking down into hers full of unbearable tenderness.

She lifted a hand to his face, too, her thumb brushing against his bottom lip as he raggedly drew in a breath.

Oh, he'd gotten this so wrong. The physical chemistry she and Alex had always had, combined with PaperGirl and Peabody's connection, wasn't just having the best of both worlds. It was an altogether *new* world, one both exhilarating and terrifying.

And it was in that moment that her body unfurled. It was more than sex, more than pleasure. The connection she felt was overwhelming, like nothing she'd ever experienced before, shaking her down to her very foundations. Her eyes stung with tears as his breathing hitched, once, twice, and then he let out a low, animal groan as he fell helplessly into his own release.

They lay in perfect bliss in the hazy aftermath, his breaths warming the side of her neck. His hair was damp with sweat as she dragged her fingers through it. He pressed a brief, soft kiss to her shoulder before shifting his weight off her. His heavy arm fell across her waist, tugging her body in tight to his. His lips

kissed the side of her hair and then her temple before
he let out his breath in an exhausted exhale.

"That was…"

"My brain stopped working the minute you started
taking off those tights."

She chuckled, nuzzling her face into the side of his
neck. "The rest of you seemed to work fine."

"I guess you bring out my best. Hang on a sec."

He rolled away to dispose of the condom, leaving her feeling chilly and bare. Conscious thoughts
began to trickle back in. She'd just had sex with Alex.
Amazing, mind-blowing sex. *Wow.* Flickers of self-
consciousness about her nakedness flared, but before
she could reach for clothes or the blankets, Alex lay
back down in bed.

"Here." He worked the duvet out from under them
and held it up, making space for her next to him. The
sheets were cool and she shivered slightly as she slid
down next to him. "Come here." Without fanfare, he
scooped an arm under her shoulders and rolled her
onto her side, nestled up against the length of him.

Their whole relationship to each other had just been
turned on its head. They were probably supposed to
talk, figure things out. But this felt too nice, too perfect. Warm, secure, delicious. Her head settled in on
his shoulder like she'd been snuggling with him forever, and his hand found its way to her hair, stroking
it slowly and hypnotically. She was gone before she
realized it.

Chapter Twenty-Three

Alex came awake to a brutal case of pins and needles in his right arm. When he turned his head on the pillow, the tumble of silky dark brown hair and the small, pale hand curled loosely against his chest brought everything back.

Jess. Here in his bed. Naked.

Holy hell, what a night.

For a long time, he lay still, just absorbing the moment. He'd wanted this—*her*—for so many years, it hardly felt real. Surely tonight was just a dream, and he'd wake up hard, still imagining her naked body laid out on his bed.

But the numbness and pain in his arm reminded him this was no fevered sex dream. Jess was real. And cutting off the circulation in his shoulder. Gently, he eased out from underneath her, lowering her head back to the pillow. She barely stirred. This day must have been hell for her.

PaperGirl told him she'd been fired from her job. Which meant Jess had gotten fired from the *Daily Post*. Jess getting fired under any circumstances from any job was inconceivable. She was the hardest-working person he knew. Dedicated and loyal to a fault. Something horrible must have happened. He'd get it out of her later. For now, he'd let her sleep and see what he could manage in the way of food, since they'd missed dinner in the midst of the drama.

Leaving her sleeping, he pulled on some sweats and made his way out into the kitchen. He was bent over, examining the bare expanse of the inside of his fridge when her voice startled him.

"For a second, I thought you'd pulled another runner, except this is your house, so that would have been awkward."

She was leaning on the island that divided the kitchen from the living room, wearing his DeWitt U Swim Team T-shirt and nothing else, her dark hair in a wild tangle around her shoulders, eyes sleepy and sexy all at once. Yep. This was a fantasy straight from the spank bank. He was still gaping at her when she began to look uneasy, tugging the hem of his T-shirt down over the tops of her thighs.

"What?"

He shook his head, eyes roving over her in wonder. "Just you…looking like this…here. I, um…" Would it be disgusting to tell her how often he'd jerked off to this image? Yeah, too soon. "I might have fantasized about this once or twice."

Relaxing, she smiled and tucked her hair behind one ear. "Wow, a fantasy is a lot for a girl to live up to."

He strode toward her, pinning her against the kitchen island. "Trust me, you're leaving the fantasy in the dust right now."

He kissed her, her mouth hot and sweet against his. Never before had one kiss been enough to reduce him to shaking lust. Was it too soon to drag her back to bed? Suddenly her stomach growled, answering the question for him.

"Sorry," she mumbled when he pulled away. "I skipped dinner."

"Me, too. I was trying to find something to eat, but the situation is pretty grim. I have beer and ketchup. How about a pizza?"

"Pizza's perfect." Scooting out from under his body, she hoisted herself up on one of the bar stools along the kitchen island.

He ordered a pizza on his phone and joined her at the kitchen island to wait. "So…" He leaned over to press another quick kiss to her lips before he launched into it. "Want to tell me about what drove you here tonight?"

She was still smiling dreamily at him. "Huh?"

"You got fired."

In an instant, the smile faded and the spark drained out of her eyes. "Oh…right."

Reaching out, he tucked her hair behind her ear and curled his palm around the back of her neck. "Tell me what happened."

She let out a wry chuckle. "It's all your fault, actually."

"*My* fault?"

"No, not really. Um…" She straightened on her stool, putting some space between them in a way that set off a tremor of unease in his gut. "Okay, you're not going to like what I'm about to say, but here it goes. Three *Brooklyn Daily Post* stories have shown up on ClickNews in the past month."

"And? Reporters are chasing the same stories all the time. Sometimes one scoops the other. It happens." The fact that a ClickNews reporter managed to scoop any-body on anything was mildly surprising, but he sus-pected they weren't all hacks. One or two seemed like they might be talented, under different circumstances.

"Yeah, I know. That's what we thought with the first two. Just bad timing, bad luck. But this last one was Lina's. Her source was supposed to be exclusive—"

"Sources sometimes lie." Surely she knew all this. No source was truly exclusive until you broke the story.

"I know that. But there's more. She's been work-ing on it for weeks. I helped her with the research. It wasn't just the source who showed up in ClickNews's article. Some of her notes and my research did, too."

"And you think someone at ClickNews stole it?"

"Alex, there's no other explanation. Some of Lina's notes showed up word-for-word in your article. There's a leak. Someone at the *Daily Post* is passing stories to ClickNews."

He dropped his hand and sat back, absorbing the information. His instinct was to defend ClickNews. And if it was just the first two stories, there was noth-ing to this suspicion. But the third, Lina's story... He trusted Jess on this one, and if she said there was no way it could have been a coincidence, then— Shit, he had a huge problem.

He closed his eyes and dropped his head back. "Fuck."

"Do you know who it is?"

"There's only one person it can be. Chase."

The buzz of the intercom gave him a few minutes of cover to collect his thoughts. Jess said nothing as he retrieved plates and worked through this startling piece of information.

Okay, so Chase didn't always have the truest moral compass, but he'd always assumed that was just where his sex life was concerned. He was familiar enough with that sort of moral relativism with his father. But he really hadn't thought Chase capable of a betrayal like this.

Although the news was a shock, it didn't hurt as much as he'd have thought. Maybe because his friendship with Chase had ebbed years ago. Yes, he had some great memories of high school and college parties, but they'd largely drifted apart by graduation, and Alex had done nothing to keep it together. They'd only reconnected when Chase called him out of the blue to invite him out for a drink.

Where he casually mentioned Drake's acquisition of ClickNews. And before that conversation was over, somehow Alex had been offering to put in a good word for him.

It had all been a setup. What a fucking asshole.

Jess tossed her half-eaten pizza on her plate and swiveled to face him. "Okay, you know I'm no fan of his, and it looks bad, but let's be logical. Are you sure it's Chase?"

"There's no one else it can be. The journalists' pool at ClickNews…" He broke off and let out a scoff of laughter. "It's a stretch to call them journalists. Some of them are, but a lot of them have no real training. They're just freelancers we bring on for short stints. It's something I wanted to change, if… Whatever. It doesn't matter. The head of the journalism division gathers the stories and assigns them to writers in the pool to work up. Sometimes they run down some info on their own, but the story…that comes from Chase. That asshole."

That lucky, ungrateful asshole. His shock was rapidly giving way to a roiling fury. How he'd envied Chase when he took over that position. Alex had dreamed of what he could do with that news division. But Dan Drake had different plans for his only child. A stint overseeing the whole site, to learn it from the inside, before he would move on to some other branch of the Drake Media empire. That was his fate.

"So it has to be him," Jess said. "But who's feeding him the stories from the *Daily Post*? Unlike you, he doesn't have a connection to anyone on the staff. Lina and I know him, but it's safe to say, we're not friendly—"

The revelation about Chase had been such a blow that he'd failed to put together the rest of the story. Now he reached out for Jess, taking her hands in his. "Wait a minute. Is *that* why Mariel fired you? She thinks *you* leaked the stories?"

Jess nodded miserably. "Yes. To you."

Another piece of the puzzle fell into place. "Because that woman from your office…she saw us together. She's the one who's been giving you a hard time, isn't she? She's your dragon."

Her mouth quirked up in a wry smile. "Right. My dragon. Of course you know all about that. It wasn't me, but I can't prove it, and it's true that I have a connection to someone at ClickNews. So Mariel fired me." She let out a quavering breath. "It was so awful, sitting there as she accused me of that. *Mariel*, of all people."

"This is bullshit!" he exploded in fury. "There was nothing underhanded going on between us. I'll go in and tell her that."

Touching his arm, she smiled weakly. "Alex, with

all due respect, you're the one they think I'm leaking to. Your dad owns the website. Mariel's not going to believe you any more than she believed me."

"Jess, I'm so sorry that being seen with me has wrecked this for you. This isn't fair."

She let out a wry chuckle. "I *really* wanted to blame you for it. But you didn't do anything wrong, any more than I did. And I have to admit, my connection to you looked bad. So did all the Twitter stuff, once that came out. I can understand what it must have looked like to everyone at the paper."

"Lina knows you'd never steal her story that way. Didn't *she* defend you?"

Without warning, Jess's eyes filled with tears. "She thinks I did it," she whispered.

"Come on. This is Lina. There's no way she thinks that."

Jess shook her head. "You didn't see the way she was looking at me. She doubted me, and that's just…" The tears slipped free, streaking down her cheeks.

"Ah, Jess—" Her tears wrecked him. She was so tough and still so relentlessly *hopeful*. This despair didn't sit right on her.

"Sorry." She swiped her fingers under her eyes. "Sorry, sorry. I'm sure it's no fun having a girl burst into tears right after she sleeps with you."

"Come here." Grasping her by the elbows, he pulled her off her stool to stand between his legs. He reached up and took her face in his palms, swiping away her tears.

"We'll figure this out," he murmured, pressing a kiss first to one cheek, then the other, and finally to her mouth.

"It's not your problem to fix, Alex."

"Excuse me? First of all, my fucking former best

friend is running stolen stories on my father's web-site. This hurts more than you. He's putting the entire company at risk. God—" He broke off, shaking his head at a memory. "I *got* him that job."

"You did?"

"Yeah, I put in a word for him with my dad."

"Hardly seems like he'd need you for that."

"What do you mean?"

She shrugged. "Just that he seems like he's in pretty tight with your father all on his own."

"That's recent," Alex said, although now that Jess had brought it up, Chase had been attempting to in-gratiate himself with his father ever since he started working at the site. Seemed Chase had big plans for himself—plans Alex was going to take great delight in crushing into dust.

"Okay, take care of Chase, but what happened to me—"

He cut her off with a brief, hard kiss. "You're in trouble because I couldn't make myself stay away from you."

"Couldn't make yourself—"

He rolled his eyes. "Come on. If I liked Ému's cof-fee *that* much, I could have hired a barista and set one up in the ClickNews lobby. I showed up every morning because chances were good that I'd see you. I wasn't always honest with myself about my motivations, but deep down, that's what I was doing."

"Maybe I was, too." Jess ran a hand up his bare arm, her fingertips skating along his skin and setting him ablaze. "The coffee's good, but not that good."

"Think how much time we wasted standing in that

line and arguing every morning when we could have been doing this."

"Fighting with you wasn't all bad, though."

She caught her bottom lip with her teeth as she glanced up at him. That gesture had always slayed him, and when she aimed it straight at him? Dead.

"No?"

"No. It was kind of…fun. If that makes sense."

"It makes perfect sense. Being near you always made me feel…"

Leaning in closer, she braced her palms on his thighs. "What?"

"Awake. You made me feel awake, when I didn't even realize I'd been sleeping before."

Jess blinked, and Alex reveled in rendering her— for once—speechless, before pulling her closer and kissing her with a slow thoroughness. His hands slid down to explore her luscious little body as his tongue explored her perfect mouth.

"How do you feel about cold pizza?" he whispered in her ear before moving to kiss the side of her neck. Her breath left her body in a long, wavering sigh as her hands slid higher on his thighs and gripped him. His cock swelled as he imagined sliding into the warmth of her body again.

"I like it better cold."

He stood and swept her up in his arms. So small, so perfect, her legs bared all the way to the crease of her thighs as his T-shirt rode up on her. "It might be very cold by the time I'm done."

Her arms wound around his neck. "Do you promise?"

Chapter Twenty-Four

Jess woke to the unfamiliar sensation of someone moving around the room. Then she registered the sheets, way softer than anything the Romanos owned, and the pillow, like a downy cloud under her head. Cracking an eye open, she saw bright morning sunlight leaking in all around the wall of curtains across from the bed. Not a window, glass doors—that was what was behind the curtains.

"I tried not to wake you." Alex's deep rumble startled her, as did the bed shifting as he sat down on it behind her. She rolled to her back to look at him. He was wearing a plain white T-shirt and dark pants, his hair wet from the shower. "You can stay as long as you want, but I need to get going."

Grimacing, she pushed herself upright, holding the blankets to her chest. "Guess I'm not rushing to get to the office this morning. Or ever again."

"Hey." His hand came up to cup her face. "This is temporary. We'll figure it out and get your job back. In the meantime, you might as well sleep in, right?"

She shook her head. "I have to get home. I have a lot to explain to my family. They don't even know I got fired." That was a conversation she was dreading, but putting it off wouldn't make it any easier.

"I'm out of coffee down here, but Lucia's probably put a pot on upstairs. We can have a cup before we go."

"Who's Lucia?"

"My dad's housekeeper."

"Your dad…"

Alex slid off the bed, turning away to pull a crisp white dress shirt from his closet. "The rest of the house is his. I told you that last night."

Regretfully leaving the heavenly warmth of Alex's bed, she began retrieving the various items of her clothing scattered around the room. "Right. I forgot. There was a lot going on."

Alex flashed a wicked grin over his shoulder. "That's an understatement."

That grin set off a pulse of arousal strong enough to make her blush and drop her eyes away. Everything had changed so completely and quickly. Alex and Peabody and confessions and sex…*so* much sex.

"Hey." He came to stand next to her. "What's wrong?"

"It's just a little…disorienting."

"Me and you?"

"Yeah."

Alex scowled, reaching up to tug on his hair. "Do you want… Is this too much? Do you want to forget it?"

"No! No, I just feel a little lost."

"Look." He took her hands in his and placed her palms on his chest. "I'm the same guy you've been talking to all these weeks. It's me."

She exhaled. Of course, she already knew how to talk to Alex. She'd *been* talking to him forever, she just didn't know it. "I know. Lucky me. You can't imagine what I was expecting when I went to meet you last night."

"Oh, really? So I'm better than you expected?"

Smoothing her hands down the front of his shirt, she traced the shape of his chest, remembering the glory of what was underneath. "*So* much better."

"I was bracing myself, too, you know."

Her eyes flew up to his. "Really? What were you imagining?"

Blowing out a breath, he glanced skyward. When he spoke, his voice was a high singsong. "'*That* Alex Drake? Does your father really know Jay-Z? Can you get us into The Standard? Can you use that private jet whenever you want?'"

"Oh. Oh, I get it. Why you were so reluctant to meet in person."

He nodded. "I've learned the hard way to be cautious. So, really, it's a relief, discovering PaperGirl is *you*, someone I know for a fact has never been the least bit impressed by me."

"Well, I wouldn't say *that*." Her fingers toyed with the first button on his shirt, undoing it and teasing his exposed skin with her fingertips. "I'm impressed by you. Just not by any of that stuff."

Covering her hands with his, he grinned down at her. "Glad to hear it. Now, stop distracting me or I'll drag you back to bed."

"Is that supposed to be a threat?"

He rolled his eyes and laughed. "Let's go get some coffee, Jess."

Once they were both dressed, he led her back through his apartment to a door off the kitchen. It opened onto a brightly lit stairwell.

"So the whole downstairs is just for you?" she asked, following him up the pale wood stairs.

"Yeah. Dad used to have a loft in Tribeca, but when I told him I was going to DeWitt for college, he moved into this place and had the ground floor renovated for me."

"Wow. My dad just bought me a new laptop when I started college."

Alex glanced back over his shoulder. "I know you hate him, but he's not all bad, you know."

"I never said I hated your dad. He's just—"

"He can be a lot to take, I know. It's hard to see under the image, but he loves me. He always has. When I moved to New York for college, I think he realized he'd missed a lot with me and he was sorry for that."

"So he built you an apartment right downstairs so you'd never be far away?"

"Pretty much."

"Is he home right now?" She didn't exactly relish the idea of crossing paths with Daniel Drake in his kitchen, wearing yesterday's clothes, having just rolled out of a marathon sex session with his son. She might not *ever* be ready for that.

He opened a door at the top of the stairs. "I have no idea. His assistant used to keep me linked to his calendar, but all the notifications were driving me crazy, so I dropped out."

When she followed him out of the stairwell, she nearly took back everything she said downstairs about not being impressed by his money. They were standing in the middle of a cavernous, two-story entryway, a white-and-black marble floor under their feet and a massive glittering crystal chandelier over their heads. The stairwell they'd just ascended was tucked under another staircase, this one grand and sweeping, curving up and away from the entryway to the upper floors.

Oblivious to her stunned silence, Alex grabbed her hand and towed her out of the entryway. "Kitchen's back this way."

Through an arched opening lay a wide hallway, tiled in the same marble. At the end of the hall, they passed through double swinging doors to a kitchen so large, it encompassed the entire back half of the floor. Marble counters lined two walls, broken at intervals by stainless steel appliances. Glass front cabinets displayed enough plates and glasses to serve an army. An island sat in the middle of the room, with a row of high stools pushed up alongside it and a bouquet of flowers in a crystal vase on its glossy surface. French doors made up the entire back wall of the room, opening onto a deck, and stairs led from there down to a garden, bare and still dusted with snow from two nights ago. The glass doors in Alex's bedroom probably opened onto that same garden.

Alex pointed her to a bar stool at the island and crossed to one of the cabinets to retrieve coffee mugs. The coffee pot was nestled in a fancy-looking contraption that looked capable of making coffee, frothing milk, and doing your taxes.

The flowers on the kitchen island were fresh, a dozen sprays of delicate creamy orchids and some sort of glossy, dark green tropical leaves. Next to the vase, today's papers lay neatly folded, the *New York Times*, the *Wall Street Journal*, and the *Financial Times*. The brewed coffee, the fresh flowers, the papers…all set out by the elusive Lucia for a couple of bachelors who might not even be in residence, for all she knew.

"All that's on this floor is the kitchen?" She thought her tone was remarkably disinterested, considering how intimidated she was.

"There are some staff rooms on this floor, too. The living room, library, and dining room are one floor up. The bedroom suites, media room, and the gym are on the floors above that."

Staff rooms. Library. Media room. Gym.

Jess schooled her expression into nonchalance, wordlessly accepting the mug of coffee Alex brought her. She absolutely couldn't let him see she was thrown by his life. That was exactly what he was afraid of—why he'd hidden behind Peabody. Once before, she'd preemptively judged him, thinking him nothing more than the sum of his beauty and privilege. She wasn't going to make that mistake twice.

Feeling her eyes on him, he glanced over and smiled tentatively. "What are you thinking about?" It still amazed her that Alex could ever be uncertain of himself. But she'd seen a different side of him as Peabody, and she knew he wasn't as happy as he tried to appear to the rest of the world.

"So, the family business…"

He nodded tightly, his expression shuttering in an instant. She'd seen that look on his face before, always when he was in the company of his father. "Drake Media."

"He wants you to work for him?"

"I already work for him. But ClickNews is just training. I'm supposed to take over the whole thing for him one day. The whole empire."

"And you don't want to." It wasn't a question, because she knew the answer. He'd told her. "You want to report."

A grim smile tugged at his beautiful mouth. His head was tipped forward, the rust tangle of his hair falling forward across his forehead. "When I started at DeWitt, I didn't even want to be a journalist, did you know that?"

She didn't reply, because he didn't seem to be looking for an answer from her.

"Dad thought a major in either journalism or communications would be good background. I was a decent writer, so I picked journalism."

"You're a fantastic writer, Alex."

"Thanks to you."

"Me?"

"I told you how intimidated you made me feel."

"Yeah, but—"

"Listening to you talk about journalism—"

"Rant is more like it." She used to get so carried away in classes, waxing rhapsodic about the noble duty of the fourth estate. He must have thought her insufferable.

"I've been around the news all my life, but you made me think about journalism—really *think* about it—for the first time. I wanted to feel as passionate about something—*anything*—as you felt about writing. Watching you work so hard for something you loved…it opened my eyes. I wanted to be as good—as driven—as you. For the first time in my life, I expected more from myself than what came easily. Eventually, I found I loved journalism as much as you did."

Back in college, she'd resented his talent. He'd made

it look so effortless, like he'd decided to be a brilliant journalist on a whim. She'd never really understood, until recently, how passionate he was about it. And here he was, not even writing. It seemed criminal to her now.

"I thought you were just trying to beat me," she said.

"*Well*, maybe a little bit of that, too. We're both pretty competitive."

Jess tilted her head in acknowledgment, because that was certainly true.

"Mostly, I think I just wanted you to see me. Really *see* me."

"Alex, I always did, even when I was pretending otherwise."

"But not Dan Drake's entitled son. *Me*. I guess that's why I became Peabody. When I talked to PaperGirl, I knew, for the first time in my life, that you didn't have an angle. You didn't want anything more than me."

Reaching out, she laid her hand over his on the counter. "You can still trust me, you know. Even now that I know about—" She waved a hand to indicate this gajillion-dollar home they were sitting in. "All this. You're still you."

His grateful smile made her heart melt. Sliding a hand around the back of her neck, he pulled her in close. "Thank you," he whispered against her lips before capturing her mouth in a soft, slow, sensual kiss that had her nearly melting off her bar stool.

"So if we're laying blame," he said after he released her, his eyes flashing with a teasing glint over the rim of his coffee cup. "It's all *your* fault. I was just supposed to get some background at college, and ended up falling in love with it."

"If I'm responsible for you wanting to be a journalist, I'll happily take the blame, because you're brilliant. Alex, if you want to work as a reporter, can't you just tell your dad that? He gave you that entire apartment. Like you said, he's got his good points."

Alex looked pained, turning his coffee cup in circles on the counter. "He's got more than good points. He's got a huge heart, and he's generous and loyal to a fault—unless you're a woman he's sleeping with."

"So? Why not tell him what you want?"

He scowled, gathering his thoughts for a moment. "Did you know, my dad got started with one TV station in Maryland?" he asked at last.

"No. I thought he must have inherited it."

"Nope. He had an investment do well and took everything he had—everything my parents had, because they were still together back then—and sank it into this small, unremarkable local TV station in Maryland. From that, he's built everything."

"Impressive." Which was the understatement of the year.

"He's devoted his whole life to building this empire, all so he can turn it over to me. It's his legacy. How can I say no to that? It's like telling him everything he's done…everything he *is*…means nothing to me."

"But you don't want to run his company. Surely—"

"There's no one else. I'm his only child. What's he done it all for if not for me? Surely you understand that, with your family's bar."

Romano's was a far cry from a media empire, but wasn't the sense of obligation just the same? "I do understand," she conceded. "In my case, Gemma took on the bar, but—"

"If she hadn't, you would have, wouldn't you?"

Reluctantly, she nodded. "I couldn't have said no."

His smile was sad and accepting. "Neither can I."

"It feels like such a waste, though. The journalism world needs you."

"The journalism world will do fine without me. They have you."

"Yep, me, the unemployed journalist."

"Listen—"

"Oh!" A breathy, startled gasp sounded from across the kitchen. A woman was paused, half in and half out of the kitchen, her eyes wide and her hand clutching the front of her white waffle-weave bathrobe closed. "I didn't realize anyone else was here." She was very pretty, even with her makeup faded and her blond hair fresh from bed. It was easy to guess she was a "guest" of Dan's, even though she looked to be much closer to Alex's age than his father's.

Alex smiled at her, all politeness and ease, not at all bothered to discover a strange woman in his father's house. This must happen all the time. "Hi, I'm Alex. This is my friend, Jessica."

"I'm Ashley. I was hoping to find some coffee."

"Help yourself," Alex said, indicating the coffee maker on the counter. "Cups are just above."

"Thanks." Ashley's eyes raked down Alex appreciatively in a way that said she was delighted to have found more than coffee. Jess scowled and suppressed an eye roll as Ashley sauntered over to the counter, swaying her hips. "Dan didn't mention his son lived here."

"I have my own place downstairs, but I was out of coffee. I couldn't send Jess out in the world without some caffeine." He reached out and ran a hand down her arm before letting it come to rest over hers and threading their fingers together. The move was casual, but deliberate.

Ashley tracked it as she reached for a coffee cup. "Cozy."

The kitchen doors swung open again and Dan strode in wearing a gray T-shirt and navy sweats, his feet bare. Oh, hell, this was exactly what Jess had hoped to avoid. And with his hookup still present, to make it extra awkward. Having never seen Dan in anything less than a suit and tie, she had a powerful urge to avert her eyes, like she'd caught him naked.

"Ah, you've met my friend," he said, all smiles, and she suspected he wasn't quite sure of Ashley's name.

"Just pointing her toward the coffee," Alex said easily. "Dad, you remember Jessica Romano?"

Dan's hawklike gaze swung to her, registering her wrinkled dress and their joined hands in a flash. She practically had a sign tattooed across her forehead, *I fucked your son downstairs last night! Three times!* Was it possible to literally die of embarrassment?

"Jessica, of course." This time, the smile was a degree less charming, slightly more calculating, as he assessed her again in the wake of this new information. Jessica Romano, Alex's old classmate in the coffee shop was one thing. Jess, the girl his son was now sleeping with, was clearly another.

Refusing to let him make her squirm, she smiled politely at him. "Nice to see you again, Mr. Drake."

"Please, it's Dan."

"Um… Dan." That was the first and last time she would ever call him Dan out loud. It was just too weird.

"You work at the *Brooklyn Daily Post* with Mariel Kemper." He couldn't remember last night's hookup's name, but he remembered *that*? Of course he would. Dan Drake excelled at remembering pertinent details when it was important. The fact that she was now sleeping with his son had evidently made the details of her life important to him—although not, she suspected, in a good way.

How was she supposed to answer that? If there was one thing to make this morning-after encounter worse, it would be admitting that his golden boy was banging a minor league reporter who'd just been fired from her first real job. But Alex saved her from responding.

"Dad, do you need the car right away? I was going to have Omar take Jess home."

She gripped his wrist with her free hand. "What, like a chauffeur?"

"Don't worry," Alex told her. "Omar's on call. He can be here in two minutes."

"Oh, no, please, I was going to take the train—"

"It's an hour to your place from here."

"But—"

This time, Dan cut her off. "Feel free. I'm not flying out until later this morning, so I'm hitting the gym."

Ashley's gaze ping-ponged between the three of them, scowling as she registered that Jess was the overnight guest being sent home in the chauffeured car, and she'd be stuck ordering an Uber.

"Where are you heading?" Alex asked conversationally, pulling out his phone and typing out a text.

"Brazil for the rest of the week."

"Still looking at that network in Rio de Janeiro?"

Dan shrugged. "Haven't made up my mind, so I'd better go check them out in person."

"Makes sense. The Mexico network has done well for us, but South America's a whole different market." They proceeded to launch into a discussion about market shares and investor stakes and a bunch of other stuff that sounded like a foreign language to Jess.

The change in Alex was disorienting. He'd donned a whole new persona, like he'd put on a jacket. She'd seen Alex slip into this role before, but this was the first time she was struck by how very wrong it was.

When his phone buzzed, he paused and glanced at Jess. "Omar's out front."

"I need to get my coat," she mumbled, sliding off her stool. "It was nice seeing you again, Mr.…Dan. And nice to meet you, Ashley."

"Have a good day, Jessica," Dan said, shooting a cheeky grin at Alex, which he studiously ignored.

Back downstairs in his apartment, she retrieved her coat from the rack by the door. Alex moved in front of her as she wrapped her scarf around her neck. He pulled her hair free where it was caught under her coat collar. "Can I see you tonight?"

"Sure. I mean, being unemployed is really going to free up my schedule."

"Hey—"

"I don't want to talk about it now. I'm going to have to tell the whole story to my family soon, and that's enough."

"Okay, we won't talk about it anymore. For now. So what time should I send the car for you?"

"What?"

"The car. Dad's out of town, so it's no problem—"

"No, please. Stop. You can't send a limo to fetch me."

He looked adorably puzzled. "Why not?"

Flustered, she waved her hands helplessly. "Because it makes me feel like your high-class hooker or something."

"That's ridiculous."

"Whatever. I'm taking the subway," she said, imbuing the words with all the finality she could muster. "I'll see you at seven?"

Before he could protest again, she hooked a hand around the back of his neck and pulled him down for a hard, thorough kiss. Abandoning his protest, he wrapped his arms around her waist and pulled her firmly into his body, deepening the kiss. Oh, maybe she could just stay…

"Maybe you could just stay," he muttered against her mouth.

"Ugh, no, I have to go home and you have to go to work." Regretfully, she extracted herself from his arms. He followed her outside, one hand resting lightly on the small of her back. The car turned out to be a black SUV, not an actual limo.

Alex and Omar shared a brief exchange, hinting at a long-standing, comfortable relationship. He was clearly part of the Drake family. Omar opened the back door for her, but Alex caught her hand when she moved to climb in.

"Hey, Jess?" Brushing a strand of hair out of her face, he tucked it behind her ear.

"Yeah?"

"I just want you to know… Yesterday was a lot to take in, but I'm really happy about this. Us."

Oh, the butterflies would be the death of her. They beat frantically against her rib cage as his fingers skated over her shoulders and down her arms to take her hands in his.

Even though the rest of her life was currently in shambles, in this moment, with Alex, she was happy, too. So incredibly happy.

"Me, too."

His smile, shy, almost grateful, made her heart swell. Leaning down, he kissed her, then murmured against her lips, "See you tonight."

Weak-kneed and grinning like an idiot, she slid into the back seat of the SUV. Alex closed the door behind her and tapped on the roof before backing away. Omar politely asked her where she was going and she gave him her address in Brooklyn. With a nod, he pulled away from the curb. Jess glanced back at Alex, still standing on the sidewalk. He raised his hand as she drove away.

Falling back on the soft leather seat, Jess watched the winter-bare branches of the trees in Central Park slide past outside the window. Her fingertips played over her lips, still feeling Alex's kiss there, still feeling his hands on her body.

When she'd idly imagined her ideal man in the past, she'd envisioned him as a little scruffy and working class, like her. Intelligent and idealistic, like her. Alex had the second in spades, but the first…wow. All that money was going to take some getting used to. He was so much the polar opposite of her imagined working-class hero, it was laughable.

But that was on her, wasn't it? He was fine the way he was. Better than fine. It was time to admit, now that she'd quit hating him, Alex Drake was pretty close to perfect. The baggage he came with—a media empire and a controlling plutocrat who had an iron grip on his son—well, those were challenges she'd think about some other day.

Chapter Twenty-Five

After Jess had gone, Alex made his way back inside, heading up to his father's kitchen again. There was no sign of Ashley, but Dan was still there, sipping his coffee and reading one of the papers Lucia had left out.

Dan looked up at him with curiosity. "You're back, Sport."

"Yeah… I just wanted to grab a bottle of water."

As he retrieved a bottle from the fridge, he considered how to proceed. He'd come upstairs intending to tell his father everything he'd found out about Chase the night before, but something held him back.

Chase was away for Christmas, which meant there was no rush to deal with this today. Right now, he only had half the puzzle. Someone inside the *Daily Post* was feeding stories to Chase, and if he showed his hand regarding Chase too soon, Chase would be fired and that would sever the link. It wasn't enough to clear the poison out of ClickNews. He needed to clear it out at the *Daily Post*, too, and in doing so, clear Jess's name. Suspicion had only fallen on her because of him, and somehow, he was going to fix it.

"Did Ashley leave?" he asked, just to make conversation.

Dan smirked as he took another sip of coffee. "She was pissed your girlfriend got the limo."

Girlfriend? The word caught him off guard, but after last night, they were certainly…something. Something big. Something serious. *Girlfriend* felt pretty accurate, actually. It felt good.

"How long's that been going on, by the way?"

His father's voice had shifted very slightly. There was an edge to the question, as Dan prodded at him, assessing the situation from all sides. His father was defensive where women were concerned. Of course, that was largely his own fault, because he slept with a string of younger women who were clearly after his money. But it left him distrustful of any woman's motivation, and now Alex could practically feel him sizing up Jess, assessing her worth.

"It's recent."

"She's cute."

"She's brilliant, too." The words came out sharper than he'd intended, almost a rebuke.

Dan slowly lowered his coffee cup, watching him over the rim. "I'm sure she is."

Damn, he'd shown his hand. Now his father would really be on alert. "I'd better get to work—"

"Forget work," Dan interjected. "Come to Rio with me."

"What?"

Dan shrugged. "I'm going down to assess the acquisition. You might as well come and see it for yourself, since it'll be yours to manage one day."

A dull thud of dread echoed in his chest. "Ah… I'd better not. There's a lot going on at ClickNews right now, with the transition."

Dan waved off his concern. "They can manage without you. Come spend Christmas on the beach in Rio with your old man. We'll have a blast."

His father's idea of a fun Christmas in Rio would undoubtedly involve a lot of very attractive women. Maybe he thought if he dangled enough of them in front of him, Alex would forget about the one who'd just left. Not a chance.

"Sounds fun, Dad, but the holiday coverage is already set at ClickNews. I'd screw up someone's plans if I took off."

His father's eyes narrowed in a lightning-fast shrewd assessment. "Are you sure you're not sticking around the city for the girl?"

He was *totally* staying in New York for Jess, but there was no way he'd say so to his father. He was already suspicious. No sense throwing gasoline on that particular fire. "ClickNews needs me right now, that's all."

Dan shrugged, letting go of the Brazil plan as quickly as it had come. "They'd better not get too used to you there. You're only passing through. You'll be at Drake HQ soon enough."

Alex forced a smile despite the ball of misery forming in his stomach. "That may be, but for now, I don't want to take advantage of being the boss's son. Terrible for morale, especially so soon after the acquisition."

Dan grinned. "See? Already thinking like a manager. You're a natural. I've always said so."

"Yes," Alex said, nodding in grim agreement. "Yes, you have."

Chapter Twenty-Six

Closing the front door behind her, Jess listened for the telltale noises the house made when someone was home—the creak of floorboards and the muffled footsteps on carpets.

"Anybody home?" she called.

"Kitchen," came Gemma's overly prompt response, which made her think Gemma had been peering out the front window as the car pulled up and had only scurried back to the kitchen as she came in.

After hanging her coat and scarf in the hall, she made her way back to the kitchen. Livie was there, too, much to her surprise. Livie spent so much time at grad school, she practically lived there.

Gemma was leaning against the counter, eating a bowl of cereal with studied nonchalance. Livie had her laptop open on the kitchen table, an explosion of papers surrounding her. Spudge lay in a softly snoring heap under the table, his head resting on Livie's feet.

"Livie, you're not at school?"

"Winter break starts this weekend."

"So you're off for what, two weeks?"

"Three."

Gemma let out a growl of frustration. "Yes, Livie's

out of school for three weeks. Can we talk about the important stuff now?"

Jess ignored her, going to the fridge and peering inside, enjoying tormenting her sister a little. "Like?"

"Oh, I don't know...like...how I get a text that my baby sister is going off to meet her mystery man last night and then I get another text letting me know she won't be home."

"I texted you our code word," Jess protested. "You knew I was okay."

"But not a word of explanation! Or maybe we can talk about that huge, expensive SUV that just dropped you off. Who was that driving?"

"Omar."

"Who's Omar?"

"The chauffeur."

Livie and Gemma gaped at her. "Chauffeur? Okay, sit." Gemma hauled out a kitchen chair and thrust Jess toward it.

Jess dropped into the chair and Gemma took the one to her right.

"I don't know where to start."

"The beginning."

Drawing a deep breath, she braced herself. "Okay, the first part isn't so good. It's kind of terrible, actually. I got fired yesterday."

"What?" Gemma and Livie shrieked in unison.

Gemma clutched her hand. "What happened?"

So, to the best of her ability, she told her sisters what happened, the stolen stories, Lauren's discovery of her innocent meeting with Alex, and the fact that he'd been behind the Twitter feud with her, Mariel's abrupt firing, and her confrontation with Lina. This time, she managed to get through it without tears, but her throat ached with the effort.

"I can't believe Mariel!" Gemma fumed. "How dare she accuse you of something like this when she's known you for years? She's got her freaking Pulitzer because of you and this family!"

"You have to admit," Livie interjected, "given the evidence Mariel was presented with, the logical conclusion would be that Jess's been working with their rival."

"But Jess would never do something like that. She should know better. I'd like to march over to that paper and give her a piece of my mind. Nobody messes with a Romano sister."

The pain of yesterday might not ever fully fade, but her sister's full-throated defense did a lot to ease the sting. Nothing was ever truly terrible as long as she had Gemma and Livie on her side. And they were *always* on her side.

"While I appreciate the moral support, that's not necessary."

"Anyway, I can't see what your intervention could do to change Mariel's mind about newspaper business," Livie said. Gemma gave her a fond smile. Where Gemma was all heart and fierce protectiveness, Livie was a thinker, examining the evidence and drawing her conclusions. Of the three of them, Jess had always been the idealistic, passionate one, but her idealism was feeling pretty trampled right now.

"Okay," Gemma said, settling back in her chair. "On to the second big thing. You spent the night with Mystery Man?"

"I spent the night with Alex."

Gemma scowled. "Wait…the guy from the bar the other night, right?"

"You've met him?" Livie looked hurt that she'd missed it.

"What happened to Peabody?" Gemma interjected.

Jess sat forward and leaned on her elbows. "Okay, here's where it gets really crazy."

So she proceeded to tell them the rest—all about Peabody and Alex, and the sudden, miraculous merging of the two.

"But this is the guy you've hated for years, right?" Gemma asked.

"Yeah. I hated him."

"And he hated you."

"We might have gotten our signals crossed on that whole hating thing."

"I could see that coming a mile away," Gemma said to Livie.

"What? How?" Jess said.

"You should have seen the way he looked at her," Gemma continued, ignoring Jess.

Livie leaned forward eagerly. "Really?"

Gemma nodded. "And you." She pointed at Jess. "You got all…*sparkly* around him."

"I don't sparkle for anybody."

"No, not like glittery. Like…full of sparks. That's what you're like around him. Full of sparks."

"Is that good?" Livie asked.

"I don't know." Gemma shot a sly grin at Jess. "Was it good, Jess?"

The helpless smile was back. Jess slumped forward, burying her face in her arms. "Oh, my God, *so* good.

I'm going to hell. I can't ever step foot in confessional again after last night. God will strike me down."

Livie rolled her eyes as Gemma burst into laughter. "Oh, relax. Nobody's judging you in this house. Especially not when the guy has a limo. That's his, right?"

"His father's."

"Thought so. He looked like he had money."

"That's putting it mildly."

Gemma's eyes lit up and she sat up to perch on the edge of her chair. "Really? Like how rich?"

"You know that cooking network you like to watch on cable?"

"Yeah?"

"His father owns it. And the rest of the world, too. At least it seems that way."

"Holy shit," Gemma breathed. "Wait... Alex *Drake*? As in *Daniel Drake*? He's Daniel Drake's kid?"

"I don't know who that is," Livie complained.

"You don't know who anybody is, unless they've had some invisible black hole named after them."

"Black holes are usually numbered, not named. And technically, *all* black holes are invisible—"

"Okay, we get it," Jess said, bringing the conversational tangent to a close. "Yes, Alex is Dan Drake's son. Oh, and this morning, five minutes after I rolled out of bed with Alex, I ran into Papa Drake and his latest disposable bedmate in the kitchen while we were getting coffee. There aren't words for how awkward it was."

"*Wow*. So..." Gemma peered closely at her. "Do you like him?"

"Who, *Dan*? Eewww, he's as old as Dad!"

"No, I meant Alex. Do you like Alex?"

Do I like Alex? Like was far too mild of a word to describe what was rampaging through her heart right now. Her emotions felt like an exposed nerve, leaving her scared and vulnerable, and if there was anyone she could confide that to, it was her sisters. "I like him so much it's scary."

Gemma and Livie were silent as they stared at her, both of them smiling softly in wonder. Then Gemma sat up briskly and slapped her hands on the table. "Well, then you have to bring him to Sunday supper to meet the family."

"Wait, wait. I think it's pretty serious, but Sunday supper is a little too much, too fast. One step at a time."

Under the table, Spudge lifted his head and wuffed softly. A second later came the sound of the front door opening and closing. Spudge heaved to his feet and scrambled out of the room.

"Hello?" their father called. "Anybody home?"

"Back here, Dad," Gemma called out, her voice oddly tight and her eyes steadfastly focused on the tabletop.

Dad came into the kitchen a moment later, Spudge lumbering along in his wake. "Look at this. My kitchen is full of beautiful women!" He cast a beaming smile at all three of them as he made his way to the coffee maker.

"Hi, Dad," Jess said, looking from Gemma to him. Gemma was too tense and Dad was too happy. Plus he hadn't even noticed she wasn't at work. It wasn't like Dad to miss something like that. Her spidey sense tingled, but she couldn't parse out what was going on.

"Just came back from the bar," her father said, taking a sip of his coffee. "Had to meet the beer distributor for a delivery. It's a little earlier than usual, but he's got to make an extra trip out to Bay Ridge this morning, so he called and asked me if I could meet him ahead of schedule, so I got up early and headed over there to meet him."

"Sure. It happens." Jess scowled, still trying to puzzle out the weirdness. That was a rather convoluted and overly detailed explanation for a boring bar delivery.

"Well." John Romano stood at the kitchen counter for another moment, looking around the kitchen like he hadn't seen it in years. "Think I'll go catch a little more shut-eye before I have to open up for the day."

All three sisters watched him in silence as he left the kitchen. His boots stomped on the creaky wooden stairs, and down the hallway overhead. The distinctive thud of his bedroom door closing broke the tense silence in the kitchen.

"Dad's acting weird," Livie said. "Did you see the way he was smiling? And where did he get that shirt?"

"That *was* a new shirt," Jess said. And not one of his interchangeable plaid flannels. A crisp black button-down—like nothing else in John Romano's wardrobe. Leave it to Livie to notice something small like that.

Gemma leaned forward, whispering even though he was too far away to hear them. "I figured out what's going on with Dad. You're not the only Romano who didn't make it home last night."

Jess and Livie gasped. "Dad didn't come home last night?"

"Where did he go?" Livie asked, eyes wide. "What was he doing all night?"

Gemma raised her eyebrows suggestively. "What do you *think* he was doing all night?"

Livie turned pale as Gemma's meaning sank in. "No! Dad? And…"

"Who?" Jess interjected. "Who was he with?" Their dad hadn't dated anyone since their mother died. The idea that he'd been shacked up with someone last night… Jess was floored.

"Well." Gemma leaned forward, eyes alight with glee as she prepared to impart some extremely juicy gossip. "You know Teresa Fiorello?"

"She's from the neighborhood, yeah?" Jess said. "She went to school with Mom and Dad. I thought she lived in Jersey."

"She did, when she was married. But she got divorced three years ago and moved back home to Second Place, to take care of her mom. She comes into the bar sometimes with her girlfriends from the neighborhood. Girls' Night Out, white wine spritzers, and gossip, you know the deal. And, of course, she's known Dad since high school, so they always talk. Well, last night, she shows up *by herself.*"

"Alone?" Livie asked.

"That's what 'by yourself' means, Livie. Yeah, totally alone. And when Dad says hello, I could swear he wasn't surprised to see her. Like, he was expecting her or something. So she sits at the end of the bar, and for the rest of the night, whenever we're not busy, Dad's holding down that end of the bar, too, chatting with Teresa."

"Wow." Jess couldn't imagine her dad flirting with any woman. Inconceivable.

"So then he sends me home at midnight and says he'll close up on his own. When I left, Teresa was still there. But one a.m. comes and goes and he doesn't come home. So I tracked his phone, just to be sure he was okay, you know? And where do you think it told me he was? Teresa's house on Second Place."

"Oh, my God," Jess breathed.

Livie looked baffled. "Dad has a...girlfriend?"

"I guess that's..."

"It's weird," Livie said.

"Well, yeah," Jess conceded. "But Dad's only fifty-two. That's not so old."

"And he's still a good-looking guy," Gemma said.

"Eeeww," Livie protested.

"Well, it's true. Dad's a hottie, in his way. You should see the way all of Teresa's married friends check him out when they come in."

Jess held up a hand. "I don't want to know this."

"I'm just saying... Mom's been gone a long time and he hasn't dated anybody else."

"I kind of forgot he could," Livie complained, making a face.

"What's she like?" Jess asked. "Teresa?" Frankly, it was hard to imagine what kind of woman might appeal to her father, since he'd been irrevocably linked to her mother forever.

Gemma shrugged. "She's pretty. She seems nice."

Livie sat back in her chair. "Wow. Dad has a girlfriend."

The three sisters exchanged a look before Jess planted her hands on the table and shoved to her feet. "I'm officially at my limit for mind-blowing stuff happening in a twenty-four-hour period. I'm going back to bed, too."

"Wow, everybody's so *tired* today," Gemma teased.

Jess rolled her eyes and laughed, the fatigue making itself known in every inch of her body. "Shut up, Gemma." Ducking between Livie and Gemma, she kissed them each briefly on the cheek. "I'm glad we're all here."

Gemma reached up to brush a hand across her hair. "Me, too."

Upstairs, Jess shed her stale clothes and climbed into bed. A thousand things crowded the edges of her mind, so many problems she needed to solve. Whenever her thoughts touched on the paper, and what had happened yesterday, she felt sick with misery. So she pushed all thoughts of it away, to be dealt with later. As she sank into sleep, she focused on the one thing—the one *person*—that was good. She thought about Alex, remembering his kisses and his body and the way he made her feel, and she counted the hours until she would see him again.

Chapter Twenty-Seven

"I can't believe you think it's okay that the *Times* ignored the embargo on the story."

"I'm not saying I agree with what they did, but the fact of the matter is, an embargo is nothing more than a gentleman's agreement. There's no legal violation at play here."

"It violates standard journalistic practice."

"Which is changing all the time. It was already leaking all over social media. What were they supposed to do? Ignore the story?"

"But—"

Alex kissed her. Hard. Then softening until she was melting into him.

When he drew back, she blinked. "You can't always shut me up with a kiss."

He grinned. "Trust me, I'm not trying to shut you up. I like arguing with you. We just need to decide where we're eating."

"Oh, right."

Omar was still driving them south through Manhattan, with no definite destination in mind.

"There's a great place in the Meatpacking District—" Alex began, but Jess silenced him with two fingers placed across his lips.

"I know *exactly* where we're going to eat," she said. "Omar, can you drop us off at Gramercy Park?"

"Sure thing, Miss Romano."

Ten minutes later, they stood at the edge of Gramercy Park, looking east.

"You want to go to Shake Shack?" Alex asked in bewilderment.

Jess laughed. "Shake Shack is for tourists. Come on. We're going to go find Jesús." She took his hand and towed him after her through the park as she checked her food truck app. It said he was here today, but it wasn't always accurate. As they neared the north side she spotted him. "Oh, good, he's still here."

Alex slowed until he'd come to a stop. "Tell me this isn't—"

"Hot dogs!" she said brightly.

Alex groaned. "Seriously?"

"Hey, I'm starting you off easy. We're going to Jesús's food truck for gourmet dogs. I could just dive in at the deep end with some random hot dog cart in Midtown."

"I'm drawing the line at that." Alex's face was filled with a combination of apprehension and distaste. He was so adorable when he was outraged.

"Come on, you big snob. I promise you, you'll be converted."

The line at Jesús's Holy Dogs wasn't long. When they reached the front, Jess rattled off her order with an ease born of frequent practice.

"A Hail Mary Dog, with chili, cheddar, green onions, and jalapenos. And an extra-large order of fries."

Alex stared down at her. "Are you serious?"

"I would never joke about hot dog toppings. And they have great fries."

The guy working the window jerked his chin at Alex. "What'll ya have?"

"I have no idea."

"Start with the Hail Mary."

He laughed. "If you say so. A Hail Mary Dog. With mustard."

The guy at the window looked at him expectantly. "And?"

"That's it. Just mustard."

Jess rolled her eyes. "We're going to have to expand your topping horizons."

They found seats on a park bench nearby, just off the sidewalk winding through the park. It was cold out, but there was no wind, so it wasn't as unpleasant as it might have been.

"Umph." Jess let out a moan of delight through the first bite.

Alex watched her eat for a minute. "I can't believe you're going to eat all that."

"I wouldn't have ordered it if I didn't intend to eat it."

"I'm not sure if I'm terrified or impressed."

"Impressed. Here, try it." She held her hot dog up to his face, laughing at his expression. "Come *on*, try it."

"Okay, fine." Alex relented, taking a larger bite than she expected.

"Well?"

He chewed his way through it, muttering, "It's not bad."

She was still laughing when a female voice called Alex's name. "Alex? I thought that was you."

Alex hurriedly swallowed down his food and stood. "Megan...hi."

Megan was tall and elegant, fashionably turned out in a chic dark coat and high heels.

"Funny running into you here," she said. "I'm about to meet Tara Sullivan at a tapas place around the corner... Toro?"

"Ah, Toro's excellent. Enjoy."

"I'd ask you to join us, but it looks like you've already got dinner." She cast a curious glance at Jess.

"Sorry... Megan, this is Jessica Romano. Jess, this is Megan Harte. She works at Drake Media."

With the sophisticated Megan standing over her, Jess was suddenly acutely aware of the monstrous half-eaten chili dog in her hand, and the tray heaped with fries in her lap. God, she probably had onions stuck in her teeth. And Megan was off to eat tapas at some fancy Flatiron restaurant. The hot dogs, which had seemed like such a perfect idea half an hour, now seemed kind of sad. Alex was used to fancy tapas restaurants and she was making him eat hot dogs on a park bench.

"I'm afraid I'm loaded down with fries." When she started to move her dinner so she could stand, Megan stopped her.

"Oh, no, please don't get up. I didn't want to interrupt. I just wanted to say hi."

"It's nice to meet you."

Her smile was warm and genuine. "Same." She turned back to Alex. "Will we see you next week for the end-of-the-year meeting? We're bringing in the team from Mexico City, so we'll have our hands full."

"Of course. You know, we should think about moving Phil onto the in-house Mexico team. He's got experience in that market."

Megan's eyes lit up. "Of course we should. He'd be the perfect person to manage that team. Brilliant idea, Alex. I can't wait until you're with us full time."

Alex gave her a tight smile—one Jess had seen before, although she'd never connected the dots before now. That was his Drake Media smile, and it was nothing like his real one. Even his posture was different as he talked to Megan, like he'd had a steel rod implanted in his spine. She couldn't even imagine this guy teasing her about her hot dog, even though he'd been doing it five minutes earlier.

"Okay, well, I'd better go. Nice running into you, Alex. And nice to meet you, Jessica."

Megan waved back over her shoulder as she walked away through Gramercy Park. As pleasant and friendly as she'd been, Alex watched her like he was watching an invading horde.

He was quiet when he sat back down, a line etched between his eyebrows.

"She seems nice," Jess ventured.

"Hmm?" Alex glanced up at her, distracted. "Oh. Yeah. Megan's great. Smart as hell. She could run the place single-handedly."

Jess silently watched Alex as he picked through his fries. *Maybe she* should *run it*, she thought, *because it's clear you don't want to.*

"Sorry about the hot dogs."

"What?" Alex looked lost.

"Hot dogs in the park. It's not your thing. You'd probably be happier at the tapas restaurant with Megan."

"Hey." Alex reached out for her hand. "I'm happy here with you. I don't care what we're eating."

"Even hot dogs?"

He grinned, and the real Alex reappeared, like the sun coming out from behind the clouds. "Okay, I'll admit, they're not as revolting as I'd expected. But all the same, I'm picking where we go for dessert."

"Better make it good," she teased.

His eyes darkened as he stared at her. Every inch of her body tightened in response. "Oh, don't worry," he murmured. "I intend to."

Chapter Twenty-Eight

"What are you doing?"

"Kissing you."

"There?"

"I like this spot. Although this one's good, too."

Jess sucked in a breath, her skin tingling under his lips. "Or this one." This time, she moaned, feeling her body soften under the weight of his. Alex's voice was muffled against her skin, his perfect diction gone sloppy with sex and exhaustion.

His room was dark, and the quiet around them was broken only by the rustling of their naked bodies against the sheets. They'd had sex twice already, and despite the fatigue pulling at her, Jess could feel her body responding to him, yearning for more.

After hot dogs in the park, Alex had taken her to an intimate little French restaurant for dessert. As awesome as her Hail Mary Dog had been, champagne and chocolate soufflé by candlelight was very nice, too. Sharing it with Alex had been even better, once she'd managed to banish Drake Media Alex for the night.

She'd been slightly worried that things would be awkward between them when they had their clothes on. Could they really just lay aside five years of bickering? The answer was—not really. Although now when they argued, it felt more like healthy intellectual debate. And Alex was certainly fun to debate with. It was a relief to finally be able to admit to herself how much she admired his brilliant mind and his sharp wit.

As they'd sat tucked in a dark corner of the restaurant, Alex had played with her fingers as he'd talked about a recent long-form article on campaign finance reform, his eyes alight with passion as he'd fumed about dark money in politics. His journalistic integrity, she'd decided, might be the hottest thing about him.

But when they'd gotten back to his apartment, journalistic integrity lost out to uninhibited lust. Alex was all over her as soon as the alarm had armed. The first time had happened up against the wall in the hallway, with most of their clothes still on. It was a side of Alex she had never guessed existed—and she liked it very much.

Now she was lying angled across his bed, and he was kissing his way down from his favorite spot to discover more, farther south. While his lips traced a trail of fire over her rib cage, his fingers stroked up the inside of her thigh. When his mouth reached her belly button, she sensed his intention.

"Are you going to—"

His fingers slid into her wetness, stroking her, dragging a ragged little pant from her throat. "Only if you want me to."

She'd only done it—or had it done to her, to be more accurate—once before, and she hadn't actually enjoyed it all that much. Maybe she was too self-conscious. The sensation had been intense, to be sure, but she hadn't been able to let go and let in the pleasure she knew was supposed to be a part of it.

"Um… I guess? If you want to?" It seemed so…intimate. So insanely personal.

Alex chuckled, the rumble sending tremors through her lower abdomen. "Oh, I want to. I really, really want to."

"You do?"

"Yes, I do. You make the most amazing sounds when you come."

"Don't tell me that. I don't need to know that. Oh, my God, what if your father heard me?"

"He's still in Brazil and can we please not talk about him right now?"

She wrestled herself up to her elbows to look down at him. "Wait…he's in Brazil?"

Alex looked up from his spot between her thighs. "And?"

"But tomorrow is Christmas Eve."

He chuckled, reaching up to put a hand on her shoulder to push her onto her back again. "No more talking, Jess."

"But—"

Then he put his mouth on her and she couldn't have formed coherent speech if her life depended on it. There was *definitely* more to this than she'd been led to believe. It. Was. *Amazing*. And she was pretty sure she made all kinds of noises, but being embarrassed was the furthest thing from her mind in the moment. He looked insufferably smug many minutes later when he moved up her body, leaning his weight on one elbow as he grinned down at her.

"Okay, that was really good."

"I told you—"

"Shut up."

His expression sobered. "Has no one ever…?"

"Um, once? It was bad."

"Well, I'm sorry for that."

"I'm wiping it from my memory as we speak. This is the first one I want to remember."

He smiled gently, leaning down to kiss her. "It's a very good first. I'm grateful to be a part of it."

How could she tell him how many things he was first at without scaring him off? The first guy to ever make her weak in the knees with a kiss, the first to get her turned on by politely pulling out her chair, the first to engage her mind at the same time he was engaging her body, the first…well, the first she'd ever loved. Because she was pretty sure she was falling in love with Alex, and not just for his excellent oral skills.

She cupped his jaw with her palm and turned his face back to hers. "Forget the firsts, because you're the best. At pretty much everything. And don't get smug and make me regret telling you that."

His smile as he leaned down to kiss her wasn't at all smug.

"Now can we talk about your dad?"

His expression was comically horrified. "Now? In this context?"

"No, in the Christmas context. What are you doing for Christmas?"

He craned his head back to look at her. "What do you mean?"

"Are you going to Brazil? Or to your mother's house?"

"Um, neither?"

"So you're going to be by yourself?"

Another careless shrug. "Sure. It's no big deal. I've spent plenty of holidays alone."

"But…" Jess propped herself up again. "It's *Christmas*!"

"Yeah," he said cautiously. "We covered that."

How could he be so blasé about this? It was literally inconceivable to her to spend Christmas alone. What would you even *do* all day? For her, Christmas meant a house full of family, a kitchen full of food, and an all-day celebration, with the obligatory trip to church for Mass tucked in there somewhere.

"Your family is abandoning you."

Alex sputtered in laughter. "They're not *abandoning* me. I'm twenty-four. A grown adult. And if it makes you feel less militant, Dad wanted me to go to Brazil with him. I said no."

Gemma was twenty-eight and would still consider it familial abandonment if her entire family ditched her for Christmas. You were never too old for some things.

"Why did you say no?" Spending Christmas in a swanky Brazilian hotel with Dan Drake didn't exactly sound festive, but at least Dan was a relative.

Alex cupped her chin and drew her face in for a brief kiss. "Because I wanted to stay in New York. With you."

Oh.

"Oh."

And there went her emotions, unfurling and blossoming, filling her up until there was scarcely room in her heart for anything more. So even though just a couple of days ago, she'd insisted to Gemma that it was too soon to bring Alex home for Sunday supper, she found herself spontaneously proposing something much more serious.

"You should come to our house for Christmas."

"Your house?"

"Sure. I mean, it's not Rio." Suddenly, she felt bashful, imagining Alex in her house, in the middle of her loud, likely half-drunk, Italian family for a whole day. But she'd started now, so she couldn't stop. And now that she knew he was on his own for the holiday, she wouldn't be able to stop thinking about him. "But we'll have a big meal, and there will be football on all day, and—"

"Is your sister cooking?"

"She's been planning it since Thanksgiving."

"Then I'm in. And…" Alex looked down, smiling softly, then back up to meet her gaze. "Thank you. I can't imagine a better way to spend the day."

"Don't say that until you've met my family. *All* of them. I love them, but they can be a lot." The rest of the world might be impressed by the gold-plated glamor of the Drakes, but she suspected her own clan would have felt a lot more at ease if Alex really had worked at a hardware store like she'd first thought.

"I can't wait."

She hoped he still felt that way after he'd met them. And they'd met him.

Chapter Twenty-Nine

The Romano house on Christmas Day was a far cry from the quiet, dark house Alex had last seen on the night he'd walked Jess home from the bar. Even from the sidewalk, he could hear loud shouts coming from inside. The shouting was followed by a round of laughter, so it didn't seem like her family had descended into a fight, at least.

On the front stoop he took a moment to gather his wits. He'd met his fair share of parents in his day. Early on, he understood that he was good "meet the parents" material—wealthy, decent looking, polite, and friendly. Mothers found him charming. Fathers found him intelligent and reliable. Parents *loved* him. So the girls he'd dated, even casually, had been eager to trot him out for parents. He was good at it, so he'd never once been nervous at the prospect of meeting some parents.

Today, he was nervous for many reasons. First, there was only the one parent, Jess's father. He suspected fathers got more protective when there was no mother there to help run interference.

Second, as Jess had repeatedly stressed, there wasn't just her father. There were her sisters and *aaaallll* the rest of her extended family to deal with. This tangled sprawl of siblings, aunts, uncles, and cousins was all new to him. What if her father hated him? What if her sisters did? What if all those cop cousins Gemma had mentioned decided to send him packing? A million things could go wrong, and his winning smile and good manners might not be a match for any of it.

Third—and perhaps most important—he'd never truly been invested in making a good impression on any of those other parents, because he hadn't truly been invested in their daughters. He was invested in Jess. This thing between them had tumbled headlong into a serious relationship seemingly overnight. In the space of a few short days, she'd become essential to him. And while that didn't scare him, the idea that he might somehow fuck it up *did* scare him.

His fingers were going numb from the cold, so he forced himself to raise his hand and ring the doorbell. Moments later, he heard Jess bellow from inside.

"I got it!"

She flung open the door, her eyes bright with nerves. Something inside of him relaxed at the sight of her, and a calmness settled over him. Yes, a million things might go wrong, but she was the one right thing that made it worth trying.

"Hi."

Pink stained the tops of her cheekbones. Whether he was the cause or the cold, he wasn't sure, but he didn't really care, because she was adorable.

"Hi." She let out a breath that she seemed to have been holding for days, and flashed him a wide, panicky smile. "You sure you want to do this?"

He reached for her, pulling her into his arms and

pressing a kiss to her temple. "Come on. I'm sure it's not that bad."

"I don't know…everybody showed today. I mean, *everybody*. If I didn't know better, I'd think Gemma sent out a memo."

"It'll be okay. I'm good with parents," he assured her, praying that in this case, it would still be true.

Before she could reply, a voice called out from inside the house. "Jess, you gonna bring him inside or let him freeze to death on the stoop?"

Jess took a deep breath. "Ready?"

"Always."

He followed her inside and hung his coat on the overstuffed coatrack in the hall. From upstairs came the rambunctious laughter and stomping footsteps of what sounded like an elementary school's worth of children.

"They've turned the kids loose upstairs," Jess warned. "Don't go up there if you value your life."

"Duly noted." He snagged her hand as she led them into the living room, crowded with men. Immediately, he discerned the source of all the shouting. There was a football game on TV, and someone—the Jets—had just scored the first touchdown of the game.

Although several men in the room looked old enough to be Jess's father, Alex picked him out immediately, because he was the one man whose eyes immediately zeroed in on their joined hands.

"Dad, this is Alex. Alex, this is my dad, John."

John Romano's eyes raked him appraisingly from head to toe as he rose out of his armchair and stepped forward to shake his hand. He was in his fifties, and still in good shape, with Jess's dark hair and eyes, and a trim mustache.

"Alex. Nice to meet you. Merry Christmas." His handshake was firm, almost too tight. Not a challenge, just feeling him out.

Alex channeled his father and kept his eyes steadily on John Romano's as he returned the grip. "Merry Christmas, sir."

The handshake challenge met and accepted, John released his hand with a nearly imperceptible nod of his head.

"Ah…call me John." He motioned to a sideboard. "Can I get you a drink?"

"Oh, that's right." Alex held out the bag he'd been holding. "I hope you don't mind. I brought something for you."

As John drew the bottle out of the Mylar bag, his thick, dark eyebrows rose. "Richie," he said over his shoulder. "Finish up that swill. Alex here has brought us some Macallan's eighteen-year scotch."

The room exploded in appreciative murmurs. Alex almost said that it was his favorite, but caught himself at the last minute. John Romano might run a bar, but two-hundred-dollar bottles of scotch seemed to be a rare treat.

As John uncorked it and one of the uncles or cousins got up to get him a glass, Jess attempted to introduce him to the rest of the room. He was lost in a blur of "Uncle This and Cousin That," until he couldn't tell one from another. He prayed he wouldn't be forced to remember anyone's name later.

One of them—in his thirties and wearing an NYPD

sweatshirt…maybe Cousin Anthony?—addressed him. "You like the Jets, Alex?"

"Ah, I'm more of a baseball fan, personally." Another murmur, this one less appreciative. Fuck, he'd blown it already.

"Mets or Yankees?" another cousin—Tommy?—pressed.

"Mets." He'd never lie about something as sacred as his favorite baseball team, not to impress any girl's family.

Jess's pack of male relatives relaxed into smiles. *Yes!* Jess's family were Mets fans, thank *God.* He'd cleared the very first and probably most important hurdle.

"Once Jess's finished introducing you to the rest of the family," John said, waving toward the back of the house, "come on back and watch the game with us."

"Sounds good."

"This way." Jess tugged on his hand. "Livie's annoyed that she hasn't met you yet."

As they neared the kitchen, more raised voices reached them, this time all female.

"A little ketchup wouldn't hurt, that's all I'm saying."

"I'm not putting *ketchup* in my tomato sauce!" He recognized that voice as Gemma's.

"Your grandmother wasn't too fancy for ketchup."

"Grandma Giordano can't cook to save her life, Aunt Cynthia, and you know it."

Jess shot him an apologetic look. "Aunt Cynthia is my mom's older sister. She drives Gemma nuts. I might have to intervene here."

Gemma was at the stove shooting a venomous

glance at the woman beside her—Aunt Cynthia, he presumed. Aunt Cynthia, thin as a greyhound, with bleached blond hair teased into a twist, was gesturing broadly with a glass of white wine as she talked. Another older woman stood on Gemma's left, sipping her wine and wisely staying out of it, while two younger women lounged against the counter, watching Gemma square off against Aunt Cynthia with a sort of fond amusement. When he and Jess came in, they both looked him up and down with undisguised interest.

Jess's other sister, Olivia, sitting at the kitchen table, was immediately recognizable. They had the same heart-shaped face and delicate chin, the same dark eyes and expressive, arched eyebrows. Her hair, dark brown like Jess's, was much longer, falling in a heavy curtain nearly to her waist. She was staring at her laptop, oblivious to the crowd and noise around her.

"Livie," Jess said as she led him to the table.

Blinking, Olivia peered up at him. "Oh. You're him, aren't you? The rich guy?"

"Livie! God! Yes, this is Alex. Alex, this is my *socially inept* sister, Olivia."

He held a hand out to her once he'd recovered. "Nice to meet you, Olivia."

"Nice to meet you," Olivia returned. "Gemma was right. You're very handsome."

"I'm going to kill you *both*!" Jess hissed, dragging him away from Olivia as Gemma burst into laughter. "Everybody, this is my friend, Alex. Alex, this is my aunt Patti and aunt Cynthia." She gestured to the two younger women in the corner. "And my cousins Kendra and Amber."

"Oh. My. God." Aunt Cynthia breathed, gesturing

at him with her wineglass as she advanced. Droplets of white wine hit Gemma, who scowled. When she reached them, she gripped his shoulder in a vise, her French manicured nails digging into his skin. Okay, he'd charmed CEOs and senators. Surely he could handle a half-drunk Aunt Cynthia, right? "Jess, he is so *hot*! My God, look at these shoulders. And this chest. I bet he's got good abs, doesn't he, Jess?"

Jess's face turned scarlet and she slapped a hand over her eyes. "Aunt Cynthia!"

"And Gemma says he's *loaded*. You're a rich one, huh? Did you meet my daughter, Amber, yet?"

Jess went from red to white as the color drained from her face. "Ma!" Amber hissed in mortification.

He was formulating something witty to dispel the awkwardness when Gemma charged in to his rescue. "Hey! Can someone get the trays out of the fridge and take them to the living room?"

Amber pushed off the counter. "I got it! Ma." She reached for Cynthia's elbow, pulling her away from Alex. "Why don't you help me?"

"Ooh, what's this?" the other cousin—Kendra— said as Amber pulled the plastic wrap off a tray.

"Salmon dip. And in that bag there…those are toast points. They go with it. There's also a tray of antipasti in there, too, and some of those marinated shrimp Uncle Richie likes."

"Hungry?" Jess asked him.

"Maybe later."

"There is no 'later' in this family," Olivia said, snatching a handful of cheese cubes off a passing tray. "Food disappears in seconds."

The back door banged open and a cluster of smiling women, pink-cheeked from the cold, stumbled in. One had a baby encased in a puffy snowsuit bouncing on her hip. Jess made more introductions to more cousins and wives of cousins. When Gemma told them appetizers had been taken to the living room, they followed in a pack.

Jess let out an exhausted chuckle. "You've been here twenty minutes and I already need a break. You must be ready to run screaming."

"Nah. They're great. Especially Aunt Cynthia."

"I can't believe my aunt tried to set you up with my cousin right in front of me." Jess laid her head against his shoulder. "Thanks for being a good sport."

"If that woman steps foot in my kitchen again, I'm gonna strangle her!" Gemma stabbed her spoon into the air for emphasis. "*Ketchup*, she says! In *my* lasagna!"

"You have lasagna on Christmas?"

"We're Italian," Gemma said. "We're also having turkey and a ham, but we *always* have lasagna."

Jess turned to Olivia. "If Aunt Cynthia comes back, you head her off."

"How am I supposed to do that?"

"Tell her all about your dissertation."

"Aunt Cynthia's hardly going to be interested in black holes."

"So push her into one," Jess muttered. "Want to go outside for a minute?"

The backyard was still covered in patchy snow. Trying not to feel self-conscious, Jess mentally compared it to that beautiful, formal garden behind the Drake town house. The grill, which her father would dust off and

crank up once or twice at the beginning of each summer before leaving it to rust into oblivion again, hulked
under a tattered tarp on the left, against the battered
wooden fence. Gemma's herb garden, now nothing but
a patch of withered, bare twigs, lined the fence to the
right. A birdbath listed off-kilter at the very back of
the yard, next to the skeletal frames of the lilac bushes,
which no one ever bothered to trim or tame.

"I like your family," Alex said, sliding his hand
down her arm until he could twine their fingers together.

"Shut up. They're always a lot to take, but everybody's being *extra* entertaining today."

"They're great."

"Even Aunt Cynthia?"

"Aunt Cynthia thinks I'm hot. I love Aunt Cynthia."

Laughter bubbled up in her chest as Alex pulled
her into his arms. Head tipped forward, she rested
her forehead on his chest, and felt his chin settle on
the top of her head.

"If you saw her husband, Uncle Robbie, you'd understand," Jess said, her voice muffled by the soft wool
of his coat.

"Is Uncle Robbie one of those cops in there?"

"No. Well, yes, he *is* a cop—a sergeant—but he's
not here today. He's on duty. The cops that are here
are my cousins, Anthony, Christopher, and Michael."

"That's a lot of cops."

"Plus my cousin Nicole, who's a Port Authority of-
ficer. She's not here today, either. Tommy's an EMS
driver, and my uncle Jimmy and my cousin Nate are
firefighters."

"My God, you're a one-family emergency response unit. How the hell did you end up in journalism?"

After her laughter subsided, she answered honestly. "Gemma. She never wanted me and Livie to feel like we didn't have choices. She wanted us to be free to do anything."

"And little Jess decided she wanted to be the next Christiane Amanpour?"

"More like the next Mariel Kemper," she replied automatically. Then she remembered. That familiar knot of misery settled back into her stomach.

Alex, sensing the shift in her mood, dipped his head to whisper in her ear. "Hey, is Gemma watching from the window?"

"No, why?"

"I was about to kiss you senseless, but I didn't want to scandalize her on Christmas."

"Do you care what Gemma thinks?"

"She's the reason you ended up in journalism school with me, so yeah, I owe her one."

"Following that logic, I guess I owe your dad one."

Now it was Alex's mood that suddenly went dark. "Yeah, I'm not sure he'd appreciate the sentiment."

She hated—absolutely *hated*—seeing his light go out this way. Every time his father's stupid corporation came up, it was like Alex quickly and quietly morphed into a different person, and all his wit and life—all the brilliance that made him Alex—got buried under a grim mantle of responsibility. "Hey." She tugged on his coat lapels until he raised his eyes to her. "You need your own Gemma."

"What?"

"For all the amazing advantages in your life, it

seems like you're missing something really important…someone to tell you that you can be anything
you want to be. Maybe that can be my job. So here I
am, telling you you can be anything you want to be."

That dragged a reluctant smile from him. "But are
you going to go run Drake Media to allow me to do it?"

"Let your father run his own company. This is about
you."

"Drake Media is about me, too. It's mine, just as
much as it's his."

"But you don't want it."

"Not everybody gets everything they want." He
reached up to tug on a lock of her hair. "Not even
spoiled rich boys."

She refused to smile at his joke. "Alex…"

"Hey, let's forget about Drake Media for one day,
okay? It's Christmas and I haven't even given you
your present yet."

"Stop trying to change the subject. You got me a
present?"

Chuckling, he reached into the inside pocket of his
coat and drew out a long, narrow box wrapped in shiny
silver paper. "I did."

"I didn't get you one. Since we were barely speaking to each other a week ago, you didn't make it onto
my shopping list."

"Don't worry about it. That thing you did in the
shower yesterday is the best present I've ever gotten."
His lips brushed against her cheek just in front of her
ear, sending a little shower of sparks through her body.
God, Gemma was right. He filled her up with sparks,
and she *loved* it.

"Oh, my God, stop that."

"Are you *blushing*?"

"My entire Italian Catholic family is twenty feet away from us right now."

"You *are* blushing! This is the best."

"Shut up!"

His voice lost its teasing lilt, slipping into that low, coaxing timbre that made her knees go liquid. "Open your present, Jess."

Slipping the fancy red satin ribbon off the box, she lifted the lid. Her breath caught in her throat as she took in the contents. Nestled in a bed of white velvet was a bracelet, a delicate row of silver links, with two charms in the middle. The charms were a tiny dragon, enameled in green, and a shiny silver knight in armor.

"Alex...how did you do this?"

"Magic." He took the box from her hands and lifted the bracelet out, draping it over her left wrist and going to work on the clasp. The charms bounced gently against the heel of her thumb, the silver chain glinting in the bright winter light. "I thought you might like a little reminder of how we met. The second time, anyway. And to answer your question, yes, I've figured out I was one of the narcissistic knights you were talking about."

"You've redeemed yourself since then," she muttered.

"And you said we were irredeemable. Glad to hear I managed it. Because this knight hasn't stopped wanting to fight for you, even though I know you can fight your own battles."

Damn him and his stupid, swoony chivalry. As she stared at his bent head, watching the winter sunlight playing across all the shades of brown and rust and gold in his hair, the emotion hit her straight on with the force of a battering ram. *I love him. I love him* so *much.* Emotions this powerful couldn't be the work of a few days. She must have always been a little bit in love with Alex, and just too stubborn and blind to admit it to herself.

"I still don't know how you did this." It seemed safer to talk about the gift than everything the gift might represent. If she started down that path, she'd be blurting out her "I love yous" before she knew it and it was probably—*definitely*—too soon for that.

"It wasn't a big deal. I saw it online, I made a phone call, arranged a few things, and here it is, right where it belongs."

No big deal. He just moved mountains and had the perfect gift flown in on a jet or something, just to give it to her on Christmas Day. How had she spent so many years oblivious to his generous heart?

"It's perfect," she whispered. And maybe it wasn't the "I love you" about to burst from her heart, but it was true nonetheless. Everything about this moment and this man was perfect.

"Merry Christmas, Jess."

Reaching up, she took his face in her hands and stood on tiptoe to press a kiss to his lips. "Merry Christmas, Alex."

Chapter Thirty

"Why does your father keep so much food around when he's never here? Hasn't he been gone since last week?"

"Lucia's terrified he'll starve to death if she doesn't shower him with food."

"He's got six kinds of ice cream in his freezer."

"And he doesn't even eat the stuff."

Jess turned away from the fridge, holding a pint in each hand. "Well, I'm happy to take care of that for him."

Alex plucked them from her hands, setting them aside and backing her into the counter. "Maybe I should take care of you first."

She'd just sunk into his kiss, losing herself in the hot sweep of his tongue and the delicious press of his body against hers, when somewhere behind him, someone cleared their throat. Her startled scream was muffled by Alex's mouth before she shoved him back.

Dan Drake stood in the doorway, looking freshly pressed in his expensive suit and tie.

"Dad." Alex eased back from Jess enough to face his father. "Didn't expect to see you here tonight."

Dan's face twitched with amusement. "Obviously. Jessica, nice to see you again."

"You, too," she murmured, her insides twisting in embarrassment.

"We were watching a movie up in the media room and got hungry," Alex explained, finally shifting back enough to allow Jess to slide out from between him and the counter. "I thought you were flying back tomorrow."

Dan shrugged. "I'd seen everything I needed to, so I took off."

In the few moments since his father had entered the room, Alex had transformed. His playful smile was gone, replaced by a somber, serious expression. He stood up straighter, an unmistakable rigidity in his shoulders and spine. His eyes, sparkling with humor just seconds ago, were hard and flat. If Jess didn't already know him, she'd be too intimidated to ever approach him.

Time to make an escape and fortunately, she had an entirely legit reason. "Alex, I think I left my phone upstairs. I'm going to run up and get it. Nice to see you again, Mr. Drake."

"See you downstairs?" Alex said quietly, brushing her hand as she passed. She nodded and slipped past Dan Drake to scurry up the stairs. Her phone was right where she'd left it—in the Drakes' private in-home movie theater—after texting Gemma earlier.

She was almost to the last turn on the stairs when Alex's voice floated up to her. She didn't mean to listen in, she only hesitated a moment on the landing, torn between hurrying down before Dan started up or encountering him on the stairs. Before she could make a move either way, they were already in the middle of the conversation.

"How was the Brazil network?"

Dan sighed, stripped of his usual bonhomie when there was no one but Alex there. "They're a disorganized mess down there. The network has plenty of potential, but they'd need a complete overhaul in their organization if they're going to be competitive."

"Sorry to hear it. So we're passing?"

"No, I had the lawyers make an offer."

"But—"

"It'll be perfect for you," Dan said.

"Me?"

"Sure. ClickNews is coming along fine. You've learned the lay of the land and they don't need you anymore. Once you spend a year or two down in Rio bringing this network up to scratch, there won't be anything about the business you don't know from the ground up. You'll be ready to come on board at HQ."

Jess held her breath, waiting for Alex to tell his father no. No, he wouldn't rehab his new station. No, he didn't want to know this business from the ground up. No, he wasn't leaving ClickNews. He was staying, and transforming it into something so much better than it was now. Something real.

But Alex didn't say any of those things.

"Let's see what Brazil has to say about the offer first."

"They'll say yes," Dan said, his usual swagger returning. "Everybody says yes to me."

"They sure do, Dad."

"You'll love Rio, Alex. A guy your age, with nothing to tie you here… Rio will be your playground."

Her heart tightened painfully in her chest. *Me*, she mouthed silently. *Tell him* I'm *here*.

When she heard Dan start climbing the stairs, she forced her frozen limbs to move, not wanting to be caught listening in. She passed him on the steps, her eyes meeting his fleetingly. It was unmistakable, the challenge she saw there. He knew she'd heard everything. He was daring her to fight him for Alex. Was this as much about shaking her loose as it was about some stupid TV station?

"Have a good night, Jessica." Dan smiled—that dead-eyed shark smile—and dropped his gaze from her to Alex, where he stood waiting for her at the foot of the stairs. Jess couldn't make a sound in reply as she rushed past him down the stairs.

"Find your phone?" Alex asked. He was holding her ice cream haul. Jess wasn't the least bit hungry anymore. She waved her phone in the air and forced a small smile.

Wordlessly, Alex led her around to the stairs to his apartment. The silence between them felt brittle and sharp. He must have known she heard that conversation, and she waited for him to explain himself, but he didn't seem inclined to say a word about it.

"What do you want?" he asked once they reached his apartment and he'd set down the ice cream. He was talking about flavors, but that's not what she heard.

"I'm not hungry. So Brazil?"

"Huh?"

"You're moving to Brazil?"

"Don't worry about it. These deals take forever to get finalized." He still hadn't looked at her.

"But—" Frustrated, she threw her hands in the air and spun away from him. "That's not the *point*, Alex."

Finally, he faced her. "Why are you angry? It's just some deal my dad is making. It has nothing to do with you."

She spun back, face flushing with emotion. "Oh, really? He's plotting to ship you off to Brazil for two years and it has nothing to do with *me*? You didn't see the way he looked at me. I think it has a lot to do with me."

"My dad has trust issues, Jess. He doesn't know you like I do. I promise, he's not out to get you."

She wasn't so sure about that, but it was hardly the most pressing issue at the moment. "Okay, fine, he's not sending you to Brazil to get rid of me, but the result will be the same either way, right? Because you'll be there and I'll be here."

Alex held up his hands to placate her. "Look, anything can happen. Nothing's definite."

"Anything? Like you telling your father once and for all that you don't want to take over his company?"

Dropping his eyes to the floor, he slumped against the counter. "I told you, I can't do that."

"Can't or won't?"

"I thought you understood the obligation, Jess. You, of all people."

"I understand obligation, but I don't understand you doing something that makes you so miserable. Yes, my sister took on the bar so Livie and I didn't have to, but the day I see it making her as unhappy as Drake Media makes you is the day I tell her to quit. I'd rather give up the bar forever than let her spend her life tied to it that way. What about ClickNews and everything you wanted to do there?"

"I told you, that was just some fantasy. It's never going to happen."

"Why not?"

"Because *this* is my job! *This* is my life!"

"Running a TV station in Brazil? What about us?" Her courage momentarily flagged. She knew how she felt about him, but how could he possibly feel the same if he could just walk away like this? "I know this just started, Alex, but I thought it was important—"

In seconds, he'd shoved off the counter and closed the space between them, taking her face in his hands. "It *is* important. Listen to me, Jess. You matter to me. More than you can imagine. And that's not going to change, no matter where I work or what I do. Jess, it's just a job. Maybe not my dream job, but who gets that? Lots of people don't love their jobs. I'll make it work for me. We'll be okay."

He was back, her Alex, the one with the brilliant, alive eyes, the one that had been conspicuously absent for the past half hour—the one she loved so much that it hurt. It hurt, because she could see what he couldn't. This Alex and the one who belonged to Drake Media couldn't forever share space. One day, one of them would lose. And if it was her Alex…well, then she would lose, too, wouldn't she? She'd lose him.

Gently, she wrapped her fingers around his wrists and pulled his hands from her face, folding them in hers. "Will we be okay, though?"

"Jess, come on—"

"No, see, here's the thing." She had to fight to get

the words out when her throat closed painfully around them. "I love you."

His expression was nearly the end of her, so stunned, tender, happy... "Jess—"

"I love *you*. *This* you, standing in front of me. The you I talked to online for all those weeks. The *real* you. The you with passion and principles. And, Alex, I've seen what your father's company does to you."

"It's work. Of course I'm different at work."

"No, not like this. The minute you enter that world, part of you dies. You become a stranger."

"You're making this a bigger deal than it is. It's just a job."

"It's about more than a job! You're ready to sell your soul just to make someone else happy. You're abandoning your principles, yourself, everything you love, and for what?"

"What do you want from me?"

"I want you to stand up for yourself. Stand up for me! If I'm not that important to you, if you're not that important to *yourself*, then I'm not sure what I'm doing here."

"Are you saying you're going to break up with me if I go to work for my father?"

Just hearing him voice the words caused a painful knot in her chest. She didn't want to lose him. But would she have a choice about that in the end? She was only herself—just Jessica Romano from Brooklyn. Could she really take on Drake Media and Dan Drake himself and win?

"I don't know. I'm just not sure..." It was hard to get the words out, or even breathe. "I guess right now it's hard to see what kind of future we have together in this scenario."

"Jess—" He sounded like she'd punched him in the chest, her name just a painful exhalation.

"Look, I'm going to go."

"You're leaving?"

"Not for good." She shook her head, because she wasn't even sure if that was the truth or not. "I just need to think about this. And so do you, Alex. Think about what really matters to you."

Chapter Thirty-One

The day Alex had first met Jess—and she'd raked him over with that judgmental gaze—had been the first time he'd ever felt inadequate. Up until that moment, his life had unfolded before him easily. Nothing had been impossible to acquire, no one impossible to charm.

Then he'd run up against the stone wall of gorgeous Jessica Romano's idealism and found himself utterly wanting in every way that mattered. In the intervening years, he'd worked hard to be better, to be more than a handsome rich kid. He thought he'd done it. In many ways, he had.

But it seemed, in the end, she was still demanding more of him than he could give. What he saw as living up to his obligations, she saw as a fatal weakness of character, and he wasn't sure they could ever close the gap.

She wasn't wrong when she said he was sacrificing part of himself to his job. This was the price to be paid for all the advantages he'd been given. That was something he'd long ago made peace with. And she probably wasn't wrong about what Drake Media would turn him into. So maybe she was right about the rest, too. Maybe there was no future for them as he moved further down this path. Maybe, he told himself grimly as he made his way to ClickNews the next morning, his feelings for her were just a symptom, part of his reluctance to close the door on that part of himself forever.

But everyone had to face their fate eventually. No one said it would be easy. For him, if it meant leaving Jess behind, it was going to tear him to pieces.

Seeing Chase the moment he stepped off the elevator at the office didn't improve his black mood one bit. It was the first time he'd laid eyes on him since Jess's revelation, since he'd learned Chase was betraying them all. The urge to barrel straight into him and pummel him into a wall was nearly overpowering. His right hand flinched, half curling into a fist of its own accord. He was supposed to be above violence, but right now, beating the shit out of Chase sounded like an awfully satisfying way to deal with his anger and frustration.

But it wouldn't help Jess, and, despite how things ended last night, he was determined to undo the damage Chase had done to her. If he could return her life to her—if he knew she was where she always wanted to be and happy—maybe it would make leaving her behind easier. Doubtful, but maybe.

So for now, he suppressed his animal snarl of rage, plastering on that winning smile that fooled the whole world, and advanced on his former best friend.

"Hey, buddy, how was your break?"

Chase broke off flirting with the receptionist to turn and clap him on the shoulder. "Alex! Ah, you know. The British Virgin Islands with the parentals. Boring as shit. Although at least this time, they didn't talk my ear off about finding a job. I have you to thank for that one."

Another smile that felt like swallowing glass. "They have a lot to be proud of, huh?"

Chase's two older brothers were already success-fully working in his father's boutique investment firm. Chase, always the slacker, the disappointment, had been under pressure from his parents for years to get his shit together. Guess he decided lying and theft was his career path of choice.

"They're off my back, that's all I care about. Hey, how was the break? Did you go to Brazil with the old man?"

Of course Chase was keeping tabs on his father. Ass-kissing suck-up. "No, I stayed here. Went up to Killington and did a little skiing." The lie slid easily off his tongue.

"Killington, huh? Very nice. You find any luscious young ladies to keep you warm up there in the snow?"

"Nope. Just me and the slopes." He smiled so hard, it felt as if his cheek muscles were going to spasm. "I'm gonna grab a coffee. See you in the editorial meeting this morning?"

ClickNews, as a cutting-edge social media com-pany, had the requisite open-plan office, hoverboards in the hallways, and a staff masseuse, but what it didn't have was a clear chain of command. Alex wasn't Chase's supervisor, but no one else seemed to be, ei-ther, so early on, Alex had stepped in and organized weekly editorial meetings, just to bring some sense of order to the place.

Chase cast a quick glance at his phone, as if he were verifying something. "Umm, can we throw that to tomorrow morning? Just gotta tie up a few more loose ends today before I'm ready to assign this week's stories."

Bingo. Whatever Chase had just read on his phone prompted him to put off the meeting till tomorrow. Since he was just back in town after nearly a week away, Alex would bet his right arm that he was meeting up with his source from the *Brooklyn Daily Post*. Now he just needed an opportunity to check Chase's phone for the details.

Open-plan offices sucked for Alex's concentration, but it made keeping tabs on Chase throughout the day much easier. The problem was, the guy never left his phone unattended. If he was up wandering around— and he wandered around a lot, always hanging on the back of some woman's chair, flirting while she tried to work—it was in his pocket. As lunchtime approached, Alex decided to get devious.

First, he asked Andy Birnbaum in marketing to lunch. Then he stopped by Chase's desk and casually asked him to go, too, almost as an afterthought. While Chase was pulling on his coat, Alex bumped the phone, resting on the edge of Chase's desk, into the trash can. Out of sight, out of mind. Chase didn't even notice he didn't have it as they left the office. As they passed out the door, Alex hauled up short and groaned.

"Ah… I forgot I have to sit in on a conference call with my dad about the new Brazilian network. You guys go on without me."

"You sure?" Chase asked.

"Yeah. I have no idea how long it'll take."

"Want us to bring you something back?" Andy offered, like a decent friend, not a lying shit-stain like Chase.

"Nah. I'll just order in."

Still oblivious, Chase and Andy left for lunch. One benefit to his squeaky-clean rep—the one Chase had teased him about for years—was that, when he chose to lie, no one suspected a thing.

Once he was sure they were gone, he sprinted back to Chase's desk and fished the phone out of the trash. There was always the chance Chase would notice he'd left it and come back for it, so he didn't waste time. It was password protected, but that posed no challenge. He'd known Chase since middle school, and the idiot used the same password for nearly everything, including his phone.

His texts weren't very informative, other than outlining just how many women Chase was stringing along at the same time. His emails were also a bust. On a hunch, he swiped left out of the main screen of apps. On the next page, hidden in a folder called "Random" was the icon for BulletChat, the same messaging app he and Jess had used as Peabody and PaperGirl. A separate app just for his subterfuge. That was almost genius-level thinking for Chase.

There were three conversations in there. Each recipient was identified only by a series of letters—BDP, DN, and NYP. The first one proved to be his contact at the *Brooklyn Daily Post*. A quick glance at the other two conversations proved his suspicions were correct. Chase was stealing stories from more than one paper.

The conversation with his contact at the *Daily Post* was sparse, but the pertinent info was there. They were meeting tonight, at some bar in Greenpoint. He jotted down the bar and the time on a Post-It, carefully backed out of the app, and placed Chase's phone on the floor, just under his chair, as if it had fallen there.

Then he grabbed his coat and headed for the door. He had a few more things to arrange, and to get all the pieces into place, he was going to need some help.

Walking through the lobby of the Drake Tower, with its soaring ceilings and imported Italian marble floor, usually left Alex swimming in dread. Today, driven by anger and a thirst for retribution, he strode through like he owned the place. Which he kind of did.

Seymour, the daytime head of security, smiled and waved him through the automated turnstiles. Bypassing the banks of public elevators, he beelined to the last one on the right, his father's private express elevator, and punched in the security code. The elevator ascended with enough speed to make his ears pop.

On the forty-third floor, Zofia, his father's receptionist, flashed him the stern grimace that passed as her smile.

"Good afternoon, Mr. Drake. Are you here to see your father?"

"That would be great. Does he have time?"

"I'd say you've got four minutes. Maybe five."

"Thanks, Zofia."

His father's office door was cracked open and he could hear Dan on the phone. Pushing the door open, he stepped inside, motioning to his wrist to ask his father for a minute of his time.

"We'll finish this up later, Pete. Alex needs me." Dan ended the call and leaned back in his chair. He was silhouetted against the bright expanse of the glass wall behind him, and beyond that, a sweeping view of Central Park. "Alex, to what do I owe this rare pleasure?"

It was true Alex spent as little time at Drake Tower as he could manage, for someone being groomed to take it over one day. Drake Tower and this office, despite the luxury and glorious views, had always made him feel suffocated.

"I need you to make a phone call for me."

Dan grinned. "You must really need some pull if you're hitting up your old man for favors. What is it? Knicks tickets? You want to borrow the jet?"

"Nothing like that. I want you to call Mariel Kemper and ask her to meet you for a drink tonight."

One of Dan Drake's greatest attributes was the expansive imagination that allowed him to instantly envision countless outcomes from every situation. It made him very hard to surprise or shock. Alex experienced a small moment of satisfaction in rendering his father momentarily speechless.

Dan blinked in consternation, then cleared his throat. "Mariel Kemper? You want me to ask out Mariel Kemper."

"Yes. Tonight. It has to be tonight."

"Son, you'd better back up and start at the beginning, because I'm willing to bet my right leg that there's a hell of a story here."

"You could say that."

So, as succinctly as possible, Alex told his father what he'd learned of Chase's betrayal.

"I hope to God you fired the little shit on the spot," he fumed when Alex finished.

"No, not yet. He's only part of the problem, Dad.

Someone at the *Brooklyn Daily Post* is feeding him those stories, and we need to find out who it is."

"Alex, that isn't our problem. Mariel Kemper can see to her own staff."

"She thinks she already has, but she's got it wrong. She fired Jess because she thinks Jess did it."

Dan was silent as he examined Alex through narrowed eyes. Looking down at his desk, he straightened his pen, his voice off-handed as he asked the question Alex knew was coming. "I know you're involved with the girl, but, Alex, what makes you so sure she didn't?"

"Because I know Jess. This isn't something she'd do. Not ever."

"I hate to be the one to point this out, but she *is* sleeping with the son of the owner of Drake Media now. Quite a position for an ambitious young lady to find herself in."

Closing his eyes, Alex counted to ten and willed away the rage. He'd gone over all of this in the cab on the way over. He knew his father would go there. Logically, it made absolute sense that he would.

"Not Jess. I promise you. And if you want proof… Well, she broke up with me last night, so I'm pretty sure that sleeping with me to get ahead is not at all on her agenda."

Dan let out a sputter of disbelieving laughter. "*She* broke up with *you*?"

"I know you don't encounter this often, Dad, but not every woman finds us irresistible."

"I saw her wrapped around you in the kitchen. I'm pretty sure she does."

Alex dropped his eyes to the thick, slate gray carpet. "That's not enough for Jess. She wants more from me…things I can't give her. She's principled, Dad, in a way few people in this world are. She's not for sale."

"Everybody's for sale."

"Not her. Working for Mariel at that paper…it's all she ever wanted out of life."

Dan's eyebrows hiked sharply. "You're right. She's not ambitious."

"She is, but in a different way. This…" He waved a hand around Dan's office. "She really doesn't care. But being a reporter for that paper? It was her dream. And someone at that paper sold her out, with Chase's help. I intend to fix it."

Dan blew out a weary breath. "And that requires me asking Mariel Kemper out on a *date*?"

"Not a date, exactly." Alex passed the Post-It with the location and time across the desk. "I just need her to be there, at that time."

"What makes you think she'll say yes to me? She's not my biggest fan."

Alex grinned at his father. "Dad, you disappoint me. Are you telling me you can't convince her?"

"I never said that."

"Well?"

"She's not exactly in my speed dial."

"Surely you can track her down. Not the paper's number. Her cell. She'll pay attention then."

With another sigh, Dan snatched up the phone receiver and stabbed a button. "Pete, get me Steve in our security division. I need him to find somebody for me."

"Thanks, Dad."

Dan pointed a finger at him as he waited to be connected to Steve. "I'll get her there. After that, it's on you."

"I've got it under control."

Chapter Thirty-Two

When all you wanted to do was lie in bed and wallow in your heartbreak, leave it to your unfeeling sister to haul you out and put you to work.

The next morning, Gemma, sensing Jess was fragile and on the verge of a total emotional meltdown, dragged her with her to the bar for the onerous monthly maintenance session.

Gemma was inventorying the liquor while Jess took apart the beer taps for deep cleaning. Livie was better than either of them at mechanical stuff, so the taps were usually her job, but she'd escaped to the library as soon as it opened. Jess didn't mind so much today. Wrestling with a crescent wrench and draining hoses kept her mind occupied just enough to keep her from going catatonic with sadness.

Walking out on Alex last night had felt *awful*. Today, it still felt awful. She'd just needed space to think, but so far, nothing was any clearer, except that she loved him and missed him.

She hadn't heard a word from him. The idea that her words last night might be final was burning away at her gut like acid. She was frozen with indecision, desperate to call him and apologize, but still feeling the issue that drove her away was valid.

"You're quiet today," Gemma said into the silence of the empty bar.

"Just concentrating on not getting a face full of Bud Light. I think we're gonna have to replace these washers soon."

"I'll add it to the list. Everything okay with Superman?"

"Who?"

"Your boyfriend."

"Oh. I always think of him as more Captain America than Superman."

"I can see that. So?"

"Um…there are just some things we have to work out." She would *not* use the words *broken up*. She refused. And if she didn't say it, it couldn't be true, right?

"Like? Is he treating you okay? I worry about guys like that, with all that money. They think they can get away with anything."

"It's not that. He treats me great. It's just…things are weird with his job."

"At the website?"

"No, that's just temporary. Eventually he's going to work for Drake Media. Actually, one day he'll take it over."

"Oh. Wow. That's a big deal."

"Yeah."

They worked in silence for a few more minutes while Jess turned it over in her mind.

"Hey, Gemma," she finally asked. "Do you like the bar?"

"What…our bar?"

"Yeah. Do you like it here?"

Gemma cast a brief glance around the room and shrugged. "Sure. It's like home."

"But…" Jess threw down the crescent wrench when she couldn't get the last nut free.

Gemma abandoned her task, too, turning to face her and leaning back against the liquor shelves. "What's this about? Spit it out."

"Do you think…if Mom hadn't died, if Dad hadn't needed you…would you have chosen to work here, anyway?"

Gemma paused. "I've been behind this bar for so long I can't imagine anything different."

"But did you? Once? Before Mom?"

Gemma considered it carefully. "I had those same fantasies that all kids have. I wanted to be a vet, and an astronaut, and a famous actress. Well, every kid but you and Livie. You guys were such little weirdos. I'd never seen a kid read the *New York Times* front-to-back the way you were doing at ten years old."

"Yeah, but when you get a little older, you want things that are real. Did you ever want something like that?"

"No, not really. I always saw myself right here."

"Are you sure?"

"Why are you pushing this?"

Jess had been quietly carrying around her feelings of guilt where Gemma was concerned for years. It was time to clear the air. If Gemma wanted something more for life, then she should get it. And Alex was right. If Jess was needed, there was no way she could say no. Could this be the silver lining to getting fired? Maybe it was time for her to step up and take her turn at the bar.

"I worry, Gemma, that you wanted something more for yourself and you gave it up so Livie and I could go for it instead. You sacrificed everything for us."

Gemma blinked, her dark eyes full of disbelief. "You feel guilty because I work at the bar?"

"Yeah?"

"Well, that's just stupid," she replied with her usual brusque directness. "This was *my* choice, working here. I told you, it's like home."

"And you don't feel... I don't know...trapped? Forced into it? Obligated?"

"Maybe I feel some obligation to keep it going but hey…" She broke off and reached for Jess's hand. "Look at me. If I feel obligated, it's for my own reasons. This place is my history. It's my legacy. *Mine.* It's important to *me* to keep it going. *That's* the obligation I feel. It's not about you and Livie."

"You swear?"

Gemma scoffed. "You think I'd let the two of you off the hook if I felt like you owed me?"

"Fair point," Jess said with a laugh, running her hands over her face in relief. "But you promise me, if you ever feel like we need to step up, you'll tell us?"

"If I think you can help, I will. But hey, I chose this. You chose something else. And that's okay. Jess, I am so proud of you and Livie. I don't want you to ever give up your lives just for some scruffy Brooklyn bar. Where is all of this coming from?"

"When I first started talking to Alex online, before I knew it was him, one of the things we had in common was our family business. He wasn't working as a reporter because he had to work for his family instead. It made me worry about you, if maybe we were doing the same thing to you."

"Well, you're not, so quit worrying about it. But Alex…his family business?"

"Drake Media."

"Hmmm. That's a lot different than a crummy bar."

"He hates it. And it changes him. Whenever he has to deal with Drake Media, he becomes this entire other person."

"And I'm guessing you don't like that guy as much?"

"It's not that. It's just…" Jess trailed off, trying to find the right words. "As long as I've known Alex, when I looked at him, I couldn't see how someone like him could ever fit with someone like me. When I got to know him…the *real* him…we turned out to be perfect together. But that guy who I used to think was so different? So out of my reach? That's the Drake Media guy. And I'm worried that I don't fit with *that* guy."

"Did he make you feel that way?"

No. No, he never had. Because he accepted and adored her just as she was. *She* was the one demanding that he change to suit her.

"No," she finally said, feeling shaken and miserable. "Not at all. But his dad wants to send him to Brazil and last night I freaked out about it."

"Freaked out how?"

Saying the words out loud drove home just how wrong she'd been. "I basically told him it was Brazil or me."

Gemma flinched. "Ouch. Ultimatums aren't good."

"I know, I know. I'm such an idiot, me and my stupid principles."

"Your principles are great. They make you fight for what you love. You love this guy, right?"

A couple of days ago, she thought she was falling in love with Alex. Now, after she'd walked away from him, she was one hundred percent certain she was in love with him. And it sucked. "Yeah, I do."

"Then you'll figure it out. Just…" Gemma paused, figuring out what she wanted to say. "Don't give in all the way, okay? Because, ultimatum aside, it sounds like you were fighting for him as much as you were fighting for yourself and your principles."

"You think?"

"Yeah, I do. And it seems like he could use you fighting in his corner."

She'd fight for Alex to the ends of the earth, but he wasn't the only issue here. "Even if it means I have to fight his father?"

"Dan Drake doesn't stand a chance." Gemma reached for her, pulling her into a tight hug. "Nobody messes with a Romano girl, right?"

The door let out its familiar squeal of poorly oiled hinges as a patron entered. Jess turned to ask what he'd like, but it wasn't one of Romano's grizzled regulars.

It was Lina.

Chapter Thirty-Three

She stood just inside the door in her long navy puffer coat, her gloved fingers clenched in front of her and her uncertain gaze fixed on Jess. Jess's brain remembered the way they'd parted, the things Lina had said that left her feeling so bruised and angry, but in that split second of recognition, her heart forgot. All she knew was that she'd missed her like air.

"Hey, Lina," Gemma said conversationally, when Jess said nothing.

"Hi, Gemma," Lina said. "I came to talk to Jess."

Seeing Lina filled her with hope, but the truth was, she didn't know why she was here. And if she was going to start lobbing accusations again, Jess couldn't afford to let her guard down.

"What's up?" There. That sounded sufficiently casual. Not at all like she'd burst into tears multiple times over the past few days about her fight with Lina.

Lina took a step forward. "Can we talk?"

"Sure. Go ahead."

"I'm gonna inventory the basement stock," Gemma said, tactfully excusing herself.

As Gemma left, Jess told herself to stay calm as she heard Lina out. At least this time, the shock of her firing had faded. She was fully in control of her emotions now.

She turned back to Lina and waited for her to begin.

"Alex called me."

That was the last thing she expected her to say. "Alex? Why?"

"He told me about Chase…that he's the one who stole my story."

"Are you going to accuse me of sleeping with him, too? Because you decided that one kiss with Alex was enough to make me into some backstabbing Benedict Arnold." She hadn't intended to be confrontational, but it seemed she was more hurt than she realized.

"I know! I'm so sorry, Jess. I was wrong. Alex told me—"

"You doubted *me*, but you're immediately ready to believe *Alex*?"

"No, Jess, stop. I already knew you didn't do it. God…" She broke off, her eyes flying up to the ceiling as she fought back tears. "I feel so, so awful. Once I calmed down and thought about it, I knew I'd screwed up. Yeah, maybe you kept one or two things to yourself, but that was no reason for me to question you. You're the most loyal, honest person I know."

Grudgingly, Jess dropped her shoulders a bit, forcing herself to ease up. Lina was acknowledging her mistake and she needed to let her. "So why did you doubt me?"

"I guess because Mariel did? And finding out about you and Alex in college…it hurt that you'd never told me that."

"I wasn't trying to deceive you, Lina. I was embarrassed by it. I wanted to pretend it never happened."

"I get it. I do. But add that to the Twitter thing, which you'd also been keeping secret...and just the day before my story was stolen...it was all coming at me at once. I'm not entitled to know all your secrets. It was wrong of me to feel betrayed just because you kept something personal to yourself."

Hearing her actions laid out by Lina, even though she was apologizing, left a bad taste in Jess's mouth. "I shouldn't have kept so much from you. That's my fault. And I was too quick to blow up at you. I just wasn't in a place to think...or react...clearly. I'm sorry, too."

Lina's eyes welled again. "God, that moment must have been awful for you."

"It was definitely not my best day."

The air was heavy with their fragile truce. What happened next?

Lina was the one to break the silence. "See, that's just what I'm here to fix. I told you I figured out almost right away that you didn't do it."

Jess blinked as Lina's implication hit her. "So where have you *been* all week? I thought you hated me."

Lina grinned. "Stop scowling at me like that. I've been trying to *prove* it. And I have. Well, I proved one part. Alex took care of the rest."

"What are you talking about?"

"Something about that tweet...that last one from that morning...kept bugging me. I was talking to Hassan about it, and he put his finger right on it."

"Right on what?"

"He said it was a stupid tweet for someone so good at Twitter. I mean, look, you've been waging this Twitter war with Alex for weeks that had all of New York enthralled. You can decimate someone with a single well-worded sentence. But that was just…clunky. Dumb. Amateurish. It didn't sound like you at all."

"Because it wasn't me."

Lina thrust a finger in the air. "Right! But who was it?"

"I'm guessing you know."

"Not right away. I kept going over and over it, and then boom! It hit me. A dangling participle."

"You got hit with a dangling participle?"

"No, the tweeter used one. Along with an apostrophe in the possessive form of 'its'—something you would never, ever do. But you know who does? All the time, because her grammar sucks for someone trained to write?"

A cold knot of anger twisted in her chest as she forced the name out around the lump in her throat. "Lauren."

They'd laughed about it, her, Lina, Zoe, and Natalie, back when they were all still friends—all of Lauren's terrible typos, grammatical errors, and malapropisms in her memos. For someone with a degree in journalism, her writing was atrocious. It didn't seem so funny anymore.

"Think about it," Lina continued. "Haven't we been saying for weeks that it's just a matter of time before Mariel cans her? That's why she's been so nasty to you."

"That explains why she'd sabotage me, but not why she'd steal stories from the paper."

"Maybe she can see the writing on the wall, the same as the rest of us, and she figured she'd better guarantee herself a nice comfy job after Mariel fires her. And if she's that much of a lying snake, why wouldn't she take down her rival on the way out the door, just to be petty?"

"I can't believe this. No, I take that back. I *can* believe it. I'm just so mad at her I could spit."

"Line up," Lina growled lowly. Of course. Poor Lina had more reason to be angry than anyone.

"But, Lina, while her grammar is admittedly bad, you know that's not proof, right?"

"I know! So I got proof. Well, Griff did."

"Griffin?"

Lina nodded. "I told him what I suspected…he didn't believe it was you, either, by the way…so he took a look at Lauren's computer after hours. Along with a ton of malware, because she's an idiot who clicks on every link in her emails, he found it."

"What?"

"The record of her logging into the Twitter account at midnight the night before you got fired."

"That's still not proof."

"Maybe not proof it was Lauren, but it's proof it *wasn't* you. Where were you when that log-in happened on a computer at the *Daily Post*?"

Midnight the night before she was fired? Oh, she remembered, all right. She was in her kitchen, kissing Alex.

"Um, I was with Alex."

The corner of Lina's mouth quirked. "That's what I figured."

"So what does he have to do with this, anyway? Did he figure out it was her?"

"Not exactly, but he did snoop around and find out that Chase is meeting his contact…in other words, Lauren, tonight. He's got it all set up and he asked me to make sure you were there when they bust them. Seems like he felt he couldn't call you himself."

Jess heard the question in Lina's voice. She didn't know everything that had happened between Jess and Alex since last week, but she could probably guess it was more than one kiss.

"It's complicated," she said, to answer the unspoken question.

Lina nodded. "Seems like it. But—"

"Yeah?"

"He wouldn't be doing all this if he didn't care, Jess."

Despite that horrible scene last night, Alex was still doing everything he could to fix things for her, including enlisting Lina to help. God, she'd been so wrong. Yes, she was fighting for his happiness, but she couldn't make the choice for him, especially not by delivering some ultimatum. All she could do was support him—love him—if he'd still let her.

"I know he cares. I care about him, too. We've got some stuff to sort out. After this—after tonight."

Lina looked down at her hands, teeth catching her bottom lip. "And me and you? Do we have stuff to sort out, too, or are you never going to speak to me again after this?"

Jess rolled her eyes. "Come on, Lina. We got through competing for senior editor of the college paper. We'll get through this."

Lina's relieved smile warmed her from the inside out. Jess didn't have words for how happy she was that Lina was back. So she did what Gemma always did when she couldn't express herself with words. She did it with food.

"Have you eaten lunch? Gemma left a huge pot of ragu in back. You want some?"

Lina scrambled up on a bar stool and unzipped her coat. "You know I will never say no to Gemma's food."

Jess filled two glasses with beer from the tap. "I think we both deserve a drink today."

"I think you are exactly right."

"Here's to busting Chase and Lauren and getting my job back."

Lina clinked her glass against Jess's. "And here's to you and Alex."

"How do you know there is a 'me and Alex'? I haven't even told you the full story."

Lina leaned forward on her elbows. "Well, then maybe you should tell me now."

So Jess started at the beginning and told Lina everything, and before she knew it, it felt just like old times. Repairing her friendship with Lina seemed like it wouldn't be so hard after all.

If only things with Alex could be so easy. Even if she convinced him to give her another chance, there was still that pesky controlling media mogul determined to scrape her off like a barnacle, and the tiny problem of a potential transcontinental long-distance relationship. But if she loved him—if he loved her—they would figure it out. Right?

Chapter Thirty-Four

Jess and Lina found the address Alex had given Lina deep in the hinterlands of Greenpoint. Like Williamsburg, Greenpoint had gentrified dramatically in recent years, evidenced by the glass-and-brick facade of the bar they faced, called the HandleBar.

"Irony. How refreshing," Lina quipped.

Jess managed to laugh despite the nerves eating her up inside. Alex was inside somewhere. Would he act like nothing had changed? Or would he be cold and distant?

"Are you going in or are you gonna watch the whole thing from the sidewalk?"

"Sorry, just nervous."

"Jess, he's doing all this for you. He could have just fired Chase."

"Right."

The HandleBar was a long, narrow space, with a bar stretching along the wall to the right. A few small tables were clustered up front and many more in the back. About halfway down on the left side, a staircase led up to a mezzanine seating area that overhung the front half of the room. No one they recognized was there yet, so Lina and Jess took seats at the bar.

They hadn't gotten around to ordering drinks when Alex's voice behind her sent her jumping out of her skin.

"Good. You made it."

She spun around, greedily drinking in the sight of him, even though it had only been a day since she'd seen him.

"They're here already." He was looking at her, talking to her, but somehow managing not to make eye contact. That was a bad sign.

"What?"

"Chase and Lauren. I had to stay out of sight, but I showed a waiter Chase's picture and he's been watching for me. He says they're in a corner upstairs."

Right. Chase and Lauren. That's why they were here. Everything else would have to wait until later.

"What are we waiting for?" Lina asked, hopping off her stool. "Let's go up there and bust some heads!"

"We're waiting for them." Alex pointed toward the front door. Jess and Lina turned just in time to see Mariel Kemper coming in. With Dan Drake.

"What—"

"I asked my dad to get Mariel here. I figured she should see it for herself. And Dad will have fun firing Chase in person."

Mariel was scowling as Dan ushered her inside. "I live on the Upper West Side, Dan. I don't understand why you dragged me all the way out to Greenpoint—"

Alex strode forward, cutting her off. "Dad, thanks for coming. And Ms. Kemper."

Mariel quickly took in Alex, then Lina and Jess standing right behind him. "What's going on here?"

Dan spoke before Alex could. "Mariel, I have to

confess, I had more than one reason for bringing you here."

"I'm still not sure what the first reason is, never mind the second," she snapped. "Why did you call me? What am I doing here?"

"This afternoon, Alex brought it to my attention that someone on the ClickNews staff has been publishing stories on the website stolen from the *Brooklyn Daily Post*."

"I know," Mariel snapped. "Stolen by her." She pointed her finger at Jess. It took all Jess had to stand still and not shrink into the floor. Then she felt a touch on her hand, Lina, wrapping her fingers around hers. Lina squeezed lightly in silent reassurance. That's right. Lina and Alex knew she didn't do this. They believed in her.

Lifting her chin, she forced herself to meet Mariel's gaze. "It wasn't me, Mariel. That's what we came here to prove."

"Our leak is upstairs right now," Alex said. "Meeting with *your* leak. Probably acquiring more of your stories to publish on our site."

Dan, grinning broadly despite the palpable tension in the air, laid his hand on Mariel's back. "Why don't we go upstairs and see if you recognize Chase's friend?"

"Sounds like a good idea," Mariel growled.

Jess hung back with Lina, letting Dan escort Mariel first, with Alex in their wake. The light, already dim downstairs, was even lower upstairs. She stopped at the top of the stairs, squinting into the murk trying to make out Chase's sandy blond hair and smug face.

She spotted him tucked into the far corner at the same moment Dan and Mariel did.

Mariel let out a colorful stream of expletives, ending with, "I can't believe this!"

"You know her, then," Dan said.

Mariel started storming across the mezzanine. As soon as Dan moved to follow her, the view was unobstructed, and Jess got a good look at Chase's table in the corner.

But he wasn't sitting with Lauren.

Lina's hand tightened around hers as her shout cut through the low-level bar chatter. "Zoe!"

The shock of it, the utter betrayal, left Jess frozen in place. *Zoe.* How many times had she and Lina laughed and gossiped with her? She was supposed to be one of their team, on their side. Ever since they'd all started at the paper, they'd pledged to look out for each other.

It's a tough business for women. We've got to have each other's backs.

That's what Zoe had told her right after she'd offered to set up an interview for Jess with Frank Gallagher.

Right before she *stole* Jess's story for herself. And Lina's. And Dana's. She'd betrayed them all. The realization was like another punch to the gut.

Zoe's head whipped in their direction, just in time for her to see Mariel and Dan descending. Chase followed her horrified gaze, and in an almost comedic moment, the smug, flirty grin slid off his face, replaced with wide-eyed dread. Zoe snatched her hand out of Chase's, but not so fast that Jess didn't register it. Of course there was more to this than stolen stories.

There was sex, too. Chase was so freaking predictable. But Zoe…that betrayal burned like acid.

Jess shook off the moment of shock and followed Alex and Lina.

"Zoe, how surprising to find you taking a meeting with… I'm sorry, I can't recall your name, but I do remember you handle the journalism division at Click-News, am I correct?"

"Mariel," Dan interjected, his jokey demeanor finally replaced with grim resolve. "This is Chase Bennett, *formerly* of ClickNews, but unemployed, effective immediately."

"Dan…" Chase began, finding his smarmy smile again. "I'm not sure what you've heard—"

"I've heard from my son that you've put the website in a precarious position, accused of theft of intellectual property."

Chase scoffed. "Sorry, Dan. Your boy's desperate to throw somebody under the bus. That's a fucking lie."

"Chase," Alex cut in. "You know as well as I do that all the stories go through you. That means you were the source."

The look of pure malice Chase leveled at Alex stole Jess's breath away. "You can't prove a fucking thing," he snarled, like the cornered dog he was.

"Yes, he can," Lina interjected. "Jess's substantiating research and some of my notes appear verbatim in your article. And now we know *exactly* who gave them to you. *This* worthless piece of trash." Lina took a menacing step toward Zoe. "I mean, Lauren didn't surprise me, but you! We trusted you."

Mariel glanced at Lina. "Lauren?"

"Another snake in the grass," Lina replied. "Looks like there were two."

"We'll discuss that later," Mariel said, turning back to Zoe. "For now there's the issue of Miss Matheson's future to discuss."

"It wasn't me! I swear it!" Zoe cried.

Mariel leveled her with a glance. "Save the tearful protests, Zoe. Consider your termination immediate."

"But—"

"This is just social," Chase said. "You can't fire us for a personal relationship."

"Maybe," Alex spoke into the chaos. "Chase can prove it by giving me that flash drive I just saw him pocket."

Chase turned his head to glare at him. "I have no idea what you're talking about. I'm just buying a girl a drink and you're storming in here with all these bullshit accusations—"

Without another word, Alex leaned down and fisted the front of Chase's neatly pressed blue Oxford shirt, hauling him halfway to his feet.

"What the fuck do you think you're doing?"

While Chase shoved ineffectually at Alex's shoulders, Alex reached his free hand into the pocket of Chase's shirt, retrieving a flash drive. He released Chase, letting him fall heavily back into his chair.

He held the flash drive up to Zoe. "I suspect we'll find the outlines of all the *Daily Post*'s latest stories on this? Am I right?"

Zoe looked uneasily from Mariel to Jess to Lina and back again. "Mariel—"

Mariel held up a hand to cut her off. "I really don't want to hear the pathetic explanation you're about to offer up. I hope whatever Mr. Bennett was able to offer you for this was worth it."

"But—"

"Zoe," Mariel said. Her voice was deceptively soft, like a sharpened steel blade hiding under a sheer silk scarf. "You know my position in this business as well as I do. I am not someone you want to cross. You've proved to be a thief and a liar. If I were you, I'd retool my resume for something outside of journalism. I have a very long reach."

"But that's not fair!"

Jess had been determined to stay out of it, but her patience finally snapped. "What's not fair is that you had every advantage imaginable…money, education, family connections, and a great job at a fantastic paper…and you still chose to cheat your way up instead of earning it on your own merit. All that bullshit about taking care of each other in a tough business, when the whole time, you were stealing from all of us."

Zoe turned to Jess, her wide-eyed innocent expression dropping away in a flash. "Look, why don't you and Lina spare me your heartwarming stories about scrappy determination? You're just as ambitious as I am and you know it. Yes, it *is* a tough business, and I did what I had to do to get ahead. You'd have done the same."

Jess shook her head in bafflement. Who *was* this person? How had she fooled them all? "No, I wouldn't betray a friend. Not for any job. And I thought that's what you were."

"You're pathetic," Lina hissed. "He must have offered you a hell of a job, because I *know* he's not that good in bed."

"You should probably also know," Alex interjected, "that you weren't the only one."

Zoe's eyes flew to Chase. "What's he talking about?"

"You want to tell her about your arrangement with reporters from the *New York Post* and the *Daily News*, Chase, or should I? Judging from the nature of your conversations with them, there was more being exchanged than stories."

Despite her career currently in flames around her, Zoe lashed out at Chase. "You lying piece of shit!"

Mariel didn't wait to see how the next chapter of the Zoe and Chase scandal unfolded. She turned to face Jess. "Jessica, we should talk."

"There's more," Lina said.

Mariel sighed wearily. "Right. You mentioned something about Lauren. I believe I need a drink for this one."

Jess and Lina began to follow her downstairs, but Jess could feel Alex behind her, his presence a magnet holding her in place. She turned back to him.

All she wanted was to go to him, to start putting this to rights, but she couldn't, at least, not yet. She and Lina owed Mariel the full story and he and his father had their own mopping up to do with Chase. This wasn't over quite yet.

But she couldn't leave him without a word. "Thank you, Alex. Thank you for doing this for me."

He nodded briefly in acknowledgment but his frozen expression, his flat eyes, gave nothing away. Not a flash of hope, not a spark of happiness.

Jess felt chilled to the bone as she turned to follow Lina downstairs.

Chapter Thirty-Five

Downstairs, Mariel turned to Jess and Lina. "Okay, fill me in on the Lauren piece of this puzzle."

"Well," Lina began. "We thought it was the *same* situation. We were as surprised as you to see Zoe up there."

"You thought *Lauren* was stealing the stories? Why?"

Lina briefly filled her in about the evidence Griffin had uncovered linking Lauren to the incriminating tweet.

"She's always had a grudge against Jess," Lina concluded. "I thought the tweet was just her way of taking a swipe at her on the way out the door, but now Zoe's turned out to be the thief, so—"

"I fired Lauren today," Mariel interjected.

Jess and Lina exchanged a glance. "You did?"

"It was based on her substandard job performance, but I wish I'd known about this, too. Ladies, I believe I owe you a drink. And probably dinner. And possibly promotions. But let's start with the drinks."

Mariel corralled the bartender with one commanding glance. "Vodka martini, dirty, two olives. Strong enough to stand up and walk out of here on its own. Ladies?"

When the drinks were delivered—Mariel's martini and beers for Jess and Lina—Mariel took a long, slow sip of hers and carefully set it down. She braced her palms on the bar and inhaled deeply. "I owe you a profound apology, Jess. I can't tell you how sorry I am for all this."

"It's okay."

Mariel shook her head angrily. "After spending so many years as a reporter, I pride myself on my ability to suss out a person. Lauren was a bad hire. Sometimes it happens, no matter how carefully you vet. But Zoe… I missed the clues."

"Trust me, there weren't any," Jess assured her. "We've been close with her since we started and neither of us ever suspected."

"But I let Lauren guide my opinion on this Twitter thing, despite my misgivings about her. And looking back, she was the first to suggest you might be behind the thefts. She planted the seed."

"Come to think of it," Lina said. "She probably truly thought it was Jess. She already hated her, and she was suspicious of Jess's relationship with Alex. She just got it wrong."

"But you saw me talking to Alex yourself, Mariel," Jess added. "And I covered up my relationship with him, which didn't help. I'm sorry. Looking at the whole thing objectively, I can see it would have been easy to believe. It looked like I was lying about something."

"I'm guessing there's more to Zoe's computer contractor story, isn't there?"

Jess nodded. "That was *my* story. Zoe said she could

land me an interview with the agency head in Albany, but afterward, she said he'd only agree to talk to her, so you told her she was the one who had to write it up."

Mariel closed her eyes and angrily exhaled. "She never mentioned your involvement. She's a talented writer. I can't believe she decided to stoop so low."

"Well, Chase is sleeping with her. That might have been a factor, too." Mariel glanced up and Jess shrugged. "We've known Chase since college. He sleeps with everybody."

"Truth," Lina murmured.

Mariel's elegantly arched eyebrows hiked up. "Well. Tonight has just been full of surprises. It goes without saying that you have your job back, Jess, along with my sincere apologies."

"Thank you. Honestly, the worst part of all of this was knowing you thought so poorly of me. You've been such a…" Earlier, she'd been running on adrenaline. Now, she felt shaky with nerves as it all began to hit home. "You've been a role model for me my whole life. It was awful, knowing that you thought I'd do something like that."

Mariel, who always seemed so polished, so ruthlessly controlled, momentarily paled. The fine skin around her eyes crinkled as she winced, as if in pain. "I should have known better. I've known you since you were a girl. I should have trusted that."

Jess wasn't sure she could speak without crying, swallowing hard around the painful lump in her throat. "I'm glad you believe me now," she finally choked out.

Mariel reached out, laying a hand on her arm. "I won't doubt your integrity and dedication again. I promise you that."

"Thank you."

"Ladies!" Dan Drake was striding across the bar toward them, arms outspread, white smile dazzling. "What an interesting night this has turned out to be."

"To put it mildly," Mariel said.

"Mariel, I believe I lured you here with the promise of a drink. At this point, I think I may owe you more than one. Shall we?" He gestured expansively toward the sparsely populated back of the bar.

"You know, Dan, after this night, I think I just might let you buy me those drinks." She scooped up her half-empty martini glass. "And you can start with buying this round. Jess? I'll see you at the paper tomorrow?"

For the first time all night, Jess felt able to smile. "You will. I can't wait to be back."

"And you'll be coming back with a killer story ready to go. Get me a draft about all of this by next Friday."

"Oh." It hadn't even occurred to her that what happened might be newsworthy. But actually, it was a *huge* story. A *juicy* story. And Mariel had just tossed it right into her lap.

"Sure thing. Absolutely. And thank you. Again."

"Thank *you*, for coming back. I wouldn't have blamed you if you didn't." Mariel turned to Lina. "Lina, ClickNews broke your story about Assemblyman Stevens, and we can't undo that. But the story isn't over. There's going to be fallout in the construction industry. Projects under new scrutiny. State criminal charges. A trial."

Lina nodded in confusion.

"I want you to cover it, Lina. Let's make it a featured series."

Lina's eyes went wide. "Are you sure? I mean, thank you. Thank you so much, Mariel."

"You're a good reporter. I was impressed with the way your story had been coming together, and you've already done the background on this. I'm looking forward to seeing your coverage of the rest of it. Dan? I'm ready for that drink now." She turned and let Dan escort her to the back of the bar.

"Well, we got you your job back and we both have great stories to work on," Lina said, tapping her glass against Jess's. "I'd say that was a huge success."

Jess forced a smile and sipped her beer. It was all good news—fantastic news—but she couldn't relax and enjoy any of it until she'd dealt with the most important thing—Alex.

Chapter Thirty-Six

Dan Drake might have spent the past twenty years ensconced in a penthouse office, leaving the nitty-gritty of running his businesses to others, but that didn't mean he'd lost his edge, as Chase was quickly finding out. He hadn't gotten where he was in life by going soft on shitheads, and right now, Alex was very much enjoying watching his father verbally strip the hide off his one-time best friend. When Dan had said his fill, he turned, smiling at Alex like nothing had happened.

"Good work, son. I'll leave you to take out the trash. There's an aggrieved woman downstairs who needs a drink."

Alex watched his father depart in silence before turning back to face Chase. Zoe had slipped away while Dan was tearing Chase apart, and now he was sitting with his arm casually draped over the back of his chair, smug expression firmly back in place. The bastard didn't even look sorry. Alex knew him well enough to know he was probably frantically scrambling through his options in his mind right now, but Chase wasn't the type to let even a hint of self-doubt appear on the surface.

"You're lucky we're still inside," Alex said conversationally. "Or you'd be dealing with my fist in your fucking face right now."

"Don't hold back, bro. Let me have it."

All day long, Alex had been channeling his rage into controlled action, but now that the goal had been achieved, he felt the fragile tether inside snap. His hand shot out, grasping Chase by his shirt, jerking him to his feet so rapidly, his chair fell over, clattering on the floor. The few patrons still seated in the balcony had long since given up attempting to have their own conversations. They were avidly observing the drama going down in the corner like it was a Jerry Springer episode. Some latent instinct warned Alex that he and his father had undoubtedly been identified and that cell phone videos of tonight's events would probably be all over social media by morning.

Oh, well. Too late to keep it quiet, so he might as well give them a really good show.

"Let you have it?" he snarled, his face just inches from Chase's. "With pleasure."

"You don't have the guts," Chase snapped, that maddening, lazy grin finally wiped off his face. "Not about this or anything else in your blessed fucking life."

"What are you talking about?"

"Why do you think I did it?"

"Because you're a lazy, greedy motherfucker without a shred of loyalty."

"You'd like to believe that, wouldn't you? But it wasn't about greed. It was about ambition."

"Obviously."

"You think my goal was running that crap news department at that crap website?"

Scowling, Alex finally released his hold on Chase and shoved him away. "Then why? What was the point of all this?"

"I was going to turn that department around and show your dad what *real* ambition looks like. Not this noble, suffering, brave face you wear all the time."

"I don't know what you're talking about."

"Poor Alex Drake," Chase sneered contemptuously. "It must be so hard to have your father's media empire dumped in your lap when you haven't done a damned thing to earn it. When you don't even want it."

Alex's breath left him in a rush, like he'd been gut-punched. "You're full of shit." The words were still full of anger, even if his voice wasn't.

"Am I? I've known you since we were twelve, Alex. You think I can't tell you hate every second of your existence?"

As furious as he still was, a tiny voice in his head was whispering that Chase was right. Chase had seen the truth he'd tried so hard to hide from everyone. "And this is how you repay that friendship."

"Hey, I just got tired of watching you drag around the opportunity of a lifetime like it was your own personal cross to bear."

"So you thought you'd cheat your way to the top in my place?"

"Eventually your father's going to have to face the fact that he backed the wrong horse with you. And when that day came, I planned to be right there, ready to step up. You might not want to be the heir to Drake Media, but I have no problem with it."

He didn't know what propelled him forward—rage or terror. His hands came up, shoving Chase hard, knocking him back into the wall. "You're never going to set one filthy hand on Dad's company."

"Maybe not anymore," Chase conceded. "Which means he's stuck with you. How long before you run it all into the ground?"

"Shut up," he bit out through clenched teeth. But now his anger had two targets—Chase and himself. Because he couldn't deny what Chase was saying. He hated Drake Media. He didn't want it. Did that mean he was doomed to ruin it, as Chase alleged? If he thought being trapped in a life he didn't want was bad, he hadn't factored in the possibility of failing at it— ruining everything his father had built. That would be even worse.

He fell back a step, his taste for blood deserting him. "Drake Media is mine to worry about. You're going to be busy picking up the pieces of your career. You'll never work in journalism again."

Chase laughed softly as he straightened his shirt and ran a hand through his hair. "You think I give a shit about being a journalist? I never did. I'll land on my feet. Drake Media hasn't seen the last of me, but next time it'll be because I'm leaving your company in the dust."

Alex didn't doubt Chase's assertion that he'd find some way out of this. He always did. He was an opportunist of the first order, and he'd find some scheme to weasel into.

"Well, then get the fuck out of my face and get started on the rest of your life. If you ever come within a hundred yards of Drake Media, you'll find yourself under arrest."

"Trust me, that's not gonna happen."

Alex let out a bitter scoff of humorless laughter. "Trust you? I've made that mistake for the last time."

Chase shoved off the wall and strode past Alex, knocking him hard in the shoulder. The temptation to haul him back by the collar and slam his fucking head against the floor was nearly overwhelming, but the last thing this night needed was police involvement, or the resulting lawsuit.

So he let him go, the frustration and rage ebbing out of his blood as his heartbeat slowed and the adrenaline stopped pumping. Downstairs, he snagged a waiter and handed him a roll of bills to cover the drinks for everyone up on the balcony, along with fat tips for the staff. When he looked for everyone else, his father and Mariel had disappeared, but Jess was with Lina by the bar. His heart gave one painful thud at the sight of the two of them, chattering away happily. Jess had her best friend and her job back. Everybody was back where they belonged. He'd done what he came here to do. Now it was time to go.

Before he left, he stayed hidden in the shadow of the staircase, watching Jess, just as he'd been doing for years. As she turned her face toward Lina and laughed at something she said, her hair slid back over her shoulder. How many times had he stared at that hair, wondering how it would feel between his fingers? Now he knew, the sense memory tingling along his fingertips. Now he knew what it felt like to wake up with her body next to his. Now he knew what it felt like to look into her eyes and see them light up with love instead of hate.

But how long would that love in her eyes last if, day after day, his life ground off all the parts of him she liked best? The animosity she'd thrown his way for so many years would pale in comparison to seeing her look at him with disappointment. Regret.

Last night, he'd been angry at Jess. But what had she said that wasn't true? How long did he think he could juggle all the disparate parts of his life before he dropped one? Jess's Peabody versus his father's Alex Drake. In the end, only one would win, and Drake Media was a behemoth, devouring everything it touched. When he inevitably slipped up in his life's balancing act and dropped Jess, how badly would she suffer at his hands?

Slowly, he made his way over to them. Jess spun around when she sensed his approach, her eyes lit up with gratitude and love. For just a moment, he let it sink into him, fill him up, warm him from the inside out.

"Mariel gave Jess her job back!" Lina said before either of them could speak.

"That's great. I knew she would."

"Alex—" Jess said, reaching a hand out to touch him. It would be so easy to take her hand, kiss her, pretend last night had never happened. But he'd only be delaying the inevitable.

"If you see my dad, will you tell him I left?"

Jess blinked and drew her hand back as if he'd slapped it.

Lina licked her lips, her eyes flicking between him

and Jess. "Are you sure you don't want to stay? We're celebrating."

The smile he produced felt foreign on his face, but he'd better get used to it. He'd be faking his smiles for a long time to come. "No thanks, I'd better go. There's a lot to do tomorrow at work to fix Chase's mess. Good night."

Turning away from the bewildered hurt in Jess's eyes, he made his way out of the bar and into the cold night.

Jess watched Alex's retreating form, the painful constriction in her throat making it hard to breathe.

"Lina…"

"Go after him," Lina said, nudging her side. *"Go."*

Jess went, half walking, half running through the bar, which had grown crowded while their drama had played out upstairs.

"Alex!"

He didn't hear her, walking out the glass front door and off down the sidewalk. She tumbled out the door after him. "Alex! Wait!"

He stopped, turned, and waited, that impossible-to-read blank expression on his face. It was his Drake Media face. His eyes were dead.

It had started to snow again, the flakes stinging against her flushed cheeks as she closed the distance to him.

"Can we talk about last night?"

"We don't have to do that," he said, so infuriatingly calm and polite. She wanted to grab him by those broad, strong shoulders and shake him hard, until he came back to life under her hands.

"Yes, we do. I didn't say it right." Helplessly, she trailed off, squeezing her eyes shut and shaking her head in frustration.

"You said it perfectly, Jess. And you were right."

"No, I wasn't. Just—"

His eyes fixed on the snow-covered pavement between them. "You were right. I've been trying to have it both ways and it's not going to work. Not in the long run."

Suddenly it was hard to breathe. She wanted to take it all back, every single stupid thing she'd said about being true to himself and sticking to his principles. Because not once as she spouted all that crap at him did she think he'd choose Drake Media instead of himself. That he'd choose to leave her behind. "No, Alex, we can figure this out. Please—"

He looked up at her, a slight, sad smile tugging at one corner of his mouth. His hair fell in a tangled sweep across his forehead, flecked with snowflakes. They caught in the tips of his eyelashes, and one landed briefly on his bottom lip before it melted away in the heat of his skin. "I've always known what my life would be, Jess. I'm sorry if I made you think I could change that."

"You don't have to. It's okay. We can work it out. I'll be fine, I promise."

With a weary shake of his head, he stuffed his hands into his coat pockets, hunching his shoulders against the cold. "You wouldn't be. Not forever. And you shouldn't be. From the very beginning, you've known who you are and what you wanted. And it wasn't this. I don't want you to compromise yourself for me."

"I wouldn't be." She was losing him. He was going

to turn around and walk away and there was nothing she could say to stop him. Taking a step closer, she reached out to touch him but he took a sudden step back, and she stumbled to a stop. "Alex—"

With a deep inhale, he straightened and flashed her a smile, this one devoid of all life and warmth. It was a hollow shell of the smile she loved. "I'm really glad you got your job back, Jess. That place is your dream come true."

Then he did turn, walking away from her up the sidewalk. His feet left a line of dark prints in the snow, growing smaller as he moved farther and farther away.

"No, it wasn't. You were," she whispered into the cold, but he was too far gone to hear it.

Chapter Thirty-Seven

When Alex arrived at the ClickNews offices the next morning, the place was in chaos. Word of Chase's betrayal had spread, along with the inevitable viral internet videos of Alex confronting him in the bar. The excited chatter paused momentarily when he stepped off the elevator, and a second later, the staff burst into enthusiastic applause and whistles.

With a half-hearted smile and wave, Alex made his way through the workroom to his desk.

"I never liked that asshole," one writer told him.

"I always knew he was a shady son of a bitch," another said.

"So." Samaira Sangar materialized in front of his desk before he'd even sat down, arms crossed over her chest and foot tapping. "What happens to our department now?"

Chase's reporting staff had been spotty at best, but Samaira was definitely one of the better ones.

"I'm going to run it for now."

A wide smile broke across her face. "Excellent."

"It's just temporary. Until we can find someone else."

"Well, we'd better get to work. Chase was out most of last week, so we're already behind."

And any stories the staff was already working on would have to be scrapped, since there was no telling where Chase had gotten them. That meant they were starting from square one.

"Um…" Alex dragged a hand through his hair. "Sure. Let's go. Call everybody into the conference room. Let's get started."

He could do this. Brainstorm a few ideas, assign the stories, get the staff to work. Then he could turn his attention to the problem of finding Chase's replacement.

Ten minutes later, he was staring down Chase's ragtag crew around the conference table.

"It goes without saying that anything you were already working on needs to be scrapped. Which means we're going to need to generate some new content quickly. Who's got something they want to pitch?"

They looked uneasily at him. "We don't usually pitch stuff," one guy—Dean?—ventured. "Chase just assigned the stuff he'd already outlined and we'd write it up."

"Well, all of that stuff was stolen, so now it's on us to get it done."

After another awkward silence, Samaira tentatively raised her hand.

"Samaira? What do you have?"

"The mayor is holding a press conference today about his bid for the 2024 Olympics. I could cover that?"

"Good. Excellent." He was about to move on, but something made him pause and think for a moment. "And, Samaira, don't just reprint his press release.

There are sure to be some protesters there, people who don't want the Olympics here. Get some statements for the anti side, to balance the pro side."

"Got it." Samaira was smiling excitedly. For the first time in days—no, weeks…no, *months*—Alex had a frisson of excitement of his own.

Another guy—Yanni?—spoke up. Yanni's writing was good. It hinted at some formal training in journalism. "I saw something on the wire about that federal judge's corruption scandal. I was poking around online this morning and there are rumors that they had his office tapped and the tapes are about to drop."

"Yes! That's good." Adrenaline shot through Alex's body as his mind came alive with possibilities. "But we're not using the wire service's story. Get down to the FBI offices in Manhattan and see if you can talk to someone. I want something original on this. What was the probable cause behind the wiretap? Somebody knows something. Find it out."

Yanni looked startled at having such an ambitious story thrust into his face, but he sat up at attention and nodded as he scribbled some notes. "You got it, boss."

"In fact," Alex continued as the story came together in his mind, "Samaira, forget the Olympic bid story. You're on the judge, too. This is his district. His offices are downtown. Get down there and start digging. Talk to his paralegals, his secretaries, the security guys, the cleaning lady, anybody… Find us something nobody else knows yet. The offshore account, the secret mistress, the corporate collusion…whatever it is."

Samaira's eyes glinted with hungry glee. "I am *on* it!" She was definitely the star reporter of this bunch and he'd just let her off the leash. Who knew what she'd drag back, but it was exciting as hell to imagine it.

"Rob." He pointed at one of the duller staffers. This guy would definitely need to be replaced, but he'd do for now. "You take the Olympic bid. But I'm serious. You get me a pros and cons write-up, understand?"

Rob nodded nervously. "Pros and cons. Got it."

"In fact, talk to someone from the Parks Department. Has anybody done an impact study yet? And the budget office. What's it going to cost us? And the tourism department. What kind of money will it bring into the city?" He ticked off departments on his fingers. "The MTA, Con Ed, the hotel industry, the TLC… Talk to everybody and get their take. Can New York reasonably host an event as complex as the Olympics? Talk to someone in LA or Atlanta and find out what it ended up costing their city in the end. Was there ever a cost/benefits analysis done? This could be a multipart exploration of the impact of hosting the Olympic games on major cities where the infrastructure is already stressed—"

His first editorial meeting with the ClickNews staff lasted well over an hour. At the end of it, when every reporter had been tasked with a story to run down, he finally collapsed into a chair, still running high on adrenaline. The staff was filing past him, reviewing their notes or already on their cell phones. Samaira paused by his chair.

"You were amazing. I've got a whole *file* of story ideas I can't wait to pitch to you. This is going to be *so great*!"

She was gone before he could remind her that this

was just temporary. She was going to have to take all her fiery ambition and undoubtedly brilliant ideas and pitch them to his replacement. They'd find someone else for this position soon enough, because he was going to Brazil, on to the next phase of Drake Media's never-ending expansion.

In the space of an instant, his high was gone, leaving him feeling hollow and cold. Nothing he'd done in his life had felt as good—as *right*—as running this news division for the past hour. For a brief, glimmering moment, it was like that dream he'd described to Jess had actually come true. He was turning this ragtag afterthought into a force to be reckoned with. But it wouldn't last, not for him, anyway. His fate lay down another road.

In the echoing silence of the conference room, he thought about walking away from this, turning it over to the qualified candidate they eventually hired, and his heart began to pound like it was about to burst right out of his chest. A cold sweat broke out across the back of his neck.

Chase was a backstabbing son of a bitch, but he'd laid out a harsh truth that was now staring Alex unrelentingly in the face. He was a coward. He hated his life yet he was frozen, unable to make a move to change it. Maybe it was done for the best reasons, because he loved and respected his father, and felt obliged to take over what his father had so diligently built for him. But did that make it right?

Running that TV station in Brazil was the last thing he wanted to do. This—what he'd done here today— *this* was what he was meant to do. He could feel the rightness of it in his bones. Anything else would be a grievous compromise of his very soul. It had already cost him Jess. In time, it would cost him himself.

If Chase didn't have what it took to step in as his father's heir, why was he so sure he did? Why did his fortunate birth automatically instill him with what it took to run this company? What if it didn't? What if he was missing that essential attribute—the drive, the passion—to succeed at this? What if he was sacrificing everything so that he wouldn't let his father down, and then he ended up failing him, anyway?

"Hey, Champ."

His father's voice startled him out of his thoughts. Dan was standing in the doorway of the conference room, smiling down at him. "I came by to see if I needed to smooth some things over after yesterday's excitement, but it seems like you've already got it under control." He hooked a thumb over his shoulder, to the reporter's pool. "Chase's department is on fire this morning. You must have really whipped them up."

Licking his lips and inhaling deeply, Alex sat forward in his chair. "Yeah, I did. Dad, close the door and sit down." He motioned to the chair at his right. "I need to talk to you about something."

Dan's smile faded. He stepped into the room and shut the door before taking a seat at the conference table. "Is this about Chase's replacement? We can have HR pull together a list of candidates by the end of the week—"

"I don't want to replace Chase, Dad. I want to take over his job."

"Well, you'll have to for a couple of weeks, but—"

"No. Dad. I want it full time. I want to run the journalism division of ClickNews. For good."

Dan blinked once, and then leaned back in his chair, hand curled under his chin as he examined Alex. Alex knew that look. His father had just sensed a critical shift in the wind and was carefully assessing his next step, reading the room and his opponent. If this were an acquisition meeting, this is when the other team would start falling apart, panicking under Daniel Drake's shark-eyed gaze. Alex couldn't afford to do that.

"And Brazil?"

The time had come for him to lay his cards fully on the table. He'd gone along with this for so long because he loved his father. What was important to Dan was important to Alex. But now Alex needed Dan's support. He could only pray that Dan's love for him would push him to make that same sacrifice in return.

"Dad," he began, folding his hands in front of him on the table. "I don't want to run Drake Media. I never have."

Dan absorbed that with no outward reaction. Alex forced himself to stay silent. The rookie mistake was to babble, to fill the silence, and in doing so, expose yourself. But Alex had learned a few things watching his father negotiate over the years. He would make his father respond first.

"It's your company, son," Dan said. His delivery was matter-of-fact, like he'd pointed out that the sun would rise tomorrow in the east, even though Alex had just stated it would rise in the west.

"What you choose to do with Drake Media in the future is entirely up to you. This has nothing to do with that decision. But we're talking about here and now. And I cannot run Drake Media."

"You're my only child, Alex. If you don't run it, who will?" Dan sat straighter in his chair, his response this time less calculated. He was officially off-script, which was just how Alex needed him. He wanted to appeal to his *father*, not engage in protracted negotiations with the head of Drake Media.

Alex shrugged and attempted a smile. "You'll have to hire a CEO, Dad. A professional, not your son."

Dan shook his head slowly. "I built this whole thing for you."

Of all the things his father could have said, this was the hardest to resist. Dan only knew one way to care, and that was to take this amazing thing he'd built and hand it over in full. Telling him that he didn't want it felt like shoving a shiv right between his father's ribs.

"I know you did," he said quietly. "It's why, for all these years, I never said anything. I knew how important it was to you, and how much it meant. It was important to me for that reason, too."

"But not enough to work for it."

Alex dropped his head forward. "Dad... I don't love it like you do. Believe me, I've tried. But I don't." Looking up again, he leaned in, trying to get through to his father. "And here's what I've finally figured out. The passion is important. It might be more important than brains or experience or hard work. Chase might have been a bastard, but he said something out loud to me that I've never been able to bring myself to acknowledge. My heart is not in this. It never has been."

Dan scoffed. "You can't let anything that little asswipe said get to you—"

"Believe me, he only said what I already knew. Let me finish, though. He did what he did because he was trying to impress you. He figured sooner or later I'd crack, and he'd be right there, ready to step into my place."

"As if that piece of shit has what it takes to run this company."

"He didn't. But Dad, neither do I."

"Of course you do!"

"Oh, don't get me wrong, I have the knowledge, the skills, the intellect. I could do it. But, Dad, I don't think I'm exaggerating when I say it would kill me. Maybe slowly, but I'd be dead just the same."

His father's eyes were burning as he stared at Alex. Alex made himself hold still as Dan worked through it. He'd been as honest as he could be. Either way, he was out. But he hoped he could step out of the business without destroying his relationship with his father in the process. That part was up to Dan.

"Is this about the girl? Jessica?"

A huff of laughter burst from his lips. "Maybe? A little? She just pressed me to take a hard look at myself. What I found there? It's all me. Anyway, I told you, we broke up."

Although that was starting to shift in his mind, too, along with his future. Why was he walking away from the thing he most wanted in life? Because that wasn't ClickNews. That was Jess. And if he was standing up to fight for the website, then he would fight for her, too.

But one thing at a time. First, his father was sitting across the table, coming to terms with the idea that the person he'd counted on above all others was walking away from him. Alex wouldn't go without making sure he was okay.

Dan made a noncommittal grunt and fidgeted in his

chair. "And…" He stopped, cleared his throat, tugged on his shirt cuff, and started again. "This is what you want to do?"

"Journalism? Yeah."

"Son, when we acquired ClickNews, it wasn't because it was a hard-hitting news source. This isn't real journalism."

"See, that's what I'm talking about, Dad. It *could* be." He sat forward, outlining what he'd done just this morning, that familiar rush of energy and excitement flooding back in. "And that's just what we came up with on the fly. I'm thinking big, I'm thinking long-term. We can put together investigative teams to go after the really big stuff, things most papers don't have the budgets to dig into anymore. We could… Fuck, we could get credentialed, put someone in the White House press pool, report on politics…what's *really* going on, not just what the advertisers want us to say."

"You're going after the Pulitzer now?" Dan chuckled.

"The Peabody. We're digital media. We'll win a Peabody Award." He smiled at his own joke. Peabody had always been the best part of himself. Right now, he felt like he was finally starting to live up to that potential. "Why not? We could be great. I want to make us great."

"We already have great media outlets. Two cable news channels and a part-ownership of a network."

"Dad, nobody under thirty pays for cable anymore. They get their news from the internet. We could be that news. But not the cheap shit we've been turning out. And not the sensational click-bait that's out there now. I want to produce real news, with high journalistic standards, and present it in a format a younger generation will respond to. All they get right now is celebrity gossip and memes, and because of that, people are growing up uninformed and disengaged. What if we did more, and what if we did it better? We could… Hell, we could change the world, Dad."

Dan pressed his lips together as he stared at Alex. "I've never seen you like this."

"I've never felt like this. Because this is *it*, what I've always wanted to do. Doesn't Drake Media deserve someone running it who feels that way about it?"

Dan grunted, shrugging one shoulder.

"Dad, that person is not me."

Silence stretched out, and Alex made no move to fill it. He let his father come to terms with the situation in his own way. Finally, Dan cleared his throat and sat forward, mirroring Alex's pose, elbows on the table, hands threaded together. Alex recognized this moment, too. They were entering the serious negotiations portion of the discussion. "You will still sit on the board of directors, is that clear?"

Alex's breath left him in a rush. "Yeah." He nodded rapidly. "Yes, of course I'll stay on the board."

"And you keep control of your stock, so we still hold the majority share. You can't sell it off."

"Dad, I would never sell off my stock."

"And…" Dan blew out a breath, his eyes flashing at the ceiling. "You come to some investor meetings. They know you. They like you. They want to see you around."

"But you have to involve the new CEO, Dad. I won't pretend I'm more involved than I am."

"Understood. Fuck." Dan sat back again, throwing

his hands in the air. "This industry is full of assholes. Where am I supposed to find a CEO I can stand?"

"You've got this Brazilian network that needs someone to take it in hand. Seems like that might be an excellent way to try out a job prospect."

Dan harrumphed, but he looked thoughtful. "Maybe. Yeah. I'll put somebody down there and see how they do."

"You should take a look at Megan."

"Megan Harte?"

Alex nodded. "She's a powerhouse."

"Huh." With a lengthy exhale, Dan sat back and examined him once more. "How did I not see this coming?"

"I did my best to keep it from you, Dad. I didn't want to disappoint you."

"You could never—" Dan broke off, letting out a huff of frustration. "I feel like I've been sacrificing my son in favor of my company and I was too blind to see it."

"That's not what you did. If you told me I had to run Drake no matter what…well, then you might have a point. But that's not what you said."

"Because I want you to be happy."

His heart, still accustomed to its daily dose of guilt, gave a hard twist. No one, outside of him, ever saw this side of him. Dan hid it from everyone else. Some part of him still wished he could be everything Dan had hoped he'd be, just to make him happy. But that wasn't good for either one of them. Dan had to learn to stop depending on him, and Alex had to learn to stop being dependable. The only way forward from now on was honesty.

"I know you do, Dad. I wanted you to be happy, too. That's why I tried so hard."

"Well, aren't we a fine pair?"

"I happen to think so. But just as father and son, not owner and CEO."

Dan's legendary grin made a dramatic comeback. "Damned straight." He pushed to his feet. "You still have time to have lunch with your old man?"

Alex smiled as he stood, too. "Always, Dad, you know that. But let's make it quick." He motioned through the glass wall at the chaos in the reporting pool outside. "I have a big job on my hands."

Dan clapped a hand firmly on his shoulder. "Kid, I'm replacing you. I know exactly how you feel."

Chapter Thirty-Eight

On her first morning back at work, it took Jess half an hour to make it from the front door of the Fiske building to her desk upstairs. First there was Cliff from security, who hustled out from behind his desk to tell her how happy he was to see her back.

Then, when she got to the front office, Sally took one look at her and burst into noisy tears of joy. Jess was still patting her back and handing her tissues when Lina found her.

"Sally, she's back at work, which means she needs to actually, you know, work."

Sally straightened up and sniffed. "Of course, of course! I'm just so happy to see you back."

Lina pulled her away before another round of sobs could erupt. When she walked through the door of the newsroom, she was greeted with the sight of every person on the *Daily Post*'s staff standing and applauding.

"Oh." The strangled little gasp was all she could manage as her eyes started to burn. Lina, who was clearly in on it, grinned smugly at her side. One by one, the staff came forward to shake her hand or hug her, and welcome her back.

Natalie was first, bursting into tears, too, apologizing profusely for not having guessed Zoe was an evil, lying snake. Isaiah grimly castigated himself for not sniffing out Zoe's duplicity himself. "Some investigative journalist I turned out to be."

"Welcome back, killer," Hassan said, forgoing both a hug and a handshake in favor of a fist bump. Dana hugged her fiercely, sniffing back tears as she welcomed her back. Caleb guiltily shook her hand, eyes on the floor. "I was an asshole to you last week, Jess, and you've always been awesome to me. You deserved more loyalty."

"It's okay," she murmured, becoming embarrassed by the show of devotion.

Griffin was next, awkwardly clapping her on the shoulder. "I knew you didn't do it."

Jess caught his hand and squeezed. "Thanks for proving it."

He shrugged. "Anytime."

How could she have sat in that meeting and assessed each one of these people for their potential to betray? The same way they'd been led to believe the worst about her, she supposed. Fuck Chase Bennett, and fuck Zoe, for making them doubt each other.

The last one up was Mariel. "Jess," she said simply, and then she pulled her into a brief but firm hug. "I'm so glad you're back."

"I'm glad to be back, Mariel."

"Well." Mariel looked at the newsroom, still gathered around Jess. "Since I have everyone's attention, I'll take advantage of it to let you know the *Daily Post* staff has been invited to a New Year's Eve party tonight."

Tonight was New Year's Eve? Things had been so

crazy that Jess had totally lost track of the date. But yes, it was tonight.

"We're having a party?" Natalie asked brightly.

"Not us. We've been invited to the Drake Media party."

Utter silence greeted Mariel's announcement.

"Drake Media?" Marc finally said. "They have some nerve."

"Actually," Mariel said. "It's Dan Drake's attempt at an apology for what our staff has gone through at the hands of one of his employees."

"Okay, that's not a shitty thing," Hassan conceded.

"He tells me it's quite the event. It's at The Standard in SoHo. Catered, cocktail attire, and an open bar…"

"Open bar?" Caleb echoed.

"I'm in!" Lina said. "And so is Jess. We can celebrate her return."

The rest of the staff was looking for the flimsiest of reasons to accept the invitation, and Jess's return seemed to do it. In moments, the room had exploded in chatter as everyone debated what to wear.

Jess wasn't much interested in the party, but she *was* interested in Alex, and he wouldn't miss Drake Media's big party.

Last night was not the end. He wanted her, she was sure of that. In her heart of hearts, she was sure he loved her. He'd just convinced himself he couldn't have her, and that was her fault. But if she was the one who screwed it up, surely she could fix it again. All that stuff he said, about her not compromising, that was her choice to make, not his. Just like his decision to stand by Drake Media.

She was still terrified at what his choice would do

to him in the long run, but walking away and leaving him to face his future alone would only make it harder. If he was really determined, then she'd stand at his side, and somehow—she hoped—figure out how to help him hold on to himself as he did what he felt he had to do.

If he'd still let her. Tonight, she'd convince him to let her, no matter what.

Chapter Thirty-Nine

"This place is freakin' *noice*!" Hassan said as soon as he walked through the entrance to the ultra-exclusive bar at the top of The Standard in the Meatpacking District.

"Hassan," Lina warned. "Be chill, please."

He spun around to face Lina and Jess, straightening his tie. "How do I look? I look good in here, don't I?"

"You look like you're way too desperate," Lina hissed.

"Sorry, but geeky Pakistani boys from Queens don't get into places like this. Not ever. I am gonna enjoy the *hell* out of this night."

Lina relented and smiled, straightening his tie. "Well, they get in now. And with a hot date."

Hassan's eyes lit up as he smiled at Lina. "So this is a date?"

She tugged flirtatiously on his tie. "If you play your cards right."

Jess's gaze roamed over the impressive space. It was all deep amber light glinting off glossy wood with gold accents. A huge circular bar dominated the middle of the room, the curving liquor shelves in the middle exploding up toward the ceiling like an umbrella opening.

Wherever she looked, the walls were glass, displaying the glittering skyline outside. Clusters of creamy leather couches hugged the edges of the room. Dance music pulsed through the air, the heavy beat underscoring the hum of conversations and laughter.

Lina leaned closer to Jess. "Dan Drake sure throws a killer party."

"I heard the bathrooms are entirely made of glass," Hassan said.

"Did you see the appetizers back there?" Lina added. "Almost too pretty to eat."

"The DJ produced Flo Rida's last album."

"There's a hot tub in the other room. With a *bar*."

"I am *not* getting in the hot tub," Jess interjected.

"Lina," Hassan murmured. "Wanna take a dip later?"

She lifted one shoulder. "We'll see how the night progresses."

"How much do you think Drake paid to rent out the whole Boom Boom Room?" Hassan marveled, his eyes going wide as a waitress slid past him. She was at least six feet tall in her mile-high heels, in a skimpy white dress with her blond hair slicked back from her face.

"It's not called the Boom Boom Room anymore. It's just the Top of The Standard now." When they turned around, Griffin had joined them on the small raised entrance overlooking the room, but he was hardly recognizable as Griffin.

"Dude, you're wearing a tux?" Hassan said appreciatively.

Griff tugged on his bowtie. "I thought I could use an upgrade." He'd left his glasses at home and even the shaggy hair had been tamed.

"There you guys are!" Natalie materialized out of the crowd, looking stunning in a tight blue minidress, her long brown hair piled up on her head. "Everybody looks great! Wow, Griff, you clean up nice!"

He gave her a lopsided grin. "Thanks, Nat."

She reached out to hook her arm in his. "Griff, I bought this dress at the Miu Miu sample sale and I've been saving it up for a special occasion. I think your tux and my dress need to get a drink together."

"Your wish is my command," he said, waving back at Jess, Lina, and Hassan.

"Well, that was interesting," Jess said.

"Very," Lina agreed.

"Why are we still standing here like tourists?" Hassan complained.

"Good question," Lina replied. "I plan on drinking my body weight in champagne tonight, on Dan Drake's dime."

"Then let's find the bar."

Jess whispered to Lina as they followed Hassan into the crowd. "So you and Hassan?"

Lina smiled softly at his back before ducking her head. "I don't know. He's nothing like the guys I usually date. I mean, he's *such* a geek. But he's *so* nice. He was so supportive with the Lauren thing."

"Well, I think it's great."

Lina shook her hair back over her shoulders. "We'll see what the night brings."

"Speaking of, have you seen Alex anywhere? I need to talk to him."

"He's the boss's son. You need to find the VIP section. Let's get a drink and then we'll make a circuit of the room and scope him out."

At the bar, while Lina flagged down the bartender, Jess fidgeted, running her fingers nervously over the charms on her bracelet, the only jewelry she'd worn tonight. Standing on tiptoe, she struggled to see over the heads of the people surrounding her. Even in heels, she was dwarfed.

"Jessica, you made it."

Something familiar in the timbre of that voice, half-drowned out by the music and chatter around her, sent a little thrill of awareness down her spine. When she spun around, disappointment quickly snuffed out that momentary flare of joy. The father, not the son.

"Mr. Drake. It's nice to see you again."

"Enjoying the party?"

"I just got here, but it's nice. Thank you for inviting the *Daily Post* staff. You made a lot of people very happy."

He waved a dismissive hand. "Least I could do. Are you happy to be back at the paper, Jessica?"

His question was anything anyone would ask if they were making polite conversation. So why did she feel like she was being circled by a shark as it planned where to take its first bite?

Don't let him scare you, she scolded herself.

Sure, he could buy and sell her entire existence six times over with the spare change in his pockets, but he was just a person. And he was Alex's dad. Alex loved this man, enough to devote the rest of his life to making him happy. There had to be something in Dan to inspire Alex's loyalty, and she was determined to discover it.

The mistake she'd made was seeing Dan as an adversary, someone she had to battle for Alex's soul, when in reality, they were on the same side. They both loved him; they both wanted what was best for him; they just had different ideas of what that was. If she got what she wanted, she and Dan were going to be in each other's lives for a long time to come, so she was going to have to figure out how to deal with him, and that meant not letting him intimidate her.

Lifting her chin, she drew herself up as tall as her five-foot frame would allow. "I'm delighted. All my life I've wanted to work for a paper like the *Daily Post*, for an editor like Mariel Kemper, doing journalism that really matters. It's a dream come true. The *Daily Post* could change the world." Maybe she was laying it on a little thick, but she wasn't about to give him an opening to take a dig at the paper.

Dan's eyes narrowed as he examined her, with that infuriating, ever-present smile. Dan would probably grin ear-to-ear when he finally faced the Grim Reaper. Just one more person to charm, right?

Then he chuckled softly and shook his head. "That's where he got it from. You know, it's all your fault."

What? What the hell was he accusing *her* of? She was the victim of his dirtbag employee, not the other way around. "Excuse me?"

"All that passion is contagious. Should have made him major in communications. Or business. A good, solid MBA." He sighed. "Too late now, I suppose."

Now she was officially lost. He was obviously talking about Alex, but nothing he said made any sense. "I'm not sure I understand you."

"Are you looking for my son?" he asked abruptly.

"Um…" This felt like she'd stumbled into a knife fight and just discovered her switchblade was really a comb. But she wasn't about to back down. He was probably about to give her some speech about how a little nobody like her was never going to be good enough for his princeling son, and she might as well go back to Brooklyn and forget all about him. Well, if he tried that, he was in for a fight, because she didn't scare that easily. "Yes," she finally said, willing her voice not to shake with nerves. "Yes, I am."

Dan took a deep breath, as if he was about to launch his first strike. "He's outside on the balcony."

What?

"What?" she said out loud, so caught off guard that she couldn't quite comprehend what he'd said.

Dan stepped forward, swept an arm around her shoulders, and firmly turned her 180 degrees. Pointing over her shoulder, he indicated a door in the wall of glass. It opened onto a small balcony overlooking the city. Her heart gave a wild leap of joy when she recognized the familiar shape of Alex's broad shoulders and the artful tussle of his hair, silhouetted against the distant lights of the Jersey shore. "Balcony," Dan said near her ear.

When she turned back to look at him, he was already backing away through the crowd as his employees cast him surreptitious, awestruck glances. "But I don't…"

"Enjoy the party, Jessica. Try to get Alex to enjoy it, too, will you? Is Mariel here yet? I should say hello."

She shook her head in bafflement. "I don't know. I haven't seen her."

Dan pointed to the door behind her. "Balcony."

Then he was gone, leaving Jessica alone with her utter confusion. What the hell had that been about? But she didn't have time to parse out Dan's eccentricities. Alex was out there alone, and she was going to win him back if she had to grovel on her knees.

A cold breeze whipped her bare shoulders as she stepped outside, but giant standing heaters were stationed in the corners of the balcony, creating a pocket of tolerable air. It didn't matter. She'd stand outside in a snowstorm if that's what it took.

"Alex."

His shoulders jerked with surprise as he turned his head and registered her presence. "Jess…"

"Hi."

His eyes skated down her. "You look beautiful."

It was the same dress she'd worn to the Newsmaker banquet. She only had the one. But when he looked at her that way—like she was the hottest woman in the room—it didn't matter that it was recycled or twenty years old. He made her feel perfect. "Thanks. Can I talk to you?"

Taking his hands out of his pockets, he took a step closer to her. "Jess, I should—"

"No." She put a hand out to stop him. "Please. Just let me say this, okay?"

He shut his mouth and watched her. Okay, time to give the most passionate speech of her life, but not to defend workers' rights or freedom of the press. She had to convince the most important person in her life to let her love him. Maybe she should have planned this out. Jotted some notes on a Post-It, at least. But it was too late for that, so she plunged in with what she knew was true.

Stepping closer to him, she pressed her palms against his chest and looked up into his face, her gaze locking with his. "I love you, Alex. It was horrible of me to say you were abandoning your principles just for doing what you feel is right, even if I disagree. You're determined to fulfill your obligation to your father, and I respect that. I know I can get carried away over things I feel are important, but none of them are as important as you are. I don't want to be principled— I don't want to be right—if it means doing it without you. It wasn't about your job, it was about *you*…the best parts of you. I don't want you to lose those, but walking away from you isn't the answer.

"So I'm staying to fight for you. It doesn't matter if you try to send me away, because I'm still going to love you. Go to Brazil and run a TV station, if you feel that's what you have to do. I'll be waiting here when you come back, loving you, reminding you of who you are. Or I'll let you spend your money on plane tickets and limousines, as long as they take me to where you are. Because that's the only place I want to be. Right beside you."

As she spoke, his eyebrows furrowed, a little vertical crease forming between them, as his gaze flicked back and forth across hers. When she'd run out of steam, and said what she needed to say, she stared back in silence, holding her breath and her heart in her hands, waiting for him to reply.

When he did, it wasn't with words. His hands came up to hold her face, gripping her hard as his mouth descended on hers, hungry and demanding. She opened her mouth to him, her little squeak of surprise softening into a moan of pleasure as his tongue swept in and found hers.

His hand left her face, his arm banding around her

waist and hauling her up to her toes and into his chest. Unbalanced, she fell into him, gripping his hard shoulders.

What was this kiss? An acceptance of her apology or a last goodbye before he walked away for good? She slid her hands into his hair, gripping hard to hold him to her. If she could hold him in this kiss forever, he couldn't ever leave her.

When he tried to end it, she chased after him, recapturing his mouth, pushing his body back into the railing. Alex moaned, the sound vibrating down her throat and straight down to her thighs. Swinging her body around like she weighed nothing, he pushed her back into the railing, his large frame caging her in, overwhelming her, as he devoured her mouth. Heat licked up her body, and she gripped him—his shoulders, his waist, his hips, holding him tight against her.

He pulled back, holding her still when she would have dragged him back again.

"I'm not going to Brazil," he murmured. His hair blew across his forehead in a disordered mess in the cold breeze off the Hudson as he examined her from under heavy lids.

"What?" People kept saying things to her tonight that made her lose her place in space and time. All she wanted to do was kiss Alex some more and he was talking about South America.

"I'm not going to Brazil or anywhere else. I'm staying here in New York."

"Oh. Well, that's okay, too. What I said still holds true. It's your life. I was wrong to tell you how you should live it."

He chuckled, a low, throaty sound she felt against

her mouth and in her belly, as his body shifted against hers. God, she wanted to be alone and naked with him. "Somebody had to say it or I might have spent the rest of my life fucking it up."

Finally, the realization that he was trying to tell her something important pierced her haze of lust. "What are you saying, Alex?"

"I quit."

"Quit what? Just tell me what happened."

Idly, he traced the neckline of her dress, making her break out in goose bumps. "I quit Drake Media. I told my dad I just couldn't do it. I'm taking over Chase's position at ClickNews and I'm going to see what I can make of it."

His news was like a small atomic bomb going off in her brain, leaving her too stunned to even react. "What…how…"

"Before you get too insufferably smug, it wasn't *all* you. Chase said some stuff to me that really hit home, too."

"Chase? Why would you ever listen to him?"

"Because he was right. About that one thing, anyway. Eventually I was going to crack. That wasn't fair to me *or* my father."

"But… Is…" She opened her mouth, then closed it again, processing the enormity of what Alex was telling her. "And he's *okay* with this?" Because she couldn't imagine Dan Drake ever letting his precious son just walk away from the empire he built for him.

"It took some convincing, but I did it. I'm out. Drake Media will have to be somebody else's baby, because I'm going to have my hands full turning ClickNews around. And…" He leaned into her again—his thighs brushing hers, his chest against her breasts—and he lifted his hands to cup her face. "I hope I'm going to be busy making my girlfriend very happy."

Abruptly, her eyes stung with tears and her throat began to ache. It was…oh, God, was there a word for this explosive release of emotions when you thought you lost everything but then you got it all and more?

"Are you *crying*?"

"Shut up," she muttered around the tightness in her throat. "It's just the breeze off the river."

He chuckled, smoothing the windblown strands of hair away from her face. "Admit it. You're happy."

"I'm happy," she whispered. "So happy I could cry. But not for me. It's not about me getting what I wanted. I'm happy for you. Because you got what *you* always wanted."

"Jess, right now, I have everything I've *ever* wanted," he said, smiling down into her face. "And never dreamed I could have."

He kissed her again, and this time, neither one of them made any attempt to stop for a very long time.

Chapter Forty

This morning, Alex had been preparing to get on with heading up Drake Media for the rest of his miserable life, and doing it without Jess. Now, twelve hours later, Drake Media was going to be someone else's problem, some eager executive who would love it the way he never could. And the thing he'd wanted most—Click-News's ragtag journalism department—was now in his hands, ready to be molded into the vision he'd cherished for so long.

And as midnight on this long day crept closer, Jess was back in his arms for good, her lips warm under his, tasting salty from her tears of happiness. When the New Year began, he would have Jess at his side and, for the first time in his life, he would be facing a future that didn't fill him with dread.

"You're shaking," he whispered against her cheek. "Are you cold?"

His hands roved down her slender neck, over her bare shoulders, and around to the exposed expanse of her back. This dress made him *hungry*.

"Not cold," she insisted, as another tremor shook her. The heating lamps staved off the worst of the winter cold out here, but the breeze off the river was relentless. Every time it gusted, Jess's skin broke out in goose bumps. He wanted to smooth his hands over that tender flesh, to warm her back up, and then maybe follow behind with his tongue.

Suddenly, the door behind him opened. "Ooops! Mr. Drake! Sorry. I didn't see you out here. I just popped out for a smoke."

He turned to look at the woman, whom he recognized from Marketing, but couldn't name.

His head finally cleared enough to allow embarrassment to creep in. His hand had been on Jess's breast until just a second ago, and the other hand was still firmly planted on her ass. The hem of her dress had ridden up, exposing her upper thighs. Okay, it hadn't ridden up. He'd pushed it up.

"Sorry," he told the woman as he discreetly tugged her hem back down. "Got a little carried away. And Mr. Drake is my father. I'm just Alex."

Stepping back, he ran his hands through his hair as Jess slid the strap of her dress back up on her shoulder. He'd done that, too.

"No problem, Alex." The woman smirked.

He turned back to Jess. "You ready to get out of here?" *Please say yes*, he pleaded with his eyes.

"Yes." When she looked up at him, the dark hunger there nearly sent him to his knees. They'd be lucky to get all the way back to his apartment before they had each other's clothes off.

"We'll leave you the balcony," he said to the woman, ushering Jess past him. "Enjoy your night."

Back inside, the space was filled with laughter and voices competing with the DJ's thumping dance beat.

"I'm going to check out the famous bathroom before we leave," Jess said. "Meet you by the front door?"

"Give me your coat check ticket and I'll get your stuff." He kissed her slowly, full of heat and promise. "What I'm gonna do to you tonight…" he growled into her ear.

She moaned and clutched briefly at his lapels. "Stop it. I can barely walk as it is."

Chuckling, he released her and watched Jess retreat to the ladies' room on unsteady legs. He wasn't feeling too in control himself. Happiness and lust and love…it was a heady mix. He nearly walked by the coat check, because the door was closed, the mirrored panels on its face blending in with the mirrored walls. Why was it closed?

When he opened the door, he discovered why. It was dark inside, and in his distraction, he only registered bodies entwined, fingers tangled in dark hair, bare skin…

"Ah! Sorry. So sorry."

He was backing up, closing the door again, when a familiar chuckle made him roll his eyes.

"*Honestly*, Dad," he muttered. "I'm taking Jess home and I need our coats. Can you just take it somewhere else for a minute?"

The voice he heard next froze him in his tracks. It was low and lethal, a whisper of steel. "Not. One. Word."

Mariel Kemper.

Mariel *fucking* Kemper was making out with his father in the coat check.

He pushed the door open again. The low amber light spilled in, illuminating first his father, casually rebuttoning his shirt, then Mariel, tugging down the hem of her dress. She straightened, tossing her mussed hair out of her flushed face, looking *exactly* like she'd just been going at it in a closet. "Not a word from you, either," she growled as she swept past Alex, regal as a queen.

Alex held his hands up in defense. "I wouldn't dream of it."

She spun around to face his father. "And *you*."

Dan sauntered toward her, looking smugly pleased with himself. "Yes, Mariel?"

She wrapped two fingers around the edge of his lapel and tugged him forward. "You owe me. Tonight you're going to buy me several very expensive cocktails."

He grinned down at her. "It's an open bar."

"Well, I'll have to come up with something else, then. I'll think creatively."

"I have no doubt you will." He held his arm out to her, as courtly as a lord. Mariel's expression softened ever so slightly, and the corner of her mouth twitched with a smile she fought to suppress.

When Alex looked back to his father, he was stunned at the expression on his face. Dan looked almost…infatuated. Mariel Kemper had *intrigued* his father, and women simply never did that. Well, he hoped Dan knew what he was doing, because if there was one woman on earth who could eat *him* alive, and not the other way around, it was this one.

They were halfway down the hall when Dan paused and looked back over his shoulder. "Everything okay, son?"

Alex smiled and nodded. "Yeah, Dad. Everything is great. Thanks for tonight."

Mariel's eyes darted between them before landing on Alex. "You mean *you're* the one who invited my staff?"

Dan chuckled. "Let's just say my son and I were both motivated to get you and your staff here."

Alex was still smiling when Jess found him a moment later. "What's so funny?"

"I caught my dad with a woman in the coat check."

She rolled her eyes. "Could he be a bigger cliché? I bet she was one of his secretaries, right?"

"Ah…actually, it was Mariel."

Jess's eyes flew wide. "Tell me you're joking."

"Nope. And from the looks of things, it was progressing fairly rapidly."

"Eww! Oh, I have to stop her!" She shot past him, headed for the coat room. Snagging her arm, he swung her around again.

"Hold up. They're not there anymore."

"But I have to find her! She's not thinking clearly—"

"Oh, she's probably not thinking much at all, but I suspect she doesn't want to. Jess." He gripped her by the shoulders. "She's an adult. So is my father. They'll make their own choices."

"But he's so… Dan."

"I don't know…" Alex said, remembering that brand-new expression on his father's face. "This might sound crazy, but I think she's different."

"Of course she's different!"

"No, I mean different for him."

"I'll believe that when I see it."

"You'll just have to wait and see, because I'm pretty

sure Mariel doesn't want saving tonight, not by you or anyone else."

Just then, Lina exploded out of the crowd and into the empty hall. She had a champagne flute in each hand and a plastic glittery tiara perched precariously on her glossy dark hair. "There you are!"

She threw her arms around Jess, splashing champagne on all three of them, and kissed Jess noisily on the cheek.

"Hey, Lina, you seem to be having a good time."

"So much fun. I've been dancing. Did you know Hassan can dance? The boy has *moves*. Can't wait to find out about the other kind. You know, the sexy-sexy kind—"

"We were just leaving, Lina." Alex made a futile attempt to peel Lina's arms off her.

Lina gasped and attempted to clap her hands over her mouth, until she remembered she was still holding two glasses. She settled for squealing with delight instead. "You guys made up!"

"Yes, we did. Actually, we're in the middle of that," Jess said, indicating the front door. "So we're gonna go—"

"No, you can't! It's almost midnight! Come on!"

"Lina—"

Just then, Hassan staggered into the hallway. "Lina, come on. I got us more drinks."

"You guys don't look like you need more drinks," Alex observed, earning him a scowl from Lina.

She thrust one glass at Jess and, once her hand was free, grasped her wrist and began tugging her into the crowd. Jess cast an apologetic look back over her shoulder. "One toast."

After all that had happened between her and Lina, he wasn't going to begrudge them their moment, even if it left him simmering in a state of frustrated lust. It would wait. They had all night. They had...well, they had forever, didn't they?

The bar was packed now, the Drake Media employees and the *Daily Post* employees tangled into a glittering, dancing, laughing, sea of people. Jess let herself be towed through the crowd by Lina, looking back now and then to make sure Alex was still there. He always was. All she had to do was reach out and she could touch him.

A group of *Daily Post* employees had commandeered a cluster of cream sofas in a corner, overlooking a breathtaking north-facing view of Manhattan. Everyone was there, Dana and her husband, cutting loose and enjoying their child-free night, Caleb and Marc, Sally, in a truly spectacular Christmas sweater, Isaiah and his partner...and Griffin, with *Natalie* perched on his lap. *Okay.* Even Mariel had joined them—alone. Jess met her eyes briefly and a flash of understanding passed between them.

Forget what Alex said. She had to make sure Mariel wasn't doing something she'd regret later.

"Is everything okay?" she murmured under her breath.

Mariel blew out a breath. "No. Everything is..." She trailed off, looking confused, dumbstruck, and a little bit...enchanted. "I really thought I hated him, you know?"

Jess nodded sympathetically. "I know *exactly* what you mean."

Alex stepped up behind her, wrapping his arms around her waist and pulling her back against his chest. The *Daily Post* employees registered that development with a frisson of interest. She'd be grilled properly at work, but for now everyone kept their mouth shut.

Hassan poured champagne—Moët, the good stuff— into everyone's glasses. When he reached Lina's side, he slid his arm around her waist. She tipped her head onto his shoulder. Guess that was her answer about the Hassan thing. Jess was glad. Lina deserved a great guy in her life.

The DJ faded out the last track. "Nearly there, friends," he announced. "So get with your favorite person and start the new year the way you want it to end."

The crowd around them began to chant the countdown.

"Ten! Nine! Eight!"

"It's almost time!" Lina shrieked.

"Seven! Six! Five!"

"I know how I want next year to end," Alex murmured in her ear. She twisted in his arms until she was facing him, that face she'd spent so many years hating for all the wrong reasons—the face that was now so precious to her that it made her heart ache. She could scarcely wrap her mind around what might lie in store for her and Alex, and after such an inauspicious start. Wasn't that always how it started, though? One person improbably encounters another, something sparks, and a glowing future grows from that tiny flicker of heat, impossible to predict.

"Four! Three! Two!"

"And the year after that," she said. "And the year after that. I want them all to begin and end with you."

"One!"

The crowd exploded in screams. Golden confetti and balloons exploded from the ceiling, raining down on their heads. People laughed, kissed, hugged. Everyone began to sing "Auld Lang Syne" out of tune. But it all faded away. There was only Alex. Only them. Now, and maybe forever.

He bent his head toward hers. "Happy New Year, Jess. I love you."

As his lips touched hers, she was sure, in the history of New Year's Eves, no new year—no new love—had ever had a better beginning. Even if the beginning of this love had taken them years to get to, and even if it had started with hate.

* * * * *

Turn the page for an excerpt from
Love and The Laws of Motion,
the next book in The Romano Sisters series
from Amanda Weaver.

Chapter One

There was only one thing about Brooklyn that Livie Romano didn't love: there were never any stars out at night. Most of the time, when you looked up, you saw...nothing. Just a flat rust-colored glow as the streetlights reflected off the clouds. The light pollution was so powerful that it managed to blot out the entirety of the universe overhead, which was saying something.

The first time she'd seen stars...actual stars, not the random sighting of Venus that managed to puncture New York's omnipresent glow...she'd been six. Vacations had been nearly nonexistent when they were kids. There was always too much work at the family bar and too little money. But one year their uncle Vincent had rented a cabin upstate on Lake George and invited them up for the weekend. Her parents—that was back when her mother was still alive—had piled the kids into the family car and off they went.

The first night, her sisters and cousins had shrieked and laughed as they chased fireflies in the woods, but a different kind of light had caught Livie's attention. Alone, she wandered to the end of the dock, lay down on the worn wood, still warm from the day's sun, and she'd stared up at the sky, at the overwhelming sight of thousands of stars. Even the Milky Way was visible—a magical, cloudy sweep across the sky, looking just like it did in books.

It was like peeking into a world that had been hidden in plain sight all her life—a world that stretched into infinity.

These days, as she pursued her PhD in astrophysics, she was no longer dependent on a clear night sky. She stargazed through computers, the telescope orbiting thousands of miles above tiny earthbound complications like clouds and light pollution. But there was still something special about just looking up and seeing the stars, silently burning away for millennia.

Pausing on the street corner, Livie glanced up. Nothing but a low-hanging wall of clouds tonight. You'd hardly even know the universe was up there. But it was, waiting for her with its mysteries to be unraveled, if only she could figure out how.

She dropped her eyes from the blank sky to a more comforting glow—the golden light of the front window of Romano's Bar, and the electric Michelob sign that was older than she was. Just like the Milky Way, Romano's lights seemed to burn on for eons.

The poorly oiled hinges on the front door shrieked to announce her as she entered. Her older sister, Gemma, glanced up from a stack of credit card receipts.

"Livie, you're ten minutes late. Were you mugged? Kidnapped? Did you fall into an open manhole? You're never late."

Flustered, she hurried across the bar and ducked under the pass-through. "Sorry, slow train." She hated being late, and anything less than ten minutes early counted as late.

"Ugh, don't get me started on the MTA," her younger sister, Jessica, growled from behind her laptop.

"What are you doing here, Jess? I thought I was covering Dad tonight."

"You are. I'm filing the quarterly taxes."

Thank God Jess handled that odious task. Gemma was hopeless at math and Livie hated accounting. She could use numbers to explain the bending of time and space, but forget about finance.

"How was the first day of classes?" Gemma asked. "You're teaching this semester, right?"

"Campus opened this week, but classes don't officially start until next week. My section of Astronomy 200 starts next Tuesday."

Hard to say who was less enthusiastic about starting classes, Livie or her incoming undergrads. Standing up in front of a room full of undergrads was her worst nightmare come to life. But it was required as part of her grad student stipend, so she was just going to have to suck it up and do her best to avoid eye contact.

"So why were you at school all day if there were no classes?"

Livie turned to face her sisters with a triumphant smile. "Because I have big news."

Jess and Gemma both looked up expectantly. Livie had been bursting to share this with someone—anyone—since she'd left campus an hour ago. And the fact was, she didn't have many people besides her sisters to share good news with.

"We got the Skylight grant. Well, Finch got the

grant. Which, since I'm working on her research for my dissertation, is like *me* getting the grant."

Jess grinned. "That's awesome, Livie!"

"The what grant? You're getting money?"

"I told you about it, Gem."

"Livie, I love you, but you know I don't understand half of what you tell me." Gem waved her hand, miming information flying over her head. Livie wished she wouldn't do that—that flippant dismissal of her lack of education. Gemma might not have gone to college like her younger sisters, but she was one of the smartest people Livie knew.

"Professor Finch—"

"Your thesis advisor," Gemma said. "See? I remember some things!"

"Anyway, Janet applied for this big grant from Skylight last year. You know...the telecommunications company?"

"I remember you helped her with the grant application," Jess said. "It took you forever."

"Thanks for proofreading it, by the way."

"Anytime."

"Well, she found out over the summer that she got it. Which means her research is fully funded. Which means I can work on it with her for my dissertation. Working on this with her is the whole reason I chose Adams. And now we've got the money to do it."

"This is so exciting," Jess said.

"It is, but it means I've got a lot of work to do. Janet wants to start purchasing as soon as possible, which means I've got to start pulling together ordering info." She sighed. "I love research, but this administrative stuff is so boring."

"Agreed," Gemma said. "Why do you think I make Jess do the bookkeeping?"

Jess made a face at her.

"I also need to find a programmer, and I have no idea where to start with that one."

Gemma held her hands up. "Don't look at me. You know I can't even reboot the cable box."

"But, Livie," Jess said. "I thought you had a programmer listed as part of the grant proposal."

"We just included a line item for it. Janet had someone in mind when we drew up the budget. The guy is good. One of the best. But he's *so* expensive. It's going to eat up a huge chunk of the money before we even get started. If I can find someone to do it for less, then the grant money will go so much further."

"Isn't there someone at Adams who can do it?" Gemma asked. "They must have a computer department. Then it'd be free."

Livie didn't say so, but she doubted anyone in Adams's Computer Science department could program their own smart phones. There were a few academic bright stars at Adams, like Janet, but it was not a powerhouse university.

"This is beyond some college programmer. This is like, NASA-level coding. People who can program at that level aren't just wandering around looking for a part-time gig."

"You need help with your computer, Livie?" Frank, one of Romano's die-hard regulars, had been listening in on their conversation, as usual. Outside of football season, Mondays were quiet at the bar. Romano's was mostly empty, just the handful of regulars, like Frank. "Dennis, you remember that DeSantis kid? Gloria De-

Santis's nephew? He was some kinda computer whiz, wasn't he?"

Dennis Mulchahey, another old-timer, rolled his eyes and set his beer down. "A troublemaker, that's what that kid was. But yeah, he was all into computers and stuff."

"No offense, Frank, but a kid who's good at video games isn't what I need." Although that's what she loved about their regulars. They felt like family, and, like family, were always ready to pitch in when there was a problem.

Frank ignored her, because…well, he was like family. "He went to some fancy college, didn't he?"

"He went to *Jess's* college," Dennis confirmed. "When he was just sixteen. Full ride, too. Those De-Witt guys were desperate to get him in there."

"He went to DeWitt at sixteen?" Jess interjected. "He's gotta have something going on if he graduated from DeWitt, Livie."

DeWitt was Ivy League, one of the best universities in the Northeast. A computer programmer who went to DeWitt sounded promising.

"Don't think he graduated, though," Dennis said. "He got into some trouble."

"Trouble?" Gemma asked. "What kind of trouble?"

Dennis and Frank looked at each other as they searched their memories. "He got mixed up with the law, I remember that," Frank finally said.

"What, like a drug bust or something?" Gemma, ever protective of her younger sisters, had taken over the interrogation.

If he was some drug dealer, then Livie wasn't interested, computer genius or not. This research was too important to risk that way.

"Nah, not NYPD," Dennis replied. Dennis and Frank, like many of Romano's patrons, were both retired cops. "This was FBI, I think. The kid was mixed up in some serious stuff. Left college and disappeared."

"Disappeared?" Livie's tiny spark of hope snuffed out. It sounded like the guy was a dead end.

Frank turned to Livie. "You want me to get his number from Gloria for you?"

She didn't have the smallest hope that Gloria De-Santis's nephew was the person for this project, but if what Dennis said was right…if he worked in computers, especially at that level…then he might be able to help her find the right person. And a tiny lead was better than no lead at all.

"Sure. Thanks, Frank."

Chapter Two

The address was in DUMBO, almost to the water. At the end of the cobblestone street, Livie could see the Manhattan Bridge, arching away into the city. This guy must be doing pretty well for himself, because real estate in this neighborhood was not cheap.

It might be a warning sign, though, one to add to all the others. Gloria DeSantis had been able to provide her nephew's name, but she didn't have his number because, in her words, "there was bad blood," whatever that meant. When Livie tried to find him online, she hit another dead end. There were mentions of him from his teenage years—stuff about his early acceptance to DeWitt, listings in the student directory, but nothing recent. No Facebook, no Twitter, no Instagram. What kind of twentysomething had zero social media presence? Well, *she* didn't, but Jess had informed her in no uncertain terms that it made her a freak.

In the end, her uncle Robert, an NYPD detective, dug up a phone number for the guy, which was not, strictly speaking, aboveboard, but she'd been getting desperate. Despite the mysterious Mr. DeSantis's incognito existence, he'd replied instantly to a texted inquiry from a complete stranger about a freelance project. There was definitely something sketchy about this whole situation.

When Livie pressed the button by his name, someone buzzed her in without even asking who she was. *Okay.* She took the elevator to the fourteenth floor, which turned out to be the top one. It opened onto a small vestibule, and there was only one door. Meaning he had the whole floor.

She knocked and had just glanced down to double check the info in his text, when the door opened in front of her. Livie's eyes flew up and she froze.

Oh.

Whatever she'd been expecting, it was certainly not this. He was incredibly, *unbelievably* good-looking. Tall, with messy dark brown hair and riveting dark eyes that made her feel pinned in place. He had one hand braced on the door frame, making his bicep flex and his tight gray T-shirt stretch across his broad shoulders.

This couldn't be right. There was no way this was Gloria DeSantis's computer geek nephew. He had to be his hot, soccer-player roommate or something, right?

"Um… Nicholas DeSantis?"

A tiny line formed between his heavy, dark brows. "It's Nick. You Olivia?"

"It's Livie."

The corner of his mouth twitched—almost a smile—and she melted inside. There was no other way to describe it. Her insides had gone all warm and golden and glowing. An absolutely ridiculous physical response to have to another human being.

"Okay," he said, backing away from the door. "We cleared that up. Come on in."

So he *was* Gloria DeSantis's computer geek nephew. And he was also spectacularly hot. Livie rarely noticed such things, and she'd never, *ever* been so rattled by a guy's appearance before. They hadn't gotten past exchanging names and she was almost too flustered to speak.

He turned and walked away, leaving Livie to come in and close the door behind herself. "How'd you get my name again?" he asked over his shoulder. There was a restless energy in his body, evident even as he casually walked across a room, like he was a steel spring, tightly wound and ready to explode.

Livie hurried after him. "Gloria DeSantis, your aunt."

The sudden appearance of the Manhattan Bridge looming just on the other side of a wall of glass stopped her in her tracks. His apartment was huge, with floor-to-ceiling windows overlooking the bridge, the East River, and the Manhattan skyline. The furniture was all that low, sleek, leather stuff you only see in magazines. There were no family photos on the walls, no opened mail scattered across the coffee table, no shoes kicked off in a pile by the door. It barely looked like anyone lived there.

He stopped and turned back to look at her. "But Aunt Gloria doesn't have my number. Nobody in my family has my number."

"I know. So I got a cop to track you down."

Nick blinked. When he looked at Livie again, his expression had changed, like he was really seeing her for the first time since he'd opened the door. "Okay, that's a little bit interesting and also alarming."

"I tried to find you online first, but you're not really online anywhere."

"You wouldn't be, either, if you'd seen what I've seen. So Livie—you said it's Livie, right?—You know my aunt Gloria?"

"She's my neighbor."

Those thick, expressive eyebrows lifted in surprise. "You're from the neighborhood?"

"Yeah. I grew up there. Romano's Bar? That's my family's place."

Nick let out a surprised huff of laughter. "Romano's? That place is still around?"

Hey. The Romanos might complain about the lousy business, but she wasn't about to let someone else slag on the bar.

"Since 1932, and still going strong." Limping along was perhaps more accurate, but he didn't have to know that.

"I haven't seen that place since I was a kid."

"It's three subway stops away."

The little line between his eyebrows came back. "I don't get home much."

He turned and kept walking across the very large open-plan living area, passing through a door on the far wall, which led to a smaller room. This one, obviously his office, was tucked into the corner of the building, with walls of windows on two sides and the same spectacular view of the bridge. Up against the windows were two long black tables, meeting at right angles in the corner. And every square inch of their surface was covered with computer equipment. Livie counted four jumbo displays, and at least three CPU towers buried in a snaking nest of cables and peripherals.

Nick dropped into a black office chair and swiveled around to face her.

"So what are you looking for?"

Her eyes were still busy cataloging his setup. Top-notch research labs didn't have this much computer equipment. There were pieces of hardware she didn't even recognize. It must have cost him a fortune.

"I need some help with a computer program."

Nick sighed. "I don't know what you might have heard about me, but I don't do tech support. Call Geek Squad."

She turned back to face him. Okay, he was extremely attractive and obviously successful, but did he have to be so arrogant? "It's a little more complicated than that. I need to write a new program for my dissertation."

Nick leaned back in his chair, stretching his legs out and crossing them at the ankles. Threading his fingers together, he rested his hands on his abdomen—which looked like it would be firm to the touch. If she were to touch it. How did this computer geek have a body that was so hard and sculpted…and distracting?

"Okay, pitch me."

Livie blinked, embarrassed that he might have caught her staring. "Excuse me?"

"Tell me why I should take on your project."

"Um, well, I'll pay you, of course." Although she had the sinking feeling that Nick was a long way from the budget-friendly alternative she was looking for.

Nick scoffed. "I don't work for money. I've done that already."

She let out a huff of surprised laughter. What a ridiculous thing to say. "And, what, you earned money once and now you have all you'll ever need?"

Nick said nothing—he just hiked an eyebrow and smiled—a slow, crooked curling of his lips that had Livie's toes curling inside her shoes in response. Butterflies set up a flutter in her stomach. Oh, he was way too attractive for his own good.

It was too bad she was never going to see him again.

"Okay, so you're not interested." She turned toward the door. "Thanks for your time. I'll just—"

"I didn't say that," he interjected. "I don't know if I'm interested until you tell me what it is."

Taking a deep breath to marshal her thoughts, Livie turned back. "It's for my dissertation."

"You said that."

"I'm getting there. We're going to be receiving a lot of data."

"Who's 'we'?"

"Me and my thesis advisor, Dr. Janet Finch. She's brilliant. It's her theory we're attempting to prove."

"Okay, so you're going to be receiving a lot of data. What kind of data? From where?"

"I'm getting to that." Did he ever let anybody finish their train of thought? "So there's already a set of standard routines to sift through Hubble data. But what we're looking for, what we hope to find, won't show up in any of the standard analysis tools—"

"Hold up." Nick's feet hit the floor hard as he sat up abruptly. "The Hubble? Like the space telescope?"

"Yes. Did I mention I'm an astrophysicist?"

Again, the corner of his mouth twitched with that toe-curling smile. His eyes, for all their darkness, danced with animation. "No, you didn't. So you're going to get to *use* the Hubble telescope?"

"We'll need to submit a proposal, but that shouldn't be a problem. We probably won't get an observing time until next spring, so between now and then, I need to write this program. Do you know anything about astronomy?"

"Not a thing. I'm in."

"Wait...so you'll do it? I haven't even told you how much the budget is." There was cheap and then there was what she'd been planning to offer him.

"Don't know. Don't care. Writing new code for Hubble data...see, *that's* interesting. I'm in. That's the pitch I was looking for."

"We can't afford to pay you what you're obviously used to." Well, they *could*, but then they might as well go with the guy they'd already scoped out and blow half the grant money on *him*. The whole point of this was to find a cheaper alternative.

Nick rolled his eyes. "I told you, I don't work for the money. I mean, yes, people pay me, but the money doesn't determine what jobs I take on."

Who *was* this guy? How did he start where she started and end up here, having built this life for himself?

"What *does* determine it? I mean, what kind of jobs do you usually take?"

He shrugged before leaning forward and hooking his ankle around another office chair and pulling it closer. "Have a seat. I do whatever appeals to me. A little banking...although not as much of that as I did in the past. Some government work, a lot of consulting. Whatever I'm interested in, really. And only what

I'm interested in. I have no interest in doing some tedious corporate gig, no matter how fat the paycheck."

Taking the offered chair, she fiddled with the strap of her messenger bag and debated asking him any one of the hundreds of questions swirling around in her head. "I've heard some things about you."

Leaning back in his chair again, Nick smiled—a full smile this time—and his eyes sparked with amusement. His voice dropped into a lower register, something flirty and sexy. "Oh, really? Like what?"

"You got kicked out of DeWitt."

If she'd expected him to get defensive, she was mistaken. His expression didn't shift in the slightest. "Kicked out, quit…it's all in your perspective. DeWitt and I chose to part ways."

"And you got arrested."

Again, not even a ripple of a response in his eyes. She envied his confidence, even if it scared her a little bit.

"Unindicted," he said with a careless shrug. "The government and I reached a mutually beneficial agreement."

"Which is?"

"They didn't file charges and in return, I did some work on their systems, to make sure nobody else can do what I did."

"Which was?"

"I hacked into the Department of Defense."

"You hacked the *government*?" That was *not* what she'd expected to hear.

Another shrug. "It wasn't that hard. Which is why they needed me. I made it hard."

"So you're a hacker." Which was super illegal, when

the hackee was the federal government. Growing up surrounded by the *other* side of law enforcement, she didn't know anyone who'd even been busted for jaywalking, never mind crimes of this level.

"Only theoretically now, to keep my skills sharp."

"Because it's illegal." Surely he'd learned his lesson now, right? Figured out the difference between right and wrong?

Nick scoffed, swiveling back and forth in his chair. "Legal, illegal. What does that even mean?"

Apparently not. "Um, one is right and one is wrong."

He spun back to face her. "Right and wrong? Right and wrong has nothing to do with what's legal or illegal. Everything in this world, every person you meet, every choice they make, is all just a murky shade of gray. You figure out right and wrong for yourself, Livie." The way he said her name…it was like he'd just whispered it in her ear, followed by something dirty.

"I'm not sure I believe that."

He chuckled, and the sound sent a shiver down her spine. "I'm sure you don't. And that is the difference between me and you."

Oh, there were so many differences between them she couldn't begin to count them all. Maybe Nick came from the same neighborhood as her, and he had an Italian last name, but the similarities began and ended there.

He was so… For all her intelligence and education, she lacked the vocabulary to describe him. Goodlooking for sure, but there was something more, some undeniable presence, something that pulled her in—enthralled her—in spite of herself. Charisma? That hinted at his power, but it didn't fully explain it.

She didn't know what to do with all this nervous, humming awareness, as it had literally never happened to her before. Men—they were definitely out of her area of expertise. She wasn't even casually familiar with the whole men/dating/sex thing. She hadn't avoided men and sex on purpose, she'd just never felt compelled to explore it with anyone she'd met. And she wasn't going to do anything just to say she did it. So here she was, twenty-five and completely inexperienced with men. That had never once bothered her—until now.

How did you talk to a guy like Nick? Oh, they were already talking—about her work and his life. But how did she *talk* to him? How did she—as a woman—engage with a guy like Nick—as a man? If there was an instruction manual on flirting with the opposite sex, Livie's had gone missing the day they handed them out.

Now, after all these years, she finally liked a guy and she had absolutely no idea what to do about it. Why did she like him, anyway? Sure, he was attractive, but he was also practically a felon—arrogant, cocky—and then there was his alarming moral flexibility. But despite all that, she did like him. To a dangerous degree.

And now they'd be working together, for who knew how long. She suspected he was way out of her league, but she couldn't help the tiny spark of excitement—hope—that flamed to life in her chest.

"So you'll help me with my coding?"

"Can't wait to get started." His grin turned that spark into a bonfire. He was talking about the computer program, but it felt like he could be alluding to so much more. "So tell me what you're looking for out there in the stars, Livie."

She could feel herself smiling back at him, feel her body beginning to lean toward him. She might not have a clue what to do next, but she was definitely going to grill Jess tonight to find out. "Well—"

Out in the other room, a door opened and closed, and a voice called out "Hello?"

A female voice.

In moments, the owner of the voice appeared in the doorway to Nick's office. She was tall, impossibly skinny, and stunning, with long, pin-straight silky dark blond hair and large blue eyes.

"Oh, hello," she said in surprise when she spotted Livie. "I didn't know Nick was working."

She was British, too. Of course. Her accent was like something from *Masterpiece Theatre*.

Nick hopped up out of his chair, practically sprinting across the room to the willowy goddess. If Livie had a single doubt left about who she was, the next moments crushed that. He leaned down to kiss her cheek before turning to Livie with a smile that lit him up from the inside. "Livie, this is Poppy, my fiancée."

Watch for Livie's story,
Love and The Laws of Motion,
out from Carina Press.

www.CarinaPress.com

Acknowledgments

Endless thanks and gratitude to my agent, Rebecca Strauss. She's fought tirelessly for me and this book, through its many iterations. It wouldn't have made it out there into the world without her.

Thanks to Anne Forlines for early pre-reading and invaluable feedback. She's the first person to read anything I write, and I never really feel like I've finished it until Anne's read it and told me what she thinks.

And thank you to my good friend, Jennifer DeMaio, an Italian girl who grew up in Brooklyn. She gave me wonderful insight into these sisters, and advice on all the little details that matter so much.

Thanks, always and forever, to my family, for putting up with my distraction and absence as I devoted hundreds of hours to this book. My husband, like countless partners of writers everywhere, listens patiently as I explain a plot conundrum, and never even laughs or says "I told you so" as I proceed to solve it myself.

Author Bio

Amanda has loved romance since she read that very first Kathleen E. Woodiwiss novel at fifteen. After a long detour into a career as a costume designer in theater, she's found her way back to romance, this time as a writer.

A native Floridian, Amanda transplanted to New York City many years ago and now considers Brooklyn home, along with her husband, daughter, two cats, and nowhere near enough space.